Eye *of the* Rainbow Serpent

by Donovan Hoult

Publishers:
Inspiring Publishers
P.O. Box 159 Calwell ACT 2905, Australia.
Email: inspiringpublishers@gmail.com

National Library of Australia Cataloguing-in-Publication entry

Author: Hoult, Donovan

Title: **Eye of the Rainbow Serpent**/*Donovan Hoult.*

ISBN: 978-0-6484592-2-4 (pbk)

Subjects: Sacred space–Western Australia–Fiction.
        Models (Persons)–Fiction.
        Murder–Fiction.
        Suspense fiction, Australian.

Dewey Number: A823.4

Cover photo: Ross McGibbon Photography
        "King-Brown"
        Western Australia
        www.rmphotography.com.au

1

Venus Downs Station, The Kimberley, Western Australia.

Carl Boyce lay on the ground with his legs splayed, his elbows firmly planted in the red earth as he steadied the rifle. His bush hat was pulled forwards to shade his eyes as he braced for the recoil and gently squeezed the trigger. The Lee Enfield's high-pitched, resonating crack shattered the silence. A baked bean tin about one hundred metres away spun into the air. Carl methodically worked the bolt of the rifle and chambered another round before sighting on an identical tin a further two hundred metres out. A shot rang out, but the tin remained stationary as a burst of dust rose behind it. His twin brother Walter reached down to take the weapon but Carl held onto it with a look of disdain. "You've got your own bloody rifle. Use that."

Walter snapped open the lever action of an ancient Martini Henry, pushed a cartridge into the breach and gently closed it, all the while keeping his eyes on the first of his two targets. The flat staccato sound of the Martini Henry was like a whiplash. As the tin flew into the air, he ejected the spent shell, then reloaded and sighted on the far tin.

"You haven't a chance in hell of hitting anything with that old crock. You may as well—" Carl's spoiling tactic was lost as the whip-crack cut him off and the distant tin disappeared in a cloud of dust.

"Wanna try another hundred out for double or quits?" Carl leered at his brother, believing it was beyond the skill of Walter and his Boer-War veteran firearm.

"You lost, you owe me five bucks. That was the bet." Walter sprang to his feet to confront his brother.

Carl put his hand on Walter's chest and pushed him away with a mocking grin. "What's the problem? You stand to win ten bucks." He swung around and shouted towards a low set outbuilding behind him. "Chloe, get your bum out here."

A girl of about sixteen untangled her long, slender legs and rose from where she had been sitting at the feet of an old man under the open veranda. She looked up at him and he nodded his approval as Carl repeated his command with irritation in his voice. The old man watched through watering eyes that had endured many decades of relentless sun and hardship. They were cold and penetrating, two brown orbs that held the secrets of an ancient civilisation. He watched the girl as she ran up to the brothers.

Carl didn't acknowledge her. "Take these two tins and set them on the posts either side of that gate." He pointed to the gate more than three hundred metres distant. The girl took the tins and began to walk towards the gate. "Stir those buns of yours!" Carl shouted, and loosed a shot into the air. The girl jumped in fright and without looking back, broke into a run. The old man's face tightened as he spat on the ground in contempt. "That got her moving." Carl chuckled. "She's getting a nice arse and those titties look as though they could do with some fondling. I might saddle her up soon."

"You can be first after me, brother," Walter said, smirking.

"Would you like to take a bet on that?"

"Yeah, but how would we know who'd won? How about the first to produce a bit of pussy hair to confirm it?" Walter sniggered, then dropped down onto his knees and folded forwards to take up his firing position. "And don't try and put me off this time, you arsehole."

Seconds later, the target spun into the air. He reloaded and remained prone as Carl slowly folded onto his stomach in the red earth and concentrated on his shot. Out of the corner of his eye, Walter could see Carl's pressure on the trigger begin to increase, but he suddenly relaxed, rocked back on his heels and took a rag out of his pocket to mop his brow. He slumped forwards again and took aim. The crack of the Lee Enfield was followed a millisecond later by the whipcrack of the Martini Henry and with it, Carl's missed target.

"You owe me ten bucks." Walter got to his feet, dusting the red earth off his jeans and shirt.

"That was my shot!" Carl protested angrily.

Walter turned to the old man under the veranda. "Johnny, did I win ten bucks or not?"

Johnny Quartpot puffed on his cigarette and nodded. There was no point in lying that he had not seen a thing, as the brothers knew he had been watching their contest intensely.

"You need glasses, you old bastard." Carl spat on the ground, threw five dollars at Walter's feet and stalked off.

Walter retrieved the money and yelled to his brother's retreating back, "What about the other five bucks?"

"Put it on the slate."

Walter made no further demand but broke into song. *"You are my sunshine, my only sunshine..."* as he followed Carl towards the homestead with a wide grin on his face. He knew Henry Boyce's nicknames for them—Sunshine for Carl and Sunset for him—had always galled his brother, and he always sang it because there was no equivalent song with the word 'sunshine' that contained such a repetitive melody. And Walter could sing in tune, whereas his brother was tone deaf. Whenever Henry yelled at Carl, which was often, or cuffed him around the head, Walter would start to hum or whistle the offending tune under his breath. Carl's explosion of anger would be instant as he went for his tormentor, but Walter was always ready for him.

The old man's eyes followed the fair-haired brothers. They had arrived at the Station as two skinny wild-eyed waifs uprooted from their lives of increasing vagrancy to be transported to the outback where no such temptations existed. Johnny had watched them as their physical form developed with the lifestyle and unrelenting hard work. "You be careful of those two," he said, disapproval deepening the wrinkles on his face.

Chloe returned to sit at Johnny's feet again, cupping her chin with an elbow rested on her folded legs. "I don't like either of them Gramps."

"Those two are cast in the same mould, girlie. They're twins all right; their personalities are also identical; they just show it in different ways. Carl's more open, like you just saw, but Walter keeps himself hidden. Remember my words. Be careful and never be alone with either of them."

"Is Henry their father?"

"No, they just arrived here one day. Henry went into town and picked 'em up off the plane. I don't know the full story and haven't asked, but I heard they were in a lot of strife in the city so they were sent up here. They were wild all right. Henry had to straighten them out. They took off a couple of times but the local cops saw them wandering around town, rounded them up and brought them back. They've quietened down, but not by much."

"Where did I come from, Gramps?"

"I brought you here. You're my granddaughter."

"You were born here weren't you, Gramps?"

"I was born under a tree down by that billabong." The old man nodded towards a nearby waterhole nestled under a towering red ochre cliff. The billabong teamed with fish and birdlife. It never ran dry, even in the years of drought common to this part of the country. "This has been the home of my people for thousands of years. Long before the whitefella came along and stole it from us. Now, as far as the eye can see in every direction it belongs to Henry Boyce. We have no rights, no legal title to anything, nothing."

"Why do they treat us the way they do?"

"It's called prejudice, Chloe. We are black, they are white. For more than forty years I've worked on this station as a jackaroo, mustering cattle for little wages." Johnny Quartpot spat into the red earth.

"Who was my father, Gramps?"

Chloe looked at the soft, mellow brown of her arms in contrast to that of the old man. Her grandfather had the prominent forehead, sunken eyes and deeply furrowed face of his aboriginality. He was very dark-skinned—almost black, the only contrast being his white hair and beard. Some of the jackaroos on the station were full-blood aborigines like her grandfather, but most had lighter skin tones and softer features, which signified the presence of European genes.

Chloe knew why she had not been told, but the origins of her father churned through her mind constantly. She had been told her mother was Dotti, the aboriginal station cook who ran the homestead with iron discipline. No point in getting inquisitive with Dotti, it only resulted in a curse and a demand to get on with the job at hand. Although Chloe accepted Dotti was her mother, she could not help but notice her own olive skin and fine features were a sharp contrast to the distinct aboriginal appearance of her mother. She was old too. It was more like Dotti and Gramps were brother and sister, not father and daughter.

"Ah, your father was the Duke." The old man grinned, dragging on the cigarette hanging precariously from the corner of his mouth. "Someday I'll tell you, but now's not the time."

"Where did you learn to read and write, Gramps?"

"My mother took me with her to a mission station run by the Jesuits. She was the cook and housekeeper. When I was about your age, she got sick and came back here to die because this was the dreaming land of our people. All our people live in the dreaming of the rainbow serpent. It's the only thing the whitefellas can't take from us, our beliefs and our dreaming lands."

"Rainbow serpent; what's that?"

"Someday I'll show you, but now is not the time."

Her reverie was broken by an angry shout from the homestead. It was Dotti.

"Chloe, get your lazy backside in here now. You've got work to do!"

Chloe needed no second bidding to obey the command. She sprang to her feet. Dotti was already banging glasses down in front of Henry and the twins, who were sitting at the long table Henry had sawn from an ancient river gum. The homestead was clad entirely with corrugated iron he had trucked in on a war-surplus Scammel flatbed thirty years previously when he took title to Venus Downs, one thousand square miles of starkly contrasting vast spinifex plains and towering ranges cut through by paleo channels of time and erosion. The corrugated cladding was tacked to a frame of ironbark uprights and beams that supported the walls and roof. The windows consisted of frames hinged at the top with a couple of loops of fencing wire. They were covered with corrugated iron shutters, which were pushed up and outwards and propped open with a length of wood. The shutters' only purpose was to afford some protection from the cyclonic winds and rain of the wet season, otherwise they were never closed. The floor was of rough-hewn hardwood resistant to relentless termite attacks.

From a heavy iron cauldron on the ancient stove, Dotti ladled out thick stew into an assortment of mismatched plates and carried them to the table. None of them took any notice that her thumbs were embedded in the gelatinous mixture as she thumped the plates down in front of them.

"Where's the eating irons, Chloe?" Carl shouted. Chloe rushed out with a fistful of knives, forks and spoons, dropping them in a pile on the table.

"Damper, Chloe!" shouted Dotti. "What hell you doin'? You get here on time, otherwise you cop my hand. You bin spending too long talkin' to that lazy old bugger and listenin' to his stories. What's he bin tellin' you now?"

Chloe did not answer as she juggled the hot damper between her hands and dropped it onto the table, where it was quickly handed around and dismembered.

Henry Boyce was watching a group of jackaroos squatting down by the billabong. He noticed old Johnny Quartpot saunter down to join them. They parted and the one who had assumed the dominant position against a large tree moved to make way for Johnny. As the elder of the mob, Johnny commanded their respect. The jackaroos were all related, some only distantly, but they were bound by tribal bloodlines. The old man said something that stirred their emotions and their voices became raised as they argued and gesticulated.

"That old bastard is trouble," Henry muttered, picking up the occasional sentence of native language as it floated up to him in the dry heat.

"Why don't you get rid of him?" Carl had rolled himself a cigarette, leaned back in his chair and lit it, blowing a ring of smoke towards the doorway. He and Walter were quite fluent in the native dialect, having played football, hunted and worked with them every day. They could easily follow what was being discussed.

Henry did not answer as he slowly chewed his food, his thoughts drifting elsewhere. He snapped back to the present and pointed his knife at Carl. "You fire that gun anywhere near Chloe again and I'll kick your arse. Do I make myself clear?"

Carl did not acknowledge his warning. Henry began to rise to his feet when he noted Carl's thin sneer. He reached across the table and slapped him hard across the face. "Do I make myself clear? Answer me, boy."

Carl reeled back with a look of defiance. "I hear you."

Henry Boyce's features were as sun dried and time worn as the ancient landscape of his surroundings. His skin was tanned to a deep brown, his eyes permanently squinting to ease the glare of the relentless blistering sun that bore down on the land for the majority of the year, until the blinding, driving rains of the monsoonal cyclone season turned the small watercourses into raging torrents kilometres wide. Over the millenniums, these walls of water had carved deep ravines through the metamorphic landscape, where only the toughest acacias and sparse grasses survived.

Then the raging fires would come, pushed on by the dry dust and debris-laden, scorching winds. The fires had vast fronts tens of kilometres wide, destroying everything in their path. Nothing survived. Not animal, nor tree, nor blade of grass. The land was scorched and ugly. Then the cycle would begin again and the land resumed its life. New growth sprang from the blackened stumps of the prickly acacia and beefwood. The cycle was complete with the sudden appearance of native bird and animal life; swirling clouds of budgerigars, a dizzying array of colourful finches, galahs and cockatoos. Pelicans crowded every billabong to gorge on the fish whose eggs and larvae morphed into life from the sands and gravels of the barren watercourses and dry clay pans. Mobs of kangaroos appeared in waves, intent on taking advantage of the life-giving green shoots of the returning grasses. The dingoes no longer had to hunt for prey, but simply killed for the thrill of killing. The only animals that could not match the pace of the native species were the cattle herds, decimated by a prolonged drought. The wet season was vital for their survival, only this year, the wet season had not arrived. Worse still, it had failed the year before—and the year before that.

Henry Boyce looked to the skies in vain. Some whispers of high stratus to the north but otherwise, the sky was clear. The heat was dry, intense. Rain would not come until the moisture-laden cumulus rolled in from the north-west to bring oppressive humidity, lightning, thunder, heavy rain and most likely, a cyclone. When and only when that happened would the drought break.

Henry watched the animated discussion amongst the jackaroos. The group suddenly fell silent as Johnny Quartpot stood and began to saunter towards the homestead. Henry went outside and sat on the veranda steps as the old man approached.

"Well, what is it Johnny?"

"The boys are unhappy, boss. They want more money."

Henry nodded but said nothing as he eyed the old man. In indigenous terms, he was very old. The ravages of the climate, backbreaking work and no healthcare meant that very few of his tribal peers had reached his age.

Henry could see the jackaroos had remained quiet and were staring in his direction. "There's no more bloody money to be had, Johnny. This season will finish me if the rains don't come again. In the meantime, I don't want to see any of them buggering off on walkabout."

"They're not happy, boss. They don't want to muster if they're not going to get a raise."

"Johnny, you're a bloody shit stirrer. What have you been telling them? I've worked my guts out developing this property and supporting you lot."

"It's not your property boss. It's ours. You whitefellas stole it from us."

"Crap. No one stole anything. Your mob has been walking bare-arsed around this country for thousands of years, living off the land. You owned nothing, no villages or fixed settlements, no gardens, no farmed livestock. You must be the only race on Earth that has established nothing in forty thousand years of existence. You speared a roo, goanna or snake, dug for yams, water lily roots, and picked wild fruits when you were hungry. The only difference now is I feed you and all your extended families on the property. Flour for your damper, all the beef you can eat, canned foods and tobacco and a few bucks a week thrown in. I'm the one footing the bill, Johnny. Look, we are two different cultures that will never assimilate or understand one another. Sit down here beside me, and let me explain."

The old aborigine looked hesitant and then did as he was beckoned. He was pleased to get off his feet. Henry took out his tobacco tin and rolled himself a cigarette before passing the tin and matches to Johnny. He waited for him to roll a cigarette, strike a match on the step and light up.

"You don't own this land and neither do I. We merely occupy it. It was inevitable some foreigner would land on these shores and claim it. If it hadn't been the English, the Portuguese, Dutch and French weren't far behind. It was not that long ago the Japanese were keen to lay claim to it. If they'd won the War your mob certainly wouldn't be alive today."

They sat in silence and finished their cigarettes. Johnny slowly pushed himself to his feet. "This is my land."

Henry fixed him with a cold expression. "It maybe your land, but I legally occupy it, and there's nothing you can do about that. There's also nothing I can do about you taking the boys on walkabout but if you do, none of them will be allowed back. They can go camp on some other billabong on the property, but I'm not going to feed them. If the rains don't come soon, you'll all be living off the land again as I'm already into the bank for too much. No rain this time I know they'll sell me up. You're stirring up the trouble, so I advise you to back off."

Henry was relying on calling Johnny's bluff, but he had to be careful because if the jackaroos went walkabout there was no telling how long they would be gone. It could be days, weeks or months before they returned with no explanation for their absence. It was not uncommon for individuals, groups or the whole mob to suddenly disappear into the night. Everything in the camp would be left as it was. Cooking utensils scattered around, mattresses lying under the trees with assortments of broken furniture, clothes lay where they discarded them. They shunned the shacks built of corrugated iron sheets some distance from the homestead, preferring to sleep out under the stars. Only in the depths of winter when the heavy desert frosts drove them to seek shelter, would they huddle in the huts and build fires on the packed earth floor for warmth. And just as quietly as they had departed without warning, they would return and resume as though there had been no time lapse; a deeply superstitious people who respected only the spirits and dreamtime of their ancestors.

"Start telling a ghost story around the campfire at night while you're out mustering and watch their reaction," an old white drover once told Henry at the pub. Henry had tried it and was amazed. The jackaroos' eyes widened in fright as the spirits and ghosts in the fable began to be revealed, their fear evident. Without a sound, they simply disappeared silently into the night. It was some time before they could trust him not to start spinning such yarns again.

Johnny was staring at Henry as though lost deep in thought. "You going mustering next week?"

Henry nodded. "That's right. We'll be gone for a week or more. I want to bring in about a thousand head closer to the homestead."

"Then Chloe's not needed here. I'll take her with me for a few days."

Henry arched his eyebrows and his face hardened. He trusted Johnny implicitly and knew no harm would come to her while in his care, but he didn't want her indoctrinated into their ancient culture. He had other plans for her. "No, I don't want you to do that. She stays here. Dotti will look after her."

"She's my granddaughter; she's going with me," Johnny answered defiantly.

Henry understood what was happening. Johnny had lost the previous argument and it was now about saving face. He could easily explain to the jackaroos why they were not getting a pay rise, but he had to show Henry he was not in complete control. "You know damned well she is not your granddaughter."

The old man turned. "She is daughter of the Duchess, and Duchess was my daughter, so she is my granddaughter. She doesn't belong to you."

"Johnny, you know the Duchess was not your daughter."

"You've got a problem there boss. Adoption papers say Duchess was my daughter. Too bad about the Duke. He's not mentioned on the papers as the father. Dunno who that Duke fella was, do you?"

"Okay, you can take her out and introduce her to your dreamtime and ancestors for a week or so, but no longer. If she's not here when I get back, I'll come looking for you."

Johnny had won this round but he couldn't resist a taunt. "You'd never find us, boss, you know that. But she'll be here when you get back."

"And you'd better tell the boys we'll be mustering."

Johnny nodded. "The rains are coming, boss."

"How do you know that?"

"The ants, boss. They're going like crazy stockin' up their mounds with food. I've been watching them." And with that, Johnny turned his back on Henry and walked away.

The escarpment behind the homestead turned brilliant orange as the first rays of the new day penetrated the dawn and two figures rode out trailing a single packhorse. The harsh 'carks' of the crows were underscored by the chortling, musical echo of magpies and the incessant chatter of thousands of budgerigars that had suddenly come to life in the surrounding trees. Chloe soaked up the sounds. It was the time of the day that was the most serene, a cacophony of melodious orchestration merely the opening scene to a grand opera of soft light that bathed and quickly enveloped the surroundings before fading into the encroaching heat of the day, when nothing stirred and the landscape appeared devoid of life.

They rode in silence all morning, stopping briefly around midday beside a permanent waterhole fed by a trickling stream that drained from within a sandstone formation.

"How far have we got to go Gramps?"

"Oh, be there this time day after tomorrow." Johnny had boiled a billy of water, thrown in a fistful of tea and poured them each a mug as they ate corned beef sandwiches Dotti had prepared for them. They idly watched the horses drink and graze around the waterhole.

"You going to show me the dreamtime Gramps?"

The old man nodded. "Yes, but you must never tell anyone or show anyone of what you see. You must promise me."

"I promise Gramps."

The remainder of the day passed quickly before they pulled up and camped under a large overhanging rock ledge, the rear and roof of which were covered in aboriginal rock paintings. Johnny unsaddled the horses and hobbled them. Their swags were rolled out under the overhanging ledge. Chloe gathered wood, started a fire and retrieved an iron camp oven from the packhorse. She threw in two cups of flour, a pinch each of salt and baking powder and then added water to make a thick dough before putting the lid on and placing it in the embers. When the damper was ready, she tipped it out and broke it into four equal portions. She was about to cut a couple of thick slices of corned beef when Johnny quietly told her to stop. He was watching a goanna as it waddled down to the waterhole. He slowly got to his feet and picked up a large rock, which he threw with unerring accuracy to hit the animal on the side of the head, momentarily stunning it. The delay was all that Johnny required as he ran forwards, picked up a stick and delivered the death blows. He had to kill it quickly as the goanna was dangerous, its razor sharp claws and teeth quite capable of delivering severe wounding. He dragged it across and threw it into the hot embers of the fire, without preparing it in any way. Chloe was not fazed by the brutal manner of the animal's death, but was rather astounded by the speed with which her grandfather reacted. She was used to his slow movements, which she knew signified his age. She was quite used to goanna and its beautiful white flesh—not unlike chicken. Half an hour later, Johnny took the animal by the tail and dragged it out of the embers. He scraped off the charred skin, and sliced off chunks of the flesh.

"Better than corned beef," he grinned.

They alternated between chewing the meat and pieces of damper, swilling each down with a mouthful of tea. The myriad of birdlife that had been scared off by Johnny's sudden actions returned to the waterhole. As daylight faded, their chatter subsided as they drifted into the surrounding trees. Johnny retrieved a fishing line from his pack and baited a couple of hooks with pieces of goanna flesh. He sauntered down to the waterhole, unwinding the line from the stick it was lapped around. He cast the line out before placing a large rock on the stick and remainder of the line.

"Let's see if we've got breakfast in the morning." He rolled a cigarette and sat with his back supported by a saddle.

"Are these part of the dreaming Gramps?" Chloe pointed at the various figures and shapes on the walls and ceiling of the overhang.

"Yes they are, but that's not what I'm going to show you. Whitefellas have seen these ones. There are many, many of them throughout this whole region. The ones I'm going to show you no whitefella has ever seen—and must never see."

He kept talking, but Chloe didn't hear him as she had drifted off to sleep.

She awoke to the sound of the horses snuffling and snorting as they nibbled on the stubble of dry grass. She could see Johnny down by the waterhole scaling and gutting fish. He had risen early to pull in his catch and bait the hooks again. Chloe walked down and stood in the cool water and leaning down, cupped some in her hands to splash over her face.

"Morning Gramps."

"You get the fire going again, girlie. Put the billy on and we'll have these for breakfast."

Chloe loved to be with her grandfather, away from the homestead and the constant demands of Dotti. The sun bathed the morning in soft light while they saddled the horses and rode on.

"How far now Gramps?"

"We'll be at the outstation late this afternoon. We'll camp there tonight and walk from there tomorrow."

After stopping around midday for tea, damper and cheese, they arrived at the outstation cabin constructed from thick planks adzed from the surrounding ancient eucalypts. Johnny unsaddled the horses and let them go into a small holding yard. The cabin consisted of a single room with a battered table and chairs, covered in dust and cobwebs. It was obvious it had not been used for years. The solitary window opening had no glass.

"We're not going to sleep in there are we Gramps?"

"No, we'll camp down near the billabong. Just use the cabin to put our gear in tomorrow morning."

"Did Henry build this cabin?"

"No, it was built by some squatter before Henry took over Venus Downs. Henry doesn't use it any more. This is not good country for cattle; too dry. He mainly runs cattle in the north. More water and better grazing."

A fire was soon burning and they shared the remainder of the cheese and damper along with two potatoes Johnny had dropped into the embers. The jackets were hard and crisp when he pulled them out, dusted them off against a rock and cut them in half, sprinkling each with a little salt, then adding a dab of butter from a sealed tin.

"We've got to be up and away before first light. We can't take the horses because they'll leave tracks, which can easily be followed. You make another damper now. That will be plenty for tomorrow. No need to carry water; there are water holes where we're going."

Chloe didn't need waking. It was not yet dawn but the landscape was still illuminated by a phosphorescent full moon. She retrieved the damper and put it in an old army kitbag, which she slung over her shoulder. Johnny put the horse tack into the cabin along with their swags and without beckoning Chloe, he began to walk towards the east.

Occasionally, he would stop as though lost in thought and look back the way they had come, then without a word he pressed on, the iron-hard soles of his feet picking a path through the rocks and low scrub. Chloe was also barefooted; her feet hardened from having never worn shoes in her life. No white man could ever follow a blackfella, Johnny had explained. Bare feet didn't leave a trace but whitefella boots and horses were like a highway; easy to follow.

They walked steadily into the dawn and towards the rising sun. Late morning, Johnny stopped on the very edge of a deep ravine and looked out towards the south-east.

"There it is." He pointed towards a range of low hills emerging out of the barren plain. The hills gradually increased in height until they stopped at a final jagged outcrop. "That is the giant frill-neck lizard."

Chloe strained to see what he was pointing out. She shook her head. "I can't see what you're showing me Gramps. I don't know what I'm supposed to be looking at."

"See how the hills rise from that smallest one and each one grows larger? The lizard appears as you come to the biggest one."

"I can see that now."

"Then what do you see at the head of the lizard?"

"I can see two big red rocks at its highest point."

"Those are the eyes. I will show you its mouth and teeth soon."

Her gaze went back to the tip of the tail and then followed each twist as the animal slithered across the landscape, surmounted by a menacing head.

"Did you find this place Gramps?"

"No, it's been the sacred site of my mob since the beginning of time. Me and now you are the only ones alive who know about it."

"What about your people back at the station?"

Johnny shook his head. "I would never show them. When they're not working, they go to town and get on the gunja and grog. One of them would start talking in the pub and quickly the whitefellas would hear about it. I don't trust them."

"Why are you showing me Gramps?"

The old man looked into the distance. "It's because I love you and want to share something you will always remember me by. When I'm gone, I want you to guard this sacred site and come out here sometimes so I can look down from the dreaming and talk to you. Will you do that for me?"

Chloe turned towards the old man. She could not tell whether it was a tear forming in his eye or was just a reflection from his moistened iris. She put her arm around his shoulders and snuggled her head into his.

"Of course I will."

"And you must promise me you'll never show or tell anyone about this place."

"I promise."

"Now I will show you the rainbow serpent. It will kill any intruder not part of the dreaming. The serpent will strike, just as you know deadly snakes will if you're not careful."

Chloe shuddered as she thought of the lethal death-adders, taipans and king-browns common on Venus Downs. If bitten, there was little hope of survival. She was somewhat bewildered by what Gramps was saying. However, Gramps had shown her how to catch and kill snakes to eat so she was not too afraid.

"We're going down into the lizard to talk with the serpent."

Chloe followed as Johnny set off down the opposite side of the long escarpment they had just climbed. Two hours later, they were at the base and he commenced walking up a dry watercourse hewn into the timeless sandstone of the surrounding chasm. The heat was oppressive as it bounced off the solid walls. He suddenly veered off into an intersecting dry stream bed. It appeared to be a dead end. Chloe was distracted momentarily by the sight of a rock wallaby on a ledge high above her. When she looked back, Johnny had vanished. She hurried on, thinking he had fallen but there was no sign of him. She came to a sheer sandstone wall.

"Gramps, where are you?"

Johnny stepped out from behind a shadow in the rock beside her. Chloe gave a start. "You frightened me." She had not noticed that the dark shadow concealed an entrance to a narrow descending passageway.

Without a word, Johnny disappeared into the shadow and Chloe gingerly followed into the darkness of half-light that penetrated through a slither of the penetrated sandstone high above. She could see the outline of her grandfather's figure ahead, as she placed a hand on either side of the descending wall and followed. She saw him turn and disappear again. She turned at the junction and he reappeared ahead of her. Eventually, they emerged into a brightly lit amphitheatre. It took her moments to adjust to the light, but she caught her breath at the scene painted completely along one wall. It was of a giant, vividly coloured snake painted in ochres ranging from black to brown to vivid orange. The most striking feature was the huge red eyes of an evil looking reptile poised to strike, its two fangs bared in an open mouth. All around the serpent were depicted smaller monotone snakes in either black or various shades of brown.

"That's the rainbow serpent, isn't it Gramps? It looks evil."

Johnny nodded and pointed back behind her. Turning towards the entrance from which she had just emerged, Chloe saw the open mouth of the giant lizard she had just walked through. On the opposite wall to the serpent, she saw the figure of a crudely drawn human with a round head with two black dots for eyes and a black slash for a mouth. From the head there appeared to be an aura of emanating rays of light. The figure was dressed in a long cloak in various shades of brown and white and around its neck hung a pendant mounted with a brilliant red object the size of a small apple in the centre.

"What does that figure mean?" Chloe asked in amazement as she studied the scene.

Johnny shook his head. "I don't know. Come, there's something more I want to show you. This is the mouth of the serpent." Johnny walked towards an ancient boab tree growing between two painted vertical rocks representing the fangs of the serpent. He knelt down before the tree and beckoned Chloe to do the same. He began to chant in a steadily rising voice, all the while staring at a small hole in the base of the cliff.

Chloe new better than to say anything. She watched and listened to her grandfather. She could follow what he was chanting. Over and over, he called softly to the guardian of the sacred site. Suddenly, she saw the head of a deadly snake and made a move to jump away. Johnny restrained her with a firm grip on her knee as he continued to chant. She remained frozen with fear as first the head and then the full length of the king-brown appeared from within the hole and moved towards them, its coal black eyes and flicking tongue sensing the presence of the intruders. Johnny could feel Chloe shivering as he increased the pressure on her knee in an effort to calm her without breaking his chant. The metres of death circled them and she could feel the touch of its smooth, chrome brown skin on her legs. Petrified, she knew she was utterly defenceless if it chose to strike. She would not see the movement; it would be over in the blink of an eye. Death would follow within minutes as the venom penetrated the nerve cells of her brain, and restricted her lungs and vital organs. She let out a sigh of relief as the snake slithered back to the hole and disappeared.

Johnny leant forwards and put his hand into the darkness of the aperture. He slowly drew out a small earthenware bowl, which contained a number of brilliant red stones. In the centre was a particularly large stone the size of a circled thumb and forefinger. All the stones appeared to be covered with an oily sheen.

"Can I have one?".

Johnny looked hesitant before picking out one of the surrounding stones the size of a bird's egg, and handed it to her. "You must never tell anyone where you got it from. Promise me again you will preserve this sacred site by never revealing it to anyone."

Chloe nodded as she studied the stone. "It's beautiful Gramps. What is it?"

"It's an eye of the serpent. Don't you ever show anyone and hide it well. Now you put the bowl back."

Chloe pulled back in horror. "I can't do that Gramps. I'm frightened."

"The rainbow serpent won't strike you. It would have already done so if it wanted to. You're safe so long as you sing to it as you put it back. Don't be in a hurry."

Chloe started to chant as she slid the bowl back into the hollow, expecting at any moment to feel the fangs bite into her wrist. She removed her hand, shaking with fear.

"Come, girlie." Johnny patted her on the shoulder. "We have to go if we are to get back to the outstation by dark."

They retraced their steps as there was no other exit. Johnny set off at a fast pace. Chloe easily kept up, but was curious as to why he was in such a hurry. They arrived back in the late afternoon.

"Put the billy on girlie." Johnny instructed abruptly and walked away. Chloe lit a fire, all the while watching as Johnny walked around the cabin in an ever-widening circle. Finally, he spotted what he was looking for and slowly followed the trail as it weaved around and over rock outcrops, careful to avoid leaving any telltale signs to the uninitiated. He walked slowly back to the campfire and sat down by his saddle and swag.

"What were you looking for Gramps?"

"Someone has been here today. They've only just left."

"You mean they followed us all day?"

Johnny shook his head. "No, I don't think so; I would have picked up some signs on the way back. I think they waited here and left when they saw us coming."

"Could have been one of the stockmen from the homestead."

"No, I would have picked up signs of that. They would have ridden up on horse or walked around in their boots leaving a trail. Whoever it was didn't want us to know he'd been here; he was good. But I found what I was looking for."

"Can you show me?"

Chloe followed him as he got up and walked a short distance to a flat rock outcrop bare of any vegetation.

"There, can you see that?"

Chloe carefully looked all over the rock but could see nothing that would signify any disturbance. "What am I supposed to be looking at?"

"Ants. See that crushed ant there?" Johnny pointed to the low end of the rock where someone had stepped. "Now look further up the rock. Can you see two more crushed ants and look, there's another one wounded. They've only just been trodden on, otherwise the other ants would have removed them along with the wounded one. Come back in half an hour and any trace of them will be gone."

"You know who it was, don't you?"

"I've got an idea, but why he would follow is a mystery. Whoever it was, he wasn't wearing boots."

"Who?"

"I'll keep that to myself for now. No point in naming someone without proof." He turned and walked back to the camp. "What have we got to eat girlie?"

Johnny picked up the tracks of a shod horse the following day, but said nothing. He recognised it as one of the station horses, but any number of people around the homestead could have been riding it. It clearly favoured its right front leg, as the imprint into the red earth was heavier on the left. He had previously observed the slight imperfection in the horse's gait. He was mystified, as he knew the horse would have been left at the homestead when Henry took every available hand on the muster. It was a former racehorse Henry had picked up in a card game, not suited to heavy mustering work.

By the time they returned to the homestead, the yards were full of cattle being branded and bulls castrated, with breeding heifers and cows separated ready to be driven back to the northern grasslands. The older cows, excess bulls and steers were yarded, ready to be sent to the nearest market. It was a chaotic scene of clouds of swirling dust, bellowing cattle and shouting stockmen as they ingested the stink and matter of manure-saturated dust, combined with the heat and clouds of moisture seeking flies that got in eyes and up nostrils. Every hand was in the thick of it along with Carl, Walter and Henry.

Johnny and Chloe rode past and unsaddled the horses, let them go and put the tack in the stables. He noted the horse he had been tracking standing quietly in the yard. He walked over and called it, noting its step as it came towards him. The gait was unmistakable. It was definitely the horse he had tracked back from the outstation, but who had been riding it was a mystery.

3

A priest was sitting on the veranda. Not old, as priests usually were; this one was younger, late twenties or early thirties, Chloe estimated. She hadn't seen him before, but she could feel his eyes on her, penetrating her clothing rather than her soul. Clergy of all denominations were irregular visitors with no set routine. They would turn up and stay for a day or more. They were welcome no matter the religious persuasion of the host; not that any station owner paid much heed to religion or the hereafter. They were too busy trying to eke out an existence in this harsh and unforgiving landscape. Everything was born, lived and died; no eternal hand guided the process. The clergy were not expected to preach religion, but to offer communication with the outside world, to counsel and simply be a welcome face to talk to, albeit an unfamiliar face.

"Hello. You must be Chloe. Dotti has been telling me about you. Is there anything I can help you with?"

"No, there's nothing." Chloe smiled shyly as she walked past. He turned and followed her with his eyes. She didn't want to stop and talk. She smelt like a horse and wanted a long cool shower to get rid of the dust and smell.

"'Bout time you got back," Dotti shouted as she saw her enter. "Father is here and I want you to help with dinner."

"I'm just going for a shower first."

"Well, you hurry it up and don't be too long. Gone for a week an' leavin' poor old Dotti to do all the work ain't good enough. What you and that doddery old fool been up to?"

Chloe ignored Dotti's question and made her way through to her room at the back of the sprawling homestead. She took a jar of coloured stones she had collected over the years and tipped them out onto the bed. She took the red stone out of her pocket and held it up to the light, turning it in her fingers, trying to peer into it. It appeared to be covered with an oily sheen, which she attempted to remove by briskly rubbing it against her shirt. She could see the brilliant red buried deep within but it was masked by the mysterious coating. She tossed it onto the bed and stripped off, but her eyes kept returning to its brilliance. Now naked, she picked it up again and turned in a circle as the light from the open bedroom window produced brilliant facets within. Fascinated, she attempted to capture the radiance, noticing flashes of a higher or lesser brilliance as she twisted the stone at various angles trying to peer into its depths.

Suddenly sensing she was not alone, she swung around to the open doorway and then the window. Satisfied no one was there, she picked up a towel and wrapping it around herself, walked to the outside shower. The shower was directly under a large water tank filled from the nearby billabong. The cubicle consisted of roughly sawn timber slabs, which didn't meet completely to give a sealed joint, nor did the door fit perfectly. The enclosure gave some privacy, but privacy was never on her mind as no one ever ventured to her end of the house or used the shower except her. She reached up, turned on the large rose-head and stood, taking in the cool flood as it washed the sweat and dirt from her hair and body. She was towelling herself down when the strange feeling she was not alone returned, only to laugh when she looked through a gap in one of the panels and saw the tethered milking goat pulling at the undergrowth. By the time she returned to her room, she could hear Dotti summoning her from the kitchen. She unwrapped the towel and standing nude, bent forwards to towel her hair. Out of the corner of her eye, she caught what she thought was a slight movement as someone pulled away from the window. She silently ran over and looked out to see the heel of a boot disappearing around the side of the building. She had not been imagining things and knew instantly who it belonged to. She placed the stone in the bottom of the jar and shovelled up the other multi-coloured stones with her cupped hands, then poured them on top. She held the jar up to make sure the red stone was invisible, shaking it until it was completely hidden.

Chloe quickly dressed and went out into the kitchen to help Dotti.

"Why you take so long to have a shower? Bet you standin' there thinking you beautiful. Preening before the mirror and all."

Chloe ignored the remark. Dotti never changed. It was one long tirade, but underneath it, Chloe knew it was all bluster.

Henry, Carl and Walter were talking to the priest on the veranda when Dotti called them in. They had showered and put on clean shirts and jeans. Henry sat opposite the priest, who was facing directly into the kitchen with Carl and Walter sitting either side of him.

Chloe served up four plates of stew with a pile of mashed potatoes and cabbage on each plate. They muttered their thanks as it was placed in front of them. The priest looked up at Chloe and gave her a smile and nod of thanks. She did not look at him as she fled back into the kitchen where she ate with Dotti.

Carl had already begun to eat when the priest bowed his head and put his hands together over the meal. Henry put down his fork of food as the priest began to say grace. Walter followed Carl's lead. He was too hungry after such a long day in the yards to listen to prayers. Finally, the priest blessed himself and picked up his knife and fork.

"Are you going to stay with us for a day or two, Father?"

"No, Henry, I'll be off in the morning. Too much ground to cover and I want to get around the parish as quickly as possible to meet everyone."

Chloe removed the plates and could feel his eyes following her into the kitchen. Next, she brought out pudding plates stacked high with treacle covered dumplings.

"Oh, this reminds me of my mother's cooking," the priest said in his gentle Irish brogue as the plate was put in front of him. "My compliments to the cook."

"Did you hear that, Dotti?" Henry shouted. "Father likes your cooking. You can stay for a while longer."

Dotti walked to the head of the table with her hands akimbo on her waist in mock anger. "You can't get rid of me, Henry Boyce. You'd all starve if Dotti left. No one can cook like Dotti, so you lot behave yourselves." With that, she spun on her heel and went back to the kitchen.

Henry and the priest laughed, but the boys were too busy attacking the dumplings. They finished and Chloe began to pick up the plates.

"C'mon, Father, let's go and sit out on the veranda and chew the fat for a while," Henry suggested.

The priest followed Henry out. Carl and Walter excused themselves and walked off towards their rooms in separate outbuildings.

"Did you notice that priest couldn't take his eyes off Chloe? He was stripping her naked." Carl commented.

"Yeah, but you're no different. You get a hard on every time she comes near you," Walter replied.

"But he's a bloody priest. They're supposed to be all fudge punchers aren't they? Something about that guy ain't right."

"'Bout time you went into town again, brother. You need to get your rocks off."

"You gonna come with me?" Carl asked.

"Sure. If the old man will let us go after this muster. See you in the morning."

Carl didn't reply as he opened the door of his room and slammed it behind him.

The priest and Henry sat on the veranda in silence while Henry rolled a cigarette and lit up. He was surprised when the priest accepted the tobacco pouch and expertly rolled one between his thumb and forefinger, licked the gummed edge and then rolled it closed.

"How long have you been a priest?"

"I graduated from the seminary six months ago. I asked for a transfer to Australia."

"Why Australia?"

"Ireland is still a troubled place, Henry. I wanted to get away from there and I've always known I would make it here one day."

"What made you take the oath of poverty, chastity and obedience then?"

The priest looked at him sharply. "What do you mean by that?"

"Just what I said." Henry didn't look at him; apparently distracted by the cloudless heavens above.

"I had a vocation to enter holy orders, become a priest and spread God's message."

"You had a rough upbringing then?"

The priest unconsciously put his left hand over his right to cover his scarred knuckles.

Henry nodded. "You either played a lot of Gaelic football or been in a lot of fights. It's one or the other; most likely both."

"Yes, I've had my fair share of fights. You can't protect your knuckles or nose when you're in a serious argument with Protestant gangs."

"I think you've been in a bit more trouble than that haven't you, Father?"

"You're very observant, Henry. Yes, I was the ringleader of a gang in Falls Road. We were always at war with the Protestants of Shankhill."

"Which brings me back to my question. Why did you become a priest?"

"The police caught up with me one day and gave me one hell of a beating. I was sixteen going on twenty-one, angry and violent. They warned me next time I'd be found in a ditch with a bullet in the brain. There'd be no investigation or search for the guilty party. The message was very clear."

"You must have been in real trouble to have suffered that threat. Did they suspect you of killing someone?" The priest ignored his question, but Henry could see he'd struck a nerve.

"The parish priest took me home, patched me up and got me out of Belfast. He gave me a bus fare, a few quid and a contact in Dublin. The contact was another priest who gave me a place to live and enrolled me in school. School was very easy for me and I went onto university. But I just couldn't apply myself; I couldn't see any future in the discipline I'd chosen. I began to drink, fight, gamble and whore around. Belfast was coming back to haunt me. The anger was still there—I couldn't shake the black dog of depression."

Henry was amazed how the priest was pouring his heart out. It was like hearing a confession the wrong way round. Henry's parents had been Catholic, as were his Irish forebears, but he had rebelled and could never get the connection between an omnipresent and omniscient divinity and the wars and pestilence the world had endured—and continued to endure. Why did people continue to believe in what was in his view little more than mythology?

"Who pulled you out of the gutter that time?"

"The same priest who looked out for me in Dublin. I'd drifted from his counselling and tried to stay clear as I didn't want him to see the life I was living, or the people I'd fallen in with. In despair one Sunday, I was just wandering around when I passed a church in another parish. The doors were open and I could hear the Mass being said. I went in and sat down in the back pew, as the church was full. The Communion chant drifted around me but I wasn't listening or paying attention. Then I felt a hand on my shoulder; it was the priest who'd helped me before. I looked around and saw the church was empty—I don't know how long I'd been sitting there alone. From that moment, with his counselling I entered a seminary and took holy orders. Father O'Connor saved me from certain destruction."

"And what is your name, Father?"

"Oh, my apologies, Henry," the priest hastily responded. "I thought I already told you. It's Dion Murphy."

Henry turned and fixed him with a hard glare. "Well, Father Murphy, I noticed you couldn't take your eyes off Chloe. Was that lust, or are you only interested in her soul?"

Murphy's face flared several shades redder than the auburn mane that betrayed his Celtic heritage. "I resent that remark, Henry. She is indeed a beautiful young girl, but I wasn't concerned with that. I was just wondering what her future is here, cut off from the outside world."

"Chloe loves it here. And she would never leave while her grandfather is still alive."

"You mean that old black fellow I saw her ride in with this afternoon is her grandfather?"

"No, he's not, but she refers to him as 'Gramps'. She adores him—and the feeling is mutual, I might add."

"What about your sons? Do you think they'll stay on the land with you? I suppose they'll inherit the property?"

"Carl and Walter are not my natural sons, but that's another story. Time will tell as to whether they stay, but at the moment they appear happy to do so."

"Will one of them marry Chloe, do you think?"

"Chloe will make up her mind who she marries, but any interest they have at the moment would be carnal, as is normal with any young buck. I've never seen any expression of feelings by her to either of them."

"Would she ever marry an aborigine?"

"No, that would never happen. She's far too intelligent for any of the boys around here. Other than Dotti and Gramps, she doesn't associate with them at all. I would like her to get away from here, go down to Perth and further her education but as I said, she won't leave while Gramps is alive. And if she did agree to go, where would she go to? She knows no one outside of Venus Downs, and there's no one she could stay with except my sister, who I haven't spoken to in some years now."

"I don't think I'd have any trouble in getting her into a good convent. The Sisters of Mercy have a particular facility for girls from the country. They also have scholarships for the bright ones. A year or two with the right tuition and in the right environment could see her go to university. I could make enquiries for you, if you like."

Henry didn't reply right away; he rolled another cigarette and lit it. "Yes, I would appreciate that, Father. As much as I love her and would like her to stay, there's nothing for her here." He turned to see Murphy giving him a curious look. "What's on your mind, Father?"

"You seem very interested in her welfare, which I cannot really understand."

"What do you mean by that?"

"Well, you say she's not related to you and knows no other existence than living on this property and being the cook's assistant, as far as I can see."

"She came to this property as a toddler and I've looked after her. I would love her to remain here, but I would also like to see her out of this environment."

"Yes, she's beautiful; a stunning figure, magnificent complexion and charming manner—and those eyes would slay any man. She's a misfit here Henry—"

Father Murphy could see that Henry was lost in thought. "What are her interests? Does she collect gemstones?"

"What a strange question. Why do you ask?"

"Nothing in particular. I just wondered what she does to amuse herself. There are some very interesting rock formations around here, rock formations as old as the planet itself."

"You're interested in rocks. Is that your hobby?"

Father Murphy laughed. "Not any longer, although they did interest me once." He could see Henry was about to pursue a line of questioning and cut him off by standing up. "Well, it's been a long day for me, driving out here. Likewise, I'm sure you've got another hard day ahead of you in the morning. I think I'll say goodnight."

Henry nodded. "Yes. The last room on the right beside Carl and Walter is yours." Henry pointed Father Murphy in the right direction. "The toilet and shower is just past that. See you in the morning."

The next day, Father Murphy was already at the table when Henry appeared from his wing of the homestead. Dotti and Chloe had set the table and doled out thick porridge, followed by damper and thick slices of fried steak topped with eggs. Chloe poured black tea into enamelled mugs. Carl reached for the can of thickened condensed milk and poured a liberal amount into his.

"No milking cows out here, mate. Would you like some?" He made to hand the can to Father Murphy.

"No thank you, I like it black."

"Just like your women, I suppose. You do like women, don't you mate?"

Henry reached across the table, grabbed a handful of Carl's shirt and twisted it around his throat, dragging him halfway across the table. "You offensive bastard. Apologise now or I'll throttle you."

Carl's face was turning red as he struggled for breath. "I didn't mean anything by it Priest. I'm sorry."

Henry thrust him backwards so that Carl sprawled backwards over the bench on which he had been sitting and hit his head on the hard floor.

"Not as smart as you thought you were eh, Sunshine?" Walter sniggered as he headed for the doorway with a mug of tea and a steak topped damper in his hands. He was not going to stick around to suffer the fury of his humiliated twin.

Dazed, Carl picked himself up and glared at the large knife lying beside the damper.

Henry matched his look of fury. "Don't even think about it boy."

Carl muttered an obscenity under his breath as he rose and followed his brother outside.

"I'm sorry about that, Father, but he's not going to be allowed to get away with a comment like that in my presence."

Father Murphy laughed. "Henry, it's obvious you've never been to Belfast. You've not had someone walk up to you with his mates and spit in your face, knowing there's nothing you could do about it unless you wanted to be beaten to a pulp or kicked to death. The boy will learn some day. Someone will take offense and give him a hiding he'll never forget. His comment was nothing. I best be getting along now."

Father Murphy rose and thanked Dotti and Chloe.

"Please come again Father. I like someone who likes my cookin'," Dotti beamed.

Father Murphy noted Chloe had turned away and was busying herself with the dishes. As Henry was following him out to his vehicle, a dog from the jackaroos camp suddenly appeared out of nowhere and buried its teeth into the heel of the priest's black boot.

Henry stepped forwards and delivered an almighty kick into the dog's ribs. The sickening crunch and sound of breaking bones was unmistakable. The dog rolled away, screaming in pain.

"Doesn't like me," Father Murphy commented, swinging open the door of the cab.

"Dogs are like people, Father. Some like you and some don't. The ones that don't can get personal; as you've just seen."

Father Murphy nodded and started the engine, put the vehicle into gear and with a wave, drove off down the track.

Henry watched him go and muttered to himself, "There's something very odd about that man." He turned and looked at the whimpering dog and again shouted towards the camp. "Shoot that bloody animal and put it out of its misery."

She was grooming her horse when she sensed someone watching her.

"Hi, Chloe. Can I give you a hand?" Walter didn't wait for a reply. He picked up a curry comb and began to work on the coat of the glistening, chestnut haired animal.

"I've already done that side."

"I can see that, but see she likes it. Don't you want me to help you?"

Chloe looked up over the back of the horse. She was expecting Walter's usual leering grin but was surprised to see a soft, questioning look on his face. "No, but you can do this side as well if you like."

Walter laughed. "I'm bored with nothing to do. Looks like the dry season is almost over. I just want to get back to work." He stood back to admire his work.

"Look out!" Chloe swung the saddle over and reached underneath for the girth. She felt Walter's hand brush hers as he reached down and handed her the offside strapping.

"You're not going riding, are you? You've only just groomed her and now you're going to get her all sweaty and dirty again."

"I'm bored too Walter, and I don't care about doing it all again when I get back."

"Can I come with you then?"

Chloe pushed her knee into the horse's barrel and tightened the girth. "If you like, but I'm not waiting; I want to go for a bit of a gallop." She swung up into the saddle and trotted over to the yard gate. She bent down, unlatched it and swung her horse through and around before dropping the latch back into place in one fluid movement.

Walter stood and watched her kick the horse into an easy canter. Quickly he retrieved a saddle and bridle from the tack room and slowly walked towards a mob of horses. He picked out a large black gelding, notorious for its fiery temperament and being difficult to handle.

"C'mon, you black bastard." He called softy as he walked slowly towards it. "I've got a young filly just dying for a challenge and I want you to help me ride her down." The animal snorted, arched its neck and attempted to shy away. Walter anticipated the move and continued to walk slowly towards it. He pulled out some damper from his pocket. The animal stood stock-still and eyed the offering. If it didn't take it, it knew Walter would hand it to one of the other horses now walking towards him. Walter continued to talk softly as he approached. The animal took the bread and did not resist as he pushed the bit into its mouth, quickly flicking the bridle over its head before swinging the saddle on. A minute later he was outside the gate and looking in the direction Chloe had gone, but she was nowhere in sight. He grinned as he nudged the horse into a canter. He was in no hurry to catch her up. As a stallion, the horse had been unrideable. Henry had given it to Carl three years previous but it was a challenge he could not handle, which the animal immediately sensed. Curses and kicks and violent digging in the flanks with spurred boots did nothing to subdue it as it lashed out with bared teeth and hooves. On one occasion, Henry had witnessed how Carl was treating the animal and tore the thick stick from his hand before he was able to lash out again at the terrified beast. He swung Carl around by the shoulder and backhanded him, sending him sprawling into the dirt.

"Don't ever let me see you treating any animal that way again!" he had shouted in anger as he threw the stick onto Carl's prone body.

"The bloody thing is dangerous. I'm not going to ride it again until you cut its balls out."

"I'm going to do that, but I should probably cut yours out at the same time so you keep your violence in check. You'd better get it through your head that animal is always going to view you as an aggressor. Balls or no balls, it will never change its attitude towards you, just as you will never change yours towards it."

"Well, give it to bloody Walter and see if he can do any better, but I'm not riding it again!" Carl stood up, brushed himself off and walked away, hearing the horse whinny behind him. Walter gave his brother a mocking grin and stroked its nose and neck to calm the animal down. It had been Walter's horse since that day.

Walter checked the horse as it constantly pulled at the bit to break into a gallop. "There's plenty of time for that," he chided gently, patting its neck. Half an hour later, he saw Chloe riding towards him. She slowed and pulled up beside him.

"You've been giving that animal a real workout," he said as he looked at its foam streaked jaw and girth. Chloe laughed. "I thought you would catch up to me."

"I could have done that easily, but I'm not into racing. I'll ride back with you."

Chloe nodded as he swung his horse around. They rode in silence, listening to the birds and looking at the landscape, pretending to be indifferent to one another's presence.

"You're scared of me, aren't you?"

Chloe looked away before answering. "You both scare me."

"Why?"

"It's the way you look at me—and I know you talk about me."

"I don't know about Carl, but I only look at you because I think you're very pretty. I'd like to be friends if you'd let me."

Chloe did not reply as she nudged her horse into a trot. Walter restrained his mount as it attempted to follow suit and watched her gradually pull away. He was a kilometre behind her as the homestead came into view when he gave his horse its head. She turned when she heard the thundering hooves approaching and laughed as she spurred her mare into a gallop. It was no contest; Walter caught her and swept past without a sideways glance. Normally it would have been close but Chloe had ridden her horse hard and it was feeling the effects. He was holding the gate open as she rode up and dismounted in front of the stable. He let his horse go into the paddock and walked over to the stable carrying his saddle and bridle. Chloe was struggling to undo the foam-coated surcingle.

"Here, let me do that." He uncoupled it and swung the saddle and blanket off while deftly removing the bridle with his free hand. She followed him into the tack room where he hung up her bridle and slung her saddle over the railing of the stall.

"Thank you. I shouldn't have ridden Bess so hard at the start, otherwise I would have been able to beat you on the way back."

Walter laughed. "You wouldn't have a hope against my gelding. I grant you that mare is quick, but she's no match. Want me to prove it to you tomorrow? Why don't we make it five bucks to make it interesting and I'll give you a two hundred metre start."

Chloe nodded and smiled as she walked away. "I don't want to bet and I don't need the head start."

"Suit yourself. Tomorrow it is then." Walter studied her firm buttocks in the tight jeans as she walked towards the homestead. He ambled towards his room, tossed his hat onto a stand, pulled off his riding boots and lay down on the bed. He had just shut his eyes when his feet were swept off the bed and Carl sat down.

"I saw that, but it ain't going to do you any good brother."

"Oh, yeah?" Walter smiled slowly in satisfaction as he sat up. "And I'm going to do it again tomorrow, so eat your heart out. I'll lay a bet I pick her cherry while you're still having wet dreams. I bet you fifty bucks."

"You're on, arsehole."

Walter anticipated and fended off the backhander Carl viciously swung at him. His long, looping right connected with Carl's jaw and slung his head onto the wooden wall. Before Carl could counter-attack, Walter had swept up his boots and hat and put distance between himself and his dazed brother. He was sitting on the veranda talking to Henry when Carl strode casually towards them with a menacing look on his face.

"You two had an argument?"

"We're always having arguments, Henry, you know that. It was nothing. Carl just made the mistake of letting his guard down and I gave his jaw a workout."

Henry shook his head. "I can't understand why you two are always at each other's throats. Why the hell can't you just get along?"

"It isn't me Henry. Carl's always looking for a fight and some day, someone will give him one he'll remember for a long time. The bugger's mad."

"What were you arguing about?" Henry had already guessed. He had seen Walter and Chloe racing and noticed Carl watching, then later storm into Walter's room.

"Nothing much," Walter replied as he rolled a cigarette. "Just a bet Carl knows he can't win."

"I can imagine what that's about, but if either of you attempt it I'll kill you."

Carl pretended not to hear the remark as he sat down. Walter blew a smoke ring into the air and smiled.

"When a mare comes into season they're aching to be serviced Henry. That's only natural, isn't it?"

Henry leant across and grabbed Walter by the shirt front, pulling his face towards his and forcing him down onto his knees. "You can service any mare you like, you smart arse, but make sure it doesn't have two legs and is named Chloe or you'll be missing your most treasured possessions."

"Okay, okay Henry," Walter replied lamely, putting his hands up in surrender. He stood up and retrieved his cigarette from the floor.

"That goes for you too, Carl. Go into town if you want to get your rocks off, but Chloe is off limits. Do I make myself clear?"

"Aren't we even allowed to talk to her Henry? She wants to race me tomorrow. Is that off limits?"

"No, Walter, you know very well what I'm referring to. She appeared to be enjoying your company today, but she's only young and doesn't realise what you two are really after. I take it one of you made a bet today and the other has accepted the challenge. I'm right, aren't I?"

Walter didn't reply as Carl slowly nodded. "I'd like to marry her Henry. Would you object to that?"

"Carl, that decision would be hers alone, but I haven't seen any sign of her showing any interest in you."

"What if she prefers me brother? What are you going to do about that?" It was a challenging taunt. Walter was revelling in his brother's discomfort.

Carl stood and looked down at his brother. "Well, if she does, she'll live to regret it. To you she's just a challenge, but I happen to love her."

Walter laughed and stood. "You're going soft sunshine. You haven't even got to first base. Well, I'm going riding with her tomorrow; you can tag along if you like."

Carl turned and walked away with Walter's laugh ringing in his ears.

"I'd be careful if I were you Walter. Carl has a very short fuse and you might be holding the wrong end of the gelignite if you taunt him like that."

"He'll get over it Henry. We've been bashing hell out of each other since we were kids, but we're always over it by the next day. That's the first I've heard him wanting to marry Chloe."

Walter knew he was being watched as he combed Chloe's horse down and saddled it. He whistled *"You are my sunshine"* repeatedly at his loudest pitch.

Chloe walked towards him with a broad smile. "You're trying to annoy Carl, aren't you?"

"Not at all Chloe, I just like the tune." He gave her a wry grin as she took the reins from him, swung up into the saddle and trotted off. Walter casually undid the reins of his gelding from the railing, mounted and trailed her slowly. He was in no hurry as he studied her backside splayed in the saddle and contemplated his next move.

Chloe could feel his eyes following her and finally turned in the saddle. "Are you just going to follow me, or are you going to ride with me?"

"I'm giving you a head start in case you break into a gallop."

Chloe laughed. "You don't stand a chance anyway, but I'll give you plenty of warning on the way home."

Walter pulled level with her. They rode in silence, each with their own thoughts and studying the changing light patterns on the landscape of the evolving day.

"It's beautiful, don't you think?"

"It is, especially at this time of the day. But that's not the only beautiful thing I can see this morning."

At first his remark didn't register, but it became clear when she glanced sideways to meet his penetrating blue eyes. His facial muscles had relaxed, which brought out a warmth in them she was unfamiliar with. She was used to the hard, belligerent look both he and his brother wore almost constantly—particularly when they were in each other's company. Chloe felt wary and confused and turned away without acknowledging his comment.

"You really are beautiful Chloe. I'm sorry if I've treated you badly. It's just I've never been able to express my feelings. I've never known how to in front of Carl or Henry. I hope you never leave Venus Downs. Would you share it with me?" His question was not blurted out, but delivered with a soft confidence.

"What about Carl?"

"What about Carl? That's not what I asked you."

"Walter, it's obvious to me you and Carl are going to inherit Henry's properties someday. But you're always at each other's throats, so I can't possibly see how you two are going to survive in each other's company as the years go by."

Walter laughed. "Yeah that's true, but Carl won't be around. I will buy him out."

"What if he doesn't want to sell?"

"Then I'll find a way to make him sell. I don't ever want to leave Venus Downs. Why don't you answer my question; will you share it with me?"

"I can't answer that Walter."

"Well, give it some thought. I realise I've just sprung this on you, but I'm in love with you—I want to marry you, Chloe."

She didn't acknowledge his proposal and they rode on in awkward silence. Walter tried to keep up his air of confidence, but finally he cracked. "I realise you probably don't like me, and I'm really sorry for the way I've treated you. It was my childhood, you see. I don't know how to express love for anyone. I've always been in love with you, but I just couldn't show it. Just tell me if you don't like me and I won't ever bring it up again."

"It's not that I don't like you, Walter. I think you can be rather sweet when you try. You and Carl are the same, always trying to compete with one another. Sometimes I've noticed you both have a tender side, just never when you're together—"

Walter did not tell her it was because they both wanted the same things. They both wanted sole possession of Venus Downs and they both wanted her. "I'll try to work on it so you only see a pleasant side of me in future then." He spurred his horse into a canter, his mind lost in thought. He was lying on the grass verge of the billabong when she slowly rode up minutes later and dismounted. She sat down beside him and idly began to throw pebbles into the water, watching as the concentric rings spread out into diminishing ripples.

"Which of us do you like the most?"

Chloe threw another pebble, lost in thought about how she was going to answer. "I'm not going to answer that, other than to say I could like you both if your attitudes changed."

Walter reached over and began to stroke her arm. "Well, you're out here alone with me now, so why don't you show me how much you like me?"

Chloe felt a cold shiver go up her spine. Slowly she stood and walked towards her horse.

"C'mon Chloe, don't go cold on me. There's no one around."

She felt his arm wrap around her waist and turn her as she was about to swing into the saddle. He kissed her softly and she felt herself respond momentarily before pulling away.

"See, you do like me, don't you? I can tell." Walter laughed. He patted Chloe on her rump as she mounted. He watched her for a few seconds as she turned her horse and slowly broke into a trot. She was trying to control the shaking of her hands and resist the urge to kick her horse into a full-on gallop for home and safety. As though he sensed what she was thinking, he was mounted in an instant and rode up alongside her. He began small talk again. She stirred her horse into a gentle canter, while pretending she was interested in what he was saying. She breathed a sigh of relief as she saw the station buildings appear in the distance.

"Anytime you like Chloe. The bet's still on, isn't it? How much head start...." He didn't finish as his horse reared into the air with a pained snort and began to turn towards the source of the infliction. Walter fought to remain in the saddle and restrain the startled animal before he realised what had happened. Chloe was already in full gallop, her head crouched low in a jockey stance to gain distance, the riding crop she had inflicted the pain with trailing from her wrist. She leaned close to the mare's neck and urged it on.

"Bitch!" Walter yelled in frustration as he steadied his horse and finally got it into a gallop. However, he could see the chase was already lost. It would have been a very close contest, even if they had started together. The mare was faster than he realised and the distance to closure was now too far. He had been out-manoeuvred and was wild he had been suckered so easily. Instead of accepting with good grace he had lost by trickery and slowing his horse down, he spurred his mount on with angry kicks into its flanks and curses of demand. Chloe was already unsaddling as he swung into the yard in a cloud of dust and jumped from the saddle. He checked an angry outburst and broke into a twisted grin and then a stifled laugh as Chloe looked up with a smile.

"You fight dirty, lady."

"It was just a race Walter," Chloe taunted as she misinterpreted his facial expression. "We didn't make any rules. It was a case of the fastest horse won." She began to laugh as she took her saddle into the tack room. She didn't notice his expression change as he unsaddled and followed her in, closing the door behind him.

"You're not annoyed, are you?" Chloe was still chuckling to herself at the deception of her win.

"Of course not," he lied. "You won fair and square. Next time though, I'll be waiting for you to pull some sort of stunt."

"How do you know there'll be a next time? I don't need to prove Bess is faster than your gelding again." She trailed off as she noticed the door had been closed and he was leering at her. The mirth had disappeared. She made to brush past him, but he grabbed her and crushed her up against bales of chaff. She became aware of the hardness in his pants, which he thrust towards her.

"You like that don't you?"

"Walter, stop it. Let me go." She tried to cry out but he smothered her mouth with his and ran a hand inside her jeans while his free arm pinned her against the bales. Chloe knew they were alone and she could not be heard from the homestead as she tried to push him away.

"C'mon Chloe. Someone's going to give it to you so it may as well be me. Yell all you like. No one's going to hear you."

She bit his lip hard, pushed him away with all her fear-shaken strength and turned to escape through a door at the back of the stables. He wiped his mouth and spat out a globule of blood as he ran to cut her off.

"You bitch! You're not going to get away that easily. Just lie down and enjoy it."

A split second too late he noticed the arcing crop. He yelped in pain as it caught him across the nose and cheek, the platted kangaroo skin instantly raising a blood-engorged, cross-hatched pattern as his nose started to stream blood. Still clutching the crop, Chloe staggered backwards, a scream of terror stifled in her throat as Walter wiped away the blood and lunged towards her. Suddenly, the door opened and Johnny Quartpot was standing between them.

"Fuck off, you old shit," Walter yelled. "This is none of your business."

A punch landed directly on his already bloody nose. Walter staggered back in surprise at the strength of the blow. "Well, if it's a fight you want old man, you're in for a hiding." He rushed forwards, swinging wildly. Johnny deftly ducked and tattooed Walter's face with a series of staccato jabs to the eyes and damaged nose before stepping back to admire his work. A broad smile broke out, Johnny's pearl-white teeth etched across his wrinkled black face, as he waited for Walter's next move. He saw his assailant's fists clench and his face screw up in fury to unleash a charge, the weight of which he knew he would not be able to resist. Johnny dropped his fists and feinted to one side as Walter, sensing the kill, rushed forwards. The first blow caught him in the solar plexus and the second on the point of his jaw. Walter doubled in pain, holding his stomach and gasping for air as he collapsed onto his knees in shock before rolling sideways. "He won't be bothering you again, girlie."

Chloe rushed into his arms sobbing hysterically. "Oh, Gramps, Gramps!" she moaned as she recalled the horror of the last few minutes. He stroked her hair and patted her back until her sobs became shorter and slowly subsided.

"You go and lie down for a while and try to put it out of your mind. I want to have a few words with Walter. Don't say anything to anyone about what just happened."

Chloe nodded and composed herself as she let herself out and began walking unsteadily towards the homestead.

Walter staggered to his feet and leaned against the sacks of chaff for support. The aggression had gone out of him as his brain tried to assimilate the events of the last few minutes.

"Touch her again and I'll beat you to a pulp. Make no mistake boy—and you give Carl that message too."

Walter's mind was too befuddled to answer coherently. He could still feel the sting of Chloe's riding crop as he ran his hand down the ugly weal on his face. Johnny's punches had felt like hammer blows, too quick for him to defend or comprehend.

"If either of you think you can just use her because she's coloured and easy meat, you've got another think coming."

Walter groggily pulled himself upright and held out his open hand in defence when he saw Johnny step towards him. "I hear you Johnny, I hear you. Holy shit, you pack a punch for an ancient. It won't happen again. How the Christ do I explain this to Henry?"

"Tell him what you like, but he won't be hearing anything from me. You've already got my message, but if Chloe says anything to him you'll be packing your bags, that's for sure."

Walter nodded and slumped back on the sacks again as Johnny walked out.

Henry whistled under his breath when Walter finally appeared for dinner. He had sensed something was amiss as Chloe appeared very subdued. He had caught Dotti's quick shake of the head when he was about to ask what was troubling her.

"So Walter, you either got kicked by a horse or you went a round with Johnny Quartpot. I'm inclined to believe it was Johnny who gave you those black eyes and re-arranged your face. Am I right?"

Carl burst into laughter. "I reckon he didn't even go a round from what I can see. A couple of punches and it was all over. Lover boy was out for the count."

Henry's face turned to stone. "Lover boy? What's this about?"

Walter didn't answer. Tearing a piece of damper to pieces, he dipped it into his plate of stew in silence. His jaw ached as he sucked at the nourishment.

Henry lowered his voice so Dotti, who was all ears listening from the kitchen, couldn't hear. "I can guess what you've been up to. You had a go at Chloe and Johnny caught you and gave you a hiding, which is exactly what I would have done. You two chumps should realise Johnny could take you both on at the same time and lay you out cold. He may look like a tired old man, but he was once one of Jimmy Sharman's prized tent fighters in touring country shows and fairs. Countless boundary riders, jackaroos and shearers tried their luck, only to find themselves lying flat on their backs in the dirt seconds after coming face to face with Johnny Quartpot, the *'Black Taipan'* as he was known. Like his namesake, the opponent never saw the lethal strike coming. It's obvious that's what happened to you Walter."

Walter didn't look up as he toyed with his food. It was too painful to chew anything. "Yeah Henry, that's what happened. I'm sorry for it and I'll apologise to Chloe before I leave."

Henry watched Walter's face carefully for any sign of sarcasm in the comment, but he could only see defeat. "You're leaving? Why's that?"

"You warned us, so now I guess you'll want me off the property and I don't blame you."

"Don't you have any balls boy? Someone gives you a hiding and you want to pack up and run. I need you here and this place needs you, along with your brother. I've no doubt Johnny made it perfectly clear what will happen if you go near his granddaughter again, so let it be a lesson. Chloe, Chloe come out here." Henry shouted towards the kitchen where he knew she would be hiding.

Chloe hesitated until Dotti hissed and gave her an impatient push. "Get out there, girl. Don't let them see you're frightened."

"Walter wants to say something to you." Henry's face was like thunder as she emerged.

Carl was enjoying the public humiliation of his brother, but restrained his smirk when Henry swung his gaze towards him. Walter put down his fork, stood up and looked directly at Chloe. "Chloe, I'm sorry for what happened. I guess I just lost my temper when you hit me with the crop, but I realise that's no excuse. Please forgive me."

Chloe remained silent, not knowing how to reply until Henry broke the impasse. "Just remember, you two, we're all family here and that includes everyone on this property. Treat everyone with respect and you will receive the same in return. That's the last I want to hear about this episode."

"Looks like the bet's off," Carl murmured to Walter as he got up from the table.

4

The billowing thermals had been building, bringing high winds, stifling heat and humidity. Henry sensed the drought of the past few years would break in the coming weeks with heavy monsoonal downpours and possible cyclones. The country would become impassable, the dry creek beds turning into raging torrents, pouring the ochre-coloured earth into the major river systems that swept away bridges, roads, livestock— anything in its path. The cattle and wildlife on the station would have to fend for themselves and seek out high ground on which to shelter. In the weeks that followed, marooned with absolutely no feed, they would slowly starve to death. Wild pigs would survive by eating the rotting carcasses of the cattle and kangaroos.

The homestead was battened down; the shutter windows lowered and tied firmly in place. Henry stood under the veranda and looked to the north-west at the cumulonimbus towering tens of thousands of feet into the air. The base of the systems was black, below which was a dark green sheet of torrential rain. All the while, the snow white tops of the cumulus could be clearly seen constantly growing and boiling upwards as the system appeared to explode, sheets of brilliant lightning appearing deep within, followed seconds later by overpowering thunderclaps that shook the homestead. The rains had arrived. It would rain for the next month or possibly two, with wave after wave of cyclonic downpours. Even when it stopped raining it would take weeks for the creeks and river systems to subside.

Then it would take weeks to muster cattle, draft, brand, separate the pregnant cows and release them back, all the while looking for fat steers, bulls and similar age cows that would make up a sufficient number to truck to market at Wyndham. Henry knew that no matter what the number—and it would not be large—it wouldn't be enough to satisfy the accumulating interest, let alone make a dent in his bank overdraft. The only consolation was the bank would not be able to do anything until the rains ceased. But Henry knew the next trip into town would involve a self-effacing confrontation with the bank manager, forced to bluntly deliver a direction from head office. There would be a few minutes of aimless small talk and then the boom would be lowered on another insolvent client. The pattern was well established and over the years, even the most established station owners had at times faced the same predicament as they struggled to survive. They faced major stock losses through times of drought, the fickle cycles of market prices followed by the cost of buying in cattle to restock their breeding herds.

Henry knew he was right on the edge. He had a good relationship with the bank; he had a good friendship with the manager. Whenever he arrived in Wyndham, which was about three times a year, they would always finish business with an evening over dinner at the Cattlemen's Club, along with a few beers and the inevitable game of snooker, but he wondered this time whether the atmosphere would be as cordial. He had noted the banks didn't act when times were tough. They simply froze the overdraft and let the interest run and compound. When the drought broke, the land came back to life and the cattle fattened, they foreclosed within weeks without compassion. The stations that survived, had not overstocked and were not reliant on the banks for support were able to pick the eyes out of the best stations on offer to increase and spread the size of their holdings. The banks got their money with interest, along with a potentially wealthier client, so they were not averse to tipping off someone who was a potential buyer that a customer was in trouble as it was only a matter of time before his loans were called and collateral destroyed. Every drought resulted in suicides as holdings were consolidated into vast tracts of adjoining cattle grazing properties. Size was the key, as drought-affected cattle could be moved for hundreds of kilometres through contiguous land holdings north or south to gain access to feed and water.

Henry's property was big, but he was bordered north and south by the giant landholdings of the rapacious Ascot Pastoral Company, which had approached him many times in the past to buy him out as Henry effectively blocked them from droving cattle overland between their holdings. It was not an advantage he sought; he had taken up his holding years before the advance of the ambitions of Ascot, but he had no intention of selling just to suit their plans. Venus Downs was his life.

He rolled a cigarette, watching and listening to the rain cascade off the roof and flood the surrounding area. Save for a small quantity of canned food, it would be corned beef, damper and tea from now until supplies could be replenished. Henry didn't know how long he had been sitting there before he realised Chloe had silently slid alongside him, squatting on the bench with her arms holding her knees up under her chin.

"Hello, princess. Do you like the sound of the rain?"

Chloe nodded but said nothing.

"You didn't like Father Murphy, did you?"

Chloe shuddered. "No."

"Why was that?"

Chloe didn't answer as she stared vacantly at the rain.

Henry didn't push the point, and changed the subject. "You can't stay here all your life Chloe. You need to get away, get a decent education and experience the world. Your mother would have wanted that."

"Who was my father?"

"A good man who would have wanted you to have the best. I promised I would look after you and ensure you come to no harm."

"Then why do you want me to go away?"

"Because there's nothing for you here."

"But I love it here. I don't want to be anywhere else. I've got you and Dotti and Gramps. I'm happy here."

Henry noted she didn't mention Carl or Walter. "Father Murphy said he could get you into a good convent in Perth where you'll be looked after, get an education and experience what the world has to offer. You're very smart and I believe you would have no problem keeping up with your peers. Believe me, there is a world beyond this cattle station. You've got to think ahead. You're nearly seventeen, you're very pretty and you've a brain. I want you to use it. If you stay here, you'll be married in a couple of years to God knows who."

"You want me to leave?"

"I don't want to get rid of you. I want you to leave to better yourself. This is your home and I'd never ask you to go forever."

"How old is Gramps?"

"He's getting old. That's why he's been taking you on walkabout. Where did he take you, as a matter of interest?"

"I can't tell you that. I promised."

"But you saw something you had never seen before, didn't you?"

Chloe nodded and her eyes sparkled. "Yes, I did and it was wonderful, but it was also very scary."

"Scary? In what way?"

"Oh, I can't tell you that either." Chloe shook her head gently as she recollected at what she had seen.

"You don't like Carl and Walter, do you?"

"Not really. Walter really gave me a scare."

"But you have no affection for either of them?"

Chloe thought for a minute, contemplating an answer that would not offend. "No, I don't love them as I would if they were my brothers. I know they're not."

"Why didn't you like Father Murphy?"

"He gave me the creeps."

"I've a feeling there's more to it than that."

"Will he be coming out here again?"

"He's the new parish priest, although as a long-lost Catholic he probably thinks he can save my soul from damnation. There's not much chance of that, but he's welcome at any time because he brings news and is someone to talk to. It gets very lonely at times and any new face, no matter what religious belief, is always welcome. He's offered to get you into a good convent in Perth. He's going to send the application papers. Would you consider going?"

"I love it here and I love Gramps. I can't—"

Henry cut her off. "But would you consider it?"

Chloe could sense the concern in his voice. She nodded. "Please don't force me, Henry."

Henry put his arm around her shoulders. "No one is going to force you, princess. The decision is entirely yours, but you can see I'm concerned for you. It would only be for a couple of years. Gramps will still be around, I'm sure. He's a tough old man. I'll look after him and when you're through you can come back here to live if you decide the outside world is not for you. How does that sound?"

"I'll think about it," Chloe replied slowly.

Henry squeezed her shoulder. "That's all I ask. I don't want you to take over from Dotti as the station cook, and I don't want to see you married to some jackaroo with no future except for rounding up cattle. I want you to see there's a world outside Venus Downs."

Chloe unclenched her arms and stood up. Henry watched as she walked inside the homestead without a further word. He felt he had made progress. At least the girl was listening, but for how long? The influence of her grandfather was holding her back. She knew he was not her natural grandfather, but it made no difference; she was glued to him. What was it the old coot had shown her? It must have been something very close to his culture, and clearly he had bound her to an oath of secrecy as she would not talk about it. Henry had ridden over every inch of his huge station and could think of nothing of particular importance. Sure, there were hundreds, possibly thousands of petroglyphs, rock paintings, bora rings and other evidence of human occupation over many thousands of years, but it all had a sameness. Nothing really stood out as being unique.

Countless anthropologists, geologists and other academics had walked over Venus Downs in the past hundred years looking for clues to the origins of the aborigines or signs of buried mineral wealth. The anthropologists wrote lengthy scientific papers of momentary peer interest before being buried in the libraries of academia, while the seekers of mineral wealth appeared in waves whenever there was a speculative demand for a particular metal or mineral driven by a rising world price. Henry had pointed anthropologists to the most significant of the sites he considered they would want to look at and photograph.

Likewise, geologists followed soon after the area had been over flown by light planes taking photos of the terrain or dragging drogues to detect a magnetic signature that could signify hidden mineral deposits. The geologists were friendly enough, but always guarded and evaded any direct questions as to what they may have found, or what may be indicated by their exploration. Henry was used to it, but he welcomed their intrusion. It was someone new to talk to and despite their secretive nature, he always learnt a little more of their science and what they were looking for. The waves of exploration activity always finished as abruptly as they started. The enthusiasm simply died overnight.

He was convinced whatever Johnny had shown Chloe, it was nothing he did not already know about. It couldn't be anything mineral, as Johnny wouldn't know the difference between a lump of coal and a mound of horse manure. It had to be something to do with a sacred site. Pointing the bone and willing someone to die a slow death was no mumbo jumbo. Henry had witnessed it before: a perfectly healthy male who had committed some tribal crime would wither and die after being cursed by an elder by pointing a bone or flint-tipped spear at him. The individual accepted his fate and went into a trance from which he did not recover. There was no explanation as to why the curse could not, or would not be resisted. Once the curse was laid, death followed soon after. Medically, it could not be explained. It was no use admitting the individual to hospital and force-feeding him, he would resist and disappear at the first opportunity.

Henry wondered if Johnny had threatened Chloe with a curse if she revealed where she had been. He dismissed the thought, as he knew Johnny would never do such a thing to the person he loved most in the world. But he had obviously shown her something that she had not seen before. After all, Chloe had often gone walkabout with Johnny and she always openly discussed with Henry where she had been and what she had seen. But this time, Henry knew it was different.

5

The rains finally stopped, the raging rivers with their torrents of red mud gradually subsided to a gentle flow. Dying systems linked by large billabongs sprang into life as fish-spawn, dormant during the dry season, ignited the never-ending cycle of creation. The roads and tracks would remain impassable for weeks to come, except by horse. Vehicle access was out of the question. Nothing moved around the station until finally one cloudless morning, Henry stood on the veranda after breakfast and turned to Carl and Walter. "We start mustering today. I want two thousand head rounded up and into the holding yards ready to move out next week. I want to be on the road well before any other station, so we get the best prices. We need every man available, so go down and tell the jackaroos the good news. I'm sure they'll want to get off their arses and get to work."

"Can I go with you?"

Dotti was about to protest when she saw Chloe's imploring expression work its charm on Henry.

"Yes, I suppose you can. Dotti doesn't need you around here and it will do you good to get away."

"And she would only go walkabout with that silly old man who keeps telling her stories," Dotti cut in, sensing Henry was about to overrule any reason for restricting Chloe to the homestead.

"Understand you're not just coming along for the ride, princess. We need every hand we can get. You're there to work, so you'll have to share the shift work as well as do all the cooking for ten of us. Do you think you can handle that?"

"Of course I can. The cooking's no problem and I'll do my share of the work," Chloe replied with a huge smile on her face.

They set out at dawn, slowly moving the bellowing herd in front of them with three flankers on either side with Henry, Carl and Walter bringing up the rear as Chloe followed some distance behind, trailing a string of packhorses carrying supplies for the trek. She was elated at the freedom, unfazed by the boredom of watching the slowly moving herd, cooking for a weary group, and taking her turn riding slowly around the cattle at night to ensure they were settled. A herd this size could be easily spooked by an unusual sound or smell of a wild dog, and it only took one animal to take fright and the whole herd would rush in panic.

Two weeks later, the Wyndham stockyards finally came into view through clouds of dust and bellowing cattle.

Henry stood on the railings and watched as Ike Shulman and three other buyers inspected the offering.

"Not in the best of condition Henry," Ike remarked. "Prices aren't the best at the moment. Be lucky if I can get you a dollar a kilo on the hoof for this lot."

Henry looked at the other buyers. "What do you lot think? We're first in. They've got to be worth more than that."

The buyers shook their heads almost in unison. "Maybe one twenty-five, but that's tops," one ventured.

Henry caught Ike's steely glare at the buyer who had obviously broken ranks.

"No, no, a buck would be top price at the moment," Ike interjected. "What do you want to do, Henry? Take it or leave it, but that's all I can offer for this mob. I'll pay you on an average carcass weight of two hundred kilos. No need to weigh them. I'll take a chance on that. "

"Ike, these cattle would average around three hundred and you bloody well know that," Henry exploded. "You can do better than that."

Henry realised he was being shafted. Ike had set up a nice little buying cartel with the other buyers complicit in the arrangement. Ike would take half of the offering and the other buyers would split the remainder.

Ike shrugged his shoulders as the other buyers, as if on cue, began to walk away. "Do I start counting them or do you want to leave them in the yards until someone else's cattle arrive? I'm expecting mobs from north of here in the next week or so. I thought they would have started to arrive by now. You won't get seventy-five cents if you wait."

Henry knew what Ike was telling him was correct. He had the brief advantage in that other stations would be waiting for the roads to dry out so the big road trains with two or three trailers attached could shift cattle to the saleyards. Ike and his co-conspirators were about setting the price using Venus Downs as the yardstick. Word would spread quickly that prices were down. Ike would make sure of that. Any expectations regarding higher prices would be quickly subdued. Within minutes of him accepting the offer, Ike would be on the phone to the local radio station to inform them of the opening sale price for the season. The mail plane pilots would also be briefed so any station within a two-hundred kilometre radius would know within days. The benchmark price had been set and Henry knew there was nothing he could do about it.

"You've got a nice little scam going with those other three, Ike. You're a pack thieves."

"It's business Henry and quite legal. There's no point in getting personal. I'm not forcing you to take my price." Ike held out his hand, which Henry reluctantly shook. "On another note Henry, your property borders Ascot Downs, doesn't it?"

"You know very well it does. What of it?"

"Nothing, but before you leave town you may want to come and have a talk with me. You know where my office is." Ike swung on his heel and walked off, closely followed the other buyers.

Henry was mystified as to why Ike would think he would want to talk further with him. The proceeds for the cattle sale would be deposited directly into Venus Downs' bank account. Henry didn't have to wait for it to be cleared or draw on the proceeds and he had no desire or reason to visit Ike in his office. It was galling enough to shake his hand, but to tolerate his obsequious chitchat—he could do without that. He had other things planned. First, he needed a bath, then a beer followed by a good meal and a good bed. The jackaroos could fend for themselves. They would quickly find relatives living in the camps on the outskirts of town.

Henry, Chloe, Carl and Walter checked into the Majestic Hotel. Marge Tilley, the publican greeted Henry with a large smile. "You're looking good Henry. Not a day over eighty." She guffawed at her joke. "And who's this? Oh my, you must be Chloe. My gosh, I haven't seen you for at least three years. How you've grown —you're a very pretty girl."

Chloe gave an embarrassed smile and nodded. "Thank you."

"Now give us some bloody keys Marge and let us clean up."

Marge handed over two keys. "You're upstairs, Henry with the men. Chloe is down here next to my room so she'll be safe. Where are Carl and Walter?"

"They've gone into the bar to have a drink. I want a shower and then I'll be down to sample your fine dining."

"Don't know about the fine dining. I'm always having trouble with cooks. The current one is a Chinaman. I reckon he jumped ship from some trawler that was in last month. He's not a bad cook, but a bit too heavy on the fried rice and chook."

"As long as the local cats haven't been disappearing, I'm not concerned," Henry replied, taking the room key. He trudged up the stairs, found his room and threw his bag on the bed. After quickly undressing, he wrapped a towel around his waist and wandered down to the communal bathroom at the end of the corridor, shaving gear in hand. After a shower and shave, he felt clean and refreshed and walked back to his room. The whole place was quiet. He dressed, lay down on the bed and closed his eyes in exhaustion.

Henry didn't know how long he had been dozing, but awoke to hear footsteps treading lightly past his door. It was the sound of someone trying to avoid attention. He judged the person was heading to the end of the corridor where a door opened onto a passageway leading to staff quarters. He heard a woman's voice and a subdued giggle. Another voice that sounded vaguely familiar muttered something, but Henry thought no more about it.

A short time later, Henry heard Carl and Walter thumping up the stairway, laughing and pushing each other along the hallway.

"You two have had too much to drink!" Henry shouted as one of them opened the door to the room next to him and slammed it shut, then the door next to that repeated the exercise. The walls of the rooms didn't go from ceiling to floor but ceased a good hand-span from the top and likewise at floor level. The rooms were more like cubicles, where every turn of the body and creak of the bed during the night could be clearly heard by light sleepers in the adjoining rooms.

Carl laughed. "I bet you'll keep us awake all night with your bloody snoring."

Henry knew better. A good meal and a few more beers after dinner and there would not be a sound out of either of them until the morning.

The doors were opened and slammed again as they headed for the bathroom, followed by laughter, the snap of towels and howls of feigned pain as the twins flicked towels at each other's bare backsides. Marge had been wise to keep Chloe downstairs.

Henry was at the bar when he saw Chloe walk through and into the dining room. He followed her and sat down opposite. "All clean and fresh now, princess?"

Chloe smiled and was about to reply when her face froze. She was staring right past him. Henry started to turn but Father Murphy was already beside him.

"Good evening Henry and to you also Chloe. May I join you for dinner, or are you expecting Carl and Walter? I saw them earlier."

"No, no Father. They won't be down for a while. Please join us." Henry indicated the chair opposite. He could tell Father Murphy had been drinking. He was no longer reserved and his eyes were lit up, as was his manner. The cautiousness and fixed look of compassion were no longer present.

"And what brings you to Wyndham? Here, let me get a bottle of wine and then we can talk."

"I'll stick with a beer, thanks."

"A beer it is and a bottle of wine. And what would you like Chloe?"

"A lemon, lime and bitters," Henry answered on Chloe's behalf.

Father Murphy nodded, his gaze lingering on Chloe as though she had given the order.

"A beer, a lemon lime and bitters and a bottle of wine. I should be able to remember that." He rose and headed for the bar, his gait slightly unsteady.

He came back with the drinks and bottle poised on a tray. He passed the drinks to Henry and Chloe before sitting down and pouring a glass of wine.

"Altar wine doesn't do much for me; this is the stuff of life along with a good Liffey Guinness, but they don't serve Guinness so this will have to do." He raised the glass. "Sláinte. To your health."

"And to yours, Father."

Father Murphy took a deep mouthful and put down his glass.

"So what brings you to Wyndham?"

"We drove a mob of cattle here overland. Too wet to get the road trains in and I wanted to be first in to get the best price."

"And were you successful?"

"The cattle drive was successful, but we didn't get the price I was hoping for," Henry replied quickly. He finished off his first glass and picked up the beer Father Murphy had put in front of him.

"Well you can thank the Lord you got a price and you have something to sell. My father was wiped out when swine fever hit Ireland and the authorities walked in and shot every animal. The bank stepped in and sold everything from under him. We moved to Belfast then and he never got over it. He died clutching a bottle of Jamesons."

Henry studied the young priest. He appeared to be taking after his father, as he was already halfway through the bottle of wine. The effects were starting to show.

"I wrote to Sister Collette at the Sisters of Mercy Convent in Perth regarding Chloe and recommended her entrance. I'm sure you'll be receiving a letter of invitation very soon."

Henry winced inwardly and pretended not to notice the startled look from Chloe. He quickly diverted the conversation. "I'll have the barramundi, salad and chips. What would you like, Chloe?" Henry was looking at the chalked menu on a board near the kitchen.

"The same, please."

"What would you like Father?"

"Nothing at the moment, thanks. I'll eat a bit later."

"Chloe, would you go and order?"

Chloe nodded to Henry and quickly got up from the table. She did not want to be anywhere near the priest. She did not return to the table, but stood talking to the cook through the kitchen slide until their meals were ready. Henry made idle chatter during the course of the meal. Chloe finished hers quickly and excused herself.

"Oh, going so early? I'd love to talk to you about your interests. I can tell you about the convent and what a great school it is. I believe you will fit in perfectly."

"Perhaps tomorrow Father. I'm very tired."

Father Murphy nodded and watched her go. Finally, he sat back and tipped the last of the wine into his glass. "Does she have any hobbies or interests? Does she collect rocks?"

"You've already asked me that."

"Oh, have I? It must be the wine."

"I don't know what her hobbies are. She doesn't appear to have any," Henry replied. "As for her interests, she spends a lot of time studying by correspondence. She has no problems academically and she spends a lot of time with her grandfather."

"Do you think that wise?"

"What do you mean?"

"She should be brought up a Christian in a Christian atmosphere and surrounds. Instead, it would appear she is being brainwashed by her so-called grandfather to believe in myths, legends and superstitions of a stone-age people. They're primitive. They'll never change. Millenniums of existence indelibly stamped in their ancient culture and beliefs."

"Which is the more legitimate Father?" Henry shot back. "A simple culture with beliefs going back since time immemorial, or Christianity with its long history of bloodshed and dogma?"

"So you have no intention of sending her to a convent, Henry?"

"I'll not send her anywhere she doesn't want to go. I will try my best to influence her, as I think it would be for her own good. She's growing into a beautiful young woman and has a lovely nature, as you've observed, but that has nothing to do with religion or saving her from the savages, as you are clearly referring to their culture. She will make up her own mind."

Father Murphy nodded slowly. "You believe I'm wasting my time being a priest in this part of the world?"

"The natives will listen to your stories and teachings, but the moment you walk away, you'll be forgotten. They love to hear about this *Jesus fella*, as they call him, but he isn't going to replace millenniums of unwritten lore handed down orally from generation to generation. Yes, you are wasting your time as far as converting them is concerned. If you're here to spread the word and do some good amongst the wider community, town folk and pastoralists such as me, you'll always be welcome but once again, don't expect too much. This is not Ireland where priests are feared and damnation is assured for non-believers. Here, it's different; you'll not convert anyone. All you can do is offer solace and a comforting presence. These are tough people who endure constant hardship, but they don't look to divinity to solve their problems."

"It is indeed tough. Not what I expected," Father Murphy replied looking at the bottom of his empty glass.

"With all due respect Father, if I may make an observation, you simply don't fit. I asked you once before whether your interest in Chloe was carnal or spiritual. You wouldn't be the first priest who was tempted by the flesh. She's scared of you—that's plain to see. It could be imagination on her part because she's never been alone with you, but something has her worried."

"My only concern is her welfare."

"Good, but while I have influence, I will look after her welfare."

"Do you feel like another beer?"

"No thanks Father. It's been a long day." Henry stood up to go.

"Can I discuss something else with you? It will only take a moment."

"Shoot."

"It's your boys. I cannot tell them apart visually, but one stands out as soon as he opens his mouth."

"That's Carl. I believe you are referring to his somewhat aggressive manner?"

"Yes, I don't know how I've offended him, but he appears to have taken a particular dislike to me. Walter hides it well, but I can sense the same smouldering anger in him."

"I wouldn't take too much notice of it Father. They had a somewhat traumatic upbringing before I took them in. It was a favour I did for Father O'Leary, a priest who was up here some years ago. They were his wards and they were headed in the wrong direction in life if they remained in Perth. They took a bit of straightening out until they learnt the rules, and both have received more than a belt around the ears from me. But they work hard and keep their noses clean and that's all I ask of them. What's the problem with Carl?"

"You say they were wards of Father O'Leary?"

"That's what he led me to believe and I had no reason to doubt him. They were wards of the State and placed in foster care before he arranged for me to take them. Are you implying something?"

"No, no, but it is interesting how trauma and abuse remains an indelible stain. You can rub and rub, but it can never be completely removed. I know it from first-hand experience and I see it in Carl. I would appreciate you having a word of warning in his ear in regard to me."

"Something you can't discuss with him yourself, Father? I took you as being stronger than that?"

"Don't mock me Henry."

"I'm not mocking you. Would you please explain what's on your mind."

"Carl and Walter were in the bar when I bought a beer and walked through to the lounge earlier this afternoon. I could tell they'd both had a few, but it was Carl who started commenting in a loud voice what he thought of *'poofter priests'*, as he called them. Other people were present in the bar. I come from a tough background Henry and unless he curbs his language and insinuations, I will not be held responsible for how I retaliate. Maybe Father O'Leary was more than an *'uncle'* to him, I don't know, but that doesn't mean he can take it out on me."

Henry contemplated his reply. "Father, I have no intention of discussing anything with either of them in regard to this. I'm not their keeper and have long since ceased being their guardian. They're only just eighteen but believe me, they consider themselves men who can take care of themselves. They're free to walk out on me any time they choose. If I warned Carl to back off, you would certainly become an even bigger target. I tried that once when he first took a swing at me. That's the only time he tried, and he learnt a very painful lesson. Now there's no warning, I always act first. Do you get my drift?"

"I just wanted to find an easy way out of it. But if I ignore him, he'll take it as a sign of weakness. Is that what you're implying? In your eyes, I've obviously made a mistake."

"You have Father, you have. Look, I know the lessons you preach are pastoral, but I think you'll have to be a bit more forceful when delivering a sermon to Carl. It mightn't be well received, but it certainly won't be forgotten. Just do me a favour and don't maim or kill him. The law will take a very dim view and I need all the help I can get at this time of the year. Priests are expendable but not good jackaroos. And be careful; he knows how to handle himself." Henry patted the priest on the shoulder and walked out.

Father Murphy smiled at Henry's parting words and walked to the bar for another drink. He began talking to the barmaid and was in animated conversation when Carl walked in. He bought a beer, walked over to the pool table and began to idly toss some remnant balls off the cushions.

"Hey priest, do you feel like a game of pool?"

Father Murphy turned around and gave him a bemused look. "You want to chance your hand do you, Carl? You know how to play the game?"

"Five bucks says I do."

Father Murphy hesitated. He could feel the effects of the alcohol, but he had to accept the challenge.

"What's the matter? You too pissed to play? If you lose, you can pinch it back off the plate on Sunday." Carl laughed as he racked up the balls and rolled the white ball to the end of the table. He was about to make the break when Father Murphy walked over, picked up a cue and sighted down its length. It was bent out of shape, as he knew it would be. He put five dollars on the edge of the table and pulled out a twenty-cent coin.

"Toss to break. Your call."

"Heads."

Father Murphy tossed the coin and watched it settle on the cloth as Carl called it. Carl bent down to line up and study the break when the priest restrained him with his cue.

"Now put your five on the table."

"Not much point in that," Carl laughed. "I'll be taking your money, not the other way around."

"That maybe the case, but let's play the game according to normal rules. After all, you laid the bet, so that means it's put up or shut up."

Carl took a roll of money out of his shirt front pocket and peeled off a five-dollar note.

"Happy now?"

"It's your break Carl. So let's get on with it."

Father Murphy studied his opponent's game, but showed no emotion as Carl sank four balls from the break and then missed the next.

Father Murphy potted the next two, miscued and swore silently to himself. The game was over in five minutes.

"You want to chance your hand again?" Carl sneered as he picked up the money. "I reckon I know how to play the game, don't you?"

"Carl, in gambling there's a great deal of luck attached. I haven't played for years, but I would like to play again. I admit you do know the game."

"Why don't we make it ten bucks this time?"

"Ten bucks it is," Father Murphy replied with obvious hesitation.

"You break then. You may get lucky."

Carl noticed Father Murphy's hands shaking as he lined up the break. The game was over just as quickly. Carl picked up the winnings.

"You feel like a beer, priest? Line up a couple for us love," he called to the barmaid who was watching the proceedings with interest.

Father Murphy sat down at a table and sipped his beer. He looked agitated. He watched as Carl downed his schooner and turned to him again.

"Do you want to make a real game of it?"

"I don't think so Carl. You're too good for me."

"Ah, c'mon you faggot. I want to clean you out. How much money have you got?'

Father Murphy rose in fury from the table and moved towards his aggressor with fists clenched.

Carl saw his taunt had the required effect. "Don't even think about it priest. I'll beat you to a pulp if you touch me."

"How much have you got to bet?"

Carl pulled out the banknotes and counted them out. "Two hundred bucks. That's all I've got on me at the moment. Wait here while I borrow another hundred from Walter." Minutes later, he was back with the money.

Father Murphy turned to the barmaid and called her over. He counted out three hundred of his own, picked up Carl's and handed both to her. "Would you be so good as to hold the stakes and hand it to the winner? Your break Carl."

The break resulted in two balls finding the pockets and then he managed to sink two more before missing.

Father Murphy chalked his cue and then coolly sank the remainder of the table. Finally, he laid his cue down and held out his hand for the winnings.

"You fucking hustler!" Carl cursed. "I want another game. You're a fucking cheat, you faggot!" He rushed at Father Murphy with fists clenched. The move was anticipated; Father Murphy raised the cue and thrust it into Carl's solar plexus. Carl doubled over in pain and collapsed on his side, gasping for air.

Father Murphy prodded him with the cue to demonstrate to his would-be assailant that he was completely at his mercy. "You haven't got any money. I won and I don't want to play anymore tonight. If you would like to challenge the same time tomorrow night I'll be happy to oblige. Goodnight Carl."

Father Murphy threw the cue onto the pool table and walked away. He had practically been born in a Belfast pool hall. He knew how to hustle the suckers, the drunken tourists or loud-mouth challengers who thought a kid apparently only just out of short trousers was an easy mark. In his youth, he would have smashed the handle of the cue into Carl's ribs or knees to ensure that broken ribs or smashed kneecaps would leave an enduring memory of the encounter—such was the lore of Belfast.

Carl and Walter were already at the breakfast table the next morning when Henry came down. He noted the pair were not talking, but Walter's face lit up with a smirk in contrast to Carl's sullen expression.

"What's up with you Carl?"

Walter began to whistle *"You are my sunshine"* softly.

"Pack it in, Walter," Henry snapped. He could see that Carl would explode at any moment.

"That bloody priest took all my money last night."

"What do you mean he took your money? Did he steal it?"

"No, he cheated at pool."

Henry laughed. "You mean you challenged him to a game of pool and he hustled you."

"Yeah, yeah. I lost three hundred bucks to that cheating bastard. I'm broke. Can you lend me some against my next pay day?"

Henry guffawed and slapped his knee. Walter could no longer contain himself and a peel of laughter burst out of him. He had delighted in hearing from the barmaid about his brother's humiliation at being hustled, severely winded and then helped to his feet by her. He quickly got up and moved away from the table. He knew Carl would retaliate, but when and where was the question.

"Boy, you've just learnt an expensive lesson. Never challenge an Irishman to pool or snooker if you haven't observed how they play. Pool is a national sport to them. You fell right into it. You got beaten fair and square, so don't blame Father Murphy."

"Will you lend me some money or not?" Carl snapped.

Henry peeled off a hundred dollars and handed it to him. "I should say no to drive home your stupidity. However, you've had your pride kicked so I doubt you'll be playing any more pool for a while, so a hundred will get you through the next few days."

"Tell Henry how Father Murphy gave you a hiding as well," Walter shouted as he looked back from the doorway. "And don't forget that hundred you owe me."

"He jammed the pool cue into my guts while I wasn't looking. I'll get the poofter for it."

"A word of advice Carl. Stay well clear of Father Murphy and if you do see him, keep your mouth shut. You're no match for him. Tell me, why do you think he's a queer?"

"They're all bloody queers. We both got mauled by them when we were in foster care."

"Father O'Leary?"

"Cyclops O'Leary. Did you notice his right eye was always weeping?"

"Yes, I did. Why? Did you have something to do with that?"

"Sure did. He was sucking on my dick so I jammed a finger into his eye. That was only one way he liked getting his rocks off. Any pretty looking kid was forced to bite the pillow while he shagged them any time he felt like it. He screamed like a pig when I stuck him. I hoped I'd blinded the bastard, but I knew that wouldn't be the end of it, and sure enough the bog-Irish pervert gave me one hell of a hiding a couple of days later. I laughed while he was doing it, because I could see he was in pain as he screwed up his eyes to deliver each blow. It only made him madder when I continued to laugh, but the fat arsehole finally ran out of steam. I should have done it earlier as he never came near me again."

"I had no idea," Henry said shaking his head. "Why haven't you told me this before?"

"What's the point? It's in the past and the bastard's dead now."

"Was Walter also subjected to the same kind of treatment?"

"You don't know much Henry, do you? Ask anyone who's been in a home or in foster care, male or female and they'll all tell you they've been molested or fucked by a preacher, a carer, an uncle, a cousin or a stranger expressing *'kindness'*. If it's not that lot, the older kids in any care situation also prey on the younger ones. I'm surprised old Johnny hasn't tried to screw Chloe. He's not her grandfather and I understand he was a real stud in his time."

Henry chose to ignore Carl's snide comment. "Have you tried?"

"No, but I'd like to; she's beautiful. One day I'd like to marry her, but I know my chances are pretty slim."

"Why's that?"

"She doesn't like me. I try to talk to her, but I just don't know how. I get angry with myself and it shows. Walter's better at it than me—you've probably noticed? I think he'll get into her pussy before I do."

It was a matter-of-fact comment but Carl was oblivious to the look of shock and anger on Henry's face.

Henry was dreading the meeting, but it was unavoidable. A ritual to be endured, but one he always managed to survive. It was a constant fight against the elements and cattle prices to stay ahead. The door to the inner office opened and he was confronted by someone he did not recognise. A deadpan face.

"Come in, Mr Boyce."

Henry followed the crumple-suited man into an office and was beckoned to sit. "Charlie Simmons on holiday?" Henry asked, feigning light-heartedness.

"No, he's been posted to Darwin. I'm the new manager. My name is Arthur Geddes."

Geddes did not offer his hand or look up as he opened a file on his desk, which Henry noted was clearly labelled 'Venus Downs'. "I've been looking at your file, which from the bank's viewpoint is most unsatisfactory."

"I've just been through years of drought. Charlie has always supported me in the past, and I've never let him down," Henry protested.

"Mr Simmons is no longer here," Geddes snapped. "This is not personal, Mr Boyce. The bank has appointed me manager and instructed me to pay particular attention to stressed accounts."

"I just sold two thousand head to Ike Shulman. The money should be in my account today."

Geddes nodded. "Those funds have already been deposited in your favour, but by my reckoning you can only survive the next three months without an extension of your overdraft."

"The drought has broken. All I need is the support of the bank for the next six months and I'll survive. But you're not prepared to do that; is that what you're saying?"

"I'm not saying anything, Mr Boyce. I'm just telling you what the bank's position is. The bank cannot extend any further overdraft facilities beyond three months."

Henry was horrified. "What the hell am I supposed to do? The overdraft is covered by a mortgage over the property. The bank has tons of collateral. We pastoralists rely on the banks for support. You know very well our business is cyclical. There must be others in the same boat."

Geddes closed the file and looked up with impassive eyes. "That is your problem, Mr Boyce. The bank cannot help you any further. Surely you must have more cattle to sell."

"I do have another ten thousand head, but they're not in good condition. I would lose too much if I was forced to do so now. Give me six months, they'll fatten up."

Geddes stood, walked past Henry and opened the door. "As I've already said Mr Boyce, it's not personal. I have my instructions."

Henry slowly got to his feet. He was about to be wiped out. The overdraft would not be extended for more than three months. Now the inevitable would happen. The bank would close him down. He would be evicted and Venus Downs would be sold. The bank would easily cover its exposure from the sale of cattle and the property, but his life's work would be lost. He had seen it happen to other pastoralists and it was about to happen to him.

"Perhaps you should have a word with Mr Shulman," Geddes murmured as Henry drew level.

Henry hesitated as he considered the remark.

"Good day Mr Boyce." The banker anticipated a question and closed the door before Henry could ask it. Why would he talk to Ike Shulman? Shulman was not a banker, but he was as good as a bank. He owned a string of properties he had bought at distressed auctions over the years. He was a bottom feeder. Was he lining up to buy Venus Downs? What was the connection between him and Geddes? Had Geddes tipped him off as to Henry's finances? He was lost in thought when he heard his name being called. He turned around to see Ike Shulman beckoning him from the doorway of his office across the street. It was all too obvious. Shulman had seen him go into the bank and waited for him to emerge. Henry walked over.

"Come inside Henry. I've something to discuss with you."

"I've got no more cattle to sell at the moment Ike, if that's what you're after."

Ike waved the question aside as he ushered him into his office, a complete contrast to the banker's stark surroundings. Ike's was furnished with a large desk, comfortable leather couch and matching chairs surrounding an expansive coffee table. Ike signalled for Henry to take one of the chairs and sat down opposite.

"You got your money for the cattle?"

"Ike, cut the crap. You know very well I've just been into the bank. What's the connection between you and Geddes?"

Ike raised his eyebrows. "I don't know what you're inferring."

Henry laughed. "Like hell you don't. You knew I had an appointment with the bank and Geddes must have phoned you when I left. It was no coincidence you were standing at your doorway and just happened to see me."

"I'm not admitting to anything Henry, but I'm well aware what a couple of years of drought must have done to your bank balance. You're suffering and I've no doubt the bank has given you an ultimatum."

Henry made to rise. "What do you really want Ike? My place is not for sale. Not yet, at least."

"I don't want to buy you out Henry. I want to help you out. Just sit down and listen to what I have to say. Would you like a tea or coffee?"

Henry shook his head as he sunk back into the seat. "Let's hear it Ike."

"My proposition will enable you to dispense with any overdraft you may have and be completely debt free within three months."

"Geddes and you are up to something, aren't you? I bet you know exactly what the extent of my overdraft is and how much I'm in hock, right down to the last cent."

"Keep your hat on Henry and calm down. Just listen. Ascot Downs adjoins your property to the north."

"So what? Where's this leading?"

"Ascot Downs, as you are well aware, is practically drought proof with permanent water, plenty of feed and around forty thousand head of cattle. They've come through the past two years completely unscathed."

Henry made no comment. He studied Ike's thin features, dark hair, aquiline nose and penetrating look of coal black eyes reflecting vitality. His fine and delicate hands danced before him as though conducting an orchestra.

He was building enthusiasm for what he was about to divulge.

"Do you know Bill Hargraves, the manager of Ascot Downs?"

"I've met him a couple of times. Don't know him that well."

"Well, he wants to—how shall I put it? Launder some cattle."

Henry looked perplexed. "Launder cattle? What are you talking about?"

"Bill can run off ten to fifteen thousand head of cleanskins a year straight onto Venus Downs. You brand them and I'll sell them. No one will be the wiser. The English owners of Ascot Downs hardly go near the place. Bill says they haven't been there in the last three years. They wouldn't have a clue how many head they're running."

"Jesus Christ, you're talking about a criminal act Ike. You're talking about stealing cattle on a grand scale."

"Grow up Henry. If unbranded cattle wander over your boundary, you're perfectly entitled to brand and sell them. Where's the crime? Bill Hargraves isn't going to lay a complaint."

"No, definitely not. I'm not getting mixed up in it. That's final and I'll forget you ever mentioned it to me. Go talk to someone else."

"We can't. Venus Downs abuts Ascot Downs and the cattle can be moved without anyone seeing them. It's a perfect fit."

Henry rose out of the chair. "I repeat, I won't be in it Ike."

"I'm afraid you are in it if you value continued ownership of Venus Downs. If you don't accept, your days are numbered. I'll buy Venus Downs when the bank forecloses. What did Geddes give you, three months?"

"You know everything!" Henry spat in anger. "But anything can happen in that time."

The sparkle in Ike's eyes suddenly faded, replaced by two penetrating pits of indifference. "You haven't got three months; you haven't even got three weeks. Geddes is going to cancel the overdraft. You're in dire straits. The bank wants its money."

"He can't call it. I had an agreement with Charlie Simmons," Henry blustered.

"Not so, banks are a law unto themselves. You can't fight them, but if you go along with my proposal, I'm sure he'll extend your overdraft. That way, you'll clear the overdraft, be debt free and have money in the bank. Otherwise, I believe you'll be out on your backside within, oh, a month."

"What's the deal if I agree?" Henry slumped back into the chair as he submitted to blackmail.

"Thirty per cent and the same for me and Hargraves."

"That adds up to ninety. Who gets the remainder? Oh, Christ, it's Geddes isn't it?"

Ike's thin lips curled into a smile. "Everyone benefits, everyone gets a fair share and everyone is bound to keep their lips sealed. It's perfect."

Henry was unconsciously drumming his fingers on the arms of the chair. "What guarantee do I have Geddes will lay off?"

"I'll arrange that with him tomorrow. Well, I need your answer. What's it to be? Do you wish to continue moralising and refuse, or do I wind up owning Venus Downs?"

Henry sighed. "Don't have much choice do I? You play dirty pool Ike and as for Geddes, I would love to catch him alone in a dark alley."

"Geddes is doing you a big favour. Life's not a dress rehearsal. Take the advantage when you see it. All your stress and financial problems are going to disappear in a matter of weeks, and while the absentee landlords of Ascot Downs remain asleep, we can repeat the process as long as Hargraves is manager."

Henry began to warm to the idea as his principles faded. It was a tough industry, in a tough environment, in a tough country.

"Henry, can't you see I could have easily hung you out to dry and let Geddes sell you up? I would have got Venus Downs for a song and split ninety per cent with Hargraves. Let Geddes have his ten per cent. It won't cost you a dime except for a bit of hard work branding mobs of cattle."

"Okay, I'll go along with it, but call off the dogs. I want a meeting with you and Geddes face to face in the morning."

Ike sprung to his feet and held out his hand. "Henry, you've made the right decision. I'll call Geddes and go guarantor for your overdraft, but promise me one thing, and that is don't make any mention to him of our arrangement. You're not supposed to know he's involved."

"Why's that? If we get busted, does he really think he'll be immune?"

"Geddes portrays himself as a pillar of society who knows everyone's financial details and therefore commands respect. He's also a staunch Christian and a lay preacher so he thinks he's above reproach. If he wants to live the illusion, why question it? As long as I get what I want, I don't care what desires and beliefs my fellow man harbours or covets. Let's make it ten in the morning at the bank."

Henry shook Ike's extended hand. It was soft, small and childlike, enveloped in Henry's calloused, sun-scaled paw. He felt he could easily break it off with a swift twist, but he knew it was not his hands but his brain that was the power of Ike Shulman.

6

arl watched from the darkness as a door opened and a figure looked left and right before stepping out into the corridor. An arm appeared from within the room and pulled him back, her long hair flowed down her naked flanks as she pulled his head towards her and kissed him. Carl had followed him and watched him go into the room an hour previous. The figure moved quickly along the corridor and through a door leading to the guest rooms of the hotel. He was about to open the door to his room when he heard footsteps behind him.

"Hello priest. You been screwing the barmaid or hearing her confession, or was it both?"

Father Murphy froze and slowly turned to his accuser with a look of utter surprise. He noted the length of wood he was holding. "What do you want?"

"I want my money back and another hundred so I don't start broadcasting what I just saw. You're finished if I do that."

The colour drained from Father Murphy's face as he gave a weak smile of defeat and nodded. "You have a point there, Carl. The sins of the flesh are a weakness I cannot overcome. It's a sin I'm ashamed of. I did hustle you last night and I know how humiliated you must feel. I only wanted to teach you a lesson not to gamble."

"Well, I'm teaching you one now priest."

"Yes, you are Carl, and I must accept the consequences." Father Murphy's shoulders slumped in complete surrender. "I don't have any money on me. I've hidden it in the car. Come down and I'll pay you. Oh, God how did I let myself get into this situation? Promise me you'll say nothing about what you witnessed? It'll ruin me."

Carl smirked. "Just confess it and all will be forgiven. Isn't that what you micks do?"

"Please Carl, don't rub it in. You've won and I must accept the consequences." He moved towards Carl, who could see the priest was a nervous wreck and let him pass. Father Murphy opened the door to the landing and Carl followed him down the stairway and out into the darkened yard behind the hotel. Carl was standing behind him when he unlocked the door of his car and reached under the seat. He pulled out a leather satchel and began to rummage in it with one hand while he held the flap with the other.

"The light's not good. Hold this for me while I get it out." Father Murphy handed the satchel to Carl who took it without thinking. It was a mistake he realised a split second before a fist crashed into his midriff. The satchel flew over his head as blow after blow crashed into his ribs and stomach. He was pinned against the car, unable to escape. He felt his ribs break and cries of pain were stifled in his throat by no breath and intense pain. His knees buckled, but

Father Murphy held him up and continued to land blow upon staggering blow. He didn't touch Carl's face; he didn't want to leave any visible evidence of the violence being inflicted. His victim could suffer in silence and not reveal his injuries and humiliation by having to explain missing teeth, swollen lips, cut eyebrows and black eyes. Carl finally passed out and slumped to the ground. Father Murphy dragged him into the unlit outside toilet and dumped him face down in the trough of the urinal.

Henry walked back into the hotel torn between elation and guilt, but it was too late to renege- he had supped with the devil. The meeting with Geddes had gone as Ike predicted. Any illusions about the criminality of what he was about to get involved in had vanished. He meant to survive and nothing and no one was going to stand in his way. He saw Chloe and Walter quietly talking in a corner of the lounge.

"Where's Carl?"

"He's in bed. He's not well," Walter replied.

"Not well? Did he get on the booze last night? Is he suffering a hangover?"

"No, he apparently fell down the stairs and broke his ribs. He's in a lot of pain and can't move."

Henry spun on his heel and went up the stairs two at a time. He had a feeling about what had really happened. Carl was moaning softly as he opened the door and looked into the darkened room. Henry walked over and opened the blind. He was relieved to see that Carl's face was unmarked. He obviously had not been in a fight.

"What happened to you?"

Carl opened his eyes slowly; his face grimaced in pain as he attempted to talk normally. "I fell down the bloody stairs."

Henry pulled back the bed sheet. Carl was fully dressed, but stank of urine. He looked in horror at the blood staining the mattress. "You're pissing blood. You've ruptured a kidney. We've got to get you to hospital."

Henry bent down and began to lift Carl by the shoulder. He immediately stopped when Carl let out a bellow of pain. He slowly unbuttoned his shirt and pulled it apart. One look at the damage was enough. Henry whistled between his teeth, imagining the pain Carl must be feeling. His chest was deep purple surrounded by a halo of exploded blood vessels.

"You didn't fall down any stairs boyo. You ran into a priest, didn't you? I did warn you what would happen."

Carl's eyes glazed over in pain and then slowly closed. Henry could see he could not be moved. He would have to get a doctor.

Marge Tilley was at the front desk as Henry walked past. "Carl's in bed and won't be moving for a few days Marge. I have to get him a doctor. By the way, have you seen Father Murphy this morning?"

"Yes, but he checked out first thing. He's gone. Why, did you want him to save your heathen soul?"

Henry ignored the publican's remark and strode out the door and down the street. Normally, he would have shared her joke, but he had more serious issues on his mind. Marge stared after him, trying to fathom how she had offended him.

Henry had stripped Carl off and cleaned him up by the time the doctor arrived an hour later. The doctor gently felt his ribs and pressed his liver and stomach.

"A couple of broken ribs and some internal injuries, including bleeding kidneys by the look of it."

"He claims he fell down the stairs."

The doctor gave Henry a knowing look. "The stairs must have had fists. He's had a hell of a thrashing. Odd though that his face is untouched. He'll have to stay here for a few days until I'm sure he's stopped passing blood. The kidney could be just bruised, but if they're ripped, he's in serious trouble. I'll give him a shot of morphine and tape those ribs, but it won't do anything to alleviate the pain when the morphine wears off."

They both watched on as the powerful painkiller took effect and Carl relaxed and remained barely conscious.

"Do you know who did this to him?"

"I've a fair idea doc, but I'm sure Carl doesn't want to lay a complaint. This has taught him one almighty lesson."

The doctor shook his head as they gently lifted Carl into a sitting position and began to tape his ribs. "Why do young fellows always drink too much booze and then get into fights? Bloody stupidity." The doctor finished taping and took a small bottle of pills out of his bag. "That's all I can do for the moment. Check on him every few hours. I'll call around again this evening. In the meantime, here's a bottle of pethidine. It's a strong painkiller that will put him on a high. They're highly addictive and dangerous if overdosed. He'll think he can walk on water and will want to get up, but don't let him. When the morphine wears off, he'll be in a lot of pain so just give him a couple of these. Keep an eye on him and if he continues to pass blood, come and get me no matter what time of the day or night. I may have to call the Flying Doctor to fly him to Darwin."

"Thanks, Doc. There are three of us here so we can take it in turns to watch him."

Henry noticed Walter and Chloe had entered the room and had been watching and listening.

Once the doctor was out of earshot Walter piped up, "Father Murphy did him over. Bloody near killed him by the look of it." He looked down at his brother without compassion.

"I'm not sure, but Father Murphy has apparently left town. There was bad blood between them and it looks like it came to a head last night."

"Are you going to lay a complaint with the cops?"

Henry shook his head. "No, no point in doing that. Carl got himself into it and I'm sure he doesn't want the law and everyone in town to know he got thumped by a priest."

"How's he going to get home Henry? He can't ride a horse in that condition."

"I want you to round up the boys and make tracks for home Walter. Then you can drive back and pick us up. I feel like a few days in town and Chloe can stay with me. Maybe she can bring Carl his meals and check on him now and again. I don't feel like being his bloody nursemaid. Would you do that Chloe?"

Chloe looked nervous, but nodded. "Yes, I could do that, I suppose."

"Just tell me if you don't want to, princess."

"No, I'll do it Henry."

Neither of them noticed Walter's wry smile.

The door was open a fraction as Chloe turned her back to it and pushed it open while steadying the tray of food. Carl opened his eyes and looked at her groggily before breaking into a broad smile of recognition.

"I've brought you some soup and there's chicken or fish if you feel up to it." She set the tray down and tried to hide her shock at the black and purple bruises on his chest.

"I must look a real picture." Carl laughed through his almost clenched teeth as he tried to stem the pain. "Would you prop me up please Chloe? I'm starving, but I don't know how I'm going to eat anything."

She carefully pulled him forwards into a sitting position and put pillows behind him. He leaned back with a sigh of relief. She could see he was exhausted as she picked up the plate of soup and began to spoon it into his mouth. Finally, he held up his hand and lay back.

"Thank you Chloe. My God, that priest packs a punch," he said as he reached over, unscrewed the cap of the pill bottle and swallowed two tablets. "These things sure relieve the pain. I'll be floating on air in five minutes."

Chloe got up to leave, but he held up his hand to restrain her. "Please sit with me for a while until I drop off. I know you're scared of me, but I'd never harm you. I just want to talk to you."

Chloe nodded and sat in silence as she watched as the narcotic overtook his senses and he drifted off. She reached behind him and carefully withdrew one of the pillows before leaving him to sleep. She thought she heard him murmur something as she picked up the tray and quietly closed the door behind her.

It was early evening when she went back up to check on him. She opened the door quietly, but he appeared to be still asleep so she made to leave.

"Hey Chloe," he murmured lifting his arm to beckon her in. "I've been waiting for Florence Nightingale to appear."

"I came to see if you would like something to eat."

"I certainly would. That soup didn't do much for me," he replied with a broad smile.

"It's steak or fish. Which would you prefer?"

"The fish please. Any chance of a large beer to go with that?"

"I'll see what I can do."

She returned with the meal and a beer and after propping him up, arranged the tray in front of him.

"Would you like me to help you?"

"No, no, I'm not a complete invalid, but these busted ribs are giving me hell." He winced as he ravenously finished the fish and then raised the beer to his lips. "That's what I've been dreaming of all afternoon. You're very kind to look after me." He reached out and squeezed her hand. "Has Henry said anything to you about what happened?"

"We all know what happened. Father Murphy gave you a hiding after you accused him of cheating."

"Yes, I was a complete bloody idiot and got what I deserved, I suppose. I dread facing the man again, but I guess I'll have to apologise to him."

"No need; he's left town."

Carl let out a sigh of relief. "I'm glad. I wouldn't want to get into an argument with him again. I owe you an apology too Chloe. I've never treated you very well, but I'm going to change that from now on. I hope we can be friends. More than just friends; I'm in love with you."

"Let's just be friends for now, Carl," Chloe replied as she took the tray. She left the room deep in thought. Maybe Carl was different to Walter? She certainly felt a warmth towards him. As the week passed, they became closer. They talked and laughed together and Chloe began to see a softer personality hidden behind his hard outer shell. At last, the doctor cleared him of any serious internal injuries and the pain in his ribs began to subside.

Henry watched as Johnny Quartpot walked slowly towards him. He could read what was on the old man's mind and he knew it was fomenting trouble. He offered Johnny his tobacco pouch as he sat down beside him on the veranda. Neither said a word as Johnny rolled himself a cigarette and lit it.

"You got a lot of cattle there boss."

Henry nodded but said nothing as he looked out over the yards filled with cattle churning up clouds of dust.

"Not your cattle, are they?"

"They're cleanskins Johnny. I'm entitled to brand them and sell them."

"They come from Ascot Downs, don't they boss?"

"I bought them from Ascot Downs. They're overstocked and I got them at a good price."

"Nah, you steal them boss. Just like you steal our land. I know what's going on."

Henry turned to his accuser. "You might assume you know what's going on, but the cattle are mine. If you're sure I've duffed them from Ascot Downs, why don't you ride over there and have a word with Bill Hargraves? He'll put you straight and probably give you a boot up the arse at the same time for your trouble. Mind your own fucking business."

"About time you gave the boys a pay rise, boss." Johnny ignored Henry's flash of anger. "They've been working seven days a week for a month now and they're tired. You're workin' them too hard."

"They've got another month to go and then they can have a couple of months break. You can all go on walkabout then."

Johnny shook his head. "No boss, unless you increase their wages I'll take them on walkabout next week. You're going to be stuck with a lot of unbranded cattle. And the police might be interested how many cattle you're running off and where they're coming from."

Henry knew he had to tread on eggs. The police cattle squad consisted of a single officer whose job was largely symbolic, as cattle theft was not considered a problem for these vast isolated properties. However, if something was brought to his attention he would have to follow it up and it would take a lot of explaining as to where all the cattle were coming from on Venus Downs. Johnny was the tribal elder and these were his tribal lands. He knew he had the upper hand and the jackaroos would follow him if he gave the command.

Henry nodded. "You keep the boys on the job for the next month and I'll give them all a pay rise."

"How much can I tell them they'll get?"

"We'll negotiate that, Johnny."

"Okay boss. Better be good and I want you to give us back some of our land so we can run our own cattle and not work for you all the time. The government stole it from us and gave it to you whitefellas, but it's not yours."

Henry had been given an ultimatum. He watched Johnny saunter across the yard to his shack. He would give them the pay rise, but he knew he had a real problem on his hands. The threats and blackmail would not cease. The past month had solved all his financial problems. His overdraft was a bad dream of the past. Ike had disposed of five thousand head and taken his cut and Henry had even overlooked his resentment of Geddes. The man was well worth his ten per cent. They had another five thousand head to brand and sell in the next month and they would repeat the exercise before the end of the season. He was too far in to quit now, but the problem of Johnny kept creeping into his subconscious. It was his problem. He could not tell Ike about it. Ike was cunning enough to claim he bought the cattle in good faith. He would plead he did not know they were duffed. Hargraves would claim ignorance that Ascot Downs was losing cattle and Geddes would claim to know nothing of the scheme. Only he, Henry Boyce would be the one holding the smoking gun.

7

It was early afternoon. Chloe slowly swam the length of the billabong close to the outstation where she and Gramps were camped. That morning, Johnny had told her there was no need to accompany him as he had something special to do. She protested. "Gramps, I want to come with you. What's so secret?"

"No secret. I just want to be alone. Don't ask me anymore. If I don't come back, you must promise not to come looking for me. I'll not be anywhere near the rainbow serpent so it would be pointless to search. You must promise me."

"I can't do that Gramps, you know that." Chloe's eyes began to water and a tear rolled down her cheek. "I love you Gramps. I will find you."

"Promise me you won't come looking!" Johnny demanded in a harsh tone Chloe had not heard before. "I'll be back late this afternoon but if I don't return, just head off home in the morning. Just tell Henry what I've told you. He'll understand."

Chloe nodded and tried to hold back the tears.

Johnny did not tell her, but he had the suspicion they were being followed again and he intended to confirm who it was. The inexplicable telepathy of his ancestors had warned him that morning, and he was not willing to expose Chloe to any danger. He had to find out who it was. He began walking out onto the plains at a tangent. Whoever was following him would risk being seen in the exposed terrain. Johnny headed for a large escarpment standing proud of the surrounding spinifex covered plains about two hour's walk away. Several times, he dropped down into a dry creek bed to wait and listen, but whoever was tracking him was an expert at remaining concealed. He knew he was not imagining things. Once he reached the escarpment he would have the advantage of being on higher ground and then it was just a matter of waiting until the pursuer made the mistake of showing himself. He hurried on in a loping gait, not bothering to conceal his tracks. On reaching the formation, he quickened his pace and began to climb swiftly as the rock wallabies took fright and fled from his intrusion. Finally, he rounded a large boulder and crested the escarpment. He froze in horror at the rifle pointed at him.

"Why you pointing that at me?" Johnny stammered as he tried to regain his breath from the arduous climb.

"Because you're a bloody shit stirrer, you old moocher. You know too much and you're a threat. I'll be taking over Venus Downs sometime soon and I don't want you around."

Johnny could see the hatred in the eyes, the murderous grin.

A shot rang out and he tumbled backwards, his already dead eyes remaining fixed on his assailant.

Chloe got out of the lagoon and lay on the soft grass to dry her naked body in the warm sun. Her mind drifted and then she thought she heard a distant sound alien to the peace and quietness of her surrounds. It was a long way away—she must have imagined it. It sounded like a gunshot, but her grandfather did not have a gun so she had to be mistaken.

She got up, dressed and walked back to the outstation to wait for his return.

The afternoon shadows deepened and night fell. Chloe knew something was wrong; something had happened to Gramps. She didn't eat, but sat beside the fire all night just staring into the darkness and up at the stars. At dawn, she packed some damper and a water bottle and set off in the direction her grandfather had taken, only to turn around after a short distance and head back to the camp. She knew it would be futile to look for him. She saddled her horse, and with Johnny's horse and the packhorse trailing behind, she slowly began the long ride back to the homestead. The midday heat radiated off the red earth when she pulled up at a large billabong that was fed by a spring. A cupola rose centimetres above the surface of the surrounding water. She sat under the spreading branches of an overhanging tree, slowly ate some of her damper and gazed into the water. Finally, she stripped off and dived down to find the source of the spring. The water grew colder as she swam through the rising flow and then came to the surface. She swam the length of the waterhole before climbing out and standing, eyes closed as the sun dried her skin and her goosebumps receded.

"My, you're beautiful."

Chloe spun around, trying to cover her nakedness as she made for her clothes. Under the shade of a nearby tree, Carl had been sitting out of sight, admiring Chloe's long, lithe limbs and slender but developed body. He stood up and walked towards her, stopping between her and her clothes. She froze, shaking with fear. "What do you want Carl? Why are you spying on me?"

"I'm not going to hurt you. I love you."

She was still shaking as he approached. He enclosed her in a gentle embrace and leaned down to kiss her. She wanted to resist but a strange feeling of desire enveloped her. It was not the crude, demanding kiss she had anticipated; it was soft and passionate, and she felt herself responding. She could feel him pressing himself to her as he moved his hands down to gently caress her buttocks. He leant down and softly kissed her breasts. They slowly sank to the grass where he gently ran his hand over the soft hair between her legs, then knelt down to kiss the spot that inflamed her. She curled one leg up to resist.

"You shouldn't be doing that, Carl."

"Why not? You play with it, don't you? Why not let me give you pleasure?

Chloe raised her hand to protest, but he anticipated it and gently restrained her action. Carl then got up, undressed and lay down beside her. Slowly and tentatively, they began to make love. Carl was passionate but gentle. He forced himself to be patient; he wanted Chloe to remember this moment—then she would be his. Walter would not stand a chance. At last, she gave a small cry and he was spent. Covered in sweat, they rolled apart and lay on the grass, lost in their thoughts.

"What if I get pregnant?"

Carl rolled onto his elbows and looked down at her. "Then we'll get married. I've always loved you, so why don't we get married anyway?"

"You've never shown any tenderness to me before. I always thought you were cruel and ruthless. I'm treated like a housemaid, at everyone's beck and call."

"I suppose I come across like that. I've never known how to express myself very well. I've always had to fight for everything I wanted. I try to hide my weaknesses but

I do have a soft side. I know I've never shown it, but I've loved you from the first day I set eyes on you, and I think your attitude towards me changed when you nursed me in the pub. At first, you just brought meals and would leave, but then I noticed you started to talk to me and stay longer. There was something happening between us, wasn't there?"

Chloe didn't reply as she looked up into his clear blue eyes.

"If you had resisted me just now, I wouldn't have forced you. I would never rape you, if that's what you think. Mind you, I'd have been sorely tempted. A beautiful girl alone in the wilderness is one hell of a situation to resist."

"Henry would have killed you."

"Yes, that too. But Henry wasn't in my thoughts when I was watching you swimming. You haven't answered my question. Will you marry me?"

"I'll have to think about that."

He watched her as she rose and started to dress. "You're beautiful Chloe. I'd do anything for you, but please don't wait too long before giving me your answer."

A thought occurred to her. "You've been watching me all day, haven't you?"

"No, I haven't. I came out to check on stock numbers. I saw your horses and came down to see who it was. It wasn't until I reached the tree I saw you swimming. I knew if I moved you would see me, so I decided to sit tight. I'm really sorry if I scared you." Carl turned to look at the horses. "Where's Johnny? That's his horse, isn't it?"

"Yes, but he told me not to wait for him if he didn't come back to our campsite by last night."

"Don't worry about him. He's gone walkabout to talk to his ancestors. He's a tough old sod. There's no way he would get lost in this country. He was born here and knows every rock and tree. He'll turn up when he's ready."

Chloe had already swung up into the saddle and was leading the horses away.

"Hang about a moment. I'll come with you. I've finished what Henry sent me out to do."

Chloe ignored him as she set the horses to the canter. He was soon beside her and grabbed her horse's bridle. "Slow up, you can't treat horses like that in this heat. They'll die beneath you." He let go of the bridle. She knew he was right, and let the horses slow to a walk.

"Are you having second thoughts now? Do you regret what we did?"

Chloe shook her head. "No, I don't regret it, but I don't believe I did it. It's hard to put out of my mind how you've treated me in the past."

"I think part of the reason is I thought you never liked me. I've never known love, so I've never known how to show it back. Until now, anyway. I've seen you looking at Walter. Why is he so different to me?"

"Walter attacked me and you didn't, that's the only difference. You're both the same otherwise."

Carl nodded in agreement. "I suppose you could say that. I never did thank you for the time you sat at my bedside after Father Murphy had finished with me. I just didn't know how to say thank you, but I'm saying it now. Walter and I both had a tough childhood. Our old man was an alcoholic who finished up dead on the banks of the Swan River and Mum, not that I can remember much about her, just didn't want to know us. It was foster care after foster care until the church finally took us in, and that was a nightmare I'd prefer to forget. If it hadn't been for Henry Boyce, we would have both been in jail by now. He took us in and knocked our heads together until we learnt to respect him and follow his directions without question. A hard man, but he's always fair. I love this land and this property and I hope Henry will leave it to me."

"What about Walter? Doesn't he want to stay?"

"Oh, he feels the same way, but I want to own Venus Downs. I would persuade him to sell me his share. What about you? Are you planning to spend your life here?"

Chloe did not answer. Her mind was in turmoil as to the safety of her grandfather. He had been acting strange that morning, wanting to go off on his own, but she understood there were many sacred rituals no woman was allowed to witness. They rode on in silence until the homestead came in sight.

"Please don't say anything to Henry about this afternoon. I feel sure he would boot me off the property if he found out. You are his princess, you know."

"I won't tell him on the condition I don't find out you've been bragging to Walter. That's how you two operate, always trying to outdo one another."

"You have my word. You go on ahead. I'll get one of the boys to unsaddle the horses and put the tack away. I'll be up in a while."

Chloe swung down and walked towards the homestead where Henry and Walter were sitting on the veranda.

"Where's Johnny?

"He wanted to do something by himself Henry. He said if he wasn't back by nightfall I was to come home without him."

Henry wrinkled his brow. "Strange, but it doesn't really surprise me, I suppose. He often goes walkabout for weeks at a time to look at sacred sites and his dreaming. But if he was going to do that, I would have thought he wouldn't have taken you with him in the first place. Where did you meet up with Carl?" Henry was watching Carl walking towards them.

"At Twenty Mile spring," Carl replied as he walked up to the veranda and sat down. He cast a worried look at Chloe and quickly changed the subject. "The cattle look to be in good condition out there. I think we should plan on a muster pretty soon."

As the three of them started to talk cattle and the weather, Chloe got up and silently went to her room. She was worried about her grandfather. Something was wrong.

The following morning, Chloe was helping Dotti in the kitchen when she noticed Joey Moonlight, the head jackaroo in deep conversation with Henry out in the yard. Henry was stroking his chin as he listened, something she had noticed him doing whenever he was deep in thought. They finally broke off and Henry walked off towards Carl and Walter's rooms. He called through Walter's open door to join them as he went into Carl's room.

Dotti rang the breakfast bell, which consisted of a length of steel hanging from a plough disc. Ten minutes went by but no one appeared. Dotti rang it again, harder. "Chloe, go and tell that mob breakfast is ready. I can't hang around all day. I got things to do."

Chloe walked up to the doorway of Carl's room. She felt an inexplicable sense of dread. Henry was sitting on a chair facing Carl and Walter, who were sitting on Carl's bed.

"Good riddance if the old bugger's carked. But how the hell do they know......" Carl trailed off when he saw Chloe in the doorway.

"Chloe!" Henry called, but she had burst into tears and was already running back towards the homestead. "That's torn it." Henry sighed as he got up.

"But how do they know he's dead, Henry?"

"Oh, they know, but don't ask me how. I suspected something was wrong last night when I heard them chanting down by the billabong."

"Will they go and look for him?"

"No Carl, they know he's dead and with his ancestors. Joey says Johnny would not want anyone to search for him. They're going to take off for a few days for their sacred ceremonies and then it will be back to normal around here. They'll never mention Johnny's name again; that's their way. I'll report it to the authorities as a matter of course when I'm next in town, but I know they won't take any action. No point in the cops coming out here to ask questions because they won't get any answers."

"Chloe'll get over it. It's not like anyone murdered him. He just up and disappeared," Carl said with a shrug of his shoulders. "Takes a load of your mind Henry."

"In what way?"

"Well, for starters you won't have to worry about him talking to the wrong people about the cleanskins from Ascot Downs we've been branding and flogging through Ike Shulman, and—"

Henry cut him off. "I purchased those cattle."

"Knock it off, Henry. Walter and I know they're stolen property. There's some deal between you and Ike and Bill Hargraves, and Johnny's been around long enough to know what's been going on." Carl held up his hands to stem any protest from Henry. "Don't worry, it's none of my business," he said laughing. "You won't have to worry about the old moocher demanding land rights or pay increases now, or threats about going to the cops. He's done you a favour by falling off his perch."

"You've got big ears."

"And big eyes as well. I've got to have both if I'm going to be running this place one day."

Walter said nothing as he watched Henry give Carl a steely look and walk out. "You reckon you're going to be boss-cocky around here? What about me?"

"Oh, I'll buy you out," Carl replied with conviction. "There's not enough room for both of us. Who knows, you might have followed Johnny into dreamland by the time Henry pops off. I'm going to marry Chloe and punch a few kids out of that gorgeous body."

"She doesn't even like you."

"Yeah, I've seen you sneaking peeks at her when you thought I wasn't looking, but you're not going to get her. She's mine, and she'll agree to marry me one day. I've seen something you've never seen—and never will."

"Oh? And what's that?"

"You'll never see it, so don't ask, but it's beautiful."

"You're full of shit."

Carl grabbed Walter around the throat with both hands and thrust him back onto the bed. He could feel pressure rising in his head as he struggled. Just as he was about to pass out, Carl released his grip and stood up.

"Just remember brother, I'm taking over this place one day and Chloe is mine. You don't have the balls to stand in my way, so when Henry goes you'd better have your bags packed because you're not staying here."

Walter slowly massaged his throat. He knew Carl was right. He could not possibly match Carl's anger, an anger that never diminished. It was always just below the surface. Walter tried to forget the past and what he had endured as a child. He got up and walked over to the homestead for breakfast. They sat and ate in silence while Dotti served them.

Henry turned to Dotti when they had finished and Carl and Walter had left. "Just let her be, Dotti. It's a terrible loss for her."

Dotti nodded with a tear in her eye. "Yeah, boss. I even had a soft spot for the old man, but that's the way it is. None of us want to go, but we all have to. I'll go easy on her."

Henry was surprised when he saw Chloe suddenly appear from her room and sit down at the table opposite him. Her eyes were red, but she was no longer crying. She clutched a handkerchief in one hand.

"How are you doing, princess? I know you loved Gramps and I'm sorry for you. We'll all miss him in our own way."

Chloe nodded. "Henry, I want to leave this place."

Henry was shocked. "You want to leave? But why? This is your home. You can't just suddenly up and leave. Where would you go and what would you do? You know nothing but this place. Please, Chloe—" Henry checked himself. He had always wanted her to go and experience the outside world, but here he was trying to hold onto her.

"I can smell death here, Henry. I want to go."

"What a strange statement. What do you mean, *'you can smell death here'*?"

Chloe shook her head and wrung the handkerchief between her hands. "Gramps was what held me here. I want to get away for a while and look what's outside this place. If I don't like it, I'll come back. I've made up my mind."

Henry could see there would be no dissuading her. "Okay, I have a sister in Perth who I'm sure will look after you. I'll contact her."

8

Elizabeth Murdoch had been watching the passengers disembark. She was looking for a young, part aboriginal girl as Henry had described her. There had been no one fitting that description when the last passengers filtered through, until she finally noticed a striking young woman looking worried and lost. She had seen her in the crowd, but dismissed her several times. It must be her, Elizabeth thought. It was just like Henry. He had described her height, length of hair and as having a "bubbly personality". The young woman she was looking at was nothing like the image she had conjured from his description. "Hello. Are you Chloe by any chance?"

"Yes, I am."

"I'm Elizabeth Murdoch, Henry's sister. Please call me Liz. My, you are a very pretty girl."

Chloe blushed and shook Liz's outstretched hand. She immediately warmed to this woman who was obviously older than Henry, elegantly dressed and with fine features. She smiled with genuine emotion.

"How was your flight down?"

"It's the first time I've flown. I was a little scared at first."

"You really have been locked away in the country, haven't you? We must get out and do things and show you around. Let's collect your bag and get out of here. I've prepared lunch so we can sit and talk at my place."

Chloe was overawed by the traffic and buildings as they drove into the city.

"Keep your mouth open like that and you'll swallow a fly." Liz laughed as she cast a sideways glance.

"I'm sorry; I've never seen anything this big before, and so many cars."

Liz entered the underground car park and they caught the lift up to her floor. She opened the door and ushered Chloe in. The view was spectacular over the Swan River. Chloe was drawn to the view and stood quietly, taking it all in.

"Come, I'll show you to your room."

The bedroom was down a hallway to the left of the lounge, but still with a view of the Swan.

"You have your own bathroom and toilet there. " Liz indicated a closed doorway. "I'm on the other side of the lounge so you have this area all to yourself."

Chloe began to laugh.

"What's so funny?"

"Nothing, nothing, Liz. It's just not what I'm used to. No snakes, lizards or frogs in the toilet and shower. No more treading warily when I have to go to the outside loo at night. Can I stay for a few days until I find somewhere to live and get a job?"

"Don't even think about how long you can stay. I live by myself since my husband Alastair died last year. I get lonely and I'm sick of mixing with old girls my age who can only talk about their ills, or play bowls or golf, which both bore me stiff. I think we'll get along just fine. I want the company of some young blood around me. Now you unpack and refresh yourself and come out when you're ready."

Liz had prepared a ham salad lunch, which Chloe picked at, her attention glued to the vista below. She turned around to see Liz looking at her strangely. She was conscious the observation had been going on for some time.

"Why are you looking at me like that?"

"I can see we'll have to work on your table etiquette. You can't hold a knife and fork like that." She leaned over to correct Chloe's grip.

"You weren't looking at my hands. You were looking at my face."

"You're observant, aren't you? Yes, I was looking at you because you remind me of someone. There's something about you I can't put my finger on..." Liz trailed off, lost in thought. "I'm sorry. I was presumptuous correcting your table manners; it was rude."

Chloe laughed. "No it wasn't, Liz. I didn't take any offense. I realise I'm part abo with no manners, but I want to learn."

"Don't ever put yourself down like that, Chloe," Liz admonished. "I don't want to ever hear you refer to yourself like that again. Be proud of yourself. You're a beautiful young woman. We'll work on your shortcomings together. In no time, you'll be knocking back the advances of countless admirers."

Chloe looked down at her plate and gave a slight shudder.

"Why did you want to leave Venus Downs?"

"My grandfather died and I promised myself I would leave when that happened. So here I am."

"You've had a bad experience of some kind. Was it a man?"

Chloe nodded. "Yes. Well, it wasn't a bad experience; it just scared me at the time."

"I take it that it was one of those boys Henry adopted? I knew their background and urged Henry not to do so."

"Yes, it was Carl. It was nothing really."

Liz smiled and gave her a knowing look. "Don't try and put that one over me. Remember, I was your age once and I still vividly remember the first time. We all do."

"He wants to marry me."

"And you're in love with him?"

"Well, we made love, but I don't know whether I'm in love with him. I saw a side of him I never knew existed. I think underneath it all he's a kind, loving person, but he has a hard outer surface he doesn't let anyone penetrate. Please don't tell Henry; he'd kill him."

Liz nodded, then leaned over and patted her hand. "Take my advice. You're not in love with him. You've had an experience you'll never forget, but that's not love."

"Yes, I suppose you're right."

"Now, tell me, how did your grandfather die? Was he ill?"

"No, he just went walkabout and never came back. However, I have my suspicions as to what happened to him, and why."

"Do you want to tell me?"

"No, I'll keep that to myself because I'll never know the answer, so what's the point of dwelling on it?"

"Do you think you'll ever go back?"

"I don't know. Carl's made no secret of the fact he wants to take over the station one day and wants me to be part of it. There's intense rivalry between him and Walter, so I don't know what will happen, but I do know they'll never be able to work together once Henry's gone. Henry has been very good to me, but I don't want to be caught up in fight between the boys. I know I've made the right move coming down here. I feel free."

Liz nodded. Henry was indeed very good to her. He had forwarded a significant sum of money to Liz to be given to Chloe, but only if and when she needed it. "You talk about your Gramps, but what of your mother and father? Are either of them still alive?"

"My father was someone called the Duke, but I never met him. Gramps said he would tell me about him one day, but that never happened. I don't know who my mother was, and I don't remember her ever being around."

Chloe didn't notice Liz's slight grin and slow knowing nod of the head. "The Duke. Is that all he said?"

"Yes. Why, do you know who the Duke is?"

"No, I don't. Probably someone married to a duchess I suppose," Liz replied with a laugh.

"I want to look for a job as soon as I can. I don't want to sponge off you, but I don't know where to look or how to go about it. Can you help me? I'll do anything."

"Of course I'm going to help you. In fact, I will be thrilled to do so. It will give me a real interest rather than gossiping with a pack of old nags at endless morning teas. You're beautiful, you speak nicely, you carry yourself with confidence and other than a few rough edges that have to be addressed, I believe you will be a complete success. I think we should enrol you in a deportment course, to learn about makeup and grooming and clothes—all things a young woman should know. We'll do that tomorrow morning."

Chloe beamed. "Thank you, I'd like that."

"Tomorrow evening I'm having some interesting friends around for drinks and canapés."

"Canapés?"

Liz laughed and patted Chloe on the wrist. "I'm not laughing at you. It's a very natural reaction. A canapé is a small piece of bread with a savoury topping. It comes from the French, meaning 'couch'. You would never have heard the word at Venus Downs. I'm sure Henry wouldn't know a canapé from a horse's hoof."

"Stew, steak, corned beef, damper, spuds, boiled cabbage and Dotti's suet pudding and dumplings is the sum of my cooking knowledge. I hope you won't ask me to cook Liz."

They laughed together. "No, but I'll teach you some interesting dishes."

Chloe was up before dawn and quietly let herself out of the apartment. She walked the silent streets. It was blustery and cold, but she revelled in her new surrounds as she walked around the promenade that fronted the Swan River. How different to the vast landscape she had known all her life. She didn't notice the police car pull up alongside her.

"What are you doing?"

Chloe jumped. She looked around to see the florid face of a fat policeman sitting in his patrol car.

"I'm just walking around, looking at the sights," Chloe replied politely.

"At this time of the morning?"

Chloe heard the door on the opposite side open. His stony-faced young colleague emerged and walked around towards her. The fat officer did not get out of the car.

"I've never seen you around here before. You a hooker?"

Chloe was confused by the young cop's demands. "A hooker?"

"Don't act dumb with me darling. Are you a prostitute?"

"No, I'm not! I'm just out for a walk."

"What's your name?" The officer took out his notebook and flipped it open.

"Chloe Quartpot."

The fat officer slapped his hand on the steering wheel and guffawed. "Quartpot! What kind of a name is that?"

"That is my name," Chloe replied indignantly.

"That's a coon name. You don't look like a coon to me. What's your real name? Where are you from? You look like one of those Asian hookers taking over the town. You working with a pimp, or on your own?" The young policeman began to write as he hammered her with questions.

"My name is Chloe Quartpot, and I'm from Venus Downs station up near Wyndham."

"What are you doing here?"

"I'm out for a walk"

"Don't get smart with me, just answer the questions. Where are you staying?"

"With my aunt, although she's not really my aunt. She's Henry Boyce's sister. He owns Venus Downs."

"And where does this so-called aunt live?"

Chloe looked around to get her bearings. She was confused. The tall buildings all looked the same. "I'm not sure. Ah, yes, I remember walking around that corner down there." She pointed back towards an intersection.

"Well, get in the car and we'll take you back. If you can't find where your aunt lives, it will be down to the station." The policeman held open the rear door of the cruiser. Chloe hesitated. She felt a firm hand on her arm propelling her into the cab. "In you go."

The officer walked around to the opposite side and slid in beside her. "Spin around, Sarge, and left at the next."

The fat sergeant turned the patrol car around and drove towards the street Chloe had indicated. She leaned forward and scanned the buildings looking for some feature that would identify Liz's building. The young officer looked at her as they reached the next intersection. "Well, perhaps you will be able to tell us the truth at the station. Let's go sergeant."

"Please, please," Chloe implored. "Could you just go back the way we've come? I know this is the street, but I didn't take any real notice of what the building looked like when I started my walk. Please."

Without a word, the sergeant spun the car around and began to drive slowly back.

"Stop! I think that's it."

The car pulled up and Chloe made to get out. The officer put his hand on her arm to restrain her.

"You just stay there until I go around and open the door. I don't want to have to chase you."

The door opened and Chloe was followed to the entrance of the large block of units. She looked at the names listed against the call buttons. There was no Boyce listed. She looked through the glass doorway and recognised the abstract sculpture just inside. "This is it. This is the building."

The officer gave her a stony smile. "Listen love, you've wasted enough of our time." He took a firm hold on Chloe's arm and was about to lead her away.

"Wait, I've been looking for the wrong name. There it is— Murdoch. E. Murdoch. That's who I'm staying with. I was looking for Boyce; I just wasn't thinking."

The officer leaned forwards and pushed the call button for a couple of seconds. They waited and then he gave it a longer push, followed by a series of quick pushes to signify urgency.

"Who is it?" The voice was muffled and sleepy. Chloe didn't recognise it.

"Police. We have a person here who claims to be staying with you."

"I have, but she's still in bed."

"Would you check, please?"

A minute later, the intercom came to life again. "No, she's not here. Is that you Chloe?"

"Yes, Liz. I went for a walk."

The door release clicked and Chloe pushed it open. The officer followed her inside.

"I'm okay now," she said.

He took no notice but followed her into the lift and pushed the button to the floor number indicated next to Liz's call button. The officer's demeanour changed immediately it began to move. He broke into a broad smile and moved closer. "I'm sorry if we scared you, but we have to be sure. You're a good looking sort. I would like to take you out sometime. Would you like that?"

Chloe said nothing. She willed the lift to go faster. Liz was waiting for them when it stopped and the doors opened.

"Where have you been, Chloe? I didn't hear you leave."

She looked past Chloe to the policeman. "Is she in trouble of some sort? She only came down from Wyndham yesterday."

"No, she's not, but she gave us some cause for concern." He was now satisfied Liz was not some madam running a few girls on the street. "A young girl walking aimlessly at this hour of the morning is most unusual. I can see she told us the truth so I'll be leaving. Don't forget the invitation." He smiled at Chloe as the lift doors closed.

Liz looked puzzled. "What invitation?"

"He wants to take me out."

Liz gave a wry smile as she guided Chloe inside. "He nearly ran you in for loitering with intent for immoral purposes, then he changes his mind when he sees you aren't what he assumed and now he wants to take you out. Steer clear of that one. Don't go out before dawn, Chloe and if you do go out, please tell me. I don't want to be scared out of my wits by the police pushing my buzzer at such an ungodly hour again."

"I always get up early Liz. I went for a walk and the police stopped me. I was in a real panic because I'd forgotten what the building looked like. I don't even know the address."

"Tried to chat her up, didn't you?"

The young officer slammed the door of the cruiser. "Yeah, she's a real looker. That beautiful complexion and that arse. I'd love to throw a leg over her."

The sergeant chuckled as he moved off. "That's the trouble with you Penisi, you've always got your dick in your hand."

"Your problem is you're too fat to even find it, let alone get it up," the young officer shot back.

"You forget who you're talking to," the older man snapped. "Another comment like that and you'll be back behind a desk shuffling paper, instead of getting laid when you feel like it and making a few bucks on the side."

The young officer nodded, but said nothing. The sergeant's threat was real. Connors was a mountain of a man in his late forties. Uncouth and overweight, his florid face betrayed his heavy drinking and smoking, but he was feared by anyone below his rank as well as the criminals about town. His hands were the size of dinner plates; hands that once pounded a punching bag or an opponent in the ring, but had now turned to softer targets. He ran his own fiefdom as he pleased. Penisi recalled the first night he had been partnered with him:

"We'll cruise down to Freo. D'you feel like a drink and a fuck?"

The young constable was stunned. "Whatever you say, Sarge."

Connors pulled the cruiser up at a bus stop outside a nightclub. "C'mon, let's go and be entertained by the *'ladies'*." He opened the door and slid his bulk out of the vehicle. The doorman stood aside without comment as they entered. Connors took no notice of the crowd drinking at the bar or milling around. The smell of cannabis was heavy in the air as they walked through a rear door and down a darkened passageway.

"Hank in?"

The heavy figure nodded and was about to knock but the sergeant brushed past him and pushed the door open. A man sitting behind a large desk looked up, startled. He spun round to close the door of a heavy safe.

"Keep it open Hank." Connors lowered his weight into a large chair, signalling to Penisi to take the other seat. "You'll only have to open it again. This is my new partner, Constable Penisi. Penisi, this is Hank Cominelli."

Cominelli broke into a broad, unctuous grin and leant forwards to shake Penisi's hand. "Good to meet you. Anything you want is on the house if you're with the sergeant. "What can I do for you Rick? The usual?"

"Got any fresh meat to get me aroused Hank?"

"Bill!" Cominelli shouted at the closed door. It opened and a large, bald head appeared. "Line Tina up with the sergeant. And get someone nice for the constable here."

The head nodded without expression as the door closed.

"She's Asian. Knows every move in the book. You'll be begging for mercy. How about a drink?" Cominelli turned to a bar fridge behind him.

"A beer for both of us."

Cominelli opened the fridge, took out two stubbies of beer, flipped off the caps and put them in front of the two officers.

"How's business?" Connors asked, sipping his beer.

Cominelli smiled and threw his hands wide. "You don't have to ask me that. You walked through the money when you came in. Couldn't be better."

The head reappeared and nodded.

"Off you go, Penisi. I want to have a word with Hank." It was not so much a suggestion from Connors but an order.

As soon as Penisi left the room, Cominelli turned, took an envelope out of the safe and tossed it over. Connors opened it and thumbed through the bank notes. Satisfied, he removed some, then folded the remainder into the envelope and tucked it into his shirt pocket.

"D'you give the young fellow a sling, or do I have to look after him?"

Connors shook his head. "No, you deal with me and me alone. When we walk out of here, he'll be fully compromised. You don't have to worry about him." He drained the stubby and got to his feet. "You sure this bird will be able to handle me?"

"Guarantee it."

"See you next week then." Connors left the room and was escorted by the bald head to Tina's room.

Penisi was leaning on the cruiser when Connors finally appeared with a satiated grin on his face. They got into the car and drove off.

"How was it, lad?"

"First time I've banged a hooker."

"Well, get used to it. I call on Hank every week." Connors pulled out a bundle of loose notes and handed them across. "Here's a little something for you."

"What's this for?" Penisi unfolded the notes and counted them. "A grand. That'll pay a few bills."

Connors laughed. "Stick with me, boy. There's more where that came from."

"Yeah, but what do I have to do for it?" Penisi had heard about it, now he was experiencing it.

"Whatever I tell you. Just remember that you're now in the club. You ever try to shit on me, we'll wind up in the same prison. That wouldn't be good for your complexion, or your arsehole."

"What if I give you the money back and tell you I'm not interested?"

"Too late. I don't think for a moment you want out. I'm a pretty good judge of character Penisi, otherwise I wouldn't have had you assigned to me. They don't pay us enough for the work we do and the risks we take. The whole world's on the make. Don't let anyone tell you he's honest, because the honest don't exist. And be flexible to that crap oath you took to uphold the law. I'm not talking about murderers, rapists and the like, of course, but what harm is Hank Cominelli doing running some girls, drugs and whatever on the side? The people buying have the money and they're prepared to pay for services and entertainment. He's not stealing from them. I say live and let live, as long as I get part of the action."

Chloe sat in the waiting room with other girls around her age at the June Summers Modelling Academy. She felt uncomfortable and awkward; completely out of her depth. Liz had refused to accompany her, saying she needed to gain confidence and she would not achieve this if she had to rely on her aunt.

"Chloe Quartpot." The receptionist looked directly at her with a warm smile.

Chloe stood. Someone sniggered behind her. "Quartpot. What sort of a name is that? It's a wonder she's not carrying a nulla nulla and a spear." The comment was made in a hushed voice, but clearly meant for the whole room to hear.

Chloe turned slightly and saw a girl laughing into the palm of her hand as she leaned towards a stony-faced, older woman, presumably her mother, who suddenly spoke up. "I believe my daughter is next. I am Jessica Upton-Hill and this is my daughter Amanda. We've been waiting half an hour. This is simply not good enough. I will be late for my next appointment."

The receptionist recognised the haughty, demanding voice for what it was and smiled. "Miss Quartpot, would you mind waiting a little longer while Amanda is interviewed?"

Chloe smiled and sat down. She was in no hurry.

Amanda Upton-Hill smirked at Chloe as she walked past while her mother sat back with a satisfied look on her face. Ten minutes later, Amanda emerged with tears in her eyes.

"What happened dear?" Jessica Upton-Hill dropped the magazine she had been browsing and sat upright, confused.

"Bitch. She doesn't think I can become a model." Amanda didn't look at Chloe as she fled the room, her distraught and humiliated mother in quick pursuit.

"Chloe, please come through." She was shown into a small brightly lit room. "Miss June will be with you soon." Chloe sat down to one side of a small coffee table containing *Vogue* and other fashion magazines. She picked one up and began casually flicking through it without actually seeing anything she was looking at. Her mind was in turmoil. She didn't belong there.

A door opened and in walked a woman Chloe gauged to be about Liz's age. She held out her hand and gave Chloe a warm smile. Chloe immediately took a liking to her and began to relax.

"Hello Chloe. I'm June Summers." She sat down and studied Chloe as if waiting for her to say something. Chloe held her gaze, trying to hide her nervousness. "Tell me something about yourself."

"What would you like to know Miss Summers?"

"Please, call me Miss June. I like it better and it's more personal. Never 'June'; always 'Miss June'."

Chloe told Miss June of her life on Venus Downs and why she had come to Perth and to the June Summers Academy. Miss June listened attentively, all the while studying this girl in front of her, her mannerisms, her features, her grooming, and particularly her speech, which she noted was soft and refined, a complete contrast to what she expected. With a name like Quartpot she had anticipated someone brought up in the harsh existence of a distant cattle station, with skin damaged by exposure to unrelenting sun, a voice too harsh to ever modulate or train, and a general lack of femininity and poise. She could train any girl to some extent, but some were unsalvageable. However, a tiny minority were immediately identifiable as having real potential. She was now looking at one of these special cases.

"May I ask who referred you to my agency?"

"I came down to look for employment. I have no qualifications other than being a station hand, but Elizabeth Murdoch suggested I apply for a department—sorry, I mean a deportment course?"

Miss June raised her eyebrows. "Liz? I thought she would have let me know she was sending you here. Elizabeth and I are old friends. But how do you know Elizabeth Murdoch?"

"She's the sister of Henry Boyce who owns Venus Downs where I come from. I wanted her to come with me today, but she refused. She said she wanted me to be independent."

"Quite right." Miss June realised her friend didn't want her to feel obligated. "Chloe, I'm sure you will fit in here perfectly. It's a three-month course initially and if you want to carry on, that's up to you. Would you like to do it?"

"Liz said you'd knock the rough edges off me and guide me in the right direction as to getting employment."

Miss June laughed. "I can't see any rough edges, just a few things that need a little polishing. Have you ever thought of modelling Chloe?"

"Modelling - what's that?"

Miss June picked up *Vanity Fair* and flicked a page open. "You see that girl? She's modelling those clothes for a fashion house. Here's another who's modelling perfume, and another modelling a new car. That's what modelling is. It's highly paid, but it's hard work and you need to be engaged by the right agencies. You have to be seen and noticed. The more work you get, the higher the fee you command. You can travel the world and meet interesting people. Don't let me get your expectations up too high at this stage—you've a long way to go, but I've every confidence you'll make it."

"Do you really think I could Miss June?"

"Yes, and I will give you all the help I can. Are you aware of the cost of the three month course."

Chloe paled when Miss June told her. "I, I simply don't have that much money. I will have to think of doing something else."

Miss June smiled and patted Chloe's arm. Liz was well aware what she charged, otherwise she would not have sent her. Surely, she had that base covered.

"You go home and discuss it with Elizabeth."

"But…" Miss June ignored her as she stood up, opened the door and showed Chloe out. As soon as she was gone, June turned to the receptionist. "Chloe will be starting with us at nine in the morning Martina. Please book her in."

Liz was arranging flowers in the kitchen when she heard Chloe return. June had already phoned her to let her know Chloe was certainly material she could work with and she would not be wasting her time, as was the case with the vast majority of young girls who aspired to become models.

"How did it go Chloe?"

"Miss June said I can start tomorrow. But I can't afford it."

"Don't concern yourself about that. Henry sent me money for just such an event. I wasn't going to say anything until I knew you had something worthwhile to spend it on. Do you want to become a model? June thinks you have the attributes for success."

Chloe beamed and threw her arms around Liz's neck. "Of course I do, and thank you for talking to Miss June about me."

"I didn't talk to her. You did it all by yourself so you should be proud you've survived your first interview, your first big test. By the way, these flowers are for you. I've put them in water. There's a card with them."

"Who are they from? I don't know anyone here." Chloe looked at the card. "James Penisi. I don't know anyone by that name."

"Yes you do. If my memory serves me correctly, he was that young policeman who brought you home the other morning."

"He wants to take me to dinner." Chloe looked at the neat writing.

"And?"

"I didn't like him that much. He was rude and demanding at first and then changed when he finally found out I wasn't a prostitute. What should I do?"

"Ignore him."

"What if he phones, or comes to the door?"

"Tell him politely, but firmly you're not interested. If he persists, I'll soon put a flea in his ear. Now get ready because we're going to a movie and then out to dinner."

Liz and Chloe were laughing and chatting as they walked home after the movie when Liz looked up and slowed as she saw the police car sitting outside her building. "I think this should be nipped in the bud right now. You go on up and I'll have a word with this young man."

Liz walked up to the car and tapped on the driver's window. It rolled down, but she didn't recognise the fat officer in the driver's seat. She leaned down and looked across to the passenger side.

"Can I ask you what you're doing here? It's Constable Penisi isn't it?"

"Police business," the driver snapped without turning to acknowledge her.

Liz ignored his remark. "I was talking to the other officer."

The young constable leaned across. "I was hoping to see Chloe. Did she get my flowers?"

"She did thank you, but she won't be accepting your dinner invitation, so please don't bother her again."

The driver started the engine and rolled up the window in Liz's face. "Don't get involved with that one, Penisi. You'll wind up facing a harassment complaint."

"It was worth a try."

"And you've got your answer, so leave it alone. That's an order."

9

*C*hloe *had been in Perth almost a year. On finishing her course, June Summers had employed her on a casual basis to train other young hopefuls in between occasional, but increasing modelling assignments she was receiving.*

"Hi there."

Chloe looked up from her book and studied the young man standing confidently before her. "Hi there yourself."

"I've noticed you often come here. Can I buy you a coffee?"

"No thanks, I've already had one."

"Well, let me buy you another. Please say yes?"

Chloe laughed and folded her book. "Okay, just make it a latte. I can only spend a minute. I've got an appointment."

She was used to it by now; the never ending approaches and variation of pitches. This one appeared to be different. It was the cheeky expression of confidence attempting to mask the insecurity. Besides, there was something about him that attracted her. Five minutes later he returned balancing the two cups and set them down.

"My name's Oliver Gibbs. Can I ask you what your's is?"

"Chloe."

"Chloe what?"

"Just Chloe."

He checked for a moment at the repulse. "Okay Chloe, I didn't mean to be nosey. I just wanted to say hello."

"And I've noticed you here a few times over the past couple of weeks. You finally plucked up the courage eh?"

"Yeah, yeah, I can't deny it. A few of my mates have tried to make out with you, but you gave them both the flick."

"So what's the bet?"

"What do you mean?"

"Your friends have given you the challenge to chat me up, haven't they? So what are you betting you can do it?

He was about to reply when Chloe cut him off. "And don't try to deny it."

"Okay, you're right," he replied sheepishly. "Don't look now, but those two guys sitting at the table off to your left are my mates. They bet me a carton of beer you would not accept the offer of a coffee, or let me talk to you."

"Well, it looks as though you've won the bet, so go and collect."

"I'm not interested in the bet, I'm interested in you Chloe."

"What do you do Oliver?"

His face lit up as he recognised he was making headway. "I'm in my final year at university. What do you do?"

"I've recently finished a modelling course and doing a bit of tutoring in between assignments."

"You're one stunning looking bird. I reckon you'll be a smash-hit as a model."

"I'm not a bird." She tersely corrected him. "I'm a person."

He held up his hands in supplication. "I'm sorry, I didn't mean it like that. It looks like I've screwed up already."

"Apology accepted," Chloe replied as she got up to leave.

"Will you be here tomorrow? I'm a destitute student, but I reckon I can afford another coffee."

"I could be." She smiled as she put on her sunglasses, picked up her book and walked out of the coffee bar into the street. She glanced sideway knowing her action could not be observed through the darkened lenses. She saw the three conspirators giving each other high-fives.

"I can see it in your face. You met someone you quite like today, didn't you?"

"Yes Liz I did. He was having a bet with his friends he could buy me a coffee. I'd seen him before, along with a couple of his friends who have tried to pick me up in the past month, but he didn't try until today."

"So, what made him so different?"

"I don't know really. I suppose it was because he admitted what his intentions were, and looked genuinely guilty about a challenge he'd accepted. He's a uni student. Also, there was something about him that attracted me."

"What was the bet?"

"A carton of beer," Chloe laughed.

"Hmmm." Liz raised her eyebrows "Typical of boys. The next bet will be whether he can get your pants off. You be careful. I don't want to see you getting hurt."

Chloe gave her a look of mock shock. "I've never heard you talk like that before Liz. I'm old enough to look after myself."

Liz sighed. "Yes, I know you are, but you know what I'm like. I worry about you the whole time. You're the daughter I never had."

Chloe threw her arms around Liz and hugged her. "And I love you."

"Hi there Chloe. I've missed you. Can I buy you a coffee?"

"Hello Oliver. Are your friends with you today?"

"Look, I'm sorry too that and I apologise. Can we start again? I would really like to get to know you."

Over the following weeks they became constant companions, and the bond grew closer. Liz could see Chloe was becoming totally infatuated with the boy and talked about him constantly.

"You two are getting real serious?"

"Oh, I don't know about that Liz , but I really like him and we hit it off so well. However, I know what you're thinking."

"And what's that?"

"You think I'm going to do something stupid? Well, I haven't slept with him yet, if that's what's on your mind."

"Chloe, if you sleep with him, it's none of my business, but I don't want you to mess up your life before it's even started. You have a career, you're already getting modelling assignments. You're on the way, and I want you to make a success of yourself."

"Liz, I cannot thank you enough for all you've done for me, but it's my life. It's really none of your concern. If you would like me to leave I will do so as I'm making enough money to be independent."

Liz bit her lip as a tear came to her eye. "Please don't do that Chloe. You are the only thing I have in my life. I'd be so lonely without you. I realise you're going to leave one of these days, but I just can't bear the thought."

"Oliver is going to pick me up on Saturday morning. We're going down the coast so he can teach me to surf. Why don't I bring him up and introduce him. He's often asked about you, so he won't be embarrassed."

Liz nodded and tried to smile. "Why don't you do that. I would certainly like to meet him." She felt guilty as she felt she already knew him. She had observed him discretely from the balcony every time he came to collect her, and it always seemed to be in an expensive car, way beyond the resources of a university student.

The meeting was cordial but swift. Oliver tried to look relaxed but was aware of the usual xray assessment by an older person. Liz was not what he had expected.

"Is she related to you?" He asked as he got into the car and started the engine.

"No, she's Henry Boyce's sister, the owner of Venus Downs where I grew up."

"I can see she really loves you. Very protective I would say."

Chloe said nothing, but smiled and just nodded. They drove out of the city and headed towards Bunbury. She felt uncomfortable as the speed began to increase.

"Could you slow down please Oliver? You frighten me."

He laughed as he put his foot down further and ignored her as he began to weave in and out of traffic.

"Oh shit," he exclaimed as he looked up into the rear vision mirror and saw the flashing lights. "Bloody cops."

He pulled to the side of the road and wound down the window. The cop pulled in behind, got out and walked up. "Any excuse for speeding?"

"None. I just wasn't aware I was speeding sir."

"Is this your car?"

"It's my mother's."

The cop took Oliver's licence and studied it. "You were thirty over the limit. I don't believe you weren't aware of that. Wait here." Five minutes later he came back and handed Oliver back his licence. "That just cost you three hundred dollars young man, and the loss of three points. Another fine and you'll be off the road for six months. Drive more carefully."

"Thank you officer, I will," Oliver replied politely as he put the car into gear and pulled back onto the highway. "Arsehole," he shouted into the mirror as he gathered speed.

"You were speeding Oliver."

"I know what I was doing Chloe, you don't have to rub it in." They drove on in silence as Chloe noticed him begin to relax his grip on the wheel and the tension leave his face.

"Yeah, I guess I had it coming to me. My old lady told me she wouldn't let me have her car again if I got another ticket. The old man's already banned me, but he's a pushover for a sob story. It's Mum that wears the pants around our place."

Half an hour later he slowed and pulled off the highway into a parking area. "Here we are, so let's enjoy the surf."

"But you haven't brought any boards?"

"There'll be a couple of my mates down here, so it'll be no problem in borrowing a board to teach you."

Chloe had an uneasy feeling as she got out. However, she was relieved when Oliver waved to some of his friends further down the beach, but made no move to join them. He walked off and came back with a board. Chloe stepped out of her shorts and unbuttoned her top to reveal her bikini.

One of Oliver's friends rocked onto his back from where he was sitting in the sand, and clasped his hands to his head. "Oh, mama mia, Gibbs has really hit the jackpot this time." The comment was clearly audible as it drifted towards them.

Chloe ignored the low wolf whistles as they walked towards the surf.

She realised she was being talked about and closely observed as he persevered for an hour, finally getting her to stand and gain her balance as she rode a small wave. She heard the outburst of clapping from along the beach.

"Oliver, can we go home please? I've really had enough."

"Sure. I shouldn't have brought you here. It was a mistake, and I'm really sorry." He picked up the board and walked back towards the group. He was halfway back when the one who had made the earlier comment suddenly shouted. "Hey Oliver, have you got your tongue between those chocolate lips yet?"

Oliver paused, spun around, but decided to ignore the remark. He picked up their towels and took Chloe by the elbow as he guided her towards the car. She pulled her clothes back over her bikini as he shook out the towels and draped them over the seats.

"I don't think much of your friends."

"Oh, they're okay. It's just they've been drinking and letting off steam before the first of the final exams starting next week. Three more weeks to go and it's all over, and then all I have to do is find a job. My days of freedom are coming to an end."

"What are you going to do?"

"I don't know really. Dad wants me to join him, but I don't like the idea. He's a tough old sod and we don't really hit it off. I may go overseas for a couple of years and just bum around. Do you want to join me? It would be a lot of fun."

Chloe laughed. "Thanks for the offer, but I've got other plans."

"Yes, I was only joking. Say, how would you like to spend a few days with me down on the Margaret River after the exams? None of my friends, just you and I? We can go surfing, eating at some excellent restaurants, visit some vineyards, drink some wine, and just generally chill out. It's a beautiful part of the world."

"And?"

He looked across at her and grinned. "Why don't we see what eventuates?"

Chloe did not answer as she looked straight ahead lost in thought. He reached across and patted her leg. "Don't look so worried. You don't have to answer me now. I've never had much tact according to my mother."

"I think I'd like that Oliver."

He hit the wheel with the palm of his hand and beamed across at her. "That's settled then. Say, the old man is throwing an afternoon party at our place for friends and business associates next weekend. He's not telling anyone, but it's his birthday. You'll meet a lot of interesting people."

"None of your friends from today there, I hope?"

"No, but there will be a few you haven't met, and I know you'll like them. I won't be able to catch up with you next week as I want to prepare for the exams. That okay with you?"

"Sure. I've got a photo shoot mid-week, so I'll be too busy anyhow."

Oliver introduced her to his mother and father. His father was a big man with a beaming smile, and florid face of someone who had just spent too long in the sun or drank too much. The loud welcoming voice marked him as the host and centre of attention among the chattering quests.

The smile disappeared momentarily as he appraised Chloe. Oliver's mother smiled and nodded, but said nothing.

"You two mingle and get yourselves a drink. Lunch will be served under the marquee." Jack Gibbs turned and raised his eyes at his wife as he walked away.

"Come on Chloe, I'll introduce you to a few people." Oliver had observed his father's reaction, and mother's coldness. He put his hand on Chloe's back and guided her away towards a group of younger people. The introductions were cordial, but she could sense an undercurrent of rejection as the casual questions became more probing. A waiter came up and said something to Oliver.

"The old man wants me front and centre to help him greet the arrivals," he said as he turned to Chloe. "I think he's invited the whole bloody business community, plus rent-a-crowd. I'll be back in a minute or two." He quickly finished the glass of champagne, while taking another from the tray of a passing waiter.

The younger group broke up and drifted away. Chloe was suddenly alone and she sat down beside an older woman on a garden bench. There were two empty glasses on a small table beside her and she was clutching another as she took an occasional drag on a cigarette.

"Where are you from my dear?"

"I come from Venus Downs in the Kimberley."

"And what's your name?"

"Chloe," she replied smiling, but she knew the inquisition was about to start.

"That's a pretty name. What mob are you from?" The thrust and malice of the question was obvious and direct and tinged with alcohol.

"The same mob as you I would imagine. I'm an Australian."

The woman was shocked and her eyes widened as her expression changed to one of disdain. "You know perfectly well what I meant. You're aboriginal aren't you?"

Chloe did not answer as she got up and walked away. She wanted to leave. She looked around for Oliver, but could not see him, and neither could she see his father until she suddenly heard his overbearing voice, and looked up to see him disappearing into the house with Oliver. She weaved her way through the crowd, and into the entrance, dodging past waiters carrying out trays of food and drinks. She walked slowly down the long hallway peering into each open room as the noise of the outside crowd receded behind her. She was about to turn and walk back when she heard raised voices from behind a partially open doorway.

"What the hell did you mean by bringing her here?"

"I didn't think you'd care Dad. She's lost in the crowd and no one's taking any notice of her."

"Oliver, wake up to yourself. Your mother nearly had apoplexy, and I don't want any son of mine seen to be running around with a gin. I've got an image to uphold and so have you."

"Dad, she may be an abo, but she's one smashing looking article, don't you agree?"

"That's not the bloody point boy. Shag her by all means, but make sure you're not responsible for a chocolate chip biting at your ankles in nine months time. That would really send your mother around the bend. Anyway, what happened to that girl you were bonking last week? I can't keep up your conquests."

"Dad, just calm down. You know that while the bird's keep dropping their nickers, I just can't say no. I'm taking Chloe down to Margaret River to break her in and that will be the end of it."

Chloe stifled her tears, and began to walk away hurriedly as she heard the loud guffaw from behind the door. "Good enough lad, but make sure you never invite her here again. Now, do your Mother and I a favour and make some excuse to get her out of sight today."

Oliver opened the door and went out to look for Chloe, churning over in his mind what excuse he would make. He walked around the entire perimeter of the gathering, acknowledging, but not really noticing any of the people trying to engage him.

"Are you looking for your darling Chloe, lover boy?" It was a girl he knew, and was clearly enjoying his discomfort. "You're too late as she's gone walkabout, or more likely runabout, judging by the speed she took off."

"Did you see which way she went?"

"Yes, just follow that cab," she replied pointing towards the roadway with a laugh. "Forget about her. Come and join us and have a drink."

Oliver nodded as he turned towards her with a look of resignation and relief. "Yes, I guess I will."

10

*I*t *was six months later when Chloe burst in.* "Liz, Liz are you home?"

Hearing the excitement in her voice, Liz put down the book she was reading in anticipation. "What is it?"

"I've been offered a job in London!" Chloe squealed in delight. "I can't believe it. Should I accept?"

"Sit down and tell me all about it."

"It's with the LeClair Agency. Miss June arranged it for me. What do you think?" She noticed Liz was not showing her usual animation, but sensed it was only a façade. "You know something, don't you? Come on, out with it. I know you've been hiding something for days now."

"Yes, I do know something. June phoned me a week ago and I went and had coffee with her. According to her, LeClair is an emerging agency. It doesn't have any top models on its books, but those they do have are making an impression. They saw a photo of you modelling some of the *Imagine* range of women's fashions a couple of months ago and liked what they saw. I was concerned, but June assured me she thought you could make it into the international spotlight rather than hiding away here in Perth, with its limited opportunities. What followed were the usual checks such as age, height, weight, measurements, experience etc. They wanted to know how natural the photos they saw of you were, had they been touched up or airbrushed, did you have any convictions, where did your surname derive from and so forth. They appeared to be amused by the name Quartpot, but didn't make an issue of it as you'll only ever be known and promoted as *'Chloe'*. I phoned Henry and discussed it with him, and he's thrilled you're going to make a name for yourself, but saddened by the fact you'll be so far away. He loves you, you know. He made me promise you'll fly up and see him before you go."

"So that's a yes. You think I should accept?"

"Grab the opportunity with both hands, Chloe. You're off to London in two weeks and LeClair is taking you to the Milan fashion week in Italy. Milan is one of the fashion capitals of the world. You're about to hit the big time! You've worked hard in the time you've been here with me and I've loved every moment of it."

"Oh Liz, I'm so excited. You've been so good to me." She threw her arms around Liz and hugged her. "I don't know how to thank you. I wouldn't have survived without your guidance and support."

Liz kissed her on the cheek and patted her back. "You'll survive. You're a strong girl with a determined personality. Just don't forget me, and phone me every month to tell me what you're doing."

"I told Miss June I'd give her my answer in the morning, as I wanted to talk to you and think about it overnight. I'd like to take you both out to lunch tomorrow."

"I've already told her you'll accept and she's arranged DiMitrio's for the three of us for tomorrow. She insists we're her guests and as her star graduate, she is honoured by your success. It will mean a lot for her agency. She's going to ask if she can promote it using your name. She'll pay you, of course."

"Of course she can but I couldn't take money from Miss June; I owe her so much."

"I was hoping you'd say that. She will be so pleased."

"I have to see Henry before I leave."

"I've already arranged the flights and I'm coming with you. I haven't seen my brother for so long and we're both getting on in years. Normally, I wouldn't go near the place. I can't stand the dust and flies of the outback and the smell of cattle, but this time I have no excuse. He didn't think you'd stay the course; he thought you'd be back at the station a few weeks after you left and he was ready to welcome you home. But you've proved him wrong, haven't you?"

Chloe shuddered at the thought of cooking and cleaning and being at Dotti's and everyone else's command again. She had found a new world and was about to embark on expanding those horizons. Venus Downs held fond memories, but they were just that: memories. The recurring dreams about Gramps' disappearance and her memories of the happy times they had spent together since she was a small child she would never forget. Chloe would always keep her promise to Gramps to respect and keep secret his sacred sites and dreaming places.

The plane touched down with a heavy thump and the turbine propellers were thrust into reverse to slow its forward speed. It taxied for a minute or two until it pulled up in front of the tiny terminal. Chloe studied the waiting crowd as she disembarked and walked towards the barrier fence. She immediately saw Carl, his face shaded by a large bush hat, his hands buried in his jeans pockets. He broke into a large grin when they came through the barrier. "Hi Chloe." He grabbed her by the arms and kissed her firmly on each cheek, then pushed her away to look her up and down. "It's fantastic to see you. You look smashing."

"Thank you, Carl." She was pleased to see him, but nothing more. Even though she had thought about him constantly while she was in Perth, Chloe felt none of the spark she had been expecting. She realised she felt alien to the man she was looking at—they lived in two different worlds now, and understood she could never return his affection. He was an unforgettable experience in the natural progression of her life.

"And you must be Aunt Liz. Can I call you Liz?"

"I prefer Liz. And who might you be?"

"I'm Carl Boyce." He thrust out his hand with a broad grin.

Liz shook it, but Chloe could see she was uncomfortable. It was obvious Liz had already confirmed her preconception of Carl.

"Where's Henry? I expected him to meet us?" Liz said.

"He has a badly swollen foot and can't walk. We were branding cattle and a bull trod on it. He's not as quick as he used to be and didn't get out of the way in time. I was delegated to pick you up."

"And your brother?"

"Walter was assigned to clean your rooms and also make sure the loo and shower are spotless. We tossed to see who would pick you up and who would be housemaid—I won of course. I always win tosses with Walter. He really is a loser. I hope he leaves when I take over. He just doesn't fit in."

"What are you taking over?"

"Venus Downs, of course Liz."

"You've seen my brother's Will then, have you? Has he told you he's leaving the place to you?"

Carl didn't realise Liz was baiting him. "Well, there's no one else capable of running the place and he's got no relations other than Walter and yourself Liz. I'll buy you both out at a good price, of course."

"I would hope so but what about Chloe? What if Henry leaves it all to her? Have you thought about that?"

"Chloe!" Carl exclaimed with a look of derision. He stifled the laugh building in his throat. "She's not related, but of course if she marries me, she'll be part of Venus Downs."

Chloe did not react to Carl's insinuation. Her memory flashed back to that day at the billabong when she lost her innocence to him. She did not regret it, but resented the familiarity Carl was now attempting to portray. "How's Dotti? I'm looking forward to seeing her."

"Dotti's stuffed with arthritis, Chloe. You should see her hands. They're all twisted and she's in a lot of pain. Henry will have to get rid of her soon. If he doesn't, I will."

Chloe hid her look of shock and was about to say something when she was cut off.

"Those two bags with the red ribbon on the handles are ours." Liz was pointing to the baggage trolley that had just arrived. "Would you get them for us, Carl?"

"He'd have to be the most arrogant, self-opinionated, dispassionate individual I've ever come across. And he's dangerous," Liz commented quietly to Chloe as they watched him retrieve their bags. "You could never have stayed on at Venus Downs. You made the right decision to get out. You may have felt something for him once, but he's not for you—not now, not ever." She gave Carl a warm smile as he returned. "Thank you Carl."

"This way, ladies. Your chariot awaits." He tossed their bags into the open tray of the Toyota. "Hop in Chloe." He swung open the passenger door so she would be seated next to him. Liz quickly moved in front of Chloe to get in, pretending not to notice the flash of anger on Carl's face. Chloe got in next to Liz and he closed the door.

"Doesn't Henry have any better transport than this?" Three across the cab, in the stifling heat was more than uncomfortable. "Is this thing even air-conditioned?" Liz complained.

"Yes, to both questions Liz." Carl started the engine and turned the air on full blast. "It'll cool down in a few minutes. The problem is I brought a pump motor and generator into town to be serviced and then picked up a load of stores, which you can see in the back. Henry's vehicle is a LandCruiser station wagon, not a tray-back like this. Great for passengers, but useless as a utility. I suppose you're used to riding around in chauffeured cars now, are you Chloe? Not getting up yourself, I hope."

"Carl, there is no call for sarcasm," Liz snapped. "Why don't you just shut up and drive? The sooner I get out of this vehicle the better."

Carl pushed the gear lever over and up, forcing Liz's leg towards Chloe. "Sorry about that, Liz, it's unavoidable." Once the vehicle began rolling, he changed gear and Liz felt her thigh being crushed again as he pulled the stick down. He held it there to prolong the discomfort. Liz suddenly covered his hand with hers and pushed the stick up and away from her. There was a grinding of gears until Carl declutched and put the vehicle into third gear and then fourth. "Hell Liz, I'll do the driving."

"Do you think I don't know what you're doing? It's bad enough being cooped in this cab without you playing games."

Carl did not reply. For the next three hours, they made small talk as he concentrated on his driving on the rough highway. The turn-off to Venus Downs finally loomed into sight, the once proud sign penetrated by dozens of bullet holes. Dust swirled up and although everything was closed, a fine red mist infiltrated the cab. It got into their hair and clothes and began to clog and irritate their noses. Liz held a handkerchief over her nose and mouth in a futile attempt to limit the effect.

Henry was waiting for them on the homestead veranda and waved to them with a walking stick. Chloe jumped out and rushed to throw her arms around him and kiss him. "Henry," she whispered in his ear. "I want to thank you for everything you've done for me. I'll never forget it."

"You don't have to thank me princess. I'm so proud of you. My, you look really beautiful. You certainly don't belong here anymore."

Liz followed, trying to shake some of the dust out of her clothes, while Carl retrieved their dust encrusted bags, dumped them on the veranda and strode off without a word.

"Liz, it's great to see you." Henry embraced his sister. "Sit down and bring me up to date."

"Henry, I want to shower and change into some clean clothes first. Then we can talk. I feel like I've been dragged behind that truck rather than riding in it."

"Yes, it's not the best form of transport if you want comfort, but you'll get used to it."

"I only have to suffer it one more time and that's when I leave. I've no intention of getting used to it. What a godforsaken part of the world this is."

Henry laughed. "Chloe will show you to your room. Hey, Walter, are you there?"

Carl's twin strolled out of the kitchen smiling broadly. "Hello Chloe, welcome home. I've been following your career—I'm really happy for you." He embraced her and kissed her on the cheek.

"Thank you Walter, that's very nice of you. This is Aunt Liz."

"Aunt Liz, welcome to Venus Downs." She shook his hand. "I've cleaned your rooms. No one's been in there since you left and it sure took me a while to remove all the cobwebs and clean up. I'll take your bags in."

"He's different to his brother," Liz commented as he dusted off the bags before taking them inside. "He's a smartarse that Carl, isn't he?"

"Yes, he can be," Henry replied dryly. "But without him and Walter, I just couldn't run this place. It's getting too much for me, but it's my whole life and I'll die here. I plan to be buried under a tree by that billabong."

"You are getting melancholy, Henry. You plan on dying soon then?"

"I see you've still got your dry sense of humour Liz. No, but I'm beginning to feel my age. Why don't you two go and get cleaned up, then we can chew the fat before dinner."

Chloe looked around her room. It was the same as when she had left it except the bed linen was fresh and there were fresh towels laid out. She sat on the edge of the bed contemplating what her life had been and how it had changed since leaving. She looked around at all her things that had been special to her as a child growing up. They were no longer special, but she could still recall how and when she had acquired each of them. She could feel Gramps' presence all around her. Her eyes fell on the jar of stones. She walked over and picked it up, shaking it to reveal the red stone of the rainbow serpent. She couldn't see it so she tipped the contents out onto the dresser. It wasn't there. It had to be Walter who had taken it. She could hear him talking to Henry on the veranda as she quickly went out and confronted him.

"Walter, I think you have something that belongs to me."

Walter looked guilty, took the stone out of his pocket and handed it to her. "I'm sorry, Chloe. While I was cleaning, I knocked the jar over and it fell out. I didn't think you'd mind as I thought you'd have long forgotten about it."

Chloe knew he was lying. The jar was too heavy to be simply knocked over. He must have picked it up and studied the contents.

"Where did you get it?"

"Gramps gave it to me. It's special."

"I've never seen a stone like that before. Did he pick it up on Venus Downs?"

"Yes, but I don't know where," Chloe lied. "He just gave it to me one day. Please don't touch my things again."

"That's the first time I've ever been in your room. I never go into that side of the homestead. I'm sorry I took it. I won't go in there again, I promise."

Chloe could see he was being genuine. At least he had owned up; Carl would have just taken it and denied he had done so. She sensed a change in Walter's attitude towards her. He had always been overshadowed by his brother, although she always considered Walter to be the smarter of the pair. His reactions were slower and more considered in contrast to Carl's explosive nature.

"Did I do a good job of your room?"

"Yes, thank you Walter and also for being honest and giving me back my stone. I'll always treasure it as it reminds me of Gramps." Chloe went back to her room and put the stone back in the jar, shaking it so it was concealed again. She would leave it here where it belonged on Venus Downs, and where the spirit of Gramps would look over it.

Dotti was in the kitchen when Chloe emerged showered and in fresh clothes. Chloe walked up behind her and threw her arms around her neck.

Dotti sniffed. "What you doin, comin' here and not sayin' hello to Dotti first. Where you been? I gotta do everythin' aroun' here." She indicated a shy, native girl trying to remain out of sight. "This one's just as lazy as you. Hey, you doing all right for yourself aren't you?" She spun around and returned Chloe's embrace. "I miss you so much Chloe," she whispered. There was a tear in the old woman's eye. She gathered herself. "Now git out of here while I git this lazy one working, or you won't git any dinner."

Chloe noticed Walter had showered and put on fresh jeans and a clean shirt when he appeared for dinner. Carl was in the same clothes he had picked them up in. He was sullen throughout the meal as he watched his brother in frequent animated discussion with Chloe. He could see she was enjoying Walter's company. It did not escape Liz's attention either, all the while keeping up with Henry's constant banter and questions.

After dinner, Carl wandered off but Walter joined them on the veranda—something he would never normally do. A hard day mustering and branding cattle or erecting fences or mending stockyards and constantly being subjected to Henry's shouts and demands left him tired and exhausted. Normally, he and Carl would eat and then disappear to their rooms.

"What do you plan on doing tomorrow, Chloe? Would you like to go for a ride?"

Henry stopped mid-sentence when he heard Walter's invitation. Was this a softer side of Walter he had never seen before? The memory and consequences of the last time they went riding together was still clear in his mind. He pointed at Walter. "You've no time to go riding. I want those bulls loaded first thing and trucked into Wyndham. It's your turn because Carl went in yesterday. Be careful, there are a couple of really dangerous ones amongst them. I want Chloe to stay here with Liz and me. You've got too much to do around here without going joy riding."

Walter nodded and without a word made to leave. Chloe caught his eye and smiled at him.

"The boy was only being polite Henry. Why were you so hard on him?"

"Liz, he's got plenty to do and I want to get those bulls away tomorrow. They've been locked in the yards for two days now. They should have gone yesterday, but I didn't think you'd want to be picked up in a stinking cattle truck."

Chloe walked down to the stables after breakfast. She spoke softly to her horse and stroked its nose, feeding it some damper she had pocketed. She heard the cattle truck pull up and turned to see Walter get out to open the gate. Carl drove through and waited. He saw Walter walk over and start talking to Chloe, but could not hear what was being said. Finally, he sounded the horn, opened his door and shouted to his brother. "What the hell are you doing? We've got work to do so let's get on with it." He saw Walter laughing and patting Chloe's arm, before shutting the gate and running over to clamber back into the cab of the truck. He had one foot on the running board and his other leg inside the open door, when Carl accelerated without warning. Walter just managed to hold on and scramble in.

"Christ, what was that all about? What were you saying to her?" Carl sneered.

Walter didn't need to look at his brother; he could sense jealousy oozing out of him. Carl gripped the wheel so tight his knuckle's were white, and the anger in his voice palpable.

"I was asking her for the next dance sunshine." Walter began to hum the familiar tune.

"She's mine you shit, you know that so keep your hands off her."

"She doesn't like you, Carl. Never has. I don't know why you think she's going to marry you. I don't think she particularly likes me either, but I like chatting her up because I know it gets you mad."

Carl flung his arm out, but Walter anticipated it and ducked the intended blow. "One day you and I are going to have it out and it's you that'll be leaving."

"You're going to have to come up with some real money to do that brother and what if I don't want to be bought out?" Walter smirked.

"There isn't enough room for both of us when Henry finally checks out, so unless you sell your share to me at a reasonable price, you could be checking out as well," Carl replied evenly.

"You're nuttier than I thought, but I'll be waiting for you."

Chloe went into the tack room and emerged with a saddle and bridle. Henry and Liz watched her as she saddled the mount and swung up in one fluid movement.

"I'll miss her."

"Yes, I would imagine so. After all, she is your daughter."

Henry swung around in surprise. Liz was looking directly at him with a smile on her face.

"Don't deny it Henry. Are you ashamed of her? Why don't you tell her?"

"How did you guess?"

"Henry, Henry, her eyes are a giveaway. And sit you both side on and your profiles would match perfectly."

Henry sank back in his chair and drew in a deep breath. There was no point in lying to his sister. "Yes, she is my daughter, but how do I tell her after all these years? Of course I'm not ashamed of her. I love her dearly and I'm thrilled she's making a success of her life. Countless times I've nearly told her the truth, but always held back at the last moment. I wanted her to stay on the property, but what sort of life would it be and who would she marry? There's no one I know who's suitable for her. Carl and Walter are out of the question. I want someone better for her than some busted-arse cow cocky scrambling to make a living. I've lost her now anyway, so there's no point in telling her. Can you imagine her reaction if I did? "

"Who was her mother?"

"The Duchess. Part aborigine and part Timorese on her mother's side. I believe that's where Chloe's olive skin and refined features come from. The European blood of her Portuguese forebears mixed with the Indonesian genes of that archipelago. I met the Duchess in Darwin where I was attending a conference and instantly fell hard for her. She was beautiful, intelligent and great fun to be around. I just couldn't resist her. We had an affair and Chloe was the unintended result. I was married to Marie at the time and couldn't admit my deceit. The Duchess didn't want the child. I had a real dilemma on my hands, as Marie would have immediately realised the connection if I'd proposed adopting her, so I came to an agreement with Johnny Quartpot."

"What happened to the Duchess?"

Henry sighed and shrugged. "I used every excuse possible to go up to Darwin to see her, but we gradually drifted apart. She liked excitement and entertainment whereas I was stuck here running cattle. It wasn't her lifestyle. Then I found out she was heavily into drink and drugs and mixing with the wrong people. She simply disappeared for days on end when the Americans were in town on navy or army exercises. She started to neglect Chloe and finally abandoned her altogether to a distant aunt who didn't want the responsibility. The tragedy was, she was found dead. She'd been seen drinking with a group of visiting marines. The next morning she was found violated and discarded in some cheap motel room. The marines' ship had already sailed, the suspects were unidentified and there were no local witnesses, so the police tossed it in the too hard bin."

"So how did you finally get hold of Chloe?"

"Well, as I said, I couldn't bring her home and present her to Marie and I knew Child Welfare wouldn't let me have her unless I could prove paternity. There lay the problem; my name isn't registered on her birth certificate. It was then I got the bright idea of paying the distant aunt and Johnny Quartpot to adopt her on the grounds they were both related to her mother. Johnny claimed to be her grandfather. Child Welfare weren't interested in delving too thoroughly. They conducted cursory interviews, were satisfied they could cover their backsides if any questions arose and signed her over. Johnny brought her back here. He was Gramps to her and she would have never left the property while he was alive. I owed him. The irony of it was that Marie and I split only a couple of months later. As you know, she died in a car accident soon after she returned to Sydney."

"The Duchess. Where did the name come from? What was her real name?"

"Emeline, but I called her the Duchess."

"And you were the Duke?"

"Yes, don't you recall when I was a kid, Dad was always telling me to put up my dukes when he adopted a boxing stance? He would be on his knees with his fists clenched in front waiting for my swing and I would attempt to get past his blocking tactics."

Liz laughed. "Yes, I remember that. He called you the Duke."

"When I first met Emeline she asked me what she would call me. I jokingly told her to call me Duke. She replied in that case I could call her the Duchess, and it just stuck."

"What happened to Johnny Quartpot?"

"That I don't know Liz. He went walkabout and just never came back. He was out with Chloe at the time and told her he wanted some time on his own, but not to look for him if he didn't come back. It was so out of character to leave Chloe on her own. It puzzles me to this day."

"Did you report it to the police?"

"Of course, but after a quick search they gave it away. How do you search for a body lost in tens of thousands of square kilometres of wilderness? Impossible. Carl and Walter said the old fellow did me a service. He was starting to blackmail me in a way. Nothing direct, but the implication was seeing he'd lied about his familial attachment to Chloe he could make demands on me and they were getting more constant. I still miss him though, and I know Chloe does too."

"What are you going to do about her?"

"What do you mean?"

"You're not going to live forever and she is your daughter. How are you going to look after her?"

"She will inherit a third share in Venus Downs. I legally adopted Carl and Walter so they also have a legal claim. Honestly, I don't know what's going to happen between that pair. Carl is the dominant one and wants to take over. He's got a hair-trigger temperament that has already got him into trouble on a number of occasions. Walter is more mild mannered, but in his own way he's just as determined. The two are an explosive mixture that's going to ignite one day."

"And they both have eyes on Chloe?"

Henry nodded. "You've noticed."

"Carl is direct. His intentions are obvious; he can't take his eyes off her. I shouldn't tell you this, but they've already had sex."

Henry sat bolt upright and exploded. "When did this happen? I'll kill him!"

"Calm down. It was consensual so it's none of your business. You perceive her as being forever virginal in your eyes, but when the hormones start boiling over, it just naturally happens. I don't think she has any love for him, although I know he is certainly keen. He's not going to show his true feelings in front of you, because he knows you won't approve."

"It would never work." Henry shook his head.

"When her grandfather disappeared, that was when she decided to leave, from what she's told me? That moment of passion with Carl is another reason she won't come back here. I can see it's over between them, but he'll never accept that."

"Perhaps it's better I keep the fact I'm her father a secret for a while longer. She appears to be very happy and you've really been wonderful looking after her. I'm so proud of her. Why tell her anything now and get her upset? I will tell her someday. By the way, if anything should happen to me, my Will is in the office safe inside."

"You'd better give me the combination before I leave then."

Henry laughed. "There's no combination; it's an old key safe. Good enough for out here. There are no safecrackers around."

Chloe's horse slowly picked its way through the rough terrain until she pulled it up atop a small rise looking down into the stockyards. She could see Carl and Walter were beginning to load the bulls. The dust was thick as the beasts milled around, unwilling to enter the race to the ramp leading up to the truck. She could clearly hear the profanities as Carl shouted at his brother and a reluctant bull.

"Don't swear at me, you dopey bastard. Can't you see why it won't move?" Walter pointed to Carl's shirt, which he had taken off and hung on the gate at the top of the ramp. It was bright yellow and flapped in the strong breeze. The enraged bull was obviously spooked by it and refused to budge as it smashed its horns into the side of the crush where Walter had it pinned.

Carl looked back. "Hold that bloody gate shut!" He shouted as he raced up the ramp to remove the shirt. He had his hand on it when he heard the roar and thunder of hooves on the ramp behind him. He spun around and looked back, his face transfixed in terror.

"What the fuck have you—?" A scream of panic cut off Carl's words. He did not see the sadistic grin on Walter's face as he ran up into the tray of the truck and attempted to gain a hand and foothold on the steel sides to pull himself up and out of danger. He slipped and turned to find an alternate escape route when a horn ripped into his side and flung him into the steel horizontal supports of the cage top. He crumpled in a groaning heap, his senses already knocked out by the shock as the bull continued to gore him with swipes of its horns.

Chloe watched on in horror. She had a clear view of what was happening and realised Carl could not survive. She watched as Walter leapt over the rails, opened the cab of the truck and pulled a gun from behind the seat. He jammed a round into the chamber, climbed over the railing again and ran up the ramp towards the bull, which was facing away from him, its lowered head intent on its victim. He knew it was too late as he aimed for its spine. The animal sank to its knees at the impact as he chambered another round and shot it in the brain.

Carl watched the blood flowing from the tears in his stomach as he tried to hold his intestines in with bloodied hands. Blood was also pumping from a torn artery in his throat. He slowly lifted his already glazing eyes towards Walter. "I never saw that coming, brother. You sure know how to fight dirty."

"I learnt from you Carl, so I thought I'd get in first—" Walter was about to continue when he heard someone running up the ramp. He turned and realised it was Chloe; he hadn't heard her ride up. Alarmed by her sudden appearance he dropped the gun, knelt down beside his brother and attempted to stem the flow of blood from Carl's neck by pressing his finger against the wound. Chloe watched on, horrified by the blood pumping between Walter's fingers.

"Chloe, high tail it back to the homestead and tell Henry there's been an accident."

She needed no encouragement as she ran and swung up into the saddle. She dug her heels into the horse's flanks, urging it into a full gallop.

Walter took his hand away. It had been a useless gesture, but necessary to show compassion and concern. How much had she seen or heard? He felt a cold shiver go up his spine as he watched his twin brother slowly dying. He did not think it would have been so easy. It came to him on the spur of the moment when he saw Carl take off up the ramp to retrieve his shirt. The bull had lunged and crashed into the gate he had been holding. He could have held it, but he let it go and watched in fascination as Carl had turned and screamed back at him with a look of pure terror. There were no witnesses. He would never be the subject of his brother's taunts and abuse again. The blood stopped pumping and Carl's head hung to one side of his slumped body. Walter sat beside the body and waited for Henry. He thought of moving it out of the tray, but realised it would be better if Henry could actually see the scene for himself and visualise what had happened.

Henry's ute arrived, surrounded by a cloud of dust. He hobbled up the ramp grasping the sides for support, the pain in his foot intense. He could see Carl was dead as Walter cried quietly and held his brother's hand. He patted Walter on the shoulder.

"How did this happen?" Henry's tone was soft rather than demanding.

"The bull wouldn't go up the race because Carl's shirt was flapping and spooking it. He ran up to move it when the bull smashed through the crush I was holding. The latch just gave away. I shot it, but it was already too late." Walter held his face in his hands and slowly shook his head in a show of grief.

Henry was aware that six hundred kilos of enraged bull would be unstoppable. Carl didn't stand a chance against those razor sharp horns.

"C'mon Walter, we've got to move him." Henry slid his arms underneath Carl's and gripped him around the chest while Walter picked up his legs. Chloe was standing beside the ute as she watched them bring the corpse down and put it on the tray. Henry covered it with a tarp.

"Let those bulls out Walter and drive the truck back. The jackaroos can get that beast out of there."

He put the vehicle into gear and began to drive slowly back. "Did you see what happened Chloe?"

"I was watching from that hill up there." She indicated the rise they were just skirting. "I wasn't paying attention, but I did hear Walter shout something and then saw Carl running up the ramp. He turned and shouted back at Walter. Then I saw the bull charging. It was horrible. I'll have nightmares for the rest of my life."

11

At Heathrow, a long queue consisting of every nationality on earth snaked backwards and forwards around the cordoned channels to finally reach the line of Customs desks. Chloe was daydreaming when an African woman behind her in a multi-coloured flowing dress, prodded her impatiently, indicating the beckoning Customs official.

"Passport and declaration please," came the polite request. The officer smiled at Chloe's look of confusion as she delved into her handbag. He studied her passport and declaration and closely studied her work permit. "You're a model, eh?"

"Yes, I am."

"Well, all the best Ms Quartpot. I've a feeling I'll be seeing you again—or reading about you. My wife follows all the fashion and gossip magazines. I'm not supposed to comment, but I think you're smashing." He slid the passport and papers back and signalled for the impatient kaleidoscope of colour behind her to step forwards.

Chloe retrieved her bag from the carousel and walked past a row of low tables where officials apparently showing little interest idly studied the endless flowing stream of incoming passengers. She caught sight of one nudging his partner as he watched her walk forwards. Their disinterested stares turned into broad smiles, which she ignored.

Aboard the Heathrow express train into London, Chloe stared out of the window as patches of countryside swept past, then rows of gloomy looking side-by-side terrace houses, factories and then modern office blocks until it finally pulled into Paddington Station. She was amazed by the myriad of life hurrying in every direction; people of all different shapes, sizes and colours bundled up against the cold.

"You're Chloe, aren't you?" A man in his early twenties, slightly built with swept back blond hair and a somewhat androgynous appearance held out his gloved hand with a smile. "I'm Cyrus Blomfeld, Paul's assistant. Please call me Cy. Welcome to England and to London, and welcome to the Paul LeClair Agency."

Chloe was aware he was studying her closely as he took her bag. She had no time to confirm her identity as he rattled on. "I can see you're going to make it Chloe. Usually when I come to meet a new model, I really have to pay close attention to identify them in the crowd. You, on the other hand, are a real standout. I was watching you from when you were at least fifty metres away, and I had no doubt you were the person Paul sent me to meet."

Cy bundled her into a taxi and kept up the chatter, but she was oblivious as she studied her new surroundings crawling with life and activity. Ten minutes later, the taxi pulled up outside a block of Georgian multi-storey houses, each house the mirror image of its neighbour. They squeezed into a small lift, which left them facing one another inches apart as it slowly ascended. It stopped with a jerk.

"Here we are." Cy picked up her bag and opened a door into a small entrance hall. "This will be your apartment until Paul decides otherwise. I must say, you've made quite an impression on Paul. Generally, he never invites novices into his home but in your case he's made an exception. You're very lucky."

The apartment had a large, comfortable sitting room with views out over the tops of plane trees shedding autumn leaves onto the street below. A large bedroom and bathroom lead off from a short hallway.

"Through there is the kitchen, but don't ever use it unless you want to invite Paul's displeasure. Cooking brings odours and cockroaches. Paul will not abide any contravention of that rule."

"Where do I eat then?"

"Tonight, Paul has invited you to dinner in his apartment downstairs. I will come up and fetch you around eight. Please ensure you wear something very smart, as Paul will be running a very critical eye over you. As for eating at other times, there are plenty of restaurants close by. You'll soon find your way around and if you need any advice on anything, here's my phone number."

Chloe was still looking at his card when she heard the door close behind him.

That evening, Cy was on time to the second and Chloe apprehensively followed him into the lift.

"Don't look so worried," he whispered as the lift opened on the lower floor.

Paul LeClair was waiting in the doorway and studied her as she stepped towards him. He flashed a beaming smile, displaying perfect white teeth. "Chloe, it's a pleasure to meet you."

She took his outstretched hand. A soft grip but controlling, Chloe thought. "The pleasure is mine, Mr LeClair. May I call you Paul?" Chloe had practised what she was going to say and delivered it with confidence, although underneath she was shaking with self-doubt.

LeClair laughed. "Of course you may. I like your confident approach and style. I can see we are going to hit it off."

He ushered her into a large sitting room furnished in complete contrast to her Victorian apartment. It was spartan, ultra-modern and all white with marble flooring and a huge leather lounge suite surrounding a glass-topped expanse of coffee table. A huge multi-coloured piece of meaningless abstract art dominated the room from its position over the fireplace.

Paul was tall and his tailored slacks and jacket fitted his lithe form perfectly. His hair was swept back, the sides showing silver through his otherwise dark mane. His features were unobtrusive except for striking pale blue eyes that seemed to sparkle.

"Please sit down. Can I get you a drink, cocktail perhaps?

"No thank you, I don't drink."

"Smoke?"

"No."

"No drugs of any sort? You may as well tell me now as I will soon find out and if I do, I will terminate you immediately."

"I don't know what drugs are."

He gave her a querulous look as he sat down opposite her and picked up the scotch Cy had poured for him. "Cocaine, heroin, weed, meth, ice. Haven't you heard of any of those?"

"Of course I've heard of them Paul. But I've never taken any, nor have I been offered any."

"I'm pleased to hear that. Modelling is a high-pressure business and the burn-out rate is very high. You will find it very stressful, so don't get the idea it's an easy road. You're on a fixed contract with my agency for three years with a probationary period of six months. I can terminate you at any time within that initial period. I've arranged a photo shoot next week with all the top fashion mags and newspaper fashion and style writers to promote you. You will simply be known as 'Chloe'; your background is to remain a mystery and you are never to divulge your surname. Tell me, is it really Quartpot?"

Paul did not notice the flash of indignation cross her face as he took a sip of his scotch. "My name is Chloe Quartpot. It says so on my birth certificate. Do you have a problem with that?"

Paul put down his glass and waved his hand in a vain attempt to dismiss the obvious sarcasm in his question. "Of course not, Chloe. Tell me how you got your name and where it derives from."

"It's my grandfather's name. He had a tribal name, but it was unpronounceable other than to someone who spoke the dialect. He started working life as a camp cook and mustering cattle in the outback. Later, he became a prize fighter in a travelling circus. He was given the name Quartpot because a quartpot is a tin mug in which food is served or used for drinking. He was known as Johnny Quartpot."

Paul slapped his knee and burst into laughter. "Oh, I love the story and its originality. If only the rest of the world were so simple instead of assuming airs and graces with implied social and class status. However Chloe, Quartpot is unacceptable I'm afraid, if you are to make it in the world of fashion. The press will make fun of your name. They will quickly Google 'quartpot' to get an idea of its derivation. I don't want you fighting to gain ground and recognition. I want you on the high ground from the very first moment, on an unassailable pedestal so you can simply ignore their questions with impunity. You're beautiful, Chloe—in fact, more so than I expected now I've seen you in the flesh rather than in the promotional photos and Australian magazines. I can see none of your photos have been airbrushed or played with in Photoshop. Along with your beauty, you have a lovely, natural olive complexion suggesting a Eurasian or eastern injection of bloodline in your past. Your demeanour, your poise and confidence in the way you express yourself and your bearing are all wonderful attributes. Another real surprise is your speech doesn't reflect the jarring Australian tones I was expecting. June Summers certainly didn't misrepresent you."

"Yes, I owe her everything. I hope I won't disappoint you—"

"Oh, I'm sure you won't. Now, why don't we eat?" He guided her through into a small dining room with a circular dining table set for two. Other than the setting, the room was completely void of furnishings except for another abstract painting occupying the entirety of one wall. He saw Chloe glance at it.

"Do you like art? Do you like that painting?"

Chloe laughed. "It's different to what I'm used to. I don't know whether I like it or not."

Paul nodded. "Abstract is an acquired taste but then again, you should be familiar with the style, as the indigenous art I've seen from Australia is all an interpretation of myths and legends. You can interpret it any way you like; it's meaningless, just as life is really."

"And you don't like living in the past?"

"Precisely, Chloe. I don't want to know about history. I abhor people who prattle on about some event or highlight of their past. Tomorrow is the only day that matters. Today is gone; that's the way I look at life. It was a good day today and that's the way I want to look at tomorrow. I don't want to know about my antecedents. They're dead and out of my thoughts. Life is for the living."

Chloe didn't know how to reply. Johnny Quartpot lived by the lore of generations past and she could vividly recall his endless stories of those generations.

"Anyway, enough of that. I hope you're hungry. Cy is an excellent chef amongst his many other talents as my personal assistant and companion."

As if on cue, a side door opened and a middle-aged woman pushed in a trolley.

"And what delights has Cy created for us, Mrs Blomfeld?"

"A lobster bisque followed by Dover sole in a cream and parsley sauce with new potatoes." She beamed as she set the soup plates down before Chloe and then Paul.

"This is Chloe, Mrs Blomfeld. She is my new discovery and the world is going to be hearing a lot about her."

"I'm very pleased to meet you Chloe. And where to do you come from?"

"Mrs Blomfeld, you know better than to ask that question," Paul admonished her in a mocking tone. "Chloe is a beautiful and mysterious woman who has arrived in London from a place known only to her and to me. The world need not know anything more than that for now."

Mrs Blomfeld patted Chloe on the arm. "You are in excellent hands, my dear. Paul will do everything he promises to launch your career. However, I can already see he won't have to put in too much effort. I'm a good judge and I can see you really have what it takes—" She was about to continue when she noticed Paul's sharp look of dismissal.

"Thank you Mrs Blomfeld. I would like a glass of pinot gris, please."

"And you Chloe?"

"Just a mineral water for me."

Paul waited until Mrs Blomfeld had disappeared with the trolley. "A very kindly, well-meaning person, but a real gossip. Don't be too taken in by her motherly understanding and charm. I want you to try to keep your distance from everyone. By that, I don't mean you should be aloof, just wary until you find your feet in this profession. For a start, your peers and indeed, competing agencies will be trying to cut you down. It's a dog-eat-dog world driven by jealousy, greed and above all, money—all vices you have yet to experience. You might not agree with it, but I want to put you into a cocoon until you emerge as a beautiful butterfly the whole world will want to touch and possess. It's human nature for people to want something they can't have. Modelling is all about selling, and to sell something you must promote it, and I'm going to promote you like no other model in my agency. Can you see what I'm getting at?"

Chloe nodded. "I suppose so. How long will you have me in this, um, 'cocoon'?"

"We'll start tomorrow. We're going to have lunch at Patrizzio's. Just a quiet lunch where the clientele will pretend they haven't noticed you. However, you will be noticed the moment you walk in and I want to judge the reaction. You're going to be very busy from now on."

"I need to find somewhere to live first. I imagine that is going to take some time from what Miss June told me about

London and London rents. I really don't know what I can afford."

Paul was silent for a moment as he twirled the half-empty wine glass in his hand. "I believe I can settle that problem. You can stay where you are until you get on your feet. I have never done it before because I don't want would-be models failing to match up to my requirements and then attempting to hit me with some sort of maintenance demand, or breach of promise, or implied undertakings while they remain under my roof, dragging me into court. However, I'm certain you're not going to fail—I'll make sure you don't."

"Thank you Paul. I won't let you down either and if you ever consider I have, I'll leave immediately and go home."

Cy walked into the room. "Coffee anyone?"

"Not for me thank you Cy. I'm starting to feel the jet-lag." Chloe smiled.

"Not for me either. I can see Chloe's tired and I've a few things to do, so that will be all. Oh, Chloe will be staying in the apartment for the foreseeable future. Will you tell the staff to attend to the make-up of the room every day, and see that anything she needs is attended to, please."

"Certainly Paul." Paul didn't see Cy raise his eyebrows in surprise. "Let me take you back up to your apartment, Chloe."

Cy opened the front door and handed her the key. "You've made a real impression. He's never let anyone spend more than a night or two here. Even his closest friends have never received such an open invitation as you have. Paul is a loner and can't stand people intruding on his private life. Mind you, I can see why he's done it and I'm totally in agreement. He's taking you to Patrizzio's tomorrow and I can tell you that's some compliment. Believe me, I had to call in a few favours to get a table at such short notice, but when I told the maître d' what it would mean to his business to have a beautiful new model bursting onto the scene at his restaurant, he relented and promised an excellent table. Paul has never represented anyone like you before. I'm sure you're going to be the talk of the fashion world in a very short time."

"That's nice of you, thanks Cy." Chloe quietly closed the door and went and sat down in a chair beside the window. It was a long way from Venus Downs she mused as she looked out at the dull surroundings.

12

The restaurant was packed, but a heavily built man immediately broke away from a table with mumbled apologies when he caught site of Paul LeClair.

"Paul, how nice to see you." Patrizzio didn't wait for a reply, turning and guiding them to a table set back from the window. He beamed as he pulled Chloe's chair back, seated her and unfolded her napkin. "Signorina, Paul, what would you like to drink?"

"A pinot gris and a mineral water please." Paul noticed the restaurateur's gaze fix on Chloe, before flicking back to his patron as the order registered on his distracted brain. Patrizzio nodded and handed them each a menu.

Chloe did not notice, but Paul pretended to ignore how the rapid, loud indecipherable chatter suddenly slowed down, and then lowered to a murmur. Whispers turned into instant gossip swept around the small restaurant.

"Anything you see on the menu that appeals?"

"Why don't you order for me please? Just something light."

As if by invisible signal, Patrizzio reappeared at their table.

"Today's special by two please Patrizzio."

"The table is to your liking?"

"Entirely so, and thank you for fitting us in—you can see why, I think?"

"I certainly can. However, the signorina would radiate from whichever table she sat."

"What was that all about?" Chloe asked.

"Patrizzio was paying you the ultimate compliment. Mind you, it works both ways. He gets the publicity. This is a place to be seen and dine at and I get a good table at short notice."

"So, who's seen me?"

Paul smiled. "Chloe, the whole restaurant has seen you. They don't know who you are, but you're with me and they know who I am, and that's good enough. Oh, don't look up, but you're about to find out what I mean."

"Paul, don't make out you didn't see me. I demand to know who this beautiful young lady is."

"Constance!" Paul rose from his chair and air-kissed her on both cheeks. "Constance, may I introduce you to Chloe, who has just joined my agency."

"Chloe, what a lovely name. But where does this Chloe I'm being introduced to come from?"

"Constance, all you need to know for now is her name is Chloe and the whole world will soon know it too. Chloe, meet Constance Faroud, a dear friend and competitor of mine. Oh, and her husband, Marcel."

Constance clasped Chloe's hand and kissed her on the cheeks. "Welcome to London and I wish you every success, but I don't think I really need to do that. I agree with Paul; I believe we are going to hear a lot more about you. This is my husband Marcel," she said turning to the person at her side.

Marcel Faroud shook Chloe's hand and kissed it. "The pleasure is mine, Chloe. If you ever get tired of LeClair's, the door is always open at Constance Picard's."

Chloe caught a flash of dismissal in Paul's eyes as he replied tersely. "Chloe is under contract to me Marcel. She will not be freelancing."

Constance pretended not to notice the sharp exchange. "Well, it's been lovely to meet you Chloe. I thought I knew all the emerging young talent, but you've crashed the party. That means you're not from Europe, so where do you come from?"

Chloe opened her mouth to reply, but was cut off by Paul. "Nice try Constance, but not this time."

Constance Faroud laughed as she walked out of the restaurant with Marcel.

"See how easy it is to get caught out? Constance is a real sweetie and in the fashion and modelling world, she knows everyone. She'll be on the phone as soon as she gets back to the office to find out about *'this Chloe who has joined Paul LeClair'*. The gossip has commenced. I was hoping she would be here today."

"I thought her husband was rather nice too."

Paul raised an eyebrow and gave her an odd look. "An interesting character, but I don't know what Constance sees in him, and where he gets his money from is a mystery. Her maiden name was Constance Picard—that's the name she trades under. She married Marcel a few years back and she's devoted to him, but there are rumours he's fond of gambling and women. Just be careful."

The following Monday, Chloe's first photo shoot had the desired effect. By Friday, she had a full list of engagements, beginning with the Milan fashion week.

"Gowns, lingerie, facial creams, you name it, you're fully booked. You're even going to be draped over the latest

Ferrari. From there, it's back to Paris and then you're off to Tokyo for a week."

For the next twelve months, the pressure was relentless as Chloe travelled the world being subjected to endless photo shoots, TV interviews, fashion press interviews, as well as meetings with vacuous politicians, sports stars, businessmen, endless lechers and celebrities, all clamouring to be seen in her company at some meaningless event. Paul was always by her side to quickly fend off some admirer getting too familiar by touching her or plying her with questions. The offers of invitations to country estates, exclusive resorts and exotic locations on private jets were endless. Dubious Russian tycoons would dismiss their hired escorts with a wave of the hand as they made for Chloe.

On one occasion, Paul was sidelined by the president of a major liquor marketing company who wanted to talk about the re-launching of a new product, which would depict Chloe holding a crystal glass of scotch or a flute of some brand of champagne. He had purposely taken Paul by the arm and led him out of earshot. Paul couldn't resist the invitation, but kept looking over his shoulder to see who might accost his prized possession. He was not listening as he immediately recognised the notorious Iranian, Amir Salargin approach her. Paul knew he was after a trophy and he did not care what he had to pay to get it. Cars and lavish gifts would soon be arriving at her feet if she fell for the overture, only to find she had been discarded a few months later when another trophy appeared on the scene. Paul had witnessed Salargin working the room while closing in on his intended target. He moved in swiftly and unobtrusively when Chloe was alone for a brief moment.

"Good evening Chloe. My name is Amir Salargin." He took her by the arm, gently turned her towards him and walked her away from Paul's watchful gaze. "I've heard so much about you. You are indeed very beautiful."

Chloe felt a chill of revulsion as she looked into the fat man's face with large protruding lips and bushy eyebrows. She had been pawed before and looked back towards Paul, but he was unable to intervene.

"Take your hand off the lady. Where are your manners, you fat oaf." The command was delivered with a hiss as a clear warning of intent. Salargin dropped his hand and scowled at his challenger.

"I was merely introducing myself. I'm an admirer."

"It's well-known who and what you are Salargin. Keep your hands to yourself."

"You will go too far one day Faroud. I never forget an insult." Salargin turned and walked away.

"That man makes me shudder. Thank you for rescuing me Marcel," Chloe smiled.

"Amir Salargin is a man to keep well clear of, my dear." Constance Faroud patted Chloe's arm. "He's been married three times. He took two of his wives back to Iran, one English and one French. After a year or so he was sick of them, but he took their passports off them so they couldn't leave the country. Despite what Iran may claim, women have no legal rights whatsoever. He's presently going out with a Ukranian gold-digger. She'll be showered with gifts and money until he gets sick of her. That's her, over there." Constance indicated a tall blonde in her early twenties talking animatedly to a group of admirers.

"He hasn't taken his eyes off you since he walked in. He shook the blonde off very quickly to make his move on you," Marcel advised.

"I think he's a horrible individual Marcel. When he touched me, my skin crawled. I'm pleased you were close at hand."

"How's it working out with Paul? You appear to be completely booked out from what I can see," Constance asked.

"Constance, some weeks I don't know what day it is or what country I'm in. I get very tired, but Paul insists we cannot refuse a demand from a major client."

"It doesn't quite work that way, Chloe. Paul is only your agent and I believe you should be more selective in what you take on. Go for quality, not quantity. You're already one of the most in-demand models in Europe and you should be at the stage of dictating your own terms. I've known Paul for years, but you are the most successful model he has ever represented or is ever likely to represent. May I ask you a very personal question?"

Chloe looked hesitant. "Yes, I suppose so."

"Do you know how much you actually earn? Why I ask that question is because I sense that you don't."

"Paul looks after all that. He has said I earn big money, but—"

"But he hasn't given you an account of just how much is 'big money' or how much is actually yours after he deducts his commission and expenses?"

"No, he hasn't, but I trust him. Are you suggesting I shouldn't?"

Constance noticed Paul had broken away from the liquor baron and was walking quickly towards them. "I think you should start asking questions, or at the very least get an accountant involved. Paul is coming over, so I won't say any more. Please don't mention I've said anything to you about this, but if at any time you feel you would like to speak to someone in private, I would be only too happy to assist you."

"What are you three talking about?" Paul sensed he was the subject of the discussion as he joined them. "What have Marcel and Constance been telling you?" The expression on his face belied the attempted casual nature of his question.

Chloe did not blink an eye. "I was just thanking Marcel for getting rid of that horrible Iranian pest."

Paul snorted and grinned. "Yes, I noted Salargin's intentions, but there was nothing I could do about it. Business comes first and I thought you would have no trouble by now in being able to handle yourself. But thank you, Marcel, very kind of you to look out for the welfare of my major asset."

He began to guide Chloe away before pausing and turning back to Constance. "Chloe is under contract to me, not the Picard agency. I sense you were talking to my client behind my back and that's something I don't appreciate."

Marcel was about to retort but stayed mute when he saw Constance give a barely perceptible shake of her head.

Chloe returned the smile of the person approaching behind Paul. She felt an inexplicable, but immediate attraction.

"Paul, my apologies." He touched the elbow of the agent without taking his eyes off Chloe. "But I've been very busy."

"No apology necessary Pietro," LeClair replied effusively as he turned. "I'm pleased you could make it."

"And you are of course Chloe." Pietro Malasardi gently turned Chloe's extended hand over and kissed it. "The photos don't do you justice signorina, you are truly beautiful."

Malasardi held her fixed with the disarming expression emitting from the depths of his hazel eyes. The smile was gentle and welcoming. He was impeccably dressed with no sign of flashiness or excess. She judged he was about five years older than her, tall and athletic, with the flaxen hair swept to one side and parted common to northern Italian preference, in contrast with the darker features and style of southern Italy. With his appearance and speech he could easily pass as being English.

"The pleasure is all mine Signor Malasardi."

"Please, please let's dispense with the formalities. It's Pietro to all my friends and associates and you will be my friend so I'm going to call you Chloe."

"I would like that Pietro." She felt a sudden surge of stimulation through her loins. It was a feeling she had never experienced before unaided.

"And now Paul, we have a lot to discuss, but now is not the time. I will have you picked up at your hotel at ten in the morning and we can run over the program."

They had been riding in the taxi for some minutes when Paul finally asked, "What was Constance discussing with you?" Chloe could sense the tension in his voice. "Was she asking about the terms of your contract?"

"We were discussing something personal."

"Well, what was it?" His normally polite tone had disappeared. "I don't want to hear any lies," he snapped.

"I've no intention of lying to you. I never have before so I don't know why you are now accusing me of doing so." Paul caught the look of determination and the defiance in Chloe's tone. She was not easily intimidated. "What Constance may have discussed with me is none of your business. From what I understand, I'm not working for you. You aren't my employer, you're merely my agent."

"Merely your agent?" he exploded. "I've made you what you are today. If I hadn't spotted you in an obscure Australian magazine, you'd still be earning peanuts from occasional modelling commissions. You're one of the highest paid, if not the highest earning model in the world today and I've only just begun to promote you. Don't ever insult me by referring to me as *'merely your agent'!*"

"Just how much am I earning, then? I've never seen any figures. I work seven days a week and I am still living in your apartment. I have absolutely no time to myself. I don't go out. I don't go to restaurants unless it's for promotional purposes arranged by you. Don't you understand that I get stressed? I see you revel in the action and the attention, but for me, it's different."

"Aha! It's clear that Constance and that husband of hers have been getting to you. What did they really say about me?"

"You're being paranoid Paul. They didn't make any comment at all about you personally. You don't really think I would have let them do that, do you? I owe you everything."

"I'm glad to hear that and I trust you'll always keep it foremost in your mind. Constance is a very good agent, but she could never have achieved what I have. As for what you've earned, I can get the accountant to go over that with you. As a model, you only have one shot at picking the fruit off the money tree. You've got to pick as much as you can in the short time you have. One day, you can be on top of the hill and the next you're rolling into obscurity and no one cares. Along comes the next sensation and you're completely forgotten. I know I should have accounted to you before this, but I will do so. Give me a month and I'll give you a full reconciliation. Can we agree on that?"

Chloe nodded. "I think it's reasonable I should have some account of what I've earned, or what the terms of my contract actually are, don't you? I've been thinking for some time I should get an apartment of my own. You've been very kind to me, but I think it's about time I became independent. I need some space of my own."

"I've seen the way Marcel looks at you, and don't think I haven't noticed you're attracted to him. My advice is to take care—you know nothing about Marcel."

"I admit, I find him very attractive, but he's married so that's as far as it will go."

"Hmm, I wonder," Paul observed as he stared out the window of the taxi, lost in thought.

13

*eClair and Malasardi were already seated
when she was shown to their table. Malasardi
immediately rose and kissed her on both cheeks
as the waiter held back her chair.*

"Are you still talking business?"

"No, certainly not. I don't mix business with pleasure. Can I offer you a drink?"

"Thank you Pietro, but I'll just settle for a sparkling mineral water." The waiter nodded and departed.

"Paul and I have finished what we had to do so let's study the menu and decide what we're having."

LeClair hardly said a word over lunch as Chloe and Malasardi talked and laughed as though they were a long established friendship. He could see the pair becoming closer as the magnetism of attraction increased.

"According to Paul you don't have any engagements for the next three weeks. Why don't you both join me on my yacht for a cruise to Capri and Ischia?"

"I don't think we'll have the time for that Pietro. I have a lot of office work to attend to, and besides I've been to Capri any number of times. I find it too crowded with tourists. Germans, French, Russians, Bulgarians and the like all jostling their obese bodies while stuffing their faces. Positively revolting. I'm sure Chloe can find something more attractive than that to pass the time."

"I would love that Pietro," Chloe cut in. "I've heard so much about Capri, and tourists or no tourists, I would love to see it. I've never been on a yacht. Do I have to pull up the sails?"

Malasardi laughed. "No, it's not that kind of yacht. It doesn't have sails. I have a captain and crew so you won't have to lift a finger." His laugh was also hiding his mirth at the expression on LeClair's face. He was livid Chloe had defied him, but knew he could not protest further. Malasardi was the scion of one of the wealthiest families in Umbria with interests in advertising, vineyards, hotels and construction. Paul LeClair could not afford to cause offence to such a powerful individual and establishment.

"Well, I'll leave you two to it. I'll see you back at the hotel Chloe." LeClair rose, shook Malasardi's extended hand and departed.

"You know what's going to happen when you get back to the hotel, don't you? He's going to put the pressure on you to decline the invitation. It's plain to see you two are not exactly in a happy working relationship."

Chloe nodded. "Yes, he'll want to catch the first plane out to London in the morning and I've no choice but to comply. We're not due to check out for another two days."

"You don't have to."

"What are you suggesting?" She was matching his infectious smile.

"Go pack your things and I'll pick you up in the foyer in half an hour."

Chloe felt that things were moving too fast, but it was the excitement of the challenge of defiance and the person now exciting that challenge. It was an urge she could not resist.

She was nervously looking around for any sign of LeClair when she saw the red Ferrari pull up and Pietro step out. He signalled for the doorman to put her bag in behind the seats as he opened the door for her.

"Ready to go? Not nervous are you?"

"Only nervous that Paul would see me leaving and cause a scene. I'm looking forward to it, but where are we going?"

"We are going to my home on Lake Como for a few days and then you can decide whether you would like to go to Capri."

Pietro drove fast but carefully as he weaved around and through the autostrada traffic crowded with trucks, slower touring cars, tiny Fiats and the powerful machines such as his that demanded right of way with a dip of the lights and burst of passing power. They talked in raised voices to overcome the howl of the engine at their backs. Finally the pace slowed as he weaved his way into Como and along the lake front before finally turning into the driveway of a magnificent villa perched above the lake with commanding views.

"Well this is home. Come and meet my mother." Pietro turned off the engine and got out.

"Ci'ao Carlo." He greeted an older man with a slap of affection on the shoulder as he handed him her bag. "Would you take it up to the guest room per favore."

Chloe felt a pang of regret at her actions. Was this to be a repeat of her earlier experience?

Pietro opened her door and helped her out. He noted her fleeting expression of hesitation and concern and laughed.

"I know what you're thinking, but you're wrong. I wouldn't have brought you here if I thought you would be intimidated or embarrassed."

As they approached the entrance, one side of the large double doors was flung open and a woman, obviously Pietro's mother, hurried out. She embraced her son and kissed him before turning to Chloe with a large smile of openness on her face. Her son had inherited that smile.

"And I know who you are. Everyone in the world knows who you are Chloe." Without hesitation she leaned forward and kissed her on both cheeks while ushering her towards the doorway.

"Come in, please come in, you are most welcome. Pietro you are a devil for ignoring your mother for months, then I get a phone call you're coming to see me, but you made no mention you were bringing a guest."

"I've been very busy Mama and I thought I'd surprise you."

"Excuses, excuses, just like your dear father, God rest his soul. And yes you have surprised me, but what a pleasant surprise. Now, now, no formalities. You must call me Celine."

Pietro walked behind his mother as she took charge and chatted incessantly to her bewildered hostage as she was shown into an expansive room with windows that took in vistas of the whole lake. The parquet floor was covered in richly coloured Persian rugs. A large unlit open fireplace dominated one wall of the oak panelled room with huge leather couches and armchairs that had the look of comfort and time scattered in various casual formations. An open book lay on a side table bathed in sunlight beside a large chair in one corner by the windows. Celine had obviously been reading when she heard the car pull up.

"Now Chloe, let me show you to your room. Carlo has already taken up your bag and Lucia here will look after you. Don't be shy to ask if there's anything you want."

Chloe smiled and nodded at the young woman about her age who had suddenly appeared.

"Bon giorno signorina."

"Bon giorno Lucia. Please call me Chloe."

"It's almost buona sera," Celine chipped in as she glanced back at the windows.

Chloe was shown into a vast bedroom on one wing of the huge villa. "And through here is your bathroom. Lucia has prepared it for you and you'll find everything you need." Celine opened the door to reveal a bathroom bigger than Chloe's London apartment. "Now we'll leave you alone to freshen up and rest." She glanced at her watch. "It's now six so we'll dine on the terrace at eight."

Chloe had no time to reply as the door closed and she was alone. She sat down on the bed and vacantly looked out at the scene. She could not believe the warmth of the reception. Her fears of rejection had evaporated, but what was the real reason she had agreed to an escapade after such a momentary encounter. Was it to be a brief interlude, a casual sexual affair for which Italian men are notorious, or was there something deeper slowly emerging. What was it about Pietro Malasardi she could not resist. She shrugged, lay back on the bed and closed her eyes.

"Chloe, Chloe." She awakened with a start as she glanced up at Lucia who had been gently shaking her arm. "It is seven thirty Chloe. If you would like to sleep, Celine said not to concern yourself about dinner."

"No, no." Chloe quickly rose in confusion. "I'll be down for dinner at eight. I'm used to quick changes and makeup."

"I've hung all your clothes in the closet and everything else is in those drawers."

"Thank you Lucia. I'm pleased you woke me."

Pietro and Celine were sitting in front of the fireplace when she hurried down the stairs and walked in with as much composure as she could muster.

"Ah, there you are," Pietro said rising. "Can I get you a pre-dinner drink?"

"A small glass of white wine please."

Lucia served dinner and joined them at Celine's insistence. Chloe could see Lucia was not only a servant, but a bright and cheerful companion to the older woman. The dinner was all small talk with Chloe keeping them entertained with her experiences in the modelling world and in particular people she had met.

"And what are you two going to do tomorrow?"

"I thought Chloe and I might drive up around the lake and have lunch at some nice little restaurant."

"You will be back for dinner though?"

"Yes Mama, but if we change our plans I'll let you know," Pietro replied raising his eyes in exasperation, an action that Celine did not see.

"Well, I'm off to bed where it's warm and I have a good book."

Pietro rose and pecked his mother on the cheek as Lucia began to clear the table.

"Come on, let's go and sit beside the fire Chloe." They sat staring into the fire without talking for several minutes each waiting for the other to break the silence.

"What are you thinking?"

"I'm thinking it strange that neither you or your mother have enquired about my background."

"I've no doubt you find intrusive questions to be very annoying which I can fully understand. You have to maintain the aura of intrigue and mystery, which I find LeClair has been extremely successful at maintaining. I'm not really interested in your background. I believe I'm a good judge of the human character and its failures."

"I'll bet you say that to all the women you bring here?"

"Chloe, you're the only woman I've ever brought here. No, that's not quite true because in my pubescent youth I was always trying to sneak girls up to my room much to the delight of my father, but disapproval of my mother. I prefer to keep my private life centred around Milan."

"Then why did you bring me here? Do I remind you of someone from your youth?"

"No, you're more beautiful and intriguing than any of the fumbling romps I've had under this roof. I brought you here for a reason and because I wanted to."

"For Celine's approval then?" Pietro caught the faint note of sarcasm.

"You've been hurt before somewhere in your life, haven't you?" His eyes were knowing and penetrating. There was no point in denying it. "Do you still love him?"

"I did, but it's a distant memory now from another time. It would never have worked out." She refrained from telling the truth of what happened.

"If he couldn't stand up for the person he loved, you were better out of the situation."

He looked down to see Chloe had drifted off. He shook her gently. "C'mon princess, it's time for bed. We've got a brand new life starting tomorrow."

Pietro and Celine were already sitting on the terrace watching the encroaching sunlight dissolving the gossamer patches of mist clinging to the surface of the lake when she came down.

"Did you sleep well?"

"Wonderfully, thank you Celine. The bed was so comfortable."

Pietro rose with a broad smile and kissed her on the cheek as she began to sit down. "Coffee?"

"Thank you Pietro. Just black please." He pushed a plate of pastries towards her.

"I'm disappointed my son is taking you away from me so soon. I had hoped you would stay for a few days."

"I've already told Mother we will be gone for a few days. We'll drive up around the lake and have lunch. Then I think we'll go over to Verona and visit our wine estates and then across to Venice for a few days. The trip to Capri and Ischia can wait for another time."

"I'm very excited Pietro. I haven't seen much of Italy outside Rome and Milan."

"By the way, Paul LeClair has tracked you down to here and wants you to contact him urgently. He phoned last night and already twice this morning. Lucia said he didn't sound very happy."

Chloe laughed. "I've got no engagements I'm aware of for the next three weeks and I'm not going to jump to his command. I certainly won't be phoning him until I get back."

"It could be a major client who wants your services."

"Celine, I'm booked solid with Pietro's clients three weeks from now. I could not possibly take on and do justice to anyone within that time. Paul can book me anytime after that. I'm taking a holiday and that's final."

"That's what I like to here, a girl with spirit."

Carlo was giving the bonnet of a Mercedes coupe a final polish as they emerged. Chloe looked around for the Ferrari.

"No Ferrari?"

"No, the Ferrari is for speed, someone in a hurry which attracts attention. The Mercedes is more comfortable with room to spread out. It's more leisurely and it doesn't turn any heads."

"Now you drive carefully Pietro," Celine said as he held the door open for Chloe. "I don't want to get a phone call from the police you've had an accident."

"Don't worry Mama we'll be just fine. I'll phone you when we're heading back." They both waved as he turned in the driveway and headed out through the electronic gates and swung over in the right hand lane to travel north. He noted a silver Alfa Romeo pull out from the side of the road some distance behind. Odd, he thought. This was a quiet side road with only a few sprawling villas along its length. He adjusted his speed to see whether it would pass in the usual manner of an Italian motorist in a hurry.

"She worries about you, doesn't she?"

"All Italian mothers worry about their sons. They just can't let go. Haven't you heard the saying that when you marry an Italian, you're actually marrying his mother and the whole fucking family? My apologies for the vulgarity, but that's a fact."

Chloe was laughing. "You're giving me a warning then? This is only a casual relationship?"

"I don't really have any close family other than Mother. Of course there are the relations, both rich and poor scattered through the country, but I seldom see them. You'll meet some of them in the Valpolicella wine region, but you'll like them.

No pretensions whatsoever, just down to earth hardworking country people."

"You haven't answered my question."

"Do you consider this a casual fling?" Pietro glanced across at her with a concerned look.

"I don't know what you're thinking, but I'm not concerned. I'm with you and I'm having a great time and I want it to last."

Pietro watched to see if the Alfa would turn off on the ramp south back towards Milan, but it remained in its trailing position until the on-ramp to the north came into sight and it suddenly accelerated past with a short blast of the horn. He noted the registration plate.

"Someone you know?"

Pietro shook his head as he ignored the on-ramp and continued along the lake shore. "No, the horn was just a courtesy to let me know he was about to overtake."

Half an hour later he pulled into the gravel driveway of a non-descript looking restaurant and parked. "The tourists don't know about this place. It looks too ordinary and they just drive past, but the food is superb. It's a secret the locals like to keep."

They were greeted in effusive Italian, but when Pietro replied in English, the maître de glanced at Chloe and broke into a broad smile.

"A table for two with a view of the lake for you and the beautiful signorina, signore Pietro," he replied in accented English as he showed them to a table and fussed over Chloe's chair and napkin.

"Two glasses of pino grigio please Tanto, and what is the specialty today?"

"A veal scallopini with olives and artichoke tapinade."

Pietro looked across at Chloe who nodded.

"That sounds excellent. Make that by two please."

A minute later the wine was served. They raised and touched their glasses, their eyes locked into each others minds, the telepathy complete.

"You know I'm going to ask you to marry me, don't you? Well, this is as good a time as any so what's your answer?"

Chloe nodded and smiled. "And I've been in love with you since you gave me that first cheeky grin, so the answer is yes. But what of my career?"

"That's a silly question, isn't it?" He reached over and covered her hand. "You've just accepted my proposal and now you're worried about your career. If it's money that concerns you, you won't ever have to worry about it. If it's the continued fame and adulation you seek, then I don't think you should accept my proposal. I want a wife and mother, I don't want a part-time partner," he trailed off. "Oh, please forgive me. I didn't mean it to come out like that."

"Pietro I know exactly how you meant it, but are you sure? You don't even know who I am or where I come from."

"You're the most adorable person I've ever met and I want you to become my wife. I don't care about your background. I'm not marrying that, I'm marrying you. Okay, okay, let's get it off your conscience. What is your name? Is Chloe your professional name or is it something else."

"My name is Chloe Quartpot. I'm part-aboriginal of Australian descent. I never knew my father and my mother died of alcoholism. I was brought up on a cattle station by my grandfather. I called him Gramps but he wasn't really my grandfather. In fact he was a full blooded aborigine. I don't have any identity and yet you want to marry me?"

Pietro broke into a peel of laughter which he choked off when he saw heads turned in their direction. "Quartpot.

What an interesting name. Malasardi and Quartpot, what an interesting combination."

"You're mocking me?"

"No I'm not. I'm in love with Chloe Quartpot and I couldn't give a damn who or what your ancestry is or was. However, I can see you've been dreading the moment you would have to tell me what you just have. I knew you were trying to suppress some imagined guilt and that's why I laughed. I was rude and I apologise."

He took her hand and squeezed it. "Chloe, I want to marry you and you've just accepted so that's the end of the guilt conscience. Okay? The contract is complete."

Chloe nodded as the tears rolled down her cheeks. She dabbed at them with the table napkin.

"Hey, come on, cut that out. You're supposed to be happy?"

"I am, I am happy Pietro. It's just happened so fast. What will Celine think?"

"What a question? What will my mother think? My mother was practically begging me to make sure you didn't escape. She loves you. I love you, so that's all that matters. Now dry those eyes because here comes lunch."

Tanto placed the plates in front of them while giving Chloe knowing smile. "Duo specialita della casa. I can see this beautiful lady is also special to you Pietro?"

"Yes, she is. Chloe I would like you to meet Tanto."

"Signorina, the pleasure is mine, although I recognised you the moment you walked in. Pietro is indeed lucky." Before Chloe could answer he had turned and walked away.

Pietro started to eat, but he noticed Chloe was only picking at it, her mind elsewhere. "You've got second thoughts? You look worried."

"No, I haven't. I'm just wondering what Paul's reaction will be. I have a contract with him and I believe one of the clauses is that I will not get married within the period of the contract."

"Leave him to me and let me have a copy. I'll have my London lawyers look at it. Don't concern yourself now about a wedding date or arrangements."

They finished their meal and Chloe excused herself to freshen up. Pietro was talking to someone in the car park when she emerged, but quickly disengaged when he saw her.

"A friend of yours?"

"No, just an acquaintance I haven't seen in some years."

Pietro distracted her as he opened the door of the car for her. "Tanto told me the hotel I was planning to take you to is undergoing extensive renovations. In that case I think we'll head across to Verona for the night or two and then we'll visit my villa in the wine country."

Chloe slid into the seat and casually noted the person who had been talking to Pietro got into a silver Alfa Romeo on the opposite side of the car park and started to move off.

"That looks like the same car that passed us when we left the villa."

Pietro smiled and shook his head. "Alfa's are made in Italy - they are Italy along with Ferrari and Maserati."

Chloe made no reply. She caught a partial view of the licence plate as the vehicle turned out onto the roadway. Somewhere in the back of her subconscious she recalled the same prefix and first two numbers – NO86 as being on the car that passed them earlier. Perhaps it was a coincidence. She put it out of her mind.

It was late afternoon when Pietro pulled up in front of the Hotel Due Torri in the centre of Verona. He handed his keys to a porter who took their bags and disappeared inside. To Chloe it appeared all pre-arranged as there was no waiting behind several American couples talking amongst themselves as they waited to check in.

"This way Signor Malasardi. I will show you to your suite." The manager smiled and nodded an acknowledgement to Chloe as he rounded the counter and indicated the lift. Not a word was spoken as it ascended.

"Our premier suite as requested signor." The door to the suite was opened and he stepped aside as they entered. "The champagne is compliments of the hotel and if there is anything I can assist you with, please call."

"Yes, there is. Do you know what is playing at the Roman Arena tonight?"

"La Traviatta."

"Excellent. The immortal Verdi. Please get two tickets if you can and I'll pick them up at the desk?"

"Certainly." The manager nodded and quietly closed the door behind him.

Pietro walked across the vast room and retrieved the champagne from an ice bucket. He slowly twisted out the cork, poured two flutes and handed one to Chloe.

"To us and the future." They touched glasses and he leaned forward and kissed her. She put down her glass and threw her arms around his neck.

"Is this really happening."

"Of course it is princess and it's only going to get better. What would you like to do now?"

"I'm going to have a shower and then I want dinner as I'm starving. Then you can take me to the opera. After that I would like to stroll around this romantic city before coming back here and making love." She disappeared into the adjoining bedroom and soon after he could hear the shower and her singing. He quickly stripped off.

She was still singing with her back turned towards him when unawares he stepped in, wrapped his arms around her and kissed her on the neck. He ran his hands down her flanks and around into the soft down of her femininity. She turned and pushed herself into him as she pulled his head towards hers. Their needs became more urgent as they began to thrust at one another and he could hear the low murmurings of her desire. He reached around and turned off the shower.

"Oh God Pietro, don't stop now," she moaned as he threw a robe around her shoulders and picked her up in his arms. He lay her on the bed and gently kissed her as he began to run his hand over her mons and gently parted her labia. Her murmurings became more urgent as she clutched his head and thrust it down to excite his teasing of her carnal surge. He moved up her body when he sensed the tremor of the first orgasmic spasm, gently thrust her legs apart and burst into her. Orgasm after orgasm surged through her being as they slowly thrust into one another. She was still murmuring softly with her eyes closed when he rolled away completely spent.

"Pietro don't stop. Play with me." She appeared to have drifted into an hypnotic trance as he pushed her hand away and began to gently satisfy her demand. They awoke several times during the night to a synchronised hormonal surge which when satisfied, sent them back into an exhausted sleep.

Chloe awoke to the sound of the shower and the pallid daylight which filtered through the opaque curtains casting the room in shadow. She put her arm out and rolled over to look at the empty side of the bed. She pulled the covers up under her chin and laughed happily to herself. She saw Pietro walk across the bathroom in the nude and begin to hum to himself as he began to shave. She studied his muscular form and could feel the hormones beginning to dance.

"Pietro, please come to bed. I want to make love to you again."

He turned and looked at her. "Not a chance. I'm lucky I can still walk. We didn't have dinner last night and I'm starving. And we didn't get to the opera."

She giggled as she threw back the bed clothes and got up. "But we did have an opera. I just loved the music, didn't you?"

"You might have thought you were singing, but then if you call groaning in ecstasy a form of opera singing, I'd have to agree with you."

Chloe dug him in the ribs and slapped his rump as she skipped past him into the shower. He smiled to himself as she started to sing softly, the title drowned out by the sound of water. Celine was right, he had made the right decision.

They were walking through the foyer together when a receptionist signalled to him. "Signor Malasardi, the manager apologises he could not obtain tickets to the opera for you last night, but he has two tickets for tonight if you would like them. If not, it is no trouble as they are in demand."

"Would you thank the manager please, and yes I will accept the tickets."

"Why didn't you tell her we've already had the opera," Chloe muttered within earshot.

"Would you behave please." Pietro tried to suppress his mirth as he guided her out into the plaza. They sauntered past the numerous restaurants until they found one that appealed. The plaza was alive with tourists strolling around. Pietro gave a running commentary on the various nationalities, the

Americans talking animatedly to one another, the subdued Germans taking everything in but making no comment, the French with their soft fluency, the sullen Russians with looks to match the harshness of their winters and the Italians busy gesticulating cheerfully mingled with shrugs of indifference. Interwoven were the myriad of youthful backpackers of every language drawn to the city of Romeo and Juliet.

"This is an exciting town. It's so full of life."

"And full of history. The Roman Arena is the most intact in Italy. It holds thirty thousand people. The acoustics are perfect no matter where you sit. You will experience that tonight. But, I'm boring you with history. Let's walk and I'll show you the more interesting sites."

He pointed out the balcony from which Juliet encouraged Romeo's seduction, with its thousands of signatures and graffiti from countless young tourists.

"Is that really Juliet's balcony?"

Pietro laughed as they studied the crowd. "The Capulets and Montagues were a figment of Shakespeare's imagination as were Romeo and Juliet and the balcony is as phony as an Eskimo pizza. But it's a fantastic money spinner for the city. It certainly attracts the tourists and their money. No point in telling them the truth as they want to believe."

They lunched in a small Osteria and whiled away the afternoon touring grand palaces, the Romanesque Duomo and the Gothic tombs of the Scaligeri family, the middle-ages rulers of Verona. Finally they sat on the sandstone wall overlooking the fast flowing Adige, each with a cone of their chosen flavours of layered gelato.

"I could easily live here Pietro."

He nodded as he tried to lick the outside of the dripping cone. "It's a lovely city, but it's too far away from Milan for me.

However, I have a place a few miles kilometres from here you will also fall in love with. We're going there in the morning and we can certainly spend time there in the summer."

Chloe was entranced by the opera. She snuggled up to Pietro as a chill enveloped the hushed audience as the love of Violetta and Alfredo played out and the crowd finally applauded Verdi's masterpiece.

The slopes and valleys of Valpolicella were covered in vines. "That's where we're going." Pietro pointed to a cluster of buildings nestled in the centre of a sea of green. "My cousin Ricardo manages it along with his wife Isabella and a tribe of kids. Every time I come here, which is not very often, there is always another addition to the family."

They pulled into the vast courtyard. Children began to appear from every doorway and from the nearby cellars. The boys clamoured for Pietro's attention while the girls hung back in shy recognition. Finally a man with his arms flung wide and a loud greeting emerged. The cousins hugged one another and broke into a stream of effusive Italian.

"Enough Ricardo, I would like you to meet Chloe."

"Where did you meet this beautiful creature Pietro?" Ricardo broke into heavily accented English. "Chloe," he said taking her hand. "If I was not married and had so many children I would steal you off him. When are you two getting married?"

Pietro cuffed him playfully around the head. "You ask too many questions Ricardo. Now where is Isabella?"

"Where every good wife should be, if not in the bed, she should be in the kitchen and that's where my darling Isabella is at the moment preparing lunch. Come, it will be ready."

The children ran ahead into the villa loudly announcing to their mother guests had arrived. Isabella was carrying a large dish out into the garden where an expansive oblong table was set up under a covering trellis of hanging grape vines. She shouted a greeting to Pietro before setting the dish down and turning to Chloe.

"Chloe, you are most welcome. I've read a lot about you and I'm so happy for you both. I hope we shall be seeing a lot more of you in future. This is a wonderful place for children rather than the confines of Milan."

Isabella's English was better than her husband's and there was no mistaking the warmth and meaning of her smile. Chloe looked confused. How had the news travelled so fast?

She caught the guilty look on Pietro's face as Isabella laughed and told them to sit down. "You must be the one Chloe. Pietro did not tell us, but in Italy it's near impossible to keep a secret, and absolutely impossible if it involves love."

"So where are you going to get married Pietro?"

"I haven't asked Chloe that question yet." He turned to say something but Chloe cut him off.

"I could not think of a more beautiful setting than this. Why not here?"

"Villa Terrarossi it is then," Pietro said as he leaned across and kissed her to the handclapping of Ricardo and Isabella. "We'll set it down for after the harvest when the vines are turning golden in late September."

"Let's drink to that," Ricardo said as he poured the wine. "This wine is from here, the Valpolicella region, famous throughout Italy and the world Chloe. Our finest from last year's vintage." Ricardo turned to cut large slices off a leg of ham and served it out to the proffered plates. The talk became noisier as people drifted in, and after being introduced to Chloe, joined the lunch as the wine continued to flow.

"Are these all your relations?" Chloe whispered when she thought she was not being observed.

"Some of them. Others are employees, but everyone is related to someone else in this region. As I said, you're marrying the whole family."

The lunch went well into the afternoon. The children had drifted away to amuse themselves away from boring elders. Pietro and Ricardo became engrossed in matters of the estate. Unconsciously, they excluded Chloe as their English drifted into Italian.

Isabella glanced at Chloe. "Chloe, they're talking business so why don't I show you next door." They walked out through the kitchen and around the courtyard to an adjoining sandstone building and a set of massive doors in which was set a smaller doorway.

"This is the main villa. Pietro owns the whole estate and this is where he should stay when he visits, but he maintains it's too lonely and remote so he always stays with us. We love to have him and the children adore him. This place just sits empty."

The expansive entrance hall was covered in triangular tiling of white and mottled light brown marble with rooms flowing off either side. At the end two glass panelled doors opened to a large room dominated by a vast open fireplace and scattered furniture. Isabella lead her up the marble stairway and opened the door to an apartment which overlooked the courtyard. It took on the same proportions as the entrance hall.

"Through there is the bedroom and bathroom. I've had the whole place cleaned with fresh linen and everything you should need. I'm sure you would like to nap after that lunch. There's a phone there, so if there's anything you want just pick it up and I'll hear it in the kitchen."

"Thank you, you're very kind."

Isabella took her hand and looked into her eyes. "I'm so pleased Pietro has found you. I know he will keep you safe. I worry about him though."

"In what way?"

"He has too many business interests. He inherited things and associations that should have died with his father."

"How did his father die?"

"He was killed in a car crash about five years ago. He was run off the road by a stolen truck when he was driving out of Naples one night. They never found the driver. I'm sure Pietro knows the truth of what happened, but he's never talked about it." Isabella suddenly looked concerned. "Please don't mention anything I've just told you."

Chloe shook her head. "I won't."

"I'm so happy for you. I can't wait to see you two married and I'm thrilled you've chosen here. Now I must be going. My children are sure to be up to mischief."

Chloe sat in a chair overlooking the courtyard and thought about what Isabella had said. Was there a side to Pietro she did not know about? Would he tell her, or should she ask? She kicked off her shoes and lay back on the bed, but her thoughts were racing. She decided to go for a walk. No one observed her as she walked away from the villa and found a track which meandered through the vines and up onto a rise overlooking a valley. She sat down and idly observed people working among the vines far below. It was like a still-life painting of serenity except for the animation of people suddenly appearing and disappearing as they stooped and then rose as they moved from vine to vine. The vintage was underway. The afternoon light was fading as she slowly walked back. She was walking around some cellars removed from the villa when she almost collided with Pietro and a man he was talking to. The heated conversation stopped immediately as Pietro first glared at her and then broke into his usual broad smile.

Chloe realised immediately what he was thinking. Had she overheard what was being said? And then he realised her Italian was not good enough to have understood.

He held up his hand for her to stay as he turned and guided the individual towards his car all the while speaking forcefully and rapidly in Italian. She watched as the car drove off.

Pietro hurried back and put his arm around her waist. "Isabella said you were resting. You surprised me?"

"Tell me, why has that person been following us?"

"Aha, very astute. You noticed the registration did you?"

"Yes, it followed us from Como and I've seen it on the road in various places and now here."

"That's Alfredo my assistant. I did not want to be disturbed with business matters. I wanted to be free of phones and out of contact while I was with you."

"So it's him who's been announcing our forthcoming wedding?"

Pietro laughed. "Yes, he's the guilty one, but he just could not help himself."

She sensed he was lying but did not show it. "And now something urgent has come up and it was important he tell you personally. Is that it?"

"I can see I'll never be able to hide anything from you, but yes, you are correct. We've got to head back to Milan tomorrow. I've disappointed you, haven't I?"

She turned and kissed him. "No you haven't. I've had a wonderful time and we've still got a lifetime to catch up on anything I've missed."

"I can see it Pietro. You're very worried about something aren't you? Please tell me what it is." Chloe had the feeling a premonition was about to become reality. "It's about us, isn't it?"

Pietro looked straight ahead at the autostrada unfolding before them and slowly shook his head. "No, it's not about us. I couldn't be more sure about you and I."

"Then what is it? Please tell me Pietro. I woke several times during the night and you weren't in bed. You weren't even in the room."

"I had to make some phone calls. I didn't want to disturb you, so I went down to the lobby and then I went for a walk."

"You can do better than that. Please tell me what's the matter?"

"Oh, it's nothing that insurance won't cover. My yacht caught on fire and was burnt to the waterline, so we won't be cruising to Capri anytime soon."

"And you sat up all night worrying about that?"

"Chloe, as you know I have many business interests and I get engrossed and diverted. I hope you will learn to live with that. Can we just leave it there please?" His tone was gentle, but firm.

"I've booked into the Principe di Savoia in Milan for three nights. I'm going to drop you off and drive onto Naples. I will be back tomorrow night or the following morning. I will phone you the moment I can get away."

Chloe tried to change the mood as she commented on the beauty of the countryside and how much she had enjoyed their time together. Although he tried to reciprocate, she could see his mind was tuned to a different wave-length. When they pulled up in front of the hotel and got out, he threw his arms around her and pulled her to him. Their kiss was long and passionate. "I do love you, so put any foolish thoughts out of your mind signora Malasardi. We are going to be married, I promise you."

She stood and watched him drive away. Somewhere in the back of her brain she recalled Isabella's concern and comments days before. The premonition was now one of despair and foreboding. She did not venture from the hotel the following day. She was not interested in window shopping, or being pestered by well-wishers who might identify her.

It happened as she feared it would. She was laying on the bed waiting for his phone call when she idly picked up the TV remote and began flicking for the evening news. His face suddenly appeared and remained fixed as the announcer spoke emotionally in Italian. She caught the word "morte" and screamed as she hurled the remote across the room.

14

C*hloe realised she had no chance of getting in unobserved by the remote cameras and braced for the confrontation as she opened the entrance door.*

Paul was holding the elevator door open waiting for her. "I'd like to talk to you. You can't disappear and ignore my phone calls. You have a contract with me. "

"Paul, I don't want to talk to anyone about anything at the moment. I'm exhausted and just want to rest and be alone."

"You went to Pietro's funeral?"

"Yes I did, and now if you will excuse me please." She brushed past him and closed the door of the lift.

The door to his apartment opened and Cy was standing there in a silk dressing gown with an agitated look on his face. "I've been waiting up for you, Paul."

"I thought you were going out tonight?"

"I changed my mind. Are you coming in?"

Chloe could hear the raised voices become muffled as the lift ascended to her floor. She had noticed Cy becoming increasingly distant towards her. There were no more cheery smiles and greetings, just a courteous nod of civility. She thought no more about it as she undressed as she got into bed. Sleep would not come as she tossed and turned, her mind flicking back to the image of the funeral in the little chapel a kilometre from Pietro's beloved Villa Terrarossi. The image kept recycling in her brain, a graphic colour image that would not diminish of a coffin being lowered into an ancient graveyard. She had watched as Celine stooped and gathered a handful of earth and let it trickle out of her hand onto the lid. *"Riposo in pace mia figlio,"* were the final words to her son.

Chloe and Isabella stood either side of her. There were no tears, there were no more tears to be had, only memories and grief.

"Good morning madam, or may I call you Chloe?" She smiled and nodded. "Welcome to Hampton's. My name is Peter Segal. How can I be of assistance?"

Chloe was not fazed by the informal greeting. She had come to accept everyone addressed her as Chloe. "I'm looking to lease an apartment."

"We can certainly assist you in that regard," the silver-haired, immaculately dressed Segal replied. "Please step into my office and I'll show you a few on my computer screen I think will suit you perfectly. You are moving out of Paul LeClair's apartment then?"

Chloe expressed no surprise. She had long recognised there was no privacy nor secrets in this town, but she ignored his question.

"Well, let me see." Segal did not wait for her to answer. Transferring his attention to his computer keyboard, he pressed a few keys and then pointed to a large screen on an adjacent wall. "I can take you on a 360 degree tour so you can see very quickly which property interests you. It saves a lot of time traipsing from one apartment to another. If you like one in particular, I can then take you for an inspection."

The fourth property Chloe pointed to. "That's the one I like the most. Could we have a look at it?"

"We certainly can. The present tenant is due to move out next month. He's the Argentinian consul, but a very agreeable fellow; I'm sure he'll let us through the place. I'll just check if tomorrow morning is convenient for him." Chloe heard a female voice answer and the agent immediately broke into fluent Spanish. He waited in silence until the voice came back on. "Mucho gracias," he said and hung up. "That was his housekeeper. He's going back to Argentina this afternoon so his housekeeper will let us in. Shall we say this time tomorrow? Is there anything else I can assist you with in the meantime?"

Chloe was about to shake her head when it occurred to her Segal may be the perfect source of information. "Yes there is, in fact. Could you recommend a firm of accountants, and also a firm of lawyers?"

Segal beamed and raised a finger in delight. He tapped into his computer and printed out a sheet of paper bearing the names of two companies. "Very prestigious, highly professional and totally discrete. You may use my name, but I don't really think you need any introduction."

"Tomorrow morning then Mr Segal, and thank you." The addresses he had given her were nearby so rather than phone for an appointment, she decided she would just walk in the door. Very presumptuous in London, but Chloe liked her chances following Segal's reaction. From the early days when she had been somewhat shy and in awe of the people she met, she had blossomed into a confident, assertive young woman.

At both firms, the receptionists asked if she had an appointment, knowing full well she did not.

"Please take a seat while I see if someone is available. It might not be possible at such short notice."

Chloe retreated to a lounge chair on the opposite side of the room as she heard the receptionist's muted tones and her name being mentioned.

In both instances, a partner emerged to greet her and usher her into their office. Half an hour with each convinced her to retain them both. Chloe was lost in thought as she stepped out into the London air again.

"Going anywhere in particular?"

She recognised the voice and turned. "Oh! Hello Marcel. It's nice to see you. What are you doing?"

"I asked first."

Chloe laughed. "I've a couple of days with nothing to do, so I'm just wandering around and attending to a little… business."

"Well in that case, why don't you have lunch with me?"

"Constance not with you?"

"No, she's busy interviewing a new client so I thought I'd get out of the office. Now, I know a quiet little place just around the corner where I can always get a table."

Before Chloe could think of a plausible excuse, Marcel had walked her to the corner and indicated the restaurant sign hanging over an alleyway. "This is a pleasant surprise Chloe. Generally you're always surrounded by people and I can never get near you."

They settled at a table and Marcel picked up the wine list. "I think a bottle of nice white wine would be appropriate. Ah, here's one I think you will enjoy, a Villa Maria sauvignon blanc—all the way from New Zealand. Now what do you fancy on the menu?"

Chloe tried to resist the wine, but Marcel insisted the waiter pour her a glass. "Just try it. If it doesn't appeal I won't be offended, or don't you drink wine at all?"

"I like a good wine Marcel, but I don't drink during the day. It makes me sleepy."

"Well, today is a new day, so at least try it and give me your opinion."

They were still sitting there long after the lunchtime clients had drifted away. Chloe enjoyed his company and witty conversation.

"Tell me Chloe, where do you come from?"

She shook her head. "No, I can't do that. Paul has instructed me not to."

"Yes, I can see what he's doing, or rather has done. It's been very successful. Chloe, nobody just arrives on the scene and stuns her audience with her beauty and such natural professionalism as you have. I want to know more about you."

"Marcel, I'm flattered by your interest, but I must respect Paul's wishes. I owe him a great deal and don't intend to betray his trust. Without his support and promotion, I doubt I would be where I am today."

"Rubbish," Marcel sniffed, "If you'd joined the Constance Picard agency you would have been just as successful, and probably a lot wealthier."

"What you do mean by that?"

Marcel toyed with his glass. "Have you any idea what your actual income is? Do you know what LeClair is creaming off in agency fees, promotion expenses and other hidden charges? Just remember Chloe, he has a reputation you may not be aware of. His influence was on the decline before you arrived. He was no longer attracting top talent. Then out of the blue you came along and regenerated his income stream. Without you, he may as well shut his door and retire to the south of France with Cyrus Blomfeld. By the way, I saw you going into Hampton's. Are you planning on moving out of his apartment?"

Chloe look startled. "Have you been following me?"

Marcel held up his hands in acknowledgement. "Yes, I suppose I have, but it was totally innocent. I saw you go into Hampton's and I thought I'd have a coffee across the street and catch you when you came out. But by the time you emerged and I'd made it across the street, you had disappeared into another office block. Who were you seeing there?"

"I—I don't think that's any of your business, Marcel. I'm constantly hounded by paparazzi without you asking personal questions."

Marcel noted the flash of displeasure as Chloe fixed him with an accusing look. "I apologise, Chloe. Please don't be angry with me. It's just I'm concerned, and it's not only me. Constance has taken a particular shine to you, but she's not going to say anything about LeClair. If you ever need any help, don't hesitate to call her, or me for that matter." He reached over and squeezed her hand. Neither of them were aware of the iPhone photo being taken.

"Thank you for your concern Marcel and yes, I do like Constance very much. She's a very warm person."

"And a person who has your interests at heart." Marcel flagged down the waiter for the bill.

A week later, Paul summoned her to his apartment. She had been reading and was startled by the angry tone in his voice. He was waiting at the door and she could see he was holding an open *People&Style* magazine. She followed him in.

"What's the meaning of this?" Paul demanded as he tossed the open magazine onto the coffee table in front of her.

"I don't know what you're inferring Paul." Chloe glanced at the photo of her and Marcel with his hand on hers. "I happened to meet Marcel in the street and he invited me to lunch. What's wrong with that?"

"Look at the headline, you stupid girl."

"Is Chloe joining Picard?" The headline queried in large type. The photo clearly showed them holding hands and smiling at each other. Chloe knew it was perfectly innocent. She realised it would inevitably be taken out of context and misconstrued. She laughed and pushed the magazine away. "I still don't see what you're worried about."

"I'm your agent," Paul snarled and glared at her. "I plan your every move so that you receive maximum publicity and maximum exposure."

"Well, isn't this publicity?"

"Not with that conniving scumbag, it isn't. He didn't meet you by chance and I daresay you worked that out very quickly. You're smart, but not smart enough to realise you can't just do as you want. The world revolves on gossip and this mag has now started the rumour mongering on you. You've exposed yourself to unwanted publicity. Despite what you may think, Marcel Faroud is not exactly viewed as a savoury type to be seen with. He uses his wife as his cover for respectability and front. He has no visible means of support and relies on Constance. The damage has been done; you're not to see him again. Do I make myself clear?"

"I find Marcel absolutely charming. There is nothing between us, but if I want to go out to lunch with him, I will," Chloe replied firmly. She was not going to be intimidated by his outburst.

He sprang to his feet and stood over her. "I'm your agent. You will take directions from me. I made you what you are today. You're no longer some bare-footed jillaroo from the boondocks of Australia, you're an international star and I put you there. I want to know where you are at all times and who you are mixing with. I'm warning you, keep away from Faroud. If you want to go out for lunch or go shopping, take Cy with you. By all means associate with people, but make sure they're of a class and status that cannot damage your image, not grubs like him!" Paul pointed at the photo.

"Is that all?" Chloe got up to leave.

"No, that's not all," he snapped. "What the hell is going on? I had a call from a Michael Frost who claims to represent you. He's demanding a copy of your contract."

"Michael Frost is my lawyer. I've asked him to advise me."

"Advise you on what?"

"I want him to look over my contract. You may recall I signed it, but l didn't understand the implications. I was so excited at the time, it didn't enter my mind to seek legal advice."

"Well, let me tell you it's watertight. You won't be joining Picard's or any other agency for that matter, nor will you be able to go freelance for some time yet. The option is mine and mine alone as to whether I care to renew your contract for another three years. You're locked into me Chloe Quartpot, and if you attempt to break our contract, I will destroy you. I want you to get rid of Mr Frost with his imperious demands. I have your interests at heart. You don't need some lawyer charging you outlandish fees for advice on a contract you cannot break. Your contract is with me personally, not the LeClair Agency."

"I've also engaged an accountant. You will no doubt be hearing from Alice LeBrereton in due course."

"You have been busy, haven't you? Did Faroud put you up to this?"

"No, he didn't. I decided it was time I got some professional help, so that's what I've done. I've also decided to find an apartment of my own. I want my independence."

"After all I've done for you and will do for you in the future, you are now going to spit in my face?"

"I'm doing no such thing Paul. I simply want to get my affairs in order. I want to fully understand what my contractual obligations are to you and my current financial position, hence the lawyer and accountant."

LeClair could see his standover tactics were not working. The supposedly ignorant, lonely and confused colonial he had signed up on his terms, had evolved naturally into a completely self-assured reversal of role.

"Chloe," Paul sat beside her and took her hand. "Forgive me for that outburst. It's just I'm so disappointed you're adopting this attitude. It's as if you don't trust me. I want you to stay in the apartment. It costs you nothing. Please don't move away."

Chloe gently pulled her hand away. "No Paul, it's not a matter of trust. I want my own space and I want to know where I stand legally and financially. I believe I can well afford to rent an apartment of my choice and make my own arrangements. I'm not looking to break my contract with you, nor have I been approached in that regard. I cannot move without Cy and you watching my every move, not just when I'm working but in my own free time."

"You need protection, Chloe. I pay Cy to handle that for me."

Chloe sniffed. "As much as I like Cy, I don't believe he could protect me from a raging bull ant."

Paul decided not to tell her that despite his charm and slight build appearance, Cy was a fitness fanatic, a black belt and a person not to be messed with as many a homophobic perpetrator of a taunt had discovered and lived to regret.

"Okay, okay Chloe. I can see I can't change your mind so I'll have to go along with it." Paul sighed deeply. All his tactics had fallen flat. He knew what he must do. "You must have realised by now I'm in love with you, Chloe. You must know that?"

She looked at him in total surprise and let out a stifled laugh. "No I didn't. What about Cy?"

"An interesting dalliance, no more than that."

Suddenly, they became aware of the door into the lounge being quietly closed, but Paul did not look around. Chloe had noticed the door had been slightly ajar during their conversation. She knew who was behind it.

"When are you planning on leaving?".

"By the end of the week, Paul."

"Well, I insist we have dinner here tomorrow night. I'll have Cy and his mother prepare something really special. Let's call it a farewell dinner. You won't deny me that, will you?"

Chloe hesitated. "All right but I'm sorry, I don't love you."

He gave a restrained laugh. "No, I suppose you don't, but I consider I possess you in every respect and I will continue to love you, despite your rejection."

The next evening, Paul was waiting at the door all smiles as he ushered her into the lounge. A pair of large doors were folded back to reveal the dining room, central to which was the round table already fully set, complete with an impressive candelabra.

Cy nodded to Chloe but remained stony-faced as he poured two flutes of Moet and offered them on a silver salver. He hesitated, obviously waiting to be invited to join, but Paul ignored him.

"To you, Chloe." Paul raised his glass. "We have a wonderful partnership and I'm sure it will continue."

Chloe politely sipped the champagne as Paul launched into an endless recount from when Chloe had joined the agency, the successful launch of her career and her continuing rise in the international world. Cy called them to dinner, a superb beef Wellington followed by petit crème caramel. Chloe drank sparingly, but felt light-headed and relaxed as she tried to follow Paul's banter and sarcastic comments about other models, agents, designers, advertisers, and the whole milieu of her existence. Her focus on his face became increasingly blurred until she could only hear his voice, which gradually faded into an incoherent awareness of her surrounds and what was being said.

She awoke with a start. She was in an unfamiliar bed, conscious she was nude, and not alone. Paul was leaning on an elbow staring down at her with an overbearing look of conquest.

"Good morning. How do you feel now that I've possessed you completely?"

Chloe lashed out, but he easily caught her wrist and held her arm down.

"You bastard. You drugged me... you raped me! You're not going to get away with this!" She screamed, and burst into tears.

"And who are you going to complain to? You're here of your own free will. You consented to sex, and more sex you're going to get." He cast the sheet aside, pinned her arms above her head and forcing her legs apart with his. Thrusting himself into her, she tried to scream, but he clamped his hand over her mouth. Suddenly, Chloe saw Cy throw open the door and rush into the room. Paul swung around. "No cause for alarm Cy. I'll get around to you next."

Cy fled the room.

Chloe endured the humiliation until he lay back, exhausted. Painfully, she got up, retrieved her clothes from the floor and dressed, sobbing inconsolably.

"Don't be in a hurry. You're completely mine. I own you, Chloe. I'll have you any time I want from now on." His taunt rang in her ears as she fled.

Michael Frost ushered her into his office. He could see his client was clearly distressed. She declined his offer of tea or coffee.

"I've had a look at your contract, Chloe, and I must say it is one of the most unconscionable documents I've ever read. Did you receive any advice before you signed it?" Frost let the question hang for a second, but he already knew the answer.

"What can I do about it?" Chloe asked quietly, her voice devoid of emotion.

"In a nutshell, absolutely nothing without spending a lot of money trying to have it overturned. LeClair has clearly taken advantage of you, but you've signed it of your own free will and not under any duress, so there's very little you can do. He's taking half of what you earn, which is totally outrageous."

Chloe could no longer hold back her tears and distress. "He drugged and raped me!" she blurted, breathing hard between her sobs.

"What! Tell me how this occurred and when?" The lawyer was shocked at Chloe's sudden outburst. Frost listened with obvious concern for his client as she recounted the previous evening's events before finally sitting back to contemplate his response. "Chloe, in making any complaint to the police about LeClair's actions, you have to assume what the defence will counter-attack with. First of all, LeClair has been your agent since you arrived in London, so it is not a casual relationship. Second, you have accepted his hospitality of a rent-free apartment during this period. Third, you told me you have enjoyed many a dinner invitation to his apartment and Fourth, how will you counter his claim it was not consensual sex?"

Chloe began to protest, but Frost held up his hand for her to stop. "Chloe, I've no doubt what you tell me is true. It's not the first time Paul LeClair has been rumoured to take advantage of young models, but they've all withdrawn their complaints for fear it will ruin their reputations and careers. You are in exactly the same boat. You are internationally known and any scandal will only rub off on you, not him. LeClair has nothing to lose. Contractually, he has you in a vice for the foreseeable future. You can't terminate the contract, only he can do that."

"What are my options?" Chloe wiped her eyes with a tissue and regained her composure.

"Virtually none. You can't stop working as he can sue you for breach of contract. However, I believe he won't physically assault you again. He's taken what he wanted from you. He's humiliated you and his conquest is complete. I'm not a psychiatrist, but I would hazard a guess he may have been demonstrating to his companion Cy that he's not indispensable."

"If he comes near me again, I'll kill him."

"I would strongly advise against that course of action, don't even make such a threat in company."

"So I'm powerless to do anything?"

"Look Chloe, my wife is your age and I love her dearly, but I would give her the same advice if she came to me as a single person with your renown and future prospects. Don't blow all that you have just to exact revenge. My blood boils at the thought of what he's done to you, but I strongly advise you to forget about the incident. As for the contract, you could fight to have it overturned, but it could cost you a great deal of money with absolutely no guarantee your action would be successful. And if the court ruled against you, you would be up for his legal costs too, and that could break you."

Chloe nodded in complete defeat as Frost rose and moved around his desk to show her out.

"And Chloe, please be assured anything you've told me in this room remains in this room. You have my total discretion." He handed her his card. "These are my direct line and mobile numbers. Call me anytime. And one final piece of advice. Get out of LeClair's apartment immediately. By staying there, you are diminishing your defence if you should ever lay a complaint."

"I've already taken steps in that regard. My next appointment is with Hampton's."

Peter Segal was waiting for her. She signed the lease documents, paid the required deposit and six months rent in advance and took the key. She wandered around the spacious apartment and then sat gazing out over the plane trees of Hyde Park before summoning the strength to return and gather her wardrobe and personal effects. She let herself into the building, all the while nervous at the thought of Paul or Cy suddenly confronting her. She quietly slid open the grill door of the ancient lift and was about to push the button for her floor when she heard the sounds of a violent argument drifting from Paul's apartment. She clearly recognised the voices and the repeated mention of her name as the cause of the argument. She retreated from the lift and began to climb the stairs slowly, listening intently. She reached the landing and reeled back just as an object shattered on the inside of the door below.

"You shit! That was a piece of priceless Lalique!" she heard Paul scream. "No, not that painting, it's a Christos…" but his pleadings were ignored as something heavy bounced off an internal wall. "Stop it, stop it Cyrus! What the hell do you want? What are you doing?" The anguished pleas were ignored as objects continued to be hurled about the room. Chloe hastily went back downstairs, bent down and lifted the flap covering the keyhole to the door.

"You know what I want. I want you! I don't want to be cast aside for some sun-tinted bit of goods from the never-never. You told me you loved me, but you kicked me out of our bed so you could fuck her. You drugged her, didn't you? Just like you've drugged all those other wannabe models.

You're lucky none of them ever complained, otherwise you'd be serving time."

"You saw me do it Cyrus. You've watched every moment with all of them. I don't know how many times I've invited you to join in, but the memories of your mother shagging you always gets in the way, doesn't it? You just can't get it up for a woman can you?" he taunted. Cyrus didn't respond. Realising he had gone too far, Paul dropped his voice to a soothing tone and he reached out to pacify his accuser. "Come here, Cyrus. You know I love you." There was silence for a few seconds as they embraced before Chloe heard a grunt and something heavy fall across what she recognised as the low coffee table. Then began the simultaneous grunts and kicks that never seemed to end. She could see and hear the impact of each blow into an apparently inert form lying on the floor. Cy finally let out a manic scream of laughter as he delivered the final kick. Chloe could see blood trickling from the side of Paul's head onto the polished wooden floor. She pulled back, realising he was staring directly at her with a fixed, vacant gaze.

"Now to get rid of you, you bag of shit." Cyrus lifted Paul under the armpits and started to drag him towards the entrance doorway. Chloe quickly fled up the stairs, but stopped on the landing and looked down through the railings. Cyrus opened the door and dragged the body along the tessellated marble flooring to a doorway that led down to the garages. Quietly she fled up to her apartment and hastily packed a few items of clothing. She would have to leave the rest, as she realised she was in danger. Cyrus would quickly come looking to see if she was in her apartment, as he would have guessed she would have heard the argument if she was there. If she moved now, she was liable to run straight into him. Her mind in turmoil, she stood by a window that looked out over the rear laneway. She could take her chances and run now, or she could wait to see if Paul's vehicle drove away. Minutes passed as she strained to hear the sound of an engine, at any moment expecting to hear the door of her apartment being tried. Finally, she let out a sigh of relief as she saw the nose of the Range Rover glide out and turn into the alleyway before accelerating away.

In the days that followed, Chloe picked up her phone more than a dozen times to tell Michael Frost what she had witnessed, but each time she put it down. She was sure Paul was dead or lying badly injured somewhere. He always phoned her at least twice a day to confirm engagements or discuss bookings and events. She decided she would not phone him at his apartment, as she knew it would be Cy who answered—or his mother. Cy had obviously witnessed her rape. She felt dirty and shuddered at the thought of Paul raping her while he looked on.

A week had passed when she was jolted by the sound of her mobile phone. She hesitated before picking it up to look at the caller ID. It was the LeClair agency office number.

"Hello Chloe, it's Cy."

"Yes, Cy. I've been waiting for Paul to call. It's been a week since I've heard from him. Is he unwell?"

"He's gone to his place in France for some rest. He'll be away for a month or more, so he's asked me to fill in for him. By the way, where are you? I've noticed you haven't been in your apartment, but most of your clothes are still there."

"I prefer not to say where I am, Cy. Would you give me Paul's number, please? I need to speak to him urgently... about work." Chloe's mind was racing.

"Let him rest. I'm running the agency while he's away so you can talk to me. I have all your bookings in front of me and we need to get together to discuss them."

Chloe had rehearsed the situation if either Paul or Cy phoned. If it was Paul, she had no option but to carry on with her contract, but if it was Cy, she knew Paul had to be dead. Seeing Paul's dead eyes through the keyhole brought back vivid memories of Carl's lifeless eyes staring at her after being gored by that bull.

"Cy, I need to speak to Paul. Paul is my agent, not you."

"He might be the principal of this agency, but I'm running it in his absence, so I'll be handling your bookings."

"Unless you put me in touch with Paul, you won't be doing any such thing." Chloe's heart was beating ever faster as she tried to keep her firm tone.

"Now listen here. I'm now in control and you will take my instructions. I demand to know where you are."

"Paul's dead, isn't he?"

There was a long pause followed by a hollow laugh. "What a stupid assumption. Paul's in France, resting."

"In that case, you can tell him I won't be taking on any assignments whatsoever until he gets back."

"Very well, I'll convey that to him. I know he's going to be very angry at the loss of income. I've no doubt there's a performance clause in your contract and you cannot just refuse to accept an assignment."

"A simple phone call confirming he's well and giving me an idea of when he's going to return will suffice. I just want to hear it from him directly and not second hand via you. Then I'll go straight back to work."

"Very well, but it could be a couple of days. In the meantime, give me your address and I'll come to you. We should at least discuss your modelling commitments and schedule."

"Once I've heard from Paul, I'll do that but in the meantime, please don't call me again." She snapped the phone shut.

A sudden thought struck her and in a panic, she dialled a number. "Is Peter Segal there, please? It's Chloe speaking."

Seconds later, she recognised his voice. "Hello Chloe, what can I do for you?"

"Peter, can I ask you to do something for me?"

"Most certainly, if it's within the ethics of Hampton's."

"If anyone enquires about my address, would you refrain from divulging it. It's very important."

"Chloe, Hampton's never gives out addresses or phone numbers of its clients. We maintain absolute privacy and discretion. Our name and reputation is of the utmost importance to us."

Chloe was relieved Cy could not locate her, but his phone calls became more persistent and increasingly threatening. She continued to ignore them. Constance and Marcel had phoned to enquire why they had not seen her make an appearance in weeks. They were concerned. Marcel wanted to come to see her but she made an excuse, saying she would call in one morning for coffee. Finally, early one morning she awoke to the sound of her phone ringing. She reached over and picked it up without thinking.

"Chloe, have you heard?"

She recognised Constance's voice immediately. "Heard what?"

"It's just been announced on the news. A body was pulled out of a disused quarry in Kent a couple of days ago—it was Paul. Did you know he was missing? I've tried to call Cyrus Blomfeld, but he's not answering his phone. Marcel's been suspicious something's not been quite right for some time now. He's called around to the agency a couple of times, but it's always shut. You must know something, Chloe. Can I help you?"

"I, I can't talk to you now, Constance," Chloe stammered. "I'm confused… I mean, I'm shocked. I'll call you later."

She fought with her demons, expecting a rap on the door or a phone call from the police, but there was nothing but silence as the rumour mill and media swung into action. Chloe knew she couldn't hold out or deny she knew anything about LeClair's death if she was confronted by the police. And every day she remained silent, she was implicating herself by perverting the course of justice. However, the day after LeClair's body was identified, a Range Rover was found parked on a track in Dartmoor. A passer-by had noticed the blood-spattered window and the pistol in the driver's lifeless hand. It was Cyrus Blomfeld. A scrawled note recorded his confession.

Two days later, Chloe was sitting in Michael Frost's office. He could see she was worried; her distress quite evident.

"If you're worried about your contract, you have no concerns in that regard. Your contract terminated on his death. Is there something else I can advise you on?"

Chloe looked down at her hands. "Yes, there is. It's about Cyrus Blomfeld and Paul's death."

Frost held up his hand. "Stop, please stop there. Don't compromise me by telling me what you know or what you may have witnessed. It's quite obvious to me you know something the police don't, but I don't want to know what that is. However, I will ask you, did you have a hand in murdering Paul LeClair? Blomfeld admitted he did it, but did you assist him at all? I'm sorry but I must ask."

"No! No, of course I didn't."

"Then you have nothing to be concerned about. Clearly, it was a murder suicide, so forget about it and get on with your life. You're now a free agent as your contract was with LeClair personally, not his agency."

University of Western Australia

The professor of history sucked on his pipe as he slowly read the Portuguese text. It was a slow and laborious task because of the faded script and evolution of the language, but it was a labour of fascination and interest as the tenuous connecting threads began to catch and spin a continuous, intriguing web.

It had been an idle day just sitting around his study, comfortable and unconcerned about the rain beating against the windows. He had been reading the text when his mind flicked back to a chance enquiry by a fellow don of his alumni. It was a passing question he had forgotten about, and the don had never chased him for the answer. However, it must have remained in his subconscious, and now it had been triggered by something mentioned in the text he was reading, rather like an insidious disease in remission that sprang back into life for no apparent reason.

His pipe smoke curled up, permeating the room lined with shelves of academic literature and research. The place reeked of stagnant tobacco. Piles of assignment papers crowded the dozen bound theses to be read to bestow philosophical doctorates on the next batch of historians.

Tom Fitzgerald idly flicked the dead match into the general direction of the rubbish bin. He sucked heavily and noted with satisfaction the first signs of a re-ignition and smoke from his pipe. It died just as quickly as he continued to read, distracted by the text. He reached for his matches again and held the flame to the bowl longer as he sucked deeper, the narcotic finally penetrating the tissue of his tar-encrusted lungs. He broke into a coughing fit before finally sitting back in his captain's chair, and running nicotine-stained fingers through his white hair.

The don's question snapped back into focus. He chuckled with delight as he got up and pulled out a large shallow drawer of a map cabinet. He was looking for a copy of an ancient map, which he located, pulled out and studied. Next, he referred to his voluminous library of journals and books and quickly located what he was looking for. He picked up the phone and dialled.

"Geoffrey, why don't you come around for a port and a cigar? I think I've found something you'll find very interesting."

Half an hour later Geoffrey Mayers was seated opposite Fitzgerald, a port bottle open and the room clouded in smoke from the combination of a pipe and a cigar. Their small talk fizzled out as the effects of several generous glasses of port took effect.

"C'mon Tom, what's this all about?"

Fitzgerald took a long pull on his pipe. "You once asked me whether the Portuguese ever had anything to do with

Western Australia. At the time, you said you were looking at diamonds."

Mayers nodded and blew a cloud of smoke into the air. "And you were bloody rude; you fobbed me off saying you would get back to me. You never did, so is this some kind of apology?"

Fitzgerald laughed. "I know you've got a thicker hide than that. No, I wasn't interested in the Portuguese at that time. I was studying other things and yes, I was particularly interested in someone else when you interrupted me that evening."

"You were busy chatting up Margaret Gates, you randy wombat. You didn't get anywhere, did you? Didn't you know she's got balls?"

Fitzgerald looked sheepish. "No, I didn't at that time. She hadn't long joined the faculty and naturally, I thought she wouldn't be able to resist my charm and good looks. Anyway, I apologise for my rudeness."

"Apology accepted. Now, get on with what you want to tell me."

"You asked me if I knew of a Portuguese explorer by the name of deAbreu and whether he had any association with this part of the world. Can I ask what the purpose of your enquiry was?"

Mayers nodded. "As you know, my particular interest is in diamonds. Now, Argyle in the Kimberleys is the largest diamond mine in the world, not by value, but by the number of diamonds mined, the bulk of which are industrial. On rare occasions, it produces the most spectacular pink diamonds that command an unbelievable premium. They're collectors items, purchased by the super wealthy to adorn the throats and limbs of wives and mistresses or eccentric hoarders who collect rare items of value and beauty. Likewise, the Ellendale mine in the same region produced spectacular yellow diamonds."

"Okay. So what has this to do with the Portuguese?"

"One of the world's greatest gems is the deAbreu diamond. It originates from India, or is supposed to have been provenanced from that source. I suspect it actually derives from here in the Kimberley region."

"What makes you think that? Isn't India renowned for its diamonds? What makes the deAbreu so special?"

"It is described as being a fabulous ruby red, larger than even the Indian Golconda or Kohinoor, which by the way were both white diamonds. Now come on, don't keep me in suspense. What have you come up with that will interest me?"

"I've been reading Portuguese texts from the fifteenth and sixteenth century when the Catholics split the world in two, half for the Spanish and half for the Portuguese," Fitzgerald said waving his hand in a deprecating manner. "I came upon the name Antonio deAbreu. It's not that I didn't know who deAbreu was, but it was something he did that rang the bells about your line of work and the question you once put to me about the Portuguese and Western Australia. You see, there's a reference to deAbreu presenting a large diamond to Affonse deAlbuquerque, the founder of Goa, in around 1518."

"Is there a mention of the colour of the diamond?"

Fitzgerald studied the text carefully. "Yes, it was described as *vermelho,* Portuguese for red.

"So it was just a single red gem?"

"No, it's recorded as being the largest of a number of similar coloured diamonds handed to deAlbuquerque."

Mayers furrowed his brow. "Okay, you may have established the existence of the deAbreu diamond, but what happened to the others? Surely, they would have turned up by now, or been historically recorded?"

"I may have the answer to that with reference to the fabulous Peacock Throne built for the Mughal emperor Shah Jahan in the early 17th century. It was recorded as one of the most splendorous thrones ever built of solid gold with its centrepiece being a red diamond the size of a child's fist. It's a stretch of the imagination, but this could have been the deAbreu. The centrepiece was surrounded by a number of smaller red diamonds. So one could assume all the diamonds given to deAlbuquerque could have eventually wound up in the hands of Jahan."

"What happened to this throne?"

"It was looted from India by the Persian invader Nader Shah who captured Delhi in 1739. He took it back to Iran, but lost it in warfare with the Kurds who apparently broke it up for the gold, diamonds, rubies and sapphires with which it was encrusted."

Mayers raised his bushy eyebrows. "Who was this fellow deAbreu?"

"DeAbreu was probably the first European to ever set eyes on Australia. He landed somewhere in the region of Napier Broome Bay, right on the northern most tip of the Kimberley in 1517."

"I was always led to believe the Dutch were the first to arrive."

Fitzgerald shook his head. "That's widely accepted, but the Dutch were latecomers. William Jantzoon arrived in 1606, long after the Portuguese. Abel Tasman, Dirk Hartog and James Cook in fact all worked off Portuguese maps, or portolans as they were known. The Portuguese were the world's greatest seafarers in the fifteenth and sixteenth centuries. They were light years ahead of their Catholic rivals, the Spanish. They had discovered the whole world by 1512, only they kept very quiet about what they found."

"DeAbreu sounds an interesting character?"

"He was. Amongst a number of other accomplishments he founded Dili in East Timor in1512. Do you realise East Timor was the world's longest established colony? It lasted until the Portuguese pulled out in 1976 when it was annexed by Indonesia. That is some 464 years of continuous occupation. Even the Romans never achieved anything like that."

"You may be pulling the threads together for me Tom. I've long suspected the deAbreu derives from the Kimberley as there are no records of red diamonds being found in India, whereas pink diamonds are readily found at Argyle. I believe there is an association."

"I can't eliminate anything else, but I can build the case for your hypothesis that the Kimberley maybe the source."

"Go on, man."

"DeAbreu landed in Australia in 1517, and I can prove that beyond doubt. He may have visited many times prior because he founded Dili in East Timor in 1512. Don't forget, Dili is only 460 kilometres from the nearest point of Australia. To claim the Portuguese didn't venture another 460 kilometres to discover a southernmost continent even referred to by Marco Polo, when they could navigate some twenty thousand kilometres from Goa to Lisbon without difficulty, gives lie to the Dutch claim of discovery some ninety years later. Anyhow, I digress. Pray tell me Mayers, what if I could prove the deAbreu diamond originates from somewhere in the Kimberley? What would it be worth?"

Mayers laughed as he dragged on his almost extinct cigar. "Commercially, it could be worth a fortune if the actual source could be found. It's worth nothing to me financially, except for the honours that will shower upon me if I'm proved correct."

"Is there enough room for two under that shower? No, don't answer that." Fitzgerald laughed and held up his hands. "I'm about to deliver what I believe to be a vital clue in your hunt." He picked up the old journal he had been reading. "Ever heard of George Grey?"

Mayers shook his head. "Probably have, but refresh my memory."

"George Grey was an Englishman born in Lisbon where his father was stationed in the service of the Duke of Wellington. Grey had a lot to do with this part of the world, being a Governor of South Australia and prior to that, New Zealand." Fitzgerald looked up. "I'm not boring you, am I? I just want to explain a bit of background so you can judge for yourself whether I'm on the right track."

"No, no, please go on. I'm all ears."

"In 1838, Grey sailed directly from England to explore northern Australia. He didn't call into Perth or Sydney, but for some unknown reason he headed straight for the Kimberley. I don't think for a moment he was looking for diamonds, but who knows? Anyway, Grey says he called into Brunswick Bay, the closest Australian point to Timor. He then walked overland to Colliers Bay, a distance of about forty kilometres, whereupon he discovered..." Fitzgerald held up his finger to emphasise his findings. "I quote Grey: *'On looking over some bushes, I suddenly saw from one of them a most extraordinary large figure peering down on me. Upon examination, it proved to be a drawing at the entrance to a cave, which upon entering proved to contain, besides many remarkable paintings on the sloping roof, the principal figure which I have alluded to.*

In order to produce the greater effect, the rock about it was painted black, and the figure itself coloured with the most vivid red and white. It thus appeared to stand out from the rock; and I was certainly rather surprised the moment I first saw this gigantic head and upper part of a body bending over and staring grimly down at me. Its head was encircled in bright red rays, something like the rays that one sees proceeding from the sun when depicted on the sign-board of a public house. Inside of this came a broad stripe of brilliant red, which was coped by lines of white. Both inside and outside of this red space were narrow stripes of a still deeper red, intended probably to mark its boundaries; the face was painted vividly white, and the eyes black, being however surrounded by red and yellow lines; the body, hands and arms were outlined in red – the body being curiously painted with red stripes and bars.' Now listen carefully to this part. Grey goes on: *'One arm of the figure was outstretched, almost within reach of a bright red object the size of a man's hand which was strung around the throat of a similarly large but undressed and unadorned figure that I assumed was that of a native. It appeared the hand was stayed by a giant snake whose head was intruding over the shoulder of the figure, its bared fangs ready to strike at the reaching hand, with its eye the bright red object hanging from the figure's throat.'"*

"You've got me going now, Fitzgerald. But what do you make of what he actually saw?"

"Judge for yourself." Fitzgerald unfolded a copy of a large watercolour painting and laid it out. It was faded, and damaged where it had been folded many times, but it adequately depicted the scene Grey described.

"Where did you get this?" Mayers was aghast as he studied the litho copy.

"That I don't know. There are two of them. I discovered them in this journal I acquired when I was a student more than forty years ago. I don't recall where I got it from, although I think I may have acquired it from Prof Porter, who held the chair here at the time. It was while reading the Portuguese text, I remembered something about Grey, and lo and behold, when I looked for his connection to the Kimberley these were folded into the book. I never knew they were there."

"Grey or one of his offsiders must have whipped them off at the time because of the uniqueness of the site. It's way out of character with the normal native cave paintings. I wonder where the original is."

"Probably in an attic somewhere in England, or lost in the archives of some museum, or destroyed long ago. It wouldn't mean much unless you happen to have Grey's journal and the painting in front of you at the same time to make the connection. Even then, it wouldn't be very important other than from an historical viewpoint. Just an interesting facet of Grey's expedition."

"And you think the red object is a diamond? My God, that would be one of the largest ever discovered." Mayers studied the watercolour intensely. "Accepting the object the figure is reaching for maybe a red diamond, how to you explain the characters and symbolism? Who's the fellow with the white face? It hardly looks European. I think that's drawing a bit of a long bow. More likely it's some aboriginal stylisation of a dreamtime figure."

"That's what I assumed at first. I will come back to that, but first let me read from Grey's journal wherein he describes a more realistic representation of a man, which he took to be a priest in cassock and cowl. I quote:

'In another cave, the principal painting was the figure of a man, ten feet six inches in height, clothed from the chin downwards in a red garment that reached to the wrists and ankles; beyond this red dress the feet and hands protruded, but were badly executed.' I don't think the first figure is a dreamtime depiction. Recall those medieval portrayals of martyrs, saints, and knights English churches derive some revenue by charging tourists to conduct brass rubbings. They invariably have a halo, and are hung with medallions and the like, and their garments are festooned around them. Considering the aborigines were mostly buck naked, they must have been drawing something they actually witnessed, otherwise they would not have conceived of drawing a clothed figure. The second cave clearly shows a garmented figure." Fitzgerald handed the second watercolour copy to Mayers. "Grey even likens the second painting to Ezekiel's *'Men portrayed on the wall, the images of the Chaldeans poutrayed with vermillion'.*"

"Chaldeans? If my memory serves me correctly, they're a religion associated with Syria dating back to Babylon before JC arrived on the scene?"

"Near enough, Geoffrey. Now let me read you another line from Grey: *'At the bottom right hand corner was painted what appeared to be a small white flower which looked strangely like a rose.'* Now look in the bottom right hand corner."

"It certainly appears to be a rose, and it is well painted." Mayers said, holding the print close. "But what is its significance?"

"Unless I'm mistaken, it's St Mary's Rose, *'Rosas da Santa Maria'.* The rose became the emblem of the Portuguese explorers. Its significance harks back to 1433 when Gil Eannes was commissioned by Prince Henry the Navigator to sail past the accepted end of the known world at that time, Cape Bojador on the African Coast. Eannes landed on the coast south of the cape, picked the only living thing in the desert and called it St Mary's Rose."

"But the aborigines were obviously unaware of the emblem or its significance. Surely, they would not have had the skills to paint it? It's so finely detailed."

"I've pondered that myself Geoffrey, but I beg to differ in regard to their painting skills. Although invariably all aboriginal art is referred to by the generic term, Wandjina, or Gwon Gwon or Bradshaws in the case of the Kimberley, it has been commented by the experts as demonstrating a fine degree of motor skill and artistic appreciation of line and form. Sure, their paintings are mostly of dreamtime figures, the mythical and the spiritual, of animals and humans, but they are fine painters. The impressionist or abstract style is not confined to the contemporary French school, you know. Here is ample evidence to suggest the Australian aborigines were doing impressions long ago and if you want to go back further, you can look to the Neolithic cave painters of France and Spain. Impressionists have been around since the dawn of civilisation."

"And you believe that is the Portuguese St Mary's Rose?"

"Let me make a further submission to support my theory," Fitzgerald continued. "It is established that St Mary's Rose was the emblem of the Portuguese seafarers, but has it been found anywhere else around the Australian coastline, or more to the point the Kimberley coast? The answer to that is yes. In 1916, HMS Encounter under the command of Captain C. Cumberledge RN entered Napier Broome Bay and discovered a small brass canon on a headland. It looked as though it had been set into a cairn of stones to mark a position. The canon was stamped with the Portuguese crown and the Rosa da Santa Maria. And it so happens that Napier Broome Bay is near enough to longitude 129° , the eastern edge of the Portuguese empire as defined by the Treaty of Tordesillas."

"I've never heard of it, but go on."

"Tordesillas was an agreement struck between the Spanish and Portuguese. It was the way the Pope kept the two Catholic nations from each other's throats."

"And I suppose the canon has disappeared into the pages of history, never to be found," Mayers added with a laugh.

"No, it hasn't actually. In fact, it was last noted as positioned outside the commandant's office on the Garden Island Naval base in Sydney."

"You say that Grey discovered the paintings in 1838. They could depict the coming of the Dutch or British."

Fitzgerald shrugged. "They could, but the style of clothing in the two paintings would suggest otherwise. I would say they are the robes of a priest. There are many references to the Portuguese carrying priests on board, as did the Spanish. They wanted God's blessing for their pillage. The Dutch never sought divine sanction of their conquests. They just came and took, and as for the English, they did on rare occasions carry clergymen who shunned any papist trappings, which does not fit with the dress in those prints. I'm convinced these depict the Portuguese. However, it's pure speculation as to what the red object on the necklace is, but it fits your description and drawing a long bow, I believe it fits with deAbreu presenting a red diamond to his patron, Albuquerque. I believe I've presented a strong case the Portuguese were indeed in the Kimberley region."

"It's certainly a reasonable hypothesis, but now for the jackpot question. If the deAbreu diamond did originate from the Kimberley from where exactly did it come? That's a vast area to search in."

"That, my dear fellow is for you to solve, but I believe I can give you a strong lead," Fitzgerald let his statement sink in while adopting a mischievous grin.

"For God's sake, get on with it, Tom. You sure know how to spin out a yarn."

"It's found once more in the writings of Grey wherein he states: *'Gulpinal the guide said legend has it that the glowing stone is the eye of the rainbow serpent of the dreamtime and comes from a sacred site some twenty days to the south-east.'*"

"Well, where would that be?"

Fitzgerald took a cadastral map off a shelf and flattened it out on his desk. "Twenty days at say fifteen to twenty kilometres a day walking in that terrain would put you about… here." Mayers followed Tom's finger. "Somewhere in that region could be the source of the red diamond, if legend is to be believed."

"And I've got just the student to do the looking," Mayers replied. "He'll be over the moon when I brief him on this. The time is long past when I would immediately pull on a pair of boots and rush off to look. Although I've long held the theory of the source of the deAbreu, I'll let him take the credit for any discovery. Mind you, some of the glory will rub off on me if he does. He's doing his thesis on diamonds and the fingerprinting, for want of more precise terminology, of the provenance of diamonds worldwide."

"You mean, you can tell where a diamond has come from?"

"You certainly can. Every diamond province produces stones of a particular character and structure. That's why if the deAbreu wasn't locked up in the Indian Treasury; it would be relatively easy to prove or disprove whether it is of Australian or Indian origin."

16

eoffrey Mayers didn't look up from his microscope when he heard the knock at his door. "Come in, come in, it's not locked." The student entered and flopped down in a battered leather armchair alongside the professor's desk.

"What are you looking at prof?"

"Brown industrial diamonds from the Argyle mine. I've been pondering as to why diamonds from one source vary so much in colour and in particular, why amongst the boart there occurs the occasional pink worth a king's ransom."

Mayers didn't take his eye from the high-powered microscope as he studied the dull, brown stone.

"And you've found the answer?"

"Maybe, but that's not why I asked you to come to see me. I believe I may have located the source of the famous deAbreu diamond, or rather I've located the general area, and it is in the Kimberley."

"I haven't heard of that one. What did you call it again?"

"DeAbreu, named after the Portuguese navigator who gave it to Affonse de Albuquerque, the governor of Goa, in around 1518. A fabulous, ruby red gem described as being the size of a goose egg. Proof of its existence is well recorded. The last noted sighting was in 1934; it was being used as a paperweight by the Seventh Nizam of Hyderabad. At the time, he was possibly the world's richest man thanks to the devotion of his seventeen million Islamic followers. How he came by the deAbreu is not recorded, but the Nizam was an avid collector of anything of great value, including gems. He apparently had untold millions worth stashed around his palace. The entire collection was confiscated by the Indian government in the late 1960s in order to protect, so they claimed, the dispersion of Indian national treasure by the then despotic eighth Nizam. At that point, the deAbreu disappeared from sight, and hasn't been on display since then."

"And you believe it came from the Kimberley and you want me to do the leg work?"

Mayers sat back in his chair, adopting a look of mock incredulity. "I'm offering you the chance of a lifetime, or would you prefer me to take all the credit? I'm too old to be walking around in the heat and flies and sleeping under the stars. Do you want to be part of it or not?"

"Of course I do. Lead me to it."

"Good, now let me explain it to you."

The student listened eagerly and became increasingly engrossed. He studied the litho copies Mayers had handed him and was attentive as the professor explained their significance. Finally, he sat back in his chair and unconsciously played with his cap, continuously pulling it forwards and pushing it back, his excitement visible.

"You said you can almost pinpoint where the diamond came from."

"I can give you the general area, but that's it. There are no guarantees. You understand this is all based on pure supposition?"

"It's a great story and I can see you've researched it well. If the deAbreu came from there, I can't wait to investigate and hopefully prove it. Any suggestions how I go about tackling such a program?"

"The same way Maureen Muggeridge found Argyle in the Kimberley in 1979, and Chuck Fipke the Lac de Gras diamond deposits in the North-West Territories of Canada. Both worked on the all important indicator minerals. In Fipke's case, he tracked them for hundreds of kilometres back from where they had been deposited by the glacial till of the last ice age. Likewise, Muggeridge just sampled the ancient paleo channels, which led to the discovery of Argyle. That's the only way you can address a professional exploration program such as this. You'll be in it for the long haul."

Mayers went over to a map cabinet and pulled out a large topographical map. "I've narrowed it down to here, or very close to here. It's covered by the Venus Downs pastoral holding." He noticed the momentary look of surprise on the student's face.

"Prof, have you ever considered the supposed red deAbreu originated from the Argyle deposit? After all, Argyle is only a couple of hundred kilometres away from Venus Downs and it produces the famous pinks, along with a few other colours. I hope I'm not tilting at windmills on this one."

Mayers nodded and looked thoughtful. "It's possible, but I believe there is one major flaw in that argument; there's no record of Argyle ever producing a pink weighing more than a couple of carats. There is a record of the odd reddish-brown of no value being found, but no true red. The deAbreu is unique. It's a monster by comparison."

"Have you ever seen it?"

"No. Believe me, I've pulled every string I can to get access. I approached the Indian Treasury and tried to use the influence of my professional contacts at the Indian Geological Survey, to no avail. Treasury wouldn't even admit they had the diamond, or that it even exists. But we know it existed because it was well recorded as being a feature on the Seventh Nizam's desk. I suppose it could have been cut up into smaller stones, but they would have certainly appeared and been noted as being worn by some notable celebrity by now. Small pinks and a few light reds have appeared, but they were not cleaved off the deAbreu, I'm certain of that. There is no record of red diamonds ever being found in India. The only true red ever recorded was the five carat Moussaieff found in Brazil. The DeYoung and Kozangian gems at about five carats each were found in South Africa, but they were described as being brownish-red. The deAbreu is absolutely unique—and I don't believe it came from India."

"So I'll use Venus Downs as a starting point?"

"I think that would be logical. There's one other long-shot I've been considering. Grey's guide mentioned the red object on the painting was the eye of the rainbow serpent. It could just be a myth or legend, but there may also be some truth in it. That country is riddled with painted caves and rock overhangs. I would ask at Venus Downs whether they are aware of any unusually large rock paintings on the property, or nearby. I envisage it will be something spectacular in graphic appearance and size."

"Anthropologists have been crawling over the Kimberley for years. Is there anyone in the faculty here I can talk to?"

"Margaret Gates is the chair of anthropology, but you're wasting your time. She hates geologists and mining companies. She lives and dreams the Kimberley. She won't tell you zip about what she's seen for fear you'll go and reveal its whereabouts."

"Who's going to pay for my program?" the student asked, suddenly becoming aware of the magnitude of the task he was taking on.

"I've arranged for a syndicate of private investors to stump up the first year's budget. At the end of that, they'll decide whether to continue or call it a day."

"If I find the actual pipe or an alluvial source it could be worth mega bucks. What do I get out of it?"

"The same as me lad. The glory and accolades and if we're really lucky, some monetary reward depending on how generous the syndicate feels."

The professor noticed a momentary furrowing of the student's brow. His eyes had lost their glow of enthusiasm. Mayers suddenly felt very uncomfortable. "Look, unfortunately the reality is that even if you're successful, any financial outcomes won't belong to either of us. Any new discovery belongs to the syndicate funding the research. The same syndicate has been funding my theoretical research for a number of years now. They've put in a lot of money for very little in return so far."

"But do they have exploration title to the area?"

"No, that would be too costly to maintain. Remember, this is a private operation and you must observe absolute discretion at all times. They have been generous with their funding to date and we are morally and ethically bound to maintain those standards."

"So what you're saying is that if I find what we're looking for, we'll have to settle for a few lousy bucks they may choose to throw our way. The discovery could be worth hundreds of millions, even more."

"Yes it could be, but the odds are your exploration efforts will result in nothing. As I said, the syndicate has indulged me for a number of years now and I rely on and appreciate their support. We have a verbal arrangement; there's no written contract but their money has arrived every year without fail. I warn you, should you divulge anything of what I've just told you I will have you thrown out of the faculty. Any career you had planned in geology will be finished. Honesty and integrity are the hallmarks of any professional and you cannot withhold and use to your personal advantage anything you may discover." A thought suddenly struck the professor. "You're not withholding anything from me now, are you?"

"No, why do you ask?"

"I thought I noticed a look of surprise on your face when I first put my finger on Venus Downs."

The student shook his head. "Never heard of the place prof. I was just surprised you'd narrowed the search down so much."

Mayers was concerned. Something about what the student said did not add up. "Tell me, you're what I would term a mature age student. What did you do before you took up geology?"

"Anything that paid me enough to exist. You name it; I've done it. But I've always had an interest in geology; that's why I'm here."

"You're exceptionally bright and I'm sure you will go a long way, but remember what I've told you. If I think you are attempting to gain financially from what you discover, I will take immediate action."

"Cool it prof. I've no intention of doing anything underhand. It just pisses me off we're going to have to hand over any discovery for peanuts. But I respect that you made the deal, so I'll just go along with it." The student pounded his knee, stood up and turned to leave.

The professor pulled open a drawer and took out an envelope. "Here's five grand for airfares, accommodation and supplies. I've arranged with the bank in Wyndham to advance you funds on the provision of invoices. You'll need to engage some field crew and hire vehicles. You may need to hire a helicopter on occasion, but I would prefer you kept expenditure to a minimum. Can you get away next week?"

"Nothing to hold me here prof. I'll call in Monday to say goodbye. Can I borrow those prints and get them copied?"

"Sure, but I want the originals back." The professor waved his hand and returned to his microscope.

Professor Margaret Gates was a tall, ascetic woman lacking charisma or warmth. Her manner was clinical and perfunctory.

"And what can I do for you, Mr Riley?"

"I wanted to see you because I think I have something that may be mutually beneficial, professor."

"Please sit down, but if you're here on behalf of professor Mayers, you're wasting your time."

He ignored the severity and tone of her voice. "I wasn't sent by professor Mayers but yes, I'm making my own enquiries. Before you show me the door, perhaps I should outline what

I have in mind. I wouldn't be here wasting your time if I didn't think you would be interested. "

Margaret Gates fixed him with an unwavering look of scepticism, but said nothing.

"I know you have a particular interest in the Kimberley and it's highly likely you've been to Venus Downs. Could you describe some of the more spectacular rock art you may have seen and photographed?"

"No I can't, Mr Riley, or more to the point, I won't. I've seen some spectacular Bradshaws, or more correctly Gwon Gwon paintings, but I'm not prepared to tell you where they are."

"Do you think the owner of Venus Downs would have seen them?"

"I doubt whether he's seen what I have, but why don't you go and ask him?

"Professor, I don't want you to lead me to them, I merely want to confirm something you may have seen and photographed. If you can do that, then I will be prepared to reveal something I think will be of vital importance to your scientific studies."

"And what would that be?"

"I'm particularly interested in a painting of a large snake, a very large snake if my guess is correct. It could be brightly coloured and of significant length. In addition, the serpent could be accompanied by very large paintings of figures and one in particular may depict a native with a large coloured object hanging on a necklace."

"Colour? What do mean by colour?"

He could see he had piqued her interest as she suddenly leaned forwards across her desk with a raised eyebrow.

"Did the figure appear to have multiple rays emanating from it?

"And if it did?"

"Then I think I can explain to you why the drawings are there and their possible significance." Riley let the statement hang, studying the professor's face without venturing further.

"I would like to make it clear, Mr Riley, so you are under no illusions, that even if you reveal to me what you have, it does not necessarily mean I will extend the same courtesy to you. My work is my life. Clearly, your approach is merely from a commercial viewpoint. After all, you're studying geology, therefore the motivation must be financial gain."

He was about to object, but was cut off.

"I've absolutely no interest in the profit motive. I detest mining with all the damage it causes and pollution of the environment. If you think you can add something of importance to my research, I will gladly accept, but don't expect anything in return."

He nodded, deep in thought. It was the classic play of a person with the advantage. She was confident he could add nothing to her field of endeavour and was playing hardball. He decided to chance his hand, although he doubted this woman was going to give him any information whatsoever. "I can see from your reaction you're aware of the possible location of both paintings, and I would venture to guess the snake and figure paintings are within spitting distance of each other."

She looked at him sharply. He could see he had struck a nerve.

"What if I could demonstrate almost identical paintings exist close to the Kimberley coast?"

Her face cracked into a cynical smile. "You're referring to Grey's writings of course. No one has ever been able to locate the paintings he referred to. Why? Do you know something I don't?"

Riley ignored her question. "Tell me something, professor. If the paintings you saw could be matched to what Grey witnessed, that would indicate the Portuguese were trading with the native aborigines, wouldn't it?"

"Why the Portuguese? It could have been the Dutch or English?"

He was beginning to enjoy the game. "Because the dress of the figure or figures you saw pre-date both the Dutch and English. Am I right? Also, the paintings are hundreds of kilometres from the coast in the middle of nowhere, which simply doesn't explain why a nomadic people painted a clothed figure."

"And you can explain it?"

"I have a plausible theory. I believe the Portuguese were trading something with the natives. What you saw is probably close to the source of whatever it was, and the coastal paintings add weight to that assumption."

"And what do you think they were trading?"

"I don't know. It could have been some sort of metal, or gold for that matter, or it could have been gems of some description, but it must have been something of value the Portuguese wanted."

Professor Gates shook her head. "No. Unlike other ancient civilisations the world over, such as the Aztecs who recognised the value of gems and gold, Australian aborigines only saw value in things that sustained life. If what you say were true, it means they could have actually recognised and put value on a precious commodity."

"But what if the Portuguese saw something of value and traded for it, or more likely, just took it?"

"So where is your proof of the coast paintings? If you haven't actually laid eyes on them, what are you offering me?'

It was time for the coup de grâce. He propped the leather folder on his knee, withdrew copies of the watercolours, unfolded them and handed them to her. She eagerly studied them and looked up in surprise. He could see her hands shaking with excitement. She opened a drawer and took out a magnifying glass.

"Where did you get these?"

"That's... classified, but they do match the paintings you've seen, don't they? I can assure you they're copies of Grey's originals. Identical paintings hundreds of kilometres apart in my opinion, suggesting there is a direct connection between the two. I see you are particularly interested in the St Mary's Rose. More or less proves the drawings depict the Portuguese, doesn't it?"

She nodded slowly. "It adds strong weight to that theory, but what you're proposing would lead to the establishment of a mining operation. I don't know what it is you're seeking, but it must be mineral of some kind. Anthropology is a lifetime study. You could destroy vital evidence in your rush to exploit the resource. We're at odds, Mr Riley; our objectives clash. I thank you sincerely for what you have revealed, but I cannot see how I can help you."

In one way, he realised his gamble had failed, yet at least he was now certain the paintings were located on Venus Downs. But he knew Venus Downs covered a vast area and to locate an isolated diamond pipe concealed under millenniums of alluvium would be a huge task, well outside the budget of Mayers' syndicate. "You disappoint me, Professor Gates. I'd hoped we could have worked on this together. Will you reconsider?"

Gates shook her head. "No, in the interests of science and my interest in protecting the environment, I cannot assist you. I would like to thank you for bringing the possible significance of the paintings to my attention. It seems to confirm what you say, the natives were indeed trading something. You have raised a whole new area of study for me."

"Well, I'm pleased to see one of us got something out of it," Riley replied curtly. "I was hoping we could share information to our mutual benefit." He reached across, picked up the prints and put them back into his folder.

"I would be prepared to make a small concession—on one condition."

"And what would that be, professor?" He noticed the falter in her voice and decided to press his advantage. "I'm somewhat reluctant to entertain anything you have in mind, as it's been a one-way street so far."

"Give me those pictures, or at least let me copy them. Then give me a few days while I consider your request."

Riley laughed as he stood up. "I think not, professor. You lead me to the site of the paintings on Venus Downs and I'll gladly hand you copies."

Gates sprang to her feet. "I will never give you the location of the paintings. That's the trouble with you mining people. You destroy the landscape, gouging massive holes into the landscape. You take, but never restore. You destroy ancient native sacred sites at will. Thousands of years of history disappear under the tracks of dozers and mining equipment. I only want copies of the pictures for my records. They're of vital historical importance to me, but I can see you don't give a damn. These pictures represent an important anthropological discovery, which could establish there was a trade link between the Portuguese and the aborigines. I demand access to them!" The anger in her voice was rising to such a pitch he became alarmed someone might hear. He held up his hands to quieten her down, but it was too late. The door suddenly opened, and a woman with a full head of white hair peered in.

"Everything alright, Margaret?"

"Yes, Mr Riley is just leaving," Gates snapped, abruptly waving the woman away.

"You should have played ball, professor. You've already confirmed my suspicions; the paintings are located somewhere on Venus Downs. With your assistance, I would have saved myself a lot of time. Now it will take me a little longer, but I'll find them just the same."

Margaret Gates slumped back into her chair, fixing him with a look of contempt. "You'll never find them as long as you live, they are so well concealed. I was shown them by an aboriginal elder who has since died. I promised I would never reveal their location or write about them. I've kept my promise and retained my integrity, something you lack, Mr Riley. Now get out of my office."

17

"*Notice anything suspicious constable?*" *The two policemen looked down at the body slumped in an armchair.*

"No Sarg. Looks as though he just popped his clogs. No signs of violence, and nothing has been disturbed as far as I can see other than a half-empty bottle of scotch and one glass. Looks like he was too fond of the Walking Johnny."

His superior nodded as the constable pointed to the label on the bottle. "Sharp detective work constable. You'll go far in the force."

"No need to call Homicide on this one. Just get a doc to sign him off to a slab in the fridge."

"You reckon? When did you make detective?"

"Well it's obvious to me. Nothing's been disturbed so it wasn't a robbery, and he hasn't been bashed, knifed, shot or garrotted."

"My, you are observant," the sergeant commented sarcastically. "How do you know he hasn't been garrotted?"

"Because I've read the eyes just pop right out and don't go back. Isn't that correct?"

"Remind me to sign your transfer to Homicide tomorrow. They're looking for geniuses like you. Just like on tele, the perfect murder solved within thirty minutes with the cry of *'book him, Danno.'*"

"Never heard of that show, sergeant. Must have been well before my time." The constable sniggered, but quickly stopped when he saw the deadpan look on his superior's face.

"Want to take a bet he died of natural causes?"

"Yeah, I'll take you on. A beer if I lose and a carton if you lose."

"Bloody awful odds, but I can't lose."

"Who reported him?"

"I did." The policemen hadn't noticed the diminutive figure standing just inside the doorway. "I'm the manager here. I hadn't seen Geoffrey for a couple of days. He's always up early, and his lights are out by ten. I came home after midnight last night and noted his lights were on. I didn't think too much about it, but I was concerned because he wasn't around at all today. And he always says hello when he goes past my office. I knocked on his door early this evening, but there was no answer so I let myself in and... well, then I called you people."

"Geoffrey who?" A voice demanded as two plain clothed detectives entered the room.

"Geoffrey Mayers. He's professor of geology at the university. Very quiet but got along well with everyone. Didn't have an enemy in the world, no relations either from what I could gather. Kept to himself."

The two detectives looked at the body. "Okay Connors, you and the constable can shove off now. Looks like natural causes to me," said one of them.

"Time for a beer sergeant," the constable muttered under his breath.

As they were leaving, a middle-aged man with an annoyed expression set on his face entered the room. He was clutching a small bag. "Someone called for me."

The older detective looked up. "Yeah doc. Give us a reading on this one, will you? Did he just die or did someone help him on his way?"

The doctor felt Mayers' neck. "I can tell you he's been dead for some time. A day or so. No wounds, no strangulation. Probably a stroke or heart attack."

"An autopsy's not required in that case, doc. Just write out the death certificate. We'll call the meat wagon and we can all go home."

The doctor prepared to write out the certificate when he paused and moved to straighten the corpse's head from where it had been leaning to one side. A frown furrowed his brow as he bent down and looked into the deceased's ear. Putting down his pad and pen, he delved into his bag for an otoscope. After examining the inner ear for a few seconds, he switched off the instrument and straightened up. "I can't confirm the cause of death. This is one for the pathologist to decide."

"What makes you say that doc?"

"His ear drum is punctured. There's a small amount of congealed blood present. I have my suspicions this man may have been murdered."

"What? But how?"

"I'd be looking for a sharp object like a fine knitting needle, a skewer or something similar that is long and very thin."

The detective scratched his chin. "This is a new one on me. You mean someone has pushed something in through his ear to penetrate his brain?"

"You've got it in one detective. Death would have been immediate. I almost missed it but as you can see here, the earlobe looks greasy where some fluid has leaked out."

"There's no sign of a struggle though. Surely he'd have seen it coming? You can't just walk up to someone and push something into their ear without them resisting."

"Not if he was asleep." The doctor pointed to the scotch bottle.

"Dammit, I was hoping for an early night. Thanks, doc". He turned to the younger detective. "This is a crime scene. Call in Forensics."

The two policemen were still parked in their squad car when the detective emerged from the foyer. As he walked past, Connors wound down his window.

"A homicide then, is it?"

The detective nodded, and kept on walking to his car.

"Looks like you owe me a carton of beer constable."

The corridor was in darkness as he crept along it, guided by the light from his small torch. He read the sign on the door signifying the occupant. He turned the handle, but it was locked, as he had anticipated it would be. He knelt down and fished out two long Allan keys from his pocket. They were rounded off and filed smooth, with small hooks cut into the long ends. Grasping the short end of the keys between thumb and forefinger for leverage, it took him only moments to spring the simple lock. He entered, turned on a desk lamp and quickly went through the contents of the desk. He turned to the locked filing cabinets; these were also quickly opened. Hundreds of files, but none contained the possible identification tag he was looking for. There was no time to study each folder in detail, as he quickly went through the four filing cabinets. He turned his attention to a locked library cabinet when he heard what he thought was a door closing in the hallway. He quickly turned out the lamp and rushed to stand behind the door. The footsteps were muffled, as though someone was walking slowly in soft shoes. It had to be an intruder, otherwise the person would have turned on the light at the entrance to the corridor. It wasn't Security; he knew the timing of their rounds. He heard the footsteps cease outside the door and could see the flashlight illumination from underneath. He held his breath and waited. He knew he was in deep trouble if the door opened. Then he heard the footsteps move on and he slowly let out his breath. Convinced he would not find what he was looking for, he waited before opening the door and stepping out into the corridor. There was no sign of the intruder, but curious as to who it could be, he switched off the torch and quietly walked in that direction.

The long corridor was familiar to him; he had walked along it countless times to talk to Professor Mayers. He slowly pushed open a dividing fire door leading to the geology faculty and was resisting the pneumatic closing spring when it slid out of his hand. He cursed as the door closed with a thud. He froze and listened, but could hear nothing. The corridor was in darkness as he began walking softly again with one hand against the wall for guidance. He turned the corner and could see light coming out into the corridor from Mayers' office. A large book cabinet had been placed in the corridor to house the overflow of his vast collection of books and papers. Just beyond was another door leading to a flight of fire stairs. He approached and looked into the office. It was empty. He spun around at the sudden sound behind him. A person was hiding on the far side of the corridor cabinet. Whoever it was broke cover and made a sudden rush for the stairwell door a few metres to the right. He sensed it was a woman by her audible gasp of fear at being discovered. Her head was covered with a beanie and her figure draped in a long coat. The woman was a few steps in front of him as she pushed open the door and attempted to slam it behind her. He pushed into it, resisting the opposite force and then pushing it open. The woman lost her footing on the small landing and began to fall backwards down the staircase. He made a grab for her, momentarily holding onto her coat belt before losing grip. There was no sound as he followed her down from the light of his torch. One look at her unseeing eyes told him she was dead, her head at a curious angle.

"Jesus, Mary and Joseph," he muttered to himself as he looked down at Margaret Gates. "What the hell were you doing in Mayers' office?" But he already knew, as he slowly opened the fire door leading to a pathway outside and let himself out. He stood still for a few seconds to get his bearings, then made his way out of the grounds. He was sure he had not been seen.

18

arge Tilley was wiping down the bar when the stranger walked in. "What's your poison?"

"I don't want poison. I want a room if you have one."

The Irish accent was unmistakable, but it took her a few moments to put the voice to the face as she dredged her memory. "Father! What are you doing back here? I thought you'd left town for good after you gave Carl Boyce that flogging. Mind you, he had it coming. You know he's dead, don't you?"

The colour drained from his face. "No, I didn't."

"Oh, don't look so worried. You had nothing to do with it. He was gored to death by a bull."

"Oh, I'm sorry to hear that."

"Are you going to say a prayer for him at Mass this Sunday then?"

"I left the priesthood some time back, but I'll say a prayer for him anyway."

Marge's eyes narrowed. "So what are you doing now?"

"I'm a geologist. I studied geology for a few years before I gave it away and entered the church. After the incident with Carl, I decided to give up the priesthood, go back to university and finish my studies. This part of the world has some very interesting geology—that's what brings me back here."

"Anything in particular you're looking for?"

He shrugged. "Copper, gold, lead, silver zinc, diamonds. Know where I can find any?" he smirked.

"You're the geologist. You go out and find a big lump of gold or a great big diamond and I'll gladly accept either of them," Marge cackled. "Just grab any room that's empty upstairs and make yourself at home. How long are you planning on staying?"

"Not sure of that yet, but I would say a couple of months. Any other geologists staying here?"

"They come and go, but none at the moment. Say, what do I call you now if you're not a priest?"

"Dion, Dion Murphy. The name hasn't changed, just the collar." He picked up his bag. "Marge, are there any charter helicopter operators around here?"

"Mark Snell is out at the airfield. He generally comes in for a beer in the evening. Be in here around six and I'll introduce you."

Snell did not need any introduction. The monogrammed cap and shirt pocket announced his identity. Dion introduced himself and shook the wiry hand of the weather-beaten man with a build to match that of his hands.

"Marge told me you wanted to see me. What can I do for you Irish?"

"I want to charter a helicopter for some reconnaissance work."

"What are you looking for? Maybe I can help you."

"I want to look at rock formations from the air. That way, I can get a clear idea of the strata and structures. I want to identify areas of particular interest so I can follow up on the ground. This could save me a lot of time."

"Any area you want to look at in particular? There's tens of thousands of square kilometres out there. It could cost you a fortune."

"I want to start in the vicinity of Venus Downs."

Snell looked thoughtful. "Yes, I'm familiar with Henry Boyce's property. Does he know you're back?"

"Probably not, but I hear the bush telegraph is very active around here." He could not resist glancing in Marge's direction.

"You're with a company, I take it? Helicopters are expensive and I don't want to be out of pocket if you shoot through again."

Dion felt the barb of sarcasm, but didn't react. "I'm with a syndicate. I'll approve and sign your invoices and you can present them to the bank for payment."

"Fair enough Irish. As long as it all stacks up, I'm at your service."

Marge pretended she was busy, but Dion knew she was listening to every word of their conversation. "Do you know where I can hire a four wheel drive?"

"You can have mine," Marge suddenly piped up. "Hundred bucks a day. You pay for the gas, servicing and any damage such as a busted windscreen and any panel-beating if you hit a roo or emu. In fact, anything that needs fixing is your responsibility."

"Sounds okay to me Marge. I accept."

Dion picked up the beer Marge had pulled and walked through to the dining room.

"Doesn't look dangerous to me," Snell muttered as he watched the departing back of the former priest.

Marge shook her head. "Don't push your luck Mark. You're already stepping out of line with your sarcasm. We all know of your amateur boxing prowess and the trophies you've won, but that was a long time ago. Push that man too far and you might find yourself with busted ribs and pissing blood for days, just like Carl Boyce did."

"My fighting days are over Marge." Snell laughed as he raised his glass. "No chance of me taking anyone on. Bloody strange though. A local priest who fled town suddenly turns up claiming to be a geologist. Don't you think that odd?"

"It's bloody odd but as long as he pays his bills, keeps his nose clean and doesn't go hassling Dolly again so she can't keep her mind on the job, I couldn't give a damn what he does."

Snell spluttered into his beer. "He shagged Dolly? He's a gin jockey then."

"Don't give me that shocked look Snell. The only reason you haven't shagged her is because she can't stand you. Anyway, how do you know he wasn't just hearing her confession?" Marge cackled with laughter. "She's married now, and I'm guessing neither you nor Murphy, nor any other dropout in this town would take on that gorilla she's hooked up with. One sideways glance at Dolly and he'd rip your pecker off."

Murphy was at the airstrip at first light. Snell had rolled the Kawasaki out of the hangar and completed his daily inspection.

"I've got a Bell as well, but this has more endurance and more room in the back. I figured you'd want to land and collect samples here and there."

"Not today. I just want to look around Venus Downs. Do you know of any rock paintings on the station?"

Snell laughed. "I can show you any number of rock art sites. They're all over the Kimberley."

"Anything really outstanding is what I'm interested in."

"I thought you were a geologist?"

"I am, but I'm also interested in anthropology. I study rocks for a living but I like to interest myself in the civilisations who've walked over those rocks."

"Sounds reasonable. I can't think of anything that really stands out. Henry Boyce may know. Do you want to drop in and talk to him?"

"We'll just do the aerial tour today. Let's get going." Dion did not want to meet up with Henry with Snell in tow. There would be some explaining to do and he wanted to tread gently.

Snell started the engine and let it run up for several minutes. Murphy sat behind the pilot in a three-seat arrangement. He reached for a headset, put it on and adjusted the volume. The sun was glaring from the east as they took off and turned south-east.

"Okay Irish, I'll head for the far eastern boundary of the property and work back, otherwise we're going to have the sun in our faces and you won't be able to see much on the ground."

"The name's Dion."

Snell caught the tone in his voice and nodded. 'Okay Dion, you tell me what you want to see."

"Just let me look at the ground features would you, Mark. I don't want to miss anything."

They flew in silence for an hour and a half until Snell came on the intercom. "We're about there. You see that old outstation hut down there? That's about five kilometres inside Henry's boundary." Snell began to turn the chopper.

"Just keep going a little further over that range ahead." Murphy knew it would be an ideal place for ancient rock art. It was rugged and inaccessible, other than on foot. There was no place for a chopper to land. He could see an occasional dry water hole, but it was a timeless and sun-scorched landscape he had no intention of walking around in alone. Suddenly, he saw a small exposed area on one of the highest points.

"Can you put down there Mark? I want to have a look at that formation."

"No problem." Snell skilfully manoeuvred the chopper and set it down. "Do you want to spend some time here?"

"Give me ten minutes."

"Okay. I need a piss and a smoke anyway so I'll shut her down and we can listen to the silence."

They moved off in opposite directions. As he took in the view, Dion knew he was in the right area. The rugged red ravines echoed an eerie silence as he looked back towards the west. High above, a wedge-tail eagle circled slowly, rising, rising and drifting down again as the thermals ebbed and flowed. There was not a breath of wind. He walked slowly towards a clump of rocks, climbing up onto the highest to get an even better panorama.

He was lost in thought when his eye level fell to a small flat area just below the rock and the bleached bones of a long-dead animal. Then he saw the human skull with a neat round hole in its temple and the distinct form of a human skeleton. There was no sign of a weapon. Whoever it was had been murdered. He was about to turn and shout to Snell when he checked himself. Reporting this would bring police to the scene. The skeleton had obviously been there some considerable time. The victim would probably never be identified, so why report it? He turned to see Snell walking towards him.

"That's enough, let's get going." Murphy sprang down from the rock and they walked back towards the chopper.

Henry recognised the vehicle as belonging to Marge Tilley, but he could see she was not driving. He was perplexed as the stranger got out and approached.

"Good afternoon Henry."

Red hair stuffed under a bush hat and the soft brogue took him by surprise, but there was no mistaking the identity. "Father Murphy! What are you doing out here? Have you been sent to look over us sinners again?"

"I think you know, Henry, I threw in the priesthood after the Bishop decided to consign me to an aboriginal mission to atone for my sins. I'm just plain Dion Murphy now."

Henry nodded. "Yes, a few stories did come to me on the wind. You certainly taught Carl a lesson for all it was worth at the time. You know he's dead, don't you?"

"Yes, I do. Most unfortunate."

"What brings you here? Is this a social visit or has it some purpose?"

"When I left the priesthood, I went back to university and qualified as a geologist. I'm up here working for a private syndicate, looking for interesting mineral prospects."

"I see. Well... welcome. Are you going to stay with us?"

"I would like to for a few days if that's alright."

"Throw your gear in Carl's old room and come over for a beer."

They were sitting together on the veranda when Walter drove into the yard, slammed the door on the ute, and walked up to the homestead.

"Fixed those fences, Henry. Hi, I'm Walter." He turned to Dion and held out his hand.

"We've met before, Walter."

Walter hesitated a few seconds until the recognition dawned on him. "Yeah, I remember, you're Father Murphy. I heard you got booted out."

Dion laughed at the barbed remark. "Yes, you could say that, but the priesthood wasn't for me anyway."

"Henry's told you Carl's dead?"

"Yes he has."

"You gave him one hell of a hiding. You king hit him, he said. Do you always fight dirty?"

"Walter, life is one long fight. I learnt long ago there's no such thing as a clean fight. The fact is, Carl challenged me and dropped his guard, so he paid the price. What would you do if I came at you with a piece of wood in my hand?"

Walter snorted derisively. "That's bullshit. Carl didn't threaten you with a piece of wood. He could have taken you apart with his bare hands. You king hit him."

"Not so Walter. Both you and Carl took an instant dislike to me the first time we met. There's no way I would have intentionally picked a fight with Carl."

Walter was about to argue when Henry cut him off. "I believe Dion is telling you the truth. He did ask me to warn you both not to test him too far. I declined, as I didn't think it would have made any difference. Unfortunately, Carl pushed his luck and learnt a very hard lesson in the process."

Walter did not answer but merely studied Dion, shaking his head dismissively.

"How's Chloe? She's not around?" Dion enquired to break the uneasy silence. He was well aware of Chloe's whereabouts and success. He had seen her modelling photos in magazines and had gone to see her when she was advertised as appearing at a large shopping centre in Perth. He had never made her aware of his presence, but just watched from the back of the plaza. She had grown into a beautiful woman, and seemed to blossom more every time he saw her.

Henry launched into a record of Chloe's success, beaming with pride. "I get a letter from her every month with copies of the magazine articles and photos she's in. She's in London now."

"And what of her grandfather?"

"Johnny went walkabout one day and never came back. That was one of the reasons she left. She would never have done so otherwise."

"Johnny was an elder of the local mob, wasn't he?"

Henry nodded. "He was. A fine old fellow in a way, but he was getting rather demanding."

"Did he ever talk about aboriginal rock art in this area?"

"No, never. Every rock painting is of sacred significance and not to be discussed with any whitefella. There's plenty of it around if you're interested though."

"It is an interest of mine. I was talking to a Professor Gates recently and she mentioned she had seen some spectacular rock art on Venus Downs."

"Professor Gates. I remember her, but you're going back ten or more years. I don't know how she did it, because he wouldn't even show me, but she managed to persuade old Johnny Quartpot to show her something quite unique. Mind you, it took her a few years to convince him she was not out to take advantage."

"Did she say where it was or take any photos?"

"No, she wouldn't talk about it and I know for a fact he made her leave her camera here. They were gone for more than a week and she was very excited when they got back."

Henry got up and walked into the homestead. "Anyone for another beer?"

Dion turned to Walter. "Do you know in what direction they went or where they camped?"

"They camped at the old eastern outstation." Walter didn't look up as he finished rolling a cigarette. "I was out there a week or so later and saw their tracks and the remains of campfires."

Dion nodded in satisfaction. He was right about the location, but where in that vast area was the unique rock art?

"Have you seen anything really out of the ordinary out there Walter?"

"What should I be looking for? There are hundreds of rock paintings all over the place." He sucked deeply on his cigarette.

"It could be a huge coloured snake and very large paintings of figures in robes."

Walter shook his head as he blew a cloud of smoke through his nostrils. "Nope, nothing like that. The only person who would know would be Chloe. Johnny used to take her on walkabout. She's the person you should ask, but I guarantee she won't tell you anything."

"Why's that?"

"Sacred sites and the dreaming of their ancestors. Chloe has a bit of abo in her and I'm picking old Johnny told her the stories and showed her everything. Some things are handed down through the male line only, but there's a lot of secret women's business too. She'd have been sworn to secrecy, and there's no way she would abuse that trust."

"Does Chloe come home often?"

"Last time she was here would have been about four years ago, when Carl walked in front of the bull that killed him. I don't think she wants to, or ever will come back again."

"But she's very attached to Henry, isn't she?."

"That'd be the only reason she would return, if something happened to him. But he's as fit as a Brahmin bull, so I can't see her coming home for a long time. It's strange but Henry took very little notice of her when she lived here, but he really looks forward to her letters and the articles she sends him."

"Do you like Chloe?"

Walter nodded. "Yeah, we got on okay, I suppose Carl really had the hots for her and I'm convinced something was going on between them."

"How did you get on with Johnny?"

"Not the best.I really didn't have much to do with him. He just hung around the place because this was his ancestral home. All the mob around here are somehow related to him."

"Any point in talking to them about what they may have seen?"

Walter gave a hollow laugh. "You may as well talk to a log. The moment you enquire about sacred sites or anything to do with their dreaming, their eyes glaze over and you'll be met with a blank stare. They're shit scared of the spirits of their ancestors. You're wasting your time."

Henry emerged, handing them each a stubby of beer. "We're mustering in the morning, but you're welcome to stay."

Dion thought for a moment. "I just might do that Henry, but only tomorrow. I'll have to get to work so I'll base myself in Wyndham, I think." He decided to direct attention from himself by referring to a subject on every pastoralist's mind; the weather, and cattle markets. "The seasons have been good for you, have they?"

"Coming into our fourth great season," Henry replied with a broad grin. "Plenty of rain, plenty of grass and good cattle prices. I've recently bought an adjoining property and a couple more further south in the Pilbara."

"And you're looking to take over someday I suppose Walter?"

Walter said nothing as he looked down at his beer.

"Probably, but there's no free rides in this life; so he'll have to work for it," Henry interjected.

"That's rich," Walter snapped. "You've been getting a free ride from Bill Hargraves over at Ascot Downs."

Henry glared at Walter and fought to suppress his anger. Dion could see he was about to explode.

"See you in the morning." Walter sensed the coming attack, quickly rose and strode out off to his room.

"Did I say something wrong?"

"No, Dion you didn't. He's easier to handle compared with Carl but underneath it all, he's cut from the same cloth." He was about to say something further when he checked himself. "Well, it's an early start tomorrow so if you'll excuse me, I'll be off to bed."

Dion watched the shadows lengthen and disappear as the sun set and the evening settled into an enveloping darkness. Henry and Walter had retired early after a long day drafting and branding cattle. The homestead was in silence but he knew Dotti and the cook were somewhere inside the sprawling premises. Once he was certain no one was around, he got up and walked around the corner to the corrugated sheet covering the window of Chloe's room. He tried to raise it, but it was obviously secured from the inside. He crept around to the rear door of Chloe's room that lead out to the shower cubicle. He gently eased it open a fraction, as he was unsure if someone was now occupying the room. Stepping inside, he closed the door quietly behind him and stood motionless, waiting for his eyes to adjust to the dark. The bed was empty. He shifted his vision to the dressing table where he could make out the shape of the jar he was looking for. Tiptoeing over, he was just about to pick it up when the beam from a flashlight blinded him.

"What do you think you're doing?"

He could not see the face but he knew it was Walter. He had been caught red-handed and there was no explanation for his presence in the room. Walter had anticipated his intentions.

"You know exactly why I'm here and what I'm looking for, don't you?"

"You're too late, mate; I have it. Let's get out of here and we can talk." Walter led Dion out through the back entrance and around onto the veranda. Nothing was said until they were both sitting at the far end of the veranda where they couldn't be heard.

"Okay, now come clean," Walter demanded. "Is this what you're after?" He opened his hand to disclose the red stone.

"May I?" Dion reached over and took it. "Shine your torch on the back while I hold it up."

"It's a diamond isn't it? But how did you know Chloe had it?"

"Yes, it is a diamond. I happened to be walking past her room on my first visit. She was standing there in the nude and I was horrified in case she'd seen me. I swear it was unintentional; I was just wandering around, lost in my thoughts. I had no idea it was her room. Anyway, she was holding the stone up to the light, looking at it. But now it's in my hand, I can confirm it is a diamond—and a very rare and valuable one at that."

"Why didn't you just ask if you could look at it?"

"That would have been too awkward. How would I explain I'd been looking through an open window at a naked girl holding up a red rock, especially as I was a priest at the time?"

Walter gave a low laugh as he took the stone back. "Well, you've seen more than I have. You're a bloody peeping Tom. We had you wrong. Carl and I thought you were just another shirt-lifting priest."

Dion ignored the remark. "Anyway, it went right out of my mind until I began studying diamonds during my university course. It came back to me when I was shown a pink diamond from Argyle. A very soft pink compared to that in your hand."

"So, the story about looking for copper and gold is complete bullshit. You came back here to steal this stone."

Dion nodded. "I suppose if I'd been able to take the stone without anyone noticing, I would have. However, my real intention is to find out where Chloe actually got it from. Where did she pick it up, do you know?

Walter shook his head. "Are you any the wiser?"

"I am in a way. I don't think she just picked it up. I believe her grandfather gave it to her."

"Old Johnny Quartpot?"

"Yes, when I was first here, I saw her ride in with him. Henry said they'd been on walkabout for a week or more. It was after that I saw her holding the stone up to the light. My guess is Johnny gave it to her during the course of that week."

"So you think it came from somewhere on Venus Downs?"

"I don't have conclusive proof. The only person who could tell me is Chloe. You must have ridden over every inch of this country, mustering cattle. Have you seen any rock art which you would describe as being spectacular?"

Walter shook his head. "You've already asked me that. I can't say I have. There are hundreds of rock art paintings all over the property, but nothing that stands out."

A phone began to ring in the homestead. "I'd better get that. I don't know who it would be at this time of night. Back in a moment."

Dion could hear Walter talking, but he had lowered his voice so the conversation was inaudible. "Okay, will do," was all he heard before the receiver was put down. Walter came back out with a strange look on his face.

"You look worried Walter. Something wrong?"

"No. Where were we? Yeah, rock art. You reckon this diamond comes from the vicinity of some outstanding rock art?"

"I believe it's possible. It must be well hidden if you've never seen it, but I believe it's out there somewhere."

"How do you normally look for diamonds?"

"It's a very expensive, long and involved process. Do you want me to tell you about it?"

"Nah, it's way above my understanding. Talk about cattle and I'm all ears, otherwise I'm not particularly interested. So what do you reckon this stone is worth?"

Dion shrugged his shoulders. "You can't tell until an expert looks at it to see what it's like structurally. It's worth money, but beyond that I don't know."

"I thought Argyle was the only diamond mine in the Kimberley?"

"No, it's not. Ellendale is a small mine by comparison, but it produces exquisite yellow diamonds and who knows how many more diamond mines will be discovered in the future. This whole area is very prospective. The Kimberley covers a huge, relatively unexplored area. There are ample records of prospectors finding diamonds when they were panning for gold in the 19th century, although Argyle's the only recorded source of pink diamonds."

"Very interesting. Say, have you ever been in trouble with the law?"

"Why do you ask?"

"Nothing in particular. You've admitted you would have stolen this diamond. What else have you been up to?"

"Walter, the diamond isn't yours either. It belongs to Chloe."

"Well it's mine now. What she doesn't know won't hurt her and I doubt whether she'll even remember it, so I'm claiming it."

"Perhaps I should tell Henry about this. He may have a different view."

"You won't have time to do that priest." Walter sneered as he got up and walked off.

Dion was sitting outside his room watching the light of the new day slowly reveal the landscape's emerging colours when he saw a Toyota LandCruiser approaching. It was a police vehicle. As it pulled up in front of the homestead, Walter's comment the previous night became clear.

"Down here." The shout came from Walter who was leaning on his doorway smoking while pointing at Dion.

Two officers approached. "Is your name Dion Riley?"

Walter laughed. "He's Dion Murphy when he's around here."

"Riley or Murphy, I'm here to take you in for questioning."

"For what, may I ask?"

"You're under arrest for one murder and possibly two."

Dion made no comment as the officer read him his rights, handcuffed him and led him towards the cruiser.

Henry Boyce came out onto the veranda. One of the officers walked up and spoke quietly to him. "This guy's in a lot of trouble. We've charged him with the murder of a Margaret Gates and there's another death he could also be charged with."

"Margaret Gates? I know her. She was out here years ago. An anthropologist if I recall. Who's the other one he's suspected of doing in?"

"Professor Geoffrey Mayers, head of geology at the university. Murphy was a student of his. Ever heard of him?"

Henry shook his head. "How did he kill them? With a gun?"

"Can't tell you that, other than to say Riley was academically connected to both of them. It'll all come out in the trial no doubt, but Perth believes they have him nailed."

"Murphy or Riley? I knew him as Father Murphy."

"Debatable. He came to Australia using a passport in the name or Riley, but his real name is Murphy. He's got form in Ireland, so after he finishes a stretch here, he'll be deported as an illegal, no doubt."

"But he's a priest... or was. How the hell did he get away with that?"

"Luck of the Irish, I suppose," the officer replied with a deadpan grin. "I'll take any gear he brought and drive back in Marge's wagon."

Henry watched until the vehicles had disappeared into a cloud of rising dust. "Who would have believed it? What the hell was his motive for knocking off Margaret Gates—and what's he really up to out here?"

Walter shrugged. "Maybe he was looking for diamonds, who knows?"

Henry swung on him. "You know something, don't you? What's the connection?"

Walter held up his hands. "I don't know any more than you do."

"You knew the cops were coming."

"I took the call last night. It was late and didn't want to disturb you."

"Bullshit. You know I'm a light sleeper. I know you two were out on the veranda for a long time. What were you talking about?"

"Nothing in particular; I was just being friendly."

"You couldn't stand the guy, and suddenly you want to be his friend? I don't believe it."

19

enry was reading a week-old newspaper when an article caught his eye. "Interesting. I see Dion Murphy was acquitted of both Gates' and Mayers' murders. The jury didn't accept the blurred fingerprint found on Gates' belt had been positively identified as his, and there was nothing to connect him to Mayers' murder other than circumstantial evidence; the case was dismissed by the magistrate."

"So he walked free?"

"Yes, he spent six months in jail on remand before his trial, but that's not the end of it. He's been referred to Immigration due to the forged passport in the name of Riley. His real name is Murphy. It's likely he'll be on a plane back to Ireland in the near future".

Walter was sitting on the other side of the table with a mug of tea cupped in his hands. "I couldn't stand the red-headed arsehole. He'd better not show his face around here again, but it wouldn't surprise me if he did turn up."

Henry made no comment as he continued to turn the pages and read.

"There's nothing doing around here for a couple of weeks, Henry. I might take a holiday to Perth."

Henry looked over his paper. "Any particular reason?"

"I'd just like to take a break. I haven't been anywhere since I came here with Carl, other than that trip to Indonesia last year to look at those feed-lot operations."

"Yes, I think it would be a good idea to put some space between us for a few weeks." Their arguments had become more frequent and heated lately. "I'm going into Wyndham next week so I'll take you in so you can catch a flight. Make sure you go and say hello to Aunt Elizabeth when you get to Perth."

"I'll do that, but I've no intention of staying with her."

Walter booked into a cheap hotel. The first thing he did when he got to his room was pick up the phone book. There were two diamond merchants listed. The name Anton Steiner appealed to him so he dialled the number. After a short conversation, an appointment was made for the following morning.

Steiner did not believe in wasting money on upmarket premises; he spent it on security instead. The doorway to his office was steel lined with two touch-pads for coded locks. Above and just out of reach was a single security camera which matched a camera directly opposite the lift doors.

"Please look into the camera and state your name," came the command after Walter pushed the doorbell. There was a heavy click as the door released and swung slightly inwards. He pushed the door open to be confronted by a tiny foyer devoid of furniture except for a large one-way mirror. The door to the right of the mirror opened.

Steiner was a small man, impeccably dressed with an unsmiling, defensive expression. "Please come in Mr Boyce."

Walter was ushered into a small, windowless office that was also devoid of any adornment. The ancient typist's chair on Steiner's side of the cheap veneer desk was matched on the visitors' side by two waiting room chairs that appeared to have been retrieved from a garage sale. The only imposing and expensive feature in the room were two Chubb safes, which took up the whole rear of the wall behind Steiner. The desk was bare, except a large magnifying light and a set of diamond scales housed in an ebony case. Steiner indicated for Walter to sit down.

"What can I do for you Mr Boyce? You said you had something that maybe of interest."

Walter reached into his satchel and withdrew the tissue-wrapped diamond from an inside pocket. "Is this a diamond and what's it worth?"

Steiner slowly unwrapped the diamond, flattening the tissue on which it was sitting.

Walter watched for a reaction. Steiner's expression remained neutral, but a nervous twitch of his long fingers betrayed his excitement. He opened a drawer, taking out a set of tweezers and a jeweller's loupe. He leant across, flipped the switch of the desk lamp and picked up the diamond with the tweezers. With his right hand, he brought the loupe to his eye, slowly turning the stone into the glare of the light. He put the loupe down, removed the cabinet covering the scales and dropped the diamond onto the pan. He noted the weight on a pad and began to write some notes.

Finally, he looked up. "It's a magnificent stone. Where did you get it, may I ask?"

"I'm not prepared to tell you that."

"It's an Argyle."

"No it's not, Mr Steiner."

"Well, I know it didn't come from anywhere else in the world. It has all the characteristics of an Argyle gem. If it is an Argyle, it is obviously stolen and you could be in big trouble."

"It's not an Argyle, and I can assure you it's not stolen."

Steiner picked up the gem again, turning it in every direction. He put it down, then picked it up on another plane to peer deep within the crystal. "Not a carbon inclusion and no crazing. It's an absolutely faultless stone with magnificent colour. Do you have any more?"

"I don't know at this stage. I really only came to get your opinion, confirm it's a diamond and guess its value."

"I'll show you what this stone is competing with." Steiner turned to one of the safes and with his back to Walter, dialled in the combination and spun the wheels to withdraw the locking pins. He slowly dragged the heavy door open, twirled another small knob on one of the many internal drawers and withdrew a couple of glycine-wrapped packages. He opened them reveal two brilliant-cut pink diamonds.

"These are priceless pinks." Steiner motioned his hand across the top of the open parcels. "As you can see, there's no comparison with the colour of your stone, which I believe would cut to at least ten carats. It is without doubt the finest coloured diamond I've ever seen—and I've been in this business more than forty years. It is the red of the finest Burmese ruby, referred to as 'pigeon blood' red, but I've never seen a diamond to match this. May I buy it from you?"

Walter shook his head. "It's actually not mine Mr Steiner. I'm committed to give it back."

"But you said it's not stolen."

"As I've already said, it's not."

"You're not going to walk around Perth with it, are you?"

"I plan to. I don't have a safe like yours."

"Let me keep it here for you. It will be safe, I guarantee that."

Walter shook his head. "I think it will be safer with me. You and I are the only ones who know about it and I can count on you being discreet, can't I? After all, other than you, who would know I'm carrying something extremely valuable?"

Steiner's expression hardened as he began to fold his diamonds away. "That's true, but to walk around with such a stone is like walking around with the Mona Lisa tucked under your arm. Unthinkable."

"If you divulge anything of its existence Mr Steiner, you can forget about ever handling this stone again—or any future dealings."

Steiner reached into a drawer and took out a wrapping, opening it to reveal the glycine inner envelope. Walter watched as he reverently folded the diamond into the paper and pushed it across to him.

"Take care Mr Boyce. You have one of the world's most precious gems in your possession. That diamond is unique, absolutely unique. Just to look at a stone such as this is a once in a lifetime experience. You will bring it back, won't you? I would really like to have a good look at it under a microscope. I will photograph and record its structure. Even if it was stolen and cut into several gems, I will be able to identify them as coming from that one stone.

"You're exaggerating, surely?"

The diamond merchant's expression hardened. Walter could see Steiner took his flippant remark seriously. "Please don't insult me Mr Boyce. I would not have said such a thing unless I meant it."

"I didn't mean to insult you. I just didn't realise it could be done."

"Diamond merchants have been fingerprinting diamonds for years. Most of us can just look at a diamond and identify its origin. That's why I want to look at your diamond in more detail."

"And you would like to determine whether it is really from Argyle; a stolen gem that escaped security?"

Steiner nodded slowly. "Yes, I want to eliminate it's an Argyle and determine what you say is correct. I don't want to be handling stolen gemstones. You must have some idea where the diamond came from. Do you or it's 'owner' have title to the ground?"

Walter ignored the question, reached over and picked up the parcel. Steiner took the cue, stood up and moved towards the door. "Remember, you can always leave the diamond with me. It will be completely safe."

"I'll be in touch Mr Steiner. Thank you for giving me your opinion."

Steiner shook his hand before showing him out the door. Walter heard the door close solidly behind him. The corridor was empty and quiet. Suddenly, he felt very vulnerable. It felt as if every criminal in the country knew what he was carrying. How trustworthy was Steiner? Not very, his instincts told him.

The hammering on the door was loud and insistent. Walter shook himself awake, glancing at the desk clock as he turned on the lamp.

"Who the hell is it?"

"Police. Open the door!"

Walter threw his covers back and made to get up just as the door was flung open and two men in plain clothes entered the room. "Walter Boyce?" The larger of the pair advanced towards him while the other stood guard in the doorway. Behind him, he could make out the figure of the night manager, who had obviously let them in.

Walter nodded. "What do you want?"

"We ask the questions, sport. You just answer them. I've got a warrant to search this room." The younger detective flashed a sheet of paper in front of Walter's face.

"Am I under arrest for something?"

"Not yet, but I would caution you that you are under investigation."

"Well, if I'm not under arrest, I've got nothing to talk to you about," Walter replied defiantly. "When you tell me why you're here and what you want, I'll be happy to co-operate, but at this time of the morning I don't see how I can assist you."

The fat detective ignored him. "Get your gear on Boyce. You're coming with us."

"Not likely. If I'm not under arrest, I don't have to go anywhere with you."

The punch hit him in the base of the stomach and doubling up he fell to the floor in excruciating pain. He fought for breath as he writhed in agony with his knees tucked up into his belly. The detective stood over him, but said nothing as he watched him slowly regain his breath and pull himself up to sit on the bed. The other detective in the doorway had not said a word, nor made any move to restrain his companion.

"When I tell you to do something arsehole, you do it. Now get your clothes on or I'll drag you down in your jocks. Your choice."

Walter needed no further bidding. He pulled on his shirt and trousers. Putting on his socks was an effort that caused him pain with every movement. He could feel the tortured muscles of his stomach as he finally slipped into his shoes and stood up. Both detectives were watching him with menace, alert to any wrong move that would result in another assault. The younger detective snapped the cuffs on, jerking him towards the door. He was bundled into the police cruiser, his head pushed down with force as he was propelled into the back seat. Not a word was spoken during the five-minute ride.

A uniformed officer looked up as they walked him past the reception desk without a word, through to the back of the station and into a small interview room. He was pushed down into a chair while the officers took chairs on the other side of the desk. "Okay Boyce, we can do this the hard way or the easy way. Which way do you want it?"

"I want a lawyer, you thug." Walter knew the routine. He was no longer intimidated.

The two officers got up without a word and left the room, slamming the door behind them. Walter waited for them to come back to work him over again. He sat there for an hour just staring into space, contemplating his predicament. He got up and tried the door, but it was locked. Finally, an officer who was not one of the original two opened the door and looked in. He looked lost and bewildered as though he was expecting to see someone he recognised. The door closed for a moment and then opened again as he walked in and sat down at the desk. He opened a folder, studying the contents for a few moments before looking up.

"You dickheads never change the routine, do you?" Walter was grinning at the thought of the times he and Carl had been picked up as juveniles and subjected to the attempted grilling he knew was about to happen.

The officer ignored him. "You've been told why you're here have you Mr Boyce?"

"I've been told nothing and I don't know why I've been roughed up by a thug and brought here."

The officer raised his eyebrows in mock surprise. "You say you were roughed up. If you wish to lay a formal complaint, you may do so later."

"One of the nameless plods who broke into my room assaulted me and dragged me here," Walter retorted angrily. "Look, just stop playing the good cop, bad cop crap, will you and tell me what this is all about?"

"I'm Detective Morrison. I thought your appearance here had been fully explained to you. You're here because you're a suspect in the theft of a diamond from the Argyle mine."

"Whoa, just a minute. Before we go any further with this, I demand to see a lawyer. This sounds serious—I want professional advice."

"If you can give me the name and number of your lawyer I'll have someone contact him. As for a lawyer on general call, there are no such species around at this time of day. Do you have someone you would like me to contact?"

"No, I don't know anyone. I wouldn't know where to start."

"Well, I suggest we get on with this interview. It will save both of us a lot of time and you can be on your way in an hour or so."

"Go to hell. I think I'll be on my way now. You haven't arrested me and cannot hold me unless you lay charges. Isn't that correct?"

Morrison snapped the folder shut, and stood up. "You are quite right Mr Boyce. You are not under arrest—yet.

But I can assure you, you cannot leave until I make further enquiries."

Walter watched as Morrison left the room, quietly closing the door behind him. He could hear the increasing sound of morning traffic when Morrison reappeared an hour later with another person. "Mr DiBrito has agreed to represent you. I'll leave you for ten minutes to get acquainted and then we'll see if we can't make some headway in this investigation."

"Elliott DiBrito, Mr Boyce." The lawyer thrust his hand out as the door closed behind Morrison. "Looks like they're investigating you for some pretty heavy shit involving the theft of a diamond from the Argyle mine. Worth millions, they say. Tell me your side of the story and let's see if I can't get you out of here."

DiBrito reached for his soft leather briefcase. A Mont Blanc pen appeared in his right hand and Walter watched as he scrawled the date and client's name at the top of the elaborately headed foolscap pad. "Okay, tell me about it."

Walter relayed the early morning events. DiBrito nodded as he wrote, his questions clinical and unemotional. Walter had his suspicions and was wary of anyone having anything to do with the law.

"Who do you work for, me or the cops?"

DiBrito folded his pad, pocketed his pen and made to stand up. "Mr Boyce, it is written all over your face you don't trust me. I advise you to get yourself another lawyer because it would be unethical for me to carry on under the circumstances. If you don't know anyone, I can give you the names of a couple of solicitors for you to contact. I don't work for the police. I represent the people who don't know, can't afford, or don't want to contact their own lawyer when apprehended. I do my rounds early because there are invariably some well-heeled drunks who'll get caught driving their cars, generally with someone other than their wife in the passenger seat. They want anonymity and discretion. Morrison is a good guy. Those two recently promoted detectives who picked you up, Connors and Penisi, are a couple of tough hombres. My advice is to keep well clear of that dynamic duo."

Walter waived his hand for the lawyer to sit down. "Apologies, I'm just furious at being treated like this."

The door opened. DiBrito's expression hardened as Connors and Penisi came into the room.

"What happened to Detective Morrison?"

"Decided to go for a coffee. This is our case, counsellor."

They slumped into the chairs opposite. Connors, the fat detective who had slugged Walter, leaned halfway across the desk.

"Boyce, you showed Anton Steiner a diamond; a red diamond to be exact. A diamond worth millions, obviously stolen from Argyle. Where did you get it? Who gave it to you?"

Walter's suspicions about Steiner were confirmed. If he had left the diamond with him, he would never have seen it again. "Do you have proof it came from Argyle?"

"You're admitting you have it then?"

Walter met the officer's gaze, but did not reply.

Connors leaned closer, his foul breath made worse by the stench of stale tobacco. "I'm investigating the theft of diamonds, in particular pink diamonds from Argyle. I want to see that diamond, and I want to know where or who you got it from. You'll sit there until I find out."

DiBrito intervened. "Detective, you're threatening my client. You know the limitations as well as I do. Either charge him or he's out of here."

Connors swung on the lawyer. "Go screw yourself, DiBrito. Your client is mixed up in some dirty business; I'll say what I like to him."

DiBrito just shrugged, completely unfazed by the insult.

Walter looked at Connors with a cynical grin. He knew he had his measure. "Steiner told you the diamond didn't come from Argyle, didn't he? He would have told you it was unique and he'd never seen anything like it. I'm not going to tell you where I got it from, or show it to you, but I can tell you it definitely did not come from Argyle."

"You're obstructing a police investigation into stolen goods."

"Well, charge him!" DiBrito snapped. "The court can direct the diamond be lodged in a bank for safekeeping while its provenance is established. That way, it won't fall into your hands and disappear."

"Watch your step, counsellor."

DiBrito smiled, satisfied his barb had hit home.

Connors leaned back in his chair, his gut flowing over the front of his tightly drawn belt. Walter could still feel the ache of his strained stomach muscles from where he had been punched hours earlier. Connors projected evil, a man to steer well clear of, Walter noted.

The door opened and two people entered: a male who looked at Connors and shook his head. The other was a female whose face was devoid of expression or emotion. Walter did not have to be a mind reader to work out what had happened. His hotel room had been thoroughly searched and they had come up empty, but he felt somewhat alarmed by the presence of the woman.

"Okay Boyce. You're going to get a physical. This lady is a police medic and she's going to look up your arse."

DeBrito began to protest. "You've got no grounds for this gross abuse of process. What the hell do you think you're doing?"

"I suspect your client is concealing something on his person," Connors replied with an offensive grin. "I want him checked out. I've all the power I need to conduct a full body and internal search. If you don't like it, go lay a complaint. Okay Boyce into the next room and get all your gear off— and I mean everything."

The small, brightly lit room had a single doctor's examination table. As he stripped off, Penisi searched through the pockets and felt along the seams of his pants and shirt.

"Lie on your side on the couch," instructed the female medic, pulling on a pair of latex gloves. "Bend your knees into your chest and hold them there." She bent down, and he felt a finger disappear into his anus. He cringed in pain as it was pushed to its full extent and moved around in the search for the diamond.

"Nothing." She stripped off the gloves and threw them into a bin before striding out of the room.

Walter rolled off the couch as Penisi finished searching his clothes and threw them to him.

"So it's not in your hotel room and it's not up your ginger— what have you done with it?" Connors snarled. Walter said nothing. "You and your client can fuck off now counsellor."

Walter was shocked at the sudden capitulation, but needed no second bidding to finish dressing and follow his lawyer from the room.

"What did he do with it?" Connors looked enquiringly at Penisi as he slowly stirred an instant coffee in an oversized mug.

"Can't be too far way. He's obviously stashed it somewhere. Did you say Steiner actually put a value on it for him?"

"Not a dollar value. He just said it was priceless."

"I thought he had more brains than that. He's getting really sloppy."

Penisi hesitated. "And there was one more thing he did."

Connors stopped stirring and a look of dread came over his face. "He fucked up, didn't he?"

"Yes, he got all excited and showed Boyce some Argyle pinks for comparison."

"He fucking what?" Connors' face went crimson. He clenched his fist so tight, he bent the teaspoon he was holding in half. "They're our pinks. I've already tipped him off he's under investigation for fencing stolen diamonds and yet he goes and shows them to a complete stranger. How did he know he wasn't being set up? The stupid schmuck could have blown us all away. I don't fancy a stretch in the can for his fucking stupidity. This is getting dangerous. That must be one hell of a stone Boyce has."

"Yep, Steiner said he'd never seen a gem like it and ruled it out as being from Argyle. Why didn't you just charge him with being in possession of stolen goods? He would have been forced to hand it over."

"DiBrito was onto that one. That little bastard is sharp and I think he smelt a rat. Lodge it with the court and it's out of our grasp. I want this kept under wraps. I want that diamond."

"We're doing okay now. Why push our luck?"

Connors slowly sipped his coffee. "Because I'm pissed off with being an underpaid cop at every bastard's command. Okay, we've got a nice little game going, but one more slip from Steiner and it's goodbye Connors and Penisi. At present, we're exposed. How do you think Steiner would hold up under some heavy pressure? I could bust that little pansy in five minutes. It would only take one of the junior constables in Internal Affairs ten minutes and they'd have us cold. Steiner would implicate us straight off. We've got to wind the operation down."

"Then why do you want the Boyce diamond?"

"Because it's worth a fortune. We only have to split the proceeds by two, and it can't be identified as being stolen from Argyle if Steiner is correct. We can take a trip up to the Kimberley and say we picked it up while prospecting. Who's to dispute that?"

"What about Boyce? He could blow the whistle."

"He could if we let him. First we find the diamond and then we take Boyce for a stroll in the sand hills."

"You're serious, aren't you?"

"You're damned right I'm serious. Argyle has woken up that diamonds are being stolen. I got that tip off from our man at the mine. Everyone in security is under investigation, including him. He used to fly down to deliver the goods personally, but he's already been questioned as to why he made the trip every month. They know very well he's an ex-copper who used to be attached to this division. Security is the natural starting point for any investigation. He's worried they'll put a tab on him and follow him straight to Steiner. He knows everyone in security has their phone tapped so that's why we've got to call an end to our nice little earner. Anyway, I'm sure Steiner has been ripping us off."

"How long before he fences what's left?"

"It could take some time. White diamonds are easy to get rid of, but pinks are a different story. They can only be fenced to collectors, or buyers who will keep shtum, but only at a severe discount to their real value. The heat's building up; it's time to get out of the kitchen."

Penisi nodded. "I've been thinking. You know that Irish character up on those murder charges a while back. Do you think there's any connection?"

"In what way?"

"What was his name? Ah, yes—Murphy, Dion Murphy. Murphy was a geologist who was arrested near Wyndham, accused of murdering two professors, Margaret Gates and Geoffrey Mayers. He was acquitted of murdering Gates but in the case of Mayers, the charges were suddenly dropped. Gates was an anthropologist who worked throughout the Kimberley, while Mayers was head of the geology department and Murphy's mentor. I recall something about diamonds came up in the course of that trial. Apparently, all of Mayers' records had disappeared."

Connors smiled at his associate. "I know about those records. In fact, I've read them. I got wind from a friend of mine in Homicide before Murphy was arrested that Mayers' death could somehow be connected with diamonds."

"You've what?"

"Yeah, I was ahead of the game on that one. Homicide were slow off the mark. As soon as I got the tip off, I started my own investigation. With a little bit of discreet enquiry, I found out Murphy—or Riley as he was known at the university, was Mayers' star pupil in the search for diamonds in the Kimberley. I went through his files at the university, but there wasn't much of interest in them. I struck gold when I searched his flat and took everything I could lay my hands on."

"Homicide weren't aware of what you were up to?"

"No, they were on overload at the time and were waiting on the results of an autopsy before they could confirm Mayers had been murdered. Remember, you lost that bet and had to buy me a carton of beer? Anyway, even when it was confirmed it took them a further week to act and by that time, there wasn't much for them to find in the way of a paper trail. They were reduced to relying on the Gates' death because they had a partial fingerprint of Murphy's. The prosecution tried to allege he threw her down a flight of stairs, but the jury didn't accept a partial fingerprint on her belt buckle was proof enough. Furthermore, the prosecution couldn't establish motive or his presence at the scene of her death. When I connected Murphy to Mayers and what they were up to, I decided to undertake a clandestine search of Mayers' apartment. From what I read, Mayers was on the hunt for the source of red diamonds and he'd even pinpointed where to look. The place was Venus Downs, and guess where our Walter Boyce with the red diamond comes from? Mayers' notes state he was being backed by a group of investors and Murphy was to take charge of the exploration. My bet is Murphy was aware of where the diamond came from and was also aware that Boyce had it."

"You mean to say Homicide didn't make the connection? But something about diamonds was mentioned at the trial?"

"True, but nothing was mentioned about *red* diamonds and Murphy didn't volunteer anything other than he was commissioned by Mayers to go to the Kimberley to look for diamonds. Any number of exploration companies have been looking for diamonds in the Kimberley for years, so that was nothing new."

"But you connected the dots and got to Murphy, didn't you?"

"Smart thinking, Penisi. But I didn't really connect the dots until I searched Murphy's flat and found his old diaries, and more of Mayers' files."

"Mayers could have given the files to him. Surely that supposition wouldn't fly in court?"

"I don't know about that. I found file after file all relating to the one subject of a particular red diamond given to some Indian wallah hundreds of years ago and its possible source coming from somewhere in the Kimberley. Years of notes and maps all neatly dated and archived. No professor would just hand over a life's work for a student to study at home like that. I believe Murphy stole them to remove all trace of Mayers' theory as to the source of the diamond and that's why the subject of a red diamond was never mentioned in evidence. Murphy knew if he eventually discovered the source of the diamond, he could claim it as his own. Such a discovery could be worth billions and Murphy wasn't prepared to share it. I don't believe Mayers got around to telling the syndicate he had pinpointed the general area, or had assigned Murphy to the search. If he had, it would have surfaced at the trial along with his diaries and files."

"When did you get to Murphy?"

"After the case was thrown out, I contacted him and we had a quiet beer. I explained I had strong evidence suggesting he murdered Mayers and had stolen his files."

"I'll bet he laughed in your face."

"That's exactly what he did, but I could see I had his measure. He must have wondered where all Mayers' stolen files, along with his own personal diaries had gone. He couldn't report the theft to the police for obvious reasons. His cockiness disappeared when I told him that I had them. I then drove another nail in. I showed him his diary note from years before where he wrote that he thought he'd seen a young girl by the name of Chloe Quartpot holding a red diamond at the Venus Downs homestead. He had been visiting as a priest newly assigned to the area. I then showed him a note written by Mayers a day or so before his murder. Mayers was a meticulous note taker. The note detailed a meeting with Murphy, then known as Riley, in which he queried his decision to give Riley the Kimberley assignment, raising concerns about his integrity and honesty. I think the professor realised he'd stuffed up but couldn't do anything about it at that stage."

"But Murphy was acquitted of the murder. He can't be tried again on new evidence; that would be double jeopardy. Your case has just fallen over boss."

Connors shook his head. "Not so, detective. He was acquitted of the murder of Gates, but he was never tried for the murder of Mayers because the evidence was dismissed at the hearing stage. The prosecution's case collapsed. Murphy thought he was in the clear."

"So you could demonstrate motive and strong circumstantial evidence of guilt in the murder of Mayers?"

"Yep, that's when Murphy folded and I knew I had him. I told him there was no statute of limitations when it came to murder. He would be going away for a long time and Ireland wouldn't be the destination. He might have got away with Gates' death, but he would have a hard job dodging the bullet for Mayers' demise."

"But wasn't Murphy deported?"

"No. He's right here. He managed to convince Immigration he was an asset to the country because of his professional qualifications and should be allowed to stay."

"I'm not with you."

"Murphy was found to have no case to answer in regards to Mayers' death, so the syndicate backing Mayers has agreed to go on financing his exploration program."

"So where do we fit in?"

"Penisi, sometimes I wonder about you. Can't you see we're in for a free ride? It will cost us nothing. If Murphy finds anything, he won't be telling the syndicate. Instead, an offshore company will suddenly apply for an exploration licence over the ground. Murphy is between a rock and a hard place and will do exactly what I tell him. Meanwhile, I want you to assign a tail on Boyce and make sure the hotel informs us the moment he checks out. Check out the post offices between Steiner's office and the hotel; he may have hired a box and posted the diamond to himself. Or he may have posted it to someone he knows in Perth or given it to someone he knows, which I think is unlikely. He had a bit of form as a kid years back, and I hardly think he would trust any of his past buddies."

Walter opened the door to his room and was faced with a total mess of bedclothes strewn across the floor. The bed's mattress was upturned, drawers had been pulled out and the bedside cabinets moved out from the wall to look for anything concealed behind them. His carryall bag was lying on top of clothing indiscriminately tossed onto the bed base. The liner of the bag had been torn from the backing. He picked up his passport from the floor. He had forgotten about it being in one of the inner pockets of his bag where he had shoved it after returning from Indonesia. In the bathroom, the contents of his toilet bag had been emptied into the sink and onto the tiled floor, his shaving brush and deodorant stick had been crushed under a heel to look for anything hidden inside.

He gave a wry smile and nodded. His suspicions about Steiner were correct. As soon as he had left his premises he had found a post office, purchased a padded envelope, addressed it, wrapped the gem in a couple of sheets of paper and tossed it into the mailbox. He found a phone outside the post office and phoned Elizabeth Murdoch. She was startled to hear from him, but agreed to hold the package for him until he retrieved it in a day or so. He was taking a risk, but he sensed something unpleasant was about to happen. The safest course was to get rid of the diamond into trusted hands.

Walter retrieved his clothes and hung them back in the robe before calling down for room service to makeup the room again. He needed a strong coffee and something to eat. The receptionist at the front desk smiled at him as he got out of the lift.

He made his way to the hotel's café and ordered a ham and cheese croissant. He sat idly stirring his coffee, watching the passers-by when he noticed a sloppily dressed person sitting on the bus stop bench facing directly into the café's entrance. His alert antenna went up as he recalled his time spent dodging the law between the ages of nine and fourteen. Maturity combined with street smarts came at an early age. When he and Carl were shoplifting, the floor detectives may as well have been wearing a neon sign, they were so easy to identify, as were plain clothes officers at the racetrack and shopping centres. He had been in and out of police stations so often it only took a glance to recognise them for what they were, no matter how hard they tried to blend in.

He studied the male. Mid-thirties, dressed in jeans and sneakers with long hair draped over the collar of a leather jacket covering a screen-printed tee-shirt. The regular stream of buses came and went, but the person remained seated. Occasionally, two buses would pull up one behind the other and the passengers would stream past, blocking the view of the café. Walter decided to confirm what he already knew as he waited for two buses to pull up before quickly rising and moving to a table obscured from the street by a pillar. The buses departed, but it took a few seconds before the tail noticed Walter had disappeared. He stood up and after looking up and down the street to see if Walter had joined the throng of movement, he headed directly for the café. Just as he was about to enter, Walter stood up from where he had been sitting in the shadowed part of the coffee bar and brushed past him without looking at him. He walked slowly down the street pretending to window-shop and finally entered a book store where he lost himself amongst the shelves of latest release fiction. He noticed a stairway leading up to another section. He ascended, to the mezzanine level, picked up a book and sat down at a table to read. He was not concerned about the tail; it just confirmed he was under surveillance. He could not concentrate. He put the book down and slowly walked back to the hotel.

The room had been made up so he kicked off his shoes and lay back on the bed while switching on the television. He took no notice, his mind deep in contemplation as to how he would get himself and the diamond out of town unobserved. He dozed on and off until late afternoon when he awoke to some nameless women's programme. He reached for the remote to change channels, but paused as the announcer's words caught his attention.

"And for those of you with an interest in what Europe will be wearing this spring, here is the latest from the House of Germaine, entitled the Celtic look." The accented female voice trailed off as a tall, elegant model strutted down the runway. Walter was fascinated. She was beautiful but had a strange,

haunted expression. Her large, soft brown eyes and soft brown skin reminded him of someone. The fine features, the aquiline nose, the black hair. There was something about those eyes that bored into his brain. He sat bolt upright.

"Chloe!" he exclaimed. He realised he had been staring at her without really taking any notice, his mind far away from the model and the Milan fashion show where she was appearing. In an instant, he knew what he had to do. He was being tailed so it was obvious his phone line would also be tapped. He put on his jacket and went out onto the street to look for a payphone. After hanging up from his first phone call, he dialled a second.

"Hello?"

"Liz, it's Walter."

"When are you coming to see me, Walter? I received the package you sent."

"I'm rather busy Liz. I'm off to Europe, you see."

"Whatever for?"

"I want to see Chloe."

There was momentary silence. "Why do you want to see her?"

"I can't tell you other than to say it's something personal. I just saw her on television modelling in Milan."

"Yes, I saw her as well. She's quite beautiful, isn't she?"

"Do you know where she lives or do you have a phone number for her?"

"I haven't heard from her since she left for London. She's just too busy, I suppose."

Walter could tell by her tone he was being lied to. "But she lives in London, doesn't she?"

Elizabeth dodged the question. "How do you know she'll want to see you? I would leave it alone if I were you, Walter."

"Then you won't help me?"

"It's not a matter of not helping you. It's just that I don't know it's what Chloe would want."

"Would you do something for me then Liz? I'll phone you from London with the address of my hotel. Would you send the package to me there?"

"Why don't you pick it up and take it with you? Come for lunch tomorrow and I'll give it to you."

"I'm sorry, I can't. I'm catching a flight on Singapore Airlines and I'm on my way to the airport now."

"Well, in that case I'll meet you at the airline counter in half an hour. I don't want to be responsible if your parcel should go missing in the post."

Walter had already sighted his new tails, sitting in a parked car about fifty metres down the road with a clear view of the hotel entrance. Surely they could do better than that, or perhaps the game plan was to let him know they were onto him at all times. He strolled back to his room to think how he would get out of the hotel and to the airport without being detected. He knew if he checked out, they would follow him to the airport and subject him to a body search again. If that happened, he would miss his flight. He did not pack his bag, but left all his clothes in the drawers and wardrobe. He had noted the receptionist lift a phone when he went out previously, and she did it again as he exited the lift and strolled out onto the street. Out of the corner of his eye, he could see his tail was still there so he turned in the opposite direction. It was only metres to the corner where he swung left. The short street was thick with traffic, all going in the opposite direction to which he was walking. It was a one-way street. He could not believe his luck as he broke into a fast walk. He slowed down and quickly entered an arcade.

"You lost him!"

"I don't know that we've lost him, chief. He just appeared to go out for a walk, but he disappeared in all the pedestrian traffic."

Connors was furious. "And I take it you two were sitting in the bloody car goofing off instead of one of you waiting in the foyer. Right, I want one of you in that hotel around the clock. I don't care if he knows he's under surveillance, just keep the pressure on him. If he hasn't returned in a couple of hours, I want his room checked. And I warn you now, you'll both be back on the beat if he's given you the slip."

The line went dead before the young constable could answer.

20

Walter was tired. He tuned out to the incessant chatter of the London cabbie.

"Any particular hotel guv?"

"Can you recommend one that's not too expensive?"

The cabbie laughed. "You're in London now guv. Nothing's cheap in this town, but the Royal Lancaster on the other side of Hyde Park as good as any. Very convenient and close to the tube."

Walter watched the terraced houses of Cromwell Road drift past as he thought about what had brought him here, and how he was going to make contact with Chloe. Once he found her, how would he approach her yet not disclose what it was she had actually been given?

It was a glorious spring morning. The plane trees of Bayswater Road were resplendent with their full canopies. Traffic hummed along Bourne on its way around to Marble Arch.

"Here you are guv." The cab pulled up in a circular driveway and the door was opened by a liveried doorman.

Walter paid the cab driver and followed the doorman, who was carrying his new bag and clothes purchased during a brief stopover in Singapore. One look at the bag would have told anyone here is a man who travels light, or perhaps a man on the run. Walter felt like the latter. The growth on his chin was like sandpaper and his shirt smelt like a Wyndham alleyway after the pubs closed.

"Did you have a good flight sir?" The receptionist was all smiles. Before he could open his mouth, she picked him as a colonial. He felt like telling her the truth about how it feels to be jammed in an economy class airplane seat for twenty-four hours, but simply returned her charming smile.

"Do you know how long you will be staying sir?"

"No, but I'd like a room for at least a week. You may be able to help me. If I wished to contact someone in the fashion modelling industry, where would I start?"

The receptionist didn't look up from her keyboard as she searched for a vacant room. "The modelling industry is huge. Without a name, I really can't help you. What is the name of the model you want to contact? I may be able to assist."

"Chloe, Chloe Quartpot, have you heard of her?"

The receptionist shook her head and giggled. "No, I've never heard of her. She mustn't be that well-known."

"I saw her on television. She was modelling for Germaine in Milan."

She looked up, her eyebrows arched in surprise. "You must mean Chloe Faroud, surely? That's the only model named Chloe I'm aware of. Mind you, she's never stayed here. I would imagine the Ritz or Savoy is more her style."

"Faroud? I don't think she would be the person I'm looking for."

"The only Chloe I know is married to Marcel Faroud, the Lebanese financier. She married him a year or so ago. It was cover to cover in *Prix* magazine. The glitterati of London turned up at the reception, including half of Lebanon."

"It can't be the Chloe I'm looking for," Walter shook his head. Surely she would have told Henry if she had married? And he doubted whether Liz would have been able to keep it a secret if it was the case.

"I'll bet she's in the latest issue of *Prix*. They would have covered Milan fashion week."

"*Prix?* I take it that's a popular magazine?"

"It certainly is Mr Boyce. If you're not in it, you don't rate. Obviously, it doesn't get down to Australia. She features in just about every issue. You'll find the latest issue over there in the magazine stall at our in-house newsagent."

Walter walked over to the shop and picked up the prominently featured magazine. He scanned the pages until he found the centrefold. On it were photos of Chloe, full page both sides walking towards the camera lens. Her long black lace dress complemented her stunning figure and dark, natural looks. Walter whistled quietly between his teeth in admiration. From Venus Downs to this. It was more than he could imagine. He continued turning the pages, which featured Chloe and her husband, sipping champagne and chatting with designers, politicians, royalty and the leading lights of the fashion industry. Walter studied the features of Marcel Faroud. He was a few inches taller than Chloe, of slim build, with striking good looks and a skin tone that matched hers. His head was tilted in an imperious pose, jet black hair swept back and carefully coiffured.

Faroud was smiling, but his eyes conveyed satisfaction as he paraded his trophy. A black dinner suit contrasted with a peacock-blue bow tie, ruffled silk shirt with matching cuffs just appearing proud of the suit sleeves to reveal matching sapphire cufflinks. And to think Carl had thought he was going to marry Chloe.

Walter paid for the magazine and walked back to reception. "I'll show you to your room, sir." The porter had picked up his bag and opened his hand to show he had the room key. Once they reached his room Walter was shown the facilities, given the obligatory demonstration of how the television remote worked, how the mini bar was accessed and then the porter began the practised hesitation of leaving the room; the same sequence Walter had noticed at the hotel in Perth. Walter pulled out two one pound coins and dropped them into the outstretched hand. He felt the English had deliberately designed the coin so its diminutive size would immediately embarrass guests into increasing the size of the tip.

He looked for a phone book, but there was none so he lay down on the bed, turned on the television, and slept properly for the first time in days. It was mid-afternoon when he awoke. The bar was already well occupied when he walked in. "What'll it be sir?"

"A beer, thanks."

"Australian beer, sir?" The experienced barman picked Walter's accent immediately.

"Yes. A Fosters please."

"A Fosters it is sir." He pulled the beer into a pint glass.

"Do you have a phone book I can look at?"

The barman reached under the counter and handed the heavy book to him. "Looking for someone in particular?"

"Yes. The surname is Faroud."

"Pretty common name. Let me help you." The barman took the book and flicked through. "Any particular area of London? I know the areas by looking at the numbers."

"It would have to be one of the most expensive, I would think. Right here in the heart of London."

The barman ran his finger down the page. "There's no Faroud within ten miles of here. Plenty out Uxbridge way though. There's an infestation of them out there. If he lives in London itself and is wealthy, he'll most likely have a silent number."

"Then how do you find someone in this city?"

"If you don't have an address or phone number, it's near impossible."

Walter was halfway through his beer when he suddenly had a thought. He went back to his room, picked up the *Prix* magazine and dialled their editorial number.

"*Prix* Editorial. How can I be of assistance?"

"I wonder if you could tell me of any upcoming fashion events?"

"We don't give out such information sir. Security is important to the people who attend these exclusive functions. I'm afraid I can't help you."

Walter thought fast. The accent on the other end of the phone sounded familiar. "Are you Australian?"

"I am, but that won't help you. The answer is still no."

"You must be from Perth then."

The girl laughed. "Why's that?"

"Because Perth birds have a hard attitude, but underneath they're all charmers."

"Listen, buster, I don't hail from Perth and it won't do you any good trying to guess where I come from. The answer is still no. Who do you want to know about anyway, not that I will tell you anything?"

"Chloe Quartpot, I mean Chloe Faroud, as she's now known."

"You know Chloe?" The voice sounded surprised.

"Yes, I know her very well."

"Why are you phoning *Prix* for information then? If you know her that well, surely you can just pick up the phone and talk to her."

"The problem is I haven't seen her in four years. I'm only here for a few days and I saw her in your mag. She's not listed in the phone book."

"Look, I've got to go; it's been nice talking to you."

"Can I buy you a drink after work?"

The request brought a loud peel of laughter. "A drink? You must think you're the last of the irresistibles. How old are you anyway? Not some dirty old geezer with a raincoat, are you?"

"No, I recently got defrocked for molesting some of my parishioners, but other than that I'm quite normal. I would still like to meet up with you and buy you that drink."

There was a long pause. "Okay, meet me at the Athenaeum Hotel in Piccadilly. The lounge bar at eight and I'll suss you out. I'm very overweight, five two, don't shave my legs or armpits and I wear thick glasses with heavy black rims. Sounds like you're the person I've been looking to walk into my life. You won't miss me. What's your name?"

Walter told her his first name, then laughed as he put down the phone. Was she joking? He hoped so. More importantly, would she show up?

It was just after seven when he set off up Bayswater Road then around Park Lane to Piccadilly. He needed some exercise after the inertia of the long flight. The lounge bar of the Athenaeum was busy when he entered. He ordered a beer and found a seat in the corner where he could observe everyone walking in. There was no one present resembling the appearance described to him. He finished his beer and looked at his watch. It was eight thirty. If she did not turn up by nine, he would give it away. He was about to get up to order another beer when a woman suddenly stopped in front of him.

"Walter?"

Walter nodded, trying to hide his surprise. Annie was neither fat, short, nor wore thick glasses. She was tall, slim and very attractive with short bobbed flaxen hair.

"Hi, I'm Annie Brittan from *Prix*. Are you the defrocked priest I'm supposed to be meeting?" She sat down opposite him with a wide grin on her face, appreciating his rugged handsomeness, and mischievous expression which appeared to mask something deeper.

Walter smiled, noticing her eyes scanning over him with appreciation. "What would you like to drink?"

"A rum and coke, thanks. I'm sorry I'm late, but we don't have set hours and I've just come from a reception at the Savoy."

"Was Chloe there?"

"Nice try, but I can tell you the answer is no. Well, let's get down to business. What can I do for you?"

Walter expressed a look of surprise. "I thought you said you couldn't give me any information about Chloe?"

"That was before I met you. Clearly you aren't some dirty old sod lusting after her. London is full of screwballs. Besides, I think you're rather good looking."

Walter was flattered. "Are all girls in this town like you? Straight to the point?"

"This is London. Anything goes and a girl no longer has to wait around for a guy to make all the moves. Now what can I tell you about Chloe?"

"I need to get in touch with her. Do you know her address or phone number?"

Annie looked at him strangely. "As I said before, if you know her as well as you say you do, I can't believe you don't know that already. What are you up to?"

"I'm not up to anything, I just want to see her before I leave town."

"I don't know her phone number because it's unlisted and without that, you can't get her address. Even if you did, it would be no use knocking on her door as you wouldn't get past Faroud's goons. I know her quite well from when I see her at functions, and I know her secretary, but it's all strictly business."

"Is Faroud a nasty character then?"

"You could say that. A very unpleasant man who surrounds himself with security. He's obsessed with Chloe; won't let her out of his sight. You won't get near her. Mind you, I don't blame him. This city is full of chancers and freaks wanting to touch or talk to her. Any celebrity or anyone with money takes every precaution to protect themselves."

"Can you get me into one of these functions?"

"You can't get in without an invitation and believe me, they check those very carefully. I don't see how I can possibly get you one. You know, I have a feeling there's something more to you wanting to meet her. What is it?"

"I want to talk to her about something at home. Something I think she knows a lot about. But it's not something I can talk to her about in front of her husband."

"You're not into something sinister, are you? Something from her past?"

"No, no, of course not. I promise it's honourable and completely above board."

"I'll see what I can do, but you must promise me you won't mention my name or that *Prix* is involved. I would get the boot on the spot. I know her secretary and can get Chloe's schedule, but getting you an invite into a function is a different matter altogether."

"I really would appreciate any help you can give me. If you can't get me an invite, just tell me where she's appearing next and I'll find some way of getting in the door."

"What's in it for me?"

"What do you want? Money?"

"No, I don't want money. I'm a journalist silly. I want a story. You say you know Chloe very well, but nothing is known about her or where she comes from. She was with the Paul LeClair Agency and that guy really knew how to promote her. The public loves a mystery and he was a master at prolonging that image. Where does she really come from? I heard a whisper she could be Australian and now you've confirmed it. Who is she really and what's her background?"

"Is it that important?"

"*Prix's* total focus is on celebrities, gossip, social life, whose been seen with whom at what parties or functions. Celebs, film stars, writers, football players, singers, merchant bankers, stockbrokers and every wannabe under the sun, all craving recognition, publicity and status. That's what I write about, that's what I get paid for and believe me, it's no easy lark; it's a seven day week job. Chloe is an enigma because no one can get near her. Her background appears to be a closed shop, and Marcel makes sure it stays that way. He calls himself a merchant banker but in my opinion, he's a professional letch. His hobbies are horses, roulette tables, blackjack and women. Why she ever married him has everyone guessing. What can you tell me?"

Walter smiled. "First things first. You get me an invite and I'll give you her life's story. Now, how about dinner, or do you have a prior engagement?"

"Sure, why not?"

"You obviously know all the interesting places to eat, so I'll let you make the choice."

Annie took Walter to a nondescript little Italian restaurant in Shepherd's Market. Annie was immediately recognised and shown a table. She greeted the patron in Italian, and kept up the banter until they were seated and menus thrust in front of them.

"I see you have influence."

"It helps when Valentino gets his photo in the mag, or his restaurant mentioned when he quietly lets it drop that someone I should know about is dining here."

"How often does that happen?"

Annie looked thoughtful. "Quite often. A couple of years ago, I gave him a few lines under a photo—I think the person we photographed with him was a well-known impresario. There are just so many restaurants in London, all fighting for attention and custom. I don't mind being shown to a good table and getting good service in return. Valentino gets recognition and I get a story with a discount thrown in."

"Do you speak languages other than Italian?"

"Italian, French and Spanish. I'm basic in them all, but when you talk to a restaurateur you're not expanding your vocabulary much beyond what each dish consists of." Annie broke off a piece of crust, dipping it in olive oil and balsamic vinegar. Try some, you'll like it." She signalled to the waiter. *"Uno bottiglia Valpolicella un duo specialita della casa."*

"They only speak Italian here?"

"No, they understand English perfectly well. I was just trying to impress you," Annie laughed.

The wine was served and minutes later, two plates of veal scaloppine were thrust in front of them without ceremony, along with the accompanying vegetables.

"I'm fascinated to know Chloe's background. You look like a country boy to me. Is that also her background? What a story. I can visualise the headline now: *"Bull Riding Super Model."*

"Could be, but we have a deal, don't we?"

"Oh yes, we do. I can sense a good story lurking." Annie pointed her knife at him accusingly. "The fact you've flown here from Australia to talk to someone you know very well but can't contact, smacks of intrigue."

"I'm not going to tell you why I must talk to her. Our deal is you make it possible for me to meet her. Then you'll get your background story."

"She's either the sole beneficiary of super-rich Uncle Bertie's estate, or she knows where there's a gold mine. Western Australia's full of gold, isn't it?"

Walter gave a strained laugh. He realised Annie had struck a chord and she knew it. He would have to be careful. She kept up her probing questions, but he parried them, changing the subject at every opportunity. They finished with coffee.

"What are you going to do now, Annie?"

"I'm going home to have a bath and flop into bed. Thanks for dinner."

"How about dinner and a show tomorrow night? Can you recommend anything?"

"That would be nice, provided I'm not assigned to attend some function at short notice. I'm free at the moment, but anything can pop up at *Prix*."

Valentino was already ushering them to the door with effusive Italian while he eyed another couple who had entered looking for a table.

Walter hailed a cab. "Which way are you going?"

"Bayswater."

"You can drop me off at Lancaster Gate on the way."

When the cab reached Walter's hotel, he handed the cabbie ten pounds and got out. He leaned in through the open rear window, his breath steamy in the cool night air.

Annie smiled. "I'll phone your hotel when I've spoken to Chloe's secretary in the morning. If you're not in, I'll leave a message. Otherwise, we'll meet in the Athenaeum at seven tomorrow evening."

Walter nodded and waved as he watched the cab pull away.

It was late afternoon when she finally called. "Be outside the front door at seven. I'll pick you up. Wear something smart. I've got you an invite to a fashion show featuring Chloe."

It was nearly seven thirty by the time a cab swept into the circular driveway. The door was thrown open. "Come on, get in. I'm running late," Annie commanded.

Walter had barely closed the door before the cab started to move off. The momentum thrust him back into the seat.

"I hope you appreciate this. I told the organisers you are a *Prix* stringer from Australia, here to report on the latest fashions. Make sure you don't open your mouth with that accent, otherwise they'll realise you're a phony with cow shit between your toes and toss you out."

The cab pulled into the narrow driveway of the Savoy. It was already crowded with cabs, Rolls Royces and Bentleys parked along the kerb. The beautiful people of London were basking in the glow of recognition from the flashing paparazzi cameras. Annie paid for the cab, tugged on Walter's sleeve and dragged him through the throng. "Just keep moving and don't lose me. Don't worry about manners, just push your way through."

The ballroom doors were closely guarded by a bevy of burley security personnel dressed in dinner suits. Annie showed their invitations and moved quickly into the huge room with an elevated runway set up along its middle. They were shown to their seats.

"Don't move unless someone puts a bomb under you. Oh, oh, here comes trouble. Don't say a word, I'll do the talking."

"Say, I think you're in my seat fella. You're not an accredited photographer." He held his camera to signify his profession.

"Hello Evan," Annie said sweetly. "I'd like you to meet Evan."

The photographer looked perplexed for a moment and then he twigged. "What the hell are you playing at, Annie? You know bloody well that's my seat. You stole my pass, didn't you? You thought I wouldn't get in the door and you'd get away with it. You know me better than that. No door stops me. On your bike fella, or I'll get security to remove you."

Annie stood up and pecked Evan on the cheek. "Evan, I'm working on a really important story and *this* Evan needs your seat." She stroked the photographer's cheek slowly. "Be a sweetie and join the other photographers in the back row and I'll let you take me out. This show is no big deal. You've seen a million of these before, there won't be any scoop photos, so please do as I ask." She held her smile and gently rubbed his arm.

"Bitch."

"Evan! I promise I'll go out with you and if you treat me right, I'll be your lover and slave for ever more."

"I want that in writing. I want you to announce that in front of the entire editorial staff," Evan replied, grinning evilly.

"I've already promised myself to all the other men, and even a few of the women, so it may be a while before we get around to consummating it. You understand, don't you?"

"God, I get horny just looking at you, Annie. One of these days—"

"You keep dreaming of that day Evan. I can't wait for it myself, but you must understand there are many in line before you. Now be a darling and piss off."

"Lovely, but a real dipstick," Annie murmured as he moved away. "And married with three kids, so I don't know how he'll find the time."

Walter chuckled to himself, shaking his head.

"What do you find so funny?"

"The way you handled that guy. You have no shame."

"Guilty as charged. Now wipe the grin off your face and look interested, the show's about to start. If our luck holds, we'll get to talk with Chloe before the evening's over."

Walter had never seen a live fashion parade before, but it was not much different to what he had seen on television; he was quickly bored with the cadaverous females parading clothes that he could not imagine any woman actually wearing in the street.

"What do you think?" Annie was amused by his deadpan look. "Yeah, I know it's all hype and crap, but that's the very basis of the fashion industry. Women want to be entertained and titillated, and that's why I have a job I enjoy. I love the invitations, the free flights, hotels and entertainment. Paris,

New York, Tokyo, Milan, you name it. Tokyo is my favourite. They really know how to lay it on and hand out rewards for favourable articles."

"You mean they bribe you?"

"Let's just say they pay for good service, just like a tip at a top restaurant. I work every angle if there's a buck in it, or a gift of some sort. That's the way the world works; you don't get anything for nothing. I'm hoping the time and effort I'm putting into you gives me a front page and centrefold, a real splash. Of course, I'll let Evan do the pics to keep him happy."

Walter shook his head. "I've never known anyone as confident or as full of bullshit as you."

"That's me," Annie grinned. "And just remember, we've got a deal. You'll never get near Chloe without me. Here she comes now."

The room was momentarily quiet, then spontaneous, polite applause began as the supermodel slowly strutted down the runway, seemingly oblivious to the ovation. Her trademark air of affected nonchalance and a slight countenance of disapproval was evident; her presence the result of countless rehearsals, a practised theatrical aura and mystery. She was a beautiful sight, an ethereal object whose impractical apparel was the subject of the display, but was totally overshadowed by her breathtaking body as it sashayed to the background music, claiming complete attention.

Walter drew in his breath. He now understood why Faroud was so protective of his trophy. She was the most beautiful woman he had ever laid eyes on. The diamond in his pocket was rough and uncut, in contrast to Chloe who was polished and perfect. They were two sides of a precious gem: one unfaceted; the other faceted to incomparable radiance.

Annie held her programme to her face and spoke in a lowered tone. "She's beautiful, isn't she? You can see now why she's paid millions. God, why wasn't I born that drop dead gorgeous?"

"You are gorgeous. Just a different type of beauty."

"You're full of it." She grabbed his arm. "Come on, that's her only appearance for tonight. Let's see if we can get into her dressing room." She thrust a notepad into his hand. "Just don't say a word while I try to get us past Faroud's minders."

Annie didn't hesitate. She barged towards the dressing rooms with an air of authority and certainty. Within seconds, she was into a smaller side room where Walter could clearly see Chloe standing bra-less in sheer panties. She took no notice of the models milling around as she slipped into a long evening dress. He was held up by people pushing in front of him while Annie slid easily through the crowd and up to Chloe, who broke into a broad smile of recognition. Someone stepped in front of him and he felt a rock hard hand in his chest. The man was the same height at Walter, but there the similarity ended. An expressionless bull-like head was facing him, with no visible neck set upon a massive torso bursting out of a dinner suit. Just as Walter was about to be shoved back into the crowd, Annie turned around to see where he was.

"Hey! He's with me. Let him through."

The Hulk took no notice of Annie and kept pushing Walter backwards.

"Let him through Massoud." The Hulk turned to see Chloe beckoning to Walter. Walter finally felt the pressure released from his chest.

"Chloe, I believe you know my friend Walter?"

Chloe had been distracted and was not really looking at the person Massoud was restraining. Her face expressed momentary shock as recognition dawned. "No, I don't believe I do. Where did we meet?"

Walter was as stunned as Annie. "Chloe, you know me. Why are you denying it?"

Chloe swung on Annie. "I've never met your friend before."

"He says he's from Australia and that you're related, or he knows you very well anyway."

"I have no family in Australia. Don't ever do this to me again," Chloe retorted angrily. She made to move past Walter, but he gently restrained her, deciding to play his ace.

He pulled the diamond out of his pocket, holding it in his cupped hand so no one other than Chloe could see what he was revealing. "I don't know what your game is, Chloe, but do you remember where you got this?"

"The eye of the rainbow serpent." She murmured quietly as the waves of memory rolled over her. "It's mine, you have no right to it!"

"Chloe, I want to know where it came from on Venus Downs." Walter closed his hand around the gem, thrusting it back into his jacket pocket.

Her expression suddenly changed. "I'm sorry, I can't help you. Now if you will excuse me."

"Can we meet somewhere? Can Annie contact you through your secretary?"

"That's not possible. I have a very busy schedule for the foreseeable future." She brushed past him.

Walter made to follow her, but was blocked by the Hulk in the dinner suit. For a moment, he thought the movement was accidental and attempted to step around him, but the

Hulk grabbed his arm to restrain him, and said nothing. It was then he noticed the reason for the obstruction.

Faroud had arrived and like a strutting peacock he held out his arm to Chloe. They were a perfect match for each other. To the unknowing, they were from the same ethnic background. He glared at Walter through hooded eyelids, his perfect white teeth set in a fixed, menacing grin.

Chloe gave Walter a quick glance as she broke into a smile to acknowledge the milling well-wishers. As she and her husband moved through into another room, Walter realised she had left him standing as probably the wealthiest man in the room. Who else amongst this lot would be walking around with a gem worth millions in their pocket? He was astounded. Why had she not acknowledged that she knew him?

"You lied to me. You don't really know her," Annie hissed.

"Annie, I can assure you I do know her, but why she carried on the way she did, I've no idea."

"Well, do I get my story?"

"Yes, I will give you the guts of her background. But first of all, I want to know where she lives. I'm going to follow her home."

"You mean 'we'. I'm coming with you. Let's wait in the lobby; it won't be any more than ten minutes before she leaves. She never stays for long."

Annie was correct. Within ten minutes, Faroud with Chloe on his arm swept past to the cloakroom. She reappeared in a long evening coat while Faroud maintained his affected air of a grandee, a fawn vicuna draped around his shoulders to leave his arms free. She glanced at Walter, but there was not a hint of acknowledgement as they waited momentarily for their limousine to pull up.

Annie was pulling at Walter's arm. "Come on, otherwise we'll lose them." She quickly walked past their limo, opened the door of a cab and climbed in, followed by Walter.

"Where to luv?"

"Just follow that limo pulling out now. Please don't lose him."

The cabbie nodded and moved in behind, turning left into the Strand, into Whitehall, then along Victoria Street, and finally into Eaton Square. They could see the limo slowing down ahead of them.

"Pull over here please cabbie. I don't want to get too close."

They watched as Faroud and Chloe alighted and arm in arm strode up to the front entrance of a mansion where the door was immediately opened by a servant.

"They do it in style, don't they?"

"There are no poor people in this neck of the woods," Annie replied. "Okay, cabbie, back to Soho."

Annie sat back, lost in thought for a minute. "I wonder why she didn't want to know you? Too late for a show now; let's find a decent restaurant."

Over a bowl of pasta, Walter told Annie everything he knew about Chloe and her background. She was fascinated, scribbling notes into her pad as he spoke.

"Is her story really of that much interest?" Walter swirled the spoon around in the froth of the cappuccino.

"Sure as hell is. Gossip centred around sex and money are what keeps the world spinning. Without gossip, no one would know who was shagging who. The more prurient and salacious the details, the better. It's what every red-blooded working girl and bored housewife wants to read and fantasise about. Gossip drives it. Look what the world was getting its rocks off on a few years ago. The president of France riding a motor scooter incognito for trysts with his lover topped off with a baguette for breakfast delivered by the secret service."

"You can't compare Chloe with his antics."

"I know, but Chloe is a real general interest story. It's a revelation Chloe is not the person we've been led to believe. We've all been assumed she's Lebanese or of some other middle eastern extraction, but she's not. She comes from the boondocks of Australia and is in fact part-aboriginal. I can't remember seeing anyone from that background matching her beauty or style."

Walter laughed. "It's like any race; there are some ugly ones and some good looking ones, but only a few stunners like Chloe."

"Is she related to you?"

"No, we're not related, but we lived on the same cattle station."

"Wonderful!" Annie chuckled. "I can imagine Faroud phoning his lawyers the moment the story appears instructing them to do a credit check to see if she owns part of the property. It wouldn't surprise me if he hasn't already done so. He must know her origins. When are you going back to Australia?"

"Not until I've spoken to Chloe and got an explanation from her. I want her to tell me the location of something only she knows about."

"What's that?"

Walter shrugged. "It's not relevant to you; it's something very personal to Chloe."

"I'm coming with you when you go. I'll talk to my editor and show her what I've got to date. I don't think it will take too much to convince her Chloe's background is well worth a follow up - just what our readers thrive on. It should shove some social-climbing tosspots and their sycophantic hangers-on off the front page and centre spread. This would be a major coup for me. You will take me back with you and show me around, won't you?"

"Sure, but I don't know when I'll be leaving. I must catch up with Chloe first, so don't go printing anything until I have. Promise me that?"

Annie nodded as she picked up the bill folder, studied it and inserted her credit card. "My shout. It's a legitimate dinner, so it's a legitimate expense."

Walter noticed the red light flashing on his phone after his shower. He dialled to retrieve the message.

"Hi Walter, Annie here. Chloe wants you to be at her place at ten sharp this morning. If you don't phone back within the next ten minutes I'll be gone, as I'm tied up for most of the morning."

Walter glanced at his watch. He was too late to return her call. He hastily got dressed and at the stipulated time was standing outside the house he had seen Chloe and her husband enter the night before. The iron gate was classical Victorian lace. It swung with the familiar squeal of unoiled hinges as he pushed it open. He reached the top step and was about to push the ancient bell when the front door suddenly opened. A maid of unknown nationality silently beckoned him to follow her into an ornate waiting room. She quickly left, closing the door quietly behind her. He looked around the room. The place reeked of money. It was a far cry from the sparse, basic furnishings of Venus Downs. He turned when he heard the door behind him open and Chloe walked in.

Although she took his breath away, he immediately noticed she wore a pained, anxious expression. "Walter, it's good to see you, but you can't stay long. Marcel is at the gym so we can talk for no more than half an hour, then you must leave. I'm sorry for my rudeness last night, but I couldn't acknowledge you in front of Marcel. He's extremely possessive."

"It was quite obvious with that goon hanging around. Are you frightened of him?"

Chloe ignored his question. "What is it you wish to know?" She rubbed her hands nervously and kept glancing out of the window.

"Chloe, the *'eye of the rainbow serpent'* as you called it, is in fact a very rare gem. It's a diamond, so it's very valuable. I know it comes from somewhere on Venus Downs. Will you tell me where you got it from?"

"I didn't know it was a diamond. Gramps gave it to me when we visited a sacred site. Do you have it with you? I'd like to see it again."

Walter took the diamond from his pocket, folded back the glycine wrapping and handed it to her. He watched her closely as she held it up almost reverently to her face. She trembled as she whispered in a lingua that Walter could not interpret, but he understood as being a sacred chant.

"Is this gem sacred to you?"

Chloe nodded. "Yes, it's sacred to the memory of Gramps. Now that I have it in my hands, the memories are flooding back. Everything he believed was steeped in superstition and lore. Every rock, ancient tree, waterhole and wandering stream, every gorge, every animal had a particular significance. He was a wonderful storyteller."

"If you are able to tell me the location where it was found, it could result in an incredible fortune, which I will share with you of course."

"I can see how important this is to you Walter, but it's also important to me. This stone is mine. It was given to me by Gramps and I'm not interested in showing you where it came from, or in sharing it with you."

"But why?"

"I loved Gramps dearly. He lived in the dreamtime of the rainbow serpent and everything it meant to him and his forbears. They were his totems and I cannot betray his trust by revealing a secret like that to you—and I know he would never have told you himself."

"Well, can I at least ask whether there's a painting of a giant snake and a large robed figure near where Gramps gave you the diamond? It would have been something quite spectacular in that neither Henry nor I have ever seen on Venus Downs."

Chloe was about to say something, but hesitated. Neither of them had heard the front door being opened, but Chloe jumped and looked frightened when she heard voices in the hallway. "It's Marcel, he's back early!" She quickly stood up just as the door began to open. Walter snatched up the diamond and hastily thrust it into his jacket pocket.

Walter's sudden movement was observed by Faroud. He stood in the doorway in an immaculate black tracksuit, a towel draped around his neck for effect. "And who might you be?" he demanded imperiously. "Oh yes, I remember you from last night. You put your hands on my wife. Don't ever do that again or I'll have you taught some manners."

"My apologies Mr Faroud," Walter replied smoothly without any sign of fear in his voice. "I was just leaving." He made to move past Faroud, but the ever present Hulk moved to block the doorway.

Faroud swung on his wife. "Why have you invited this man here? You know very well you are never to let anyone into my house without my permission."

A momentary flash of defiance flickered across Chloe's face, but it was quickly replaced by a demeanour of subservience. "This is Mr Boyce, Marcel. He's visiting London and came to tell me about his father, on whose property I grew up. I just wanted to hear all that has happened since I left."

"I can see you're lying." His hard, black eyes bored into her. "There's another reason and I will find out. We will discuss this later." It was a demonstration of his power, meant to demean and humiliate his wife. Walter knew he could easily account for the objectionable weasel, but the Hulk was another matter. What was the incredible hold this man had over Chloe? Whatever possessed her to marry him? "And as for you, get out of my house and make sure you never return."

Walter required no second bidding. The Hulk didn't move, nor did he alter his cold expression, as Walter was forced to squeeze past him in the doorway. Fear was written all over the maid's face as she led him out. Before the door closed behind him, he could hear Faroud shouting at her in some foreign tongue, obviously berating her for letting him in.

He pondered his position as he closed the gate and flagged down a taxi. He knew he was in danger. He had to get rid of the diamond, as it would only take minutes for Faroud to get the truth out of Chloe. "The Athenaeum Hotel driver."

It was pouring with rain when the taxi pulled up in front of the hotel. The door was opened by a tall, red-headed doorman holding an umbrella. "Welcome again to the Athenaeum, sir."

Walter acknowledged the greeting as he was ushered under the awning of the foyer. He walked the few steps down to reception and booked a room.

"No bags, sir?" asked the receptionist.

"No, they've been mislaid by the airline. I told them to phone me here when they recover them, but for the moment what I'm standing in is all I have."

She handed Walter the key and as he turned towards the elevators, he noticed the doorman standing at the bottom of the steps, watching him with a confused look on his face. He let himself into his room and sat down to collect his thoughts. He was in danger, he knew that much. He took an envelope from the desk, put the diamond inside it and went back down to the foyer. The receptionist who had checked him in was busy, but he caught the eye of the concierge.

"Can I put something into safe deposit?"

"Certainly sir. Would you come this way please."

Five minutes later, the diamond was secured. He felt more comfortable as he stepped outside. The redhead recognised him, and whistled for a cab. "The young lady hasn't been in today, sir."

"Do you recognise everyone who stays here?"

"Yes Mr Boyce. I make it my business to recall the names of everyone who checks in. I noticed you leave last night with the young lady."

The cab pulled up, and he opened the door. Walter slipped two pounds into his hand as he climbed in.

"I hope your bags turn up Mr Boyce." He closed the door and tipped his hat with a knowing smile.

Ten minutes later, Walter was back at Lancaster Gate. He tried Annie's work and mobile numbers, and left messages at both. One of her colleagues told him she was at a reception at the Ritz and was not expected in until late.

Although it was dangerous, he had to try to see Chloe again and persuade her to reveal more. He was so close, and yet so far. He switched on the television and watched the world news, but was not focussed on the latest wars and political events around the globe. As his ears were attuned to waiting for the phone to ring, it was several seconds before he became aware of a gentle knocking on the door. Annie was on his mind as he got up and opened it. The Hulk filled the doorway. He shoved Walter backwards so violently, he landed on the floor flat on his back. Behind him, he saw the grinning face of Marcel Faroud.

"What the hell do you think you're doing?" Walter's indignation was cut off by the heel of a shoe thrust into his lower rib cage. He doubled over in pain. A well-aimed kick caught him in the side of the head, sending him into an abyss of nausea.

"I will ask the questions Mr Boyce." Faroud stripped off his overcoat and leather gloves and sat down at a small table near the window. "You will have the privilege of answering them immediately so Massoud does not have to prolong your pain."

The pain was still searing through his side as he struggled to prop himself up on one elbow. The Hulk leaned down and effortlessly dragged him to his feet, but he was unable to stand and slumped onto the side of the bed. The Hulk was mute as he stood to one side, watching carefully for any attempt to counter-attack.

"What do you want, you arsehole?"

Walter saw the slap coming, but couldn't avoid it as it caught him with full force across the face. The world went black as he was flung back onto the bed.

"You will show some respect Mr Boyce, otherwise Massoud will lose his temper. I take disrespect very seriously."

Walter did not answer. He was still trying to establish whether he had been run over by a train or hit by a bus.

"Now we have established authority we can get on with this interview," Faroud said quietly. "You have something belonging to me and I want it returned now."

"I've nothing of yours Faroud. Now get the hell out of here. I'm calling reception." Walter reached for the phone, but the Hulk moved it out of his reach, challenging him to reach for it again.

"You are mistaken Mr Boyce. Whatever is my wife's is also mine."

"You're nothing but a blood-sucking leech."

"That remark will not go unpunished Mr Boyce, but not before you hand over my possession."

"I repeat, I don't have anything belonging to you or your wife." Walter rationalised he was technically correct, as Chloe was only holding it in trust, not that this bore much relevance in the current situation.

The Hulk quietly began searching the room. Nothing was overlooked. He stood on the desk, which protested under his weight, pulled the grills off the air conditioning ducts and felt inside. He took the covers off the neon light fittings, and looked under lampshades. The desk and chairs were turned over for anything taped underneath. He tore the bedclothes off and upended the mattress, checking for any concealment. Walter watched as his bag was emptied and the lining torn away. The pockets of his jacket were felt thoroughly. His toilet bag was upended in the bathroom and the deodorant stick crushed along with a tube of shaving cream. The Hulk grunted for him to take off his shoes and strip.

Walter did as he was told. Another king hit from the Hulk was more than he could endure at this stage. Soon he was standing in his boxers, wondering if he was about to experience the same indignity he had received at the hands of the police medic in Perth. The Hulk tossed the clothing on the floor and then without warning ran his hands up and around Walter's crutch. Walter expected Faroud would at any moment order him to bend over and part his cheeks, but the Hulk merely stood quietly waiting for further instructions.

"I can see more persuasive methods are in order Mr Boyce. If you don't tell me what you have done with the diamond, the situation is going to get very ugly for you."

"It's in the hotel safe deposit box. Take me down there and you can have it."

Faroud shook his head. "Don't take me for a fool. You have lodged nothing with hotel security. I checked. I'm not leaving here without the diamond or knowledge of its whereabouts. You could be in for a long, painful night. It's entirely up to you as to how quickly we get this over with."

The phone began to ring again and Walter reached over to snatch it up. It was knocked out of his hand by the Hulk and the receiver replaced. It rang again and then stopped after half a minute, as the call was diverted to message bank. The Hulk picked it up, punched in a number and listened. He turned to Faroud and shook his head. Walter was relieved; it obviously wasn't Annie.

Faroud nodded at the Hulk, who slowly took a roll of duct tape out of his jacket and a cut-throat razor from the inside breast pocket. Walter was horrified. Sweat began to break out on his forehead and soon he was clammy all over. He was powerless as a length of duct tape was wound around his head, covering his mouth.

"Massoud is a product of the Beirut underworld Mr Boyce. He learnt his trade in the clubs, dives and brothels of that city where life has no great value. He prides himself on being able to carve a man to pieces before he expires from loss of blood. He's literally an exponent of death by a thousand cuts—and he really enjoys his work."

The razor flashed and Walter felt the elastic of his boxers being cut.

"We don't want you making any noise when Massoud commences his delicate work. I will leave it to him where to start, but he may choose your most precious possessions first." He laughed as he looked at Walter's exposed genitals.

Walter realised he was a dead man whether he revealed the whereabouts of the diamond or not. He looked for an opening to make a break, a sudden manoeuvre that would surprise the Hulk and allow him to get out of the room.

Faroud had been watching him closely. "Massoud, I think it would be wise to tape Mr Boyce's arms and legs before you commence. Normally, Massoud's victims vent their bladder at the first sight of the razor but you haven't, so I think some precautions are in order."

The Hulk grunted, took off his jacket and smoothed it down before hanging it in the closet.

"You can see Massoud is very particular about his appearance Mr Boyce. However, you're appearance is about to change for the worse."

This had to be a bluff. Hotel CCTV cameras would quickly reveal who was responsible for his death, but he had the distinct impression Faroud wasn't bluffing.

The Hulk advanced with the tape in hand. Walter tensed his leg muscles and lashed out with all his force. The kick caught the Hulk in the pit of his stomach, eliciting a look of surprise rather than pain as the Hulk checked his stride. It was enough to give Walter time to reach over, grab the desk lamp and hurl it at his attacker's head. It struck the Hulk above his left eye, opening a large gash from which blood started to run. The Hulk grunted in rage, the cut-throat in his right hand. It was too late for negotiation. Walter realised the moment he caught him, the blade would start carving. Faroud had jumped up to stand in front of the door to block off any escape route. Walter knew he could knock him down with a single punch. Getting away from the Hulk was the problem. He turned suddenly and rushed into the bathroom, slamming the door behind him. He knew he had only moments to survive as he looked around for a solid object to defend himself. He grabbed the long handled toilet brush and reaching up, flicked out the red globe of the sprinkler system. The instant burst of water was immediately joined by the sound of the hotel fire alarm. The Hulk's arm, with razor in fist, smashed through the door just as Walter threw his full force against it. The razor fell to the tiled floor and the arm disappeared. He heard Faroud shout and a door slam shut.

Walter dared not move in case it was a ruse to make him reveal himself. He peered through the splintered cracks but could see nothing. Gingerly, he opened the door, praying the Hulk wasn't waiting on the other side. The room was empty. He feverishly unwound the tape from around his head, towelled himself down, dressed, thrust his remaining clothes into his mangled bag and got out of the room. He joined guests already in the corridor. The sound of approaching fire brigade vehicles joined in with the clanging of the hotel fire bells. Two hotel security pushed past him and entered his room.

"Here it is Clive. There's no fire. The sprinkler system's broken. Call down and have them turn it off. There's no one in the room, but we've still got to get everyone out of the building until the brigade clears it."

Walter swiftly merged with the jostling crowd that descended the fire stairs and began mustering in front of the hotel. He scanned the crowd to see if Faroud and his friend were anywhere to be seen. Satisfied they had left the vicinity, he strode towards Bayswater Road and hailed a cab.

The redhead was still on duty when the cab pulled up in front of the Athenaeum. He beamed as he held the door open. "I see you've found your bag sir. You're in luck sir. The young lady arrived about ten minutes ago. I told her you weren't here, but she said she'd wait. I admire your taste sir."

Annie was walking out of the lounge bar as he descended the short flight of steps. She looked worried and was clearly pleased to see him. "I've been looking for you. I've got an urgent message from Chloe."

"I think I've already got the message." He grabbed her arm and steered her towards the reception desk to reclaim his key.

"You can't have."

"If it's a message that Marcel is keen to talk to me, then I've already spoken to him and it wasn't a very pleasant experience. Come on up to my room."

Annie was startled. "You're staying here? I thought you were at the Lancaster?"

"I was until half an hour ago, but for the sake of my continued good health, I needed to change hotels. Faroud tracked me down. My next move is to get out of the country. This is just getting too hot for me."

Two minutes later, they were in his room. Walter opened the bar fridge and took out a couple of miniature bottles of scotch. His hands were still shaking as he poured them both into a glass, pulled out the ice tray and dropped a couple of cubes into the drink.

"Drink?"

"Yes, if there's a brandy there. Just a single, thank you."

Walter downed half of his glass before preparing and handing Annie her drink. He topped his up with another bottle before turning to her. "Cheers."

"You're so pale, you look as though you've stared death in the face. What happened?'

Walter went and sat down on a chair near the window overlooking busy Piccadilly and Green Park. He stared for long seconds as he took another drink. Annie walked over and sat opposite him. Walter explained what had happened, but left out the reason for Faroud's visit.

"What was he after? Chloe was frantic when she contacted me. She said Marcel was after you, but wouldn't say why."

"I've no doubt he meant to kill me." He drained his glass as the realisation sunk in. "He had that violent bastard Massoud with him, and he meant business."

"But why was he after you? Is it something to do with what you wanted to talk to Chloe about?"

"It sure as hell was. I can't stay here. I'll have to find another hotel and quickly."

"You can stay with me. I'm sure he'd never make the connection."

Walter shook his head. "Too dangerous. I've got to get out of London as soon as possible. Can you get a message to Chloe for me?"

"Not possible. She warned me not to phone under any circumstances. I'm to wait until she phones me." Annie rummaged in her bag for her mobile phone and checked it for messages. "What the hell is this all about? You'll have to tell me if I'm to help you."

"The less you know the better, Annie. It's for your own good, as I wouldn't like you to be threatened by Faroud's goon. If you saw what he's capable of—"

"He makes me shudder every time I see him. Gives me the creeps. If you're in that much trouble, you'd better check out immediately. Marcel has an incredible number of underworld contacts in this city; I know that from my days as a journalist on *News of the World*. He'll have his bloodhounds out already. At this precise moment, they'll be working overtime trying to locate you. There will be a price on your head, make no mistake. Come on, let's go. You'll have to stay with me until you fly out."

He knew Annie was right. He had no choice but to stay with her. He picked up his bag of meagre belongings and followed her. The reception desk was busy as usual when he asked the desk manager for access to his safety deposit box.

A few minutes later, Walter had the envelope in his hand. He quickly opened it to confirm its contents before stepping back into the foyer and looking around for Annie, but she was nowhere in sight. He heard a hiss to his left and saw her at the top of a short stairway, beckoning him urgently. She held her finger to her lips for silence. He looked around, but couldn't see the reason for her worried look.

"He missed you by inches," she hissed in his ear as she pushed him up the stairs into the foyer. "I was just coming out of the Ladies and there he was, along with Massoud only a metre in front of me hurrying for the lift. He didn't bother talking to reception, so he knows you've checked in here and obviously has your room number. I thought he'd seen you, it was so close."

"Do you think he saw you?"

"No, he was looking straight ahead. Two seconds earlier, I would have walked right into him."

Walter whistled softly. "Too close for comfort. That confirms I'll be staying at your place tonight."

The redhead tipped his top hat and beamed. "I see you found one another."

Walter pulled out a ten pound note. "Look, there are a couple of Arab looking types who may be out in a few minutes wanting to know whether you've seen me. Can I rely on you to have no recollection?"

"I know who you're talking about sir, a certain Mr Faroud and his unsavoury friend." He raised his eyebrows and slowly shook his head. "Mr Boyce, you can trust me, you are the most inconspicuous person in London tonight. Off back to Australia soon?"

"Sooner than expected."

21

nnie's flat was small but cosy, consisting of a tiny lounge-kitchen and a single bedroom in a row of terrace houses off Bayswater Road, "You can have the couch." She slung her handbag into an armchair just as her phone started to ring. She snatched the bag and fumbled around trying to retrieve it before it went to message bank.

"Annie speaking. Chloe!" Her smile disappeared quickly as she listened to the voice on the other end. She listened intently, making the usual nondescript replies of someone acknowledging instructions. Finally she said, "He's here, I'll put him on." She handed the phone to Walter.

Walter heard Chloe's frightened voice. "Walter, you're in great danger. You've got to get out of London and out of the country as quickly as possible."

"That really does defeat the purpose of my visit, Chloe. I was hoping we could meet up so we could discuss what I came for."

"He knows you have the diamond Walter. I didn't tell him of my own free will. He slapped me around, threatening to hand me over to Massoud. He phoned some of his contacts in the diamond business and described the size and colour of the stone. He was told if it was a diamond he was describing, it would be an extremely rare and priceless gem. You just don't know what an evil person he is; he won't hesitate to kill you. I had no choice Walter. He threatened to disfigure me if I ever leave him and he would kill me just as easily if I stood in his way. It's that butcher Massoud who terrifies me; I know what he can do. People who cross Marcel have simply disappeared, or I read about their horrific deaths."

Walter could sense Chloe was fast losing control of her emotions and composure.

"Calm down Chloe. He hasn't found me yet," he lied. There was no point in relaying the encounter and getting her more upset. "But thank you for warning me. Is there somewhere we could meet tomorrow? In view of the danger, I must fly out tomorrow evening, so it's my last chance to talk to you." There was a long silence. "Are you still there, Chloe?"

"Yes Walter. I'm trying to think. I'm attending a luncheon at the Albert Museum tomorrow. I will meet you in the Egyptian section if I can. If I don't show up, you will know I cannot get away from Marcel. Bring Annie with you." The line went dead.

He turned to Annie. "She said she would meet me at the Albert Museum tomorrow. Can you fit it into your schedule to come with me?"

"That's no problem, as long as I can produce something to write about from the event. However, the Albert is not a very private place. I'll bet Massoud will be lingering somewhere inside the building. You'd better be very careful, and now that I'm giving you room and lodgings, you'd better start explaining what this is all about. I sense something big here and I don't want anything to get in the way of a good article."

"I don't want you involved Annie. The less you know the better, especially if Faroud sees us together. I promised you the background on Chloe and I've given it to you, but there is more—I promise I'll do that when I get back to Australia."

"I'm sure Faroud probably suspects I'm involved somewhere in this after seeing you with me at the Savoy."

The landline on her side table began to ring. Annie looked at it quizzically. "I wonder who that could be? No one I know rings me on that number any longer. Probably some telemarketer."

Before Walter could stop her, she had picked it up. "Annie Brittan speaking." She listened for a few seconds and slowly put it down again. "I know there was someone on the other end, but they didn't speak. Curious."

Walter did not want to alarm her, but it had to be Faroud. The man certainly worked fast. He got up and picked up his bag.

"I'd better go. You're in danger with me around. In fact, it would be better if you stay with a friend until we leave town tomorrow night. Have you cleared it with your editor?"

Annie nodded. "Yes, all approved, but who do you think that was?"

"I believe that was Faroud checking whether you're here. Come with me now."

Annie looked alarmed. "I suppose you're right, but I'll be okay. I'll just go and see Diane down the corridor for an hour or so, but you go now. I'll see you tomorrow." She quickly kissed him on the cheek, then opened the door and let him out. "Take care."

Walter quickly descended the stairs and was about to swing around the landing onto the final flight when he heard footsteps below him. He paused and waited. The footsteps continued slowly as though unsure, like a person listening for sound. They were not the tread of a weary resident returning from work. Walter froze as the footsteps stopped and then began to climb again, barely audible above the muted sound of a television behind the door opposite to where he was standing. He tensed and waited. His chances were fifty-fifty of the person looking his way when they reached the top of the stairs, or looking away from him down the corridor. It was either going to be his lucky day, or it was not. He recognised the back of the bald head the moment it leaned forwards from the top step and peered tentatively to the left. In the second it took for it to turn back to the right, it was already too late. Walter's shoe was aimed at his head but it caught Massoud full in the throat. His head jerked back as he gasped for breath and clutched at his shattered larynx. His face turned a brilliant red, his pupils rolled back so just the whites of his eyes were showing. He staggered backwards and tried to steady himself while his lungs fought for air. A deep gurgle emitted from within his diaphragm. He flung his arms out in desperation as he went over backwards and down the flight of stairs.

Walter did not follow immediately, but watched as Massoud cartwheeled and hit the marble floor with a sickening thud. Walter could see his neck was broken, the head twisted at an acute angle. He slowly descended the stairs. At any moment, he expected someone to walk in, or a door to open. It remained quiet except for the background noise of the television. He stepped around Massoud, his mind racing as to what to do next. He could not leave the body where it was.

He knelt down and threw one lifeless arm over his shoulder, dragging the corpse upright with the dead weight across his back. He reached down and with a quick movement, hefted the body in a fireman's lift. Massoud's bulk was barely manageable.

Walter pushed his way through the rear entrance doors of the apartments and out into the car park. It was dark and rain was falling steadily. He had the advantage as long as a car did not turn in and focus on him and his burden in its headlights. He would have a lot of explaining to do and did not like his chances of getting out of London the following day if that happened. In the corner of the dark car park, two partly open dumpsters were visible. He headed towards them, heaved his burden into one of them and covered it with bags of garbage. Where he belongs, Walter reflected as he pulled down the lid.

He went back to retrieve his bag from the foyer and was about to leave when he noticed Massoud's razor lying in the corner near the doorway. He picked it up and shoved it into his pocket then started up the stairs to alert Annie, but stopped abruptly when he heard a doorway on the landing above open and two people saying their goodbyes. He did not want to be identified anywhere near the scene, so he retreated through the dark car park entrance and around the side of the building.

He was about to step around the overhanging branches of a tree and out onto the pavement when he froze in his tracks. The sudden glow from a cigarette lighter lit up Faroud's face as he waited in his Mercedes. Walter was not more than two metres from him when he lifted his head and exhaled a stream of smoke, which drifted out through the open window. Faroud was distracted as he tapped his fingers on the sill of the open window in time with the music playing on the car's stereo.

Walter slowly retreated into the shadows, expecting Faroud to turn his head slightly at any second and spot him. He circled around behind the large, rambling tree and climbed over a low brick wall, coming out onto the pavement behind Massoud's car. With a few quick steps, he drew level and slammed his fist into the side of Faroud's exposed head. It whipped sideways and then bounced back into the doorframe. He was out cold. To anyone passing, it would appear the man had gone to sleep while listening to the radio. He reached into Faroud's inside jacket pocket and pulled out an expensive crocodile skin wallet. He tried the other side and came up with an identical matching wallet and a Mont Blanc pen. Walter then stripped the heavy gold Rolex and a gold bracelet from his wrist. A diamond-mounted pinkie ring also slipped off easily. He ripped the gold chain necklace from around his neck and took the keys out of the ignition for good measure. In one final act of humiliation, he opened the door and bent down, slipping off the expensive handmade shoes. He was sure Faroud had not recognised him and would assume he had been the victim of a very expensive, opportunistic robbery.

Walter went back through the car park past the dumpsters. He felt for the razor in his pocket, lifted the lid and thrust it, along with the empty wallets, watch, ring, pen, chains, car keys and shoes into a mess of household waste. The two thousand pounds in crisp new notes he had found in the wallets could be put to good use, he mused. Compensation for the belting he had received from that gorilla. It was a pity about the jewellery, but it was too easily traceable if he was apprehended. He jumped over a low fence and made his way down the side of an adjacent block. Within minutes, he had hailed a cab and found a small, unobtrusive hotel near St James Station.

Annie answered on the third ring. "Annie, Walter here, did you get away okay?"

"Yes, I'm with Diane."

"Okay, okay, well the coast is clear. You won't be hearing from Massoud again and I think Faroud will have too much of a headache to do anything tonight."

"What are you talking about?"

"You would have been in real trouble if I hadn't run into Massoud when I left you. I'm afraid he had a nasty accident and won't be working with Faroud again. As for Faroud, turn out the lights and look out the window. See if there's a Mercedes parked down the street to your left."

"Hold on, I'll just go back to my place. "

He heard Annie making some excuse to her friend and her hurried footsteps down the hallway.

Annie switched off the light and slowly pulled back the curtain. "Yes, but it's being pulled up onto a tow truck and Faroud is just getting into a taxi. He doesn't appear to be wearing any shoes."

Walter laughed. "I thought they'd fit me, but they didn't."

"What did you mean about Massoud having an accident? Is he dead?"

"Fraid so. He was coming up the stairs as I was going down. He must have been sent to find me, or beat the hell out of you as to my whereabouts. We met at the top of the stairs and I was just a fraction quicker than him. Well, he fell down the bloody stairwell and broke his neck, didn't he."

"Oh my God, he's not still there, is he?"

"No, I put him out with the rubbish, where he belongs. He's in a dumpster at the back of your block. When's rubbish removal day?"

Annie laughed nervously. "Would you believe at around five tomorrow morning. Damned truck wakes the whole street."

"Well, hopefully Massoud will be under a thousand tonnes of rotting trash before anyone raises the alarm, if anyone ever does. I'm not sure Faroud will report him missing. He may have to answer too many awkward questions."

"What about Marcel?"

"Marcel got mugged for his money and other valuables. I doubt he'll report it to the police. He didn't see what, or who hit him. I dare say he's gone home nursing a very sore head."

"What did you do with his bling? Don't tell me you chucked that into the dumpster too?"

"I had to, after I emptied his wallets. I couldn't walk around with all that jewellery on me."

"What should I do now?"

"Absolutely nothing. You're safe for now. You don't know anything and you haven't seen anything. Faroud will be trying to work out what happened to Massoud and will no doubt be furious about being mugged. He was a sitting duck waiting in a car in a dark street with no protection with all that jewellery and money on him."

Annie burst out laughing.

"What's so funny?"

"Marcel is all front. Can you imagine what will be said behind his back if this ever gets out? His reputation will be trashed with his underworld contacts. Mind you, he'll immediately put the word out he's lost some important personal items and if anyone tries to fence them, there'll a big reward for their recovery. He might even suspect it was Massoud, especially when neither he nor his bling are anywhere to be found. He really has had his arse kicked tonight. Say, what are you doing now? Why don't you come back for coffee now the pressure is off?"

Walter chuckled. "I'd love to, but I'm in a nice room in a nice little hotel and it's been a very stressful day. I could probably drag myself away if there's anything being offered after the coffee though—"

"Go screw yourself Boyce. I'm not an easy lay. I'll see you tomorrow; don't be late."

Walter was at the museum an hour before the arranged time. He went inside and found a spot from where he could observe everyone entering without being seen. He saw Annie enter in a hurry about half an hour before the luncheon was due to commence. She glanced around the crowd. Walter waited until she was close by, then stepped out from where he was hiding and grabbed her arm.

"Oh God, Walter!" She gasped in relief and surprise. "You've got to get out of here now before Faroud turns up. Chloe phoned to say Faroud came home last night with one side of his face swollen and all his jewellery missing. He started one hell of an argument, accusing her of being complicit with you."

"You didn't tell her anything about what happened last night?"

"Hell no, but you're a dead man if he catches up with you. Chloe rang me this morning while he was in the shower. He's guessed you had something to do with Massoud's sudden disappearance and he's brought in a couple of assassins from Manchester; Serbs or Croats, I believe. He's paying them big money to find you and the diamond and then kill you. Chloe's a wreck. She told me she finally broke down and told him she could lead him to where the diamond came from but in return, she wants a divorce. You can imagine how that went down. Faroud was not about to lose his money tree."

Annie paused and let the statement sink in. "Yes, I now know why you're here, and not only do I want more on Chloe's background, I also want the scoop on this fabulous red diamond—" Annie suddenly stopped, grabbed his arm and spun him around. "Faroud just walked in with a couple of unsavoury looking types. I think they're the killers Chloe mentioned." She pulled him behind a pillar. They waited until the men had passed, then Annie led him towards the front of the building and down the steps into the street. She hailed a cab and within a minute, they were lost in the traffic of Cromwell Road.

"Was Chloe with them?"

"No. Marcel wouldn't have wanted her around when the goons grabbed you. She would have attracted too much attention by her presence and it could have caused a scene. He got it out of her about your meeting with her here today. She must have rebelled as she guessed what would happen to you. You have a lot to thank her for. I hope she's okay."

22

t Perth's international terminal, Walter and Annie followed the scurrying passengers as they streamed along the air bridge. When the plane had taken off from London, they had all been given the usual spiel to "sit back, relax and enjoy the flight." But it had been a long flight and the inevitable tired, glassy-eyed, short tempered and sweaty throng were now stampeding for Customs clearance and the exit. Walter was suffering like the rest of them, but he knew it was nothing a shower and a few hours' sleep in a comfortable bed couldn't fix.

He and Annie looked for the shortest queue and walked swiftly towards it. In Walter's peripheral vision, he noticed two men in plain clothes detach themselves from a group of uniformed Customs officials and move towards the booth they were approaching. At first, his tired brain didn't register until it snapped a warning.

Annie had not said a word since getting off the plane. She was walking slightly behind him as he reached into his pocket and took out the package. He stopped suddenly and Annie walked into him. With a deft movement, he thrust his hand into her jacket pocket. Passengers crowded past, blocking the view of the two plain clothes detectives about to detain him.

"You don't know me," he said out of the corner of his mouth. "Don't follow me. Just go through and catch a cab to the Parmelia Hotel and check in as Mr and Mrs Brittan. I don't know how long I'll be, but just wait. I've got a problem about to happen and I don't know how long it will take to sort out."

Annie opened her mouth to say something but Walter cut her off. "Don't bloody argue, otherwise we'll both be detained." He casually moved to another queue so as not to be identified with her.

The two policemen were waiting for him as he was cleared through Customs. He heaved a sigh of relief. They had not seen his contact with Annie. She did not look back as she was cleared and walked towards the baggage carousel.

Walter pretended not to notice as Connors stepped forwards to stop him. "Mr Boyce, we've been expecting you. Would you follow us, please?"

Walter said nothing as Penisi and a uniformed Customs officer fell in and they escorted him to one side. A fourth person joined them. He was dressed in a grey suit, but did not introduce himself. They ushered him into a small interview room.

"Sit down, please. We have a few questions to ask you."

"What's this about? Am I under arrest?"

Connors shook his head. "No, but that doesn't mean you can call a lawyer or walk out of here until we're finished. You're being detained under the Customs and Immigration Act on suspicion of carrying stolen goods, which we have an interest in retrieving. And Detective Watters here is investigating a death in London that you may have some knowledge of. Talk about killing two birds with one gemstone." Connors chuckled at his own joke.

Walter said nothing but his mind raced. Thank God he had unloaded the diamond onto Annie and they were unaware who he had travelled with. They studied him in silence for a long minute, watching for any signs of unease. Walter said nothing as he waited them out. It was Connors who finally broke the silence.

"I believe you have a stolen diamond in your possession, a very valuable diamond I've asked you about previously. It comes, as you know, from the Argyle diamond mine in the Kimberley. We also have a report you stole a similar diamond from someone in London, or are we talking about the same gem? If it's not, it seems you're getting to be a habitual diamond thief."

"I don't know what you're talking about. I don't have a stolen diamond from Argyle, and I haven't stolen a diamond from anyone in London."

"Well in that case, let's get on with it. Strip off; you know the drill. We don't have the authority to search you, but Officer Peters here does."

Peters picked up the phone and muttered something into it, watching as Walter stood up and began to strip off. Peters then began to methodically go through his discarded clothes, when a balding man with thick glasses and the stoop of someone used to leaning over a mortuary slab walked in and pulled on a pair of latex gloves.

"Oh Christ, don't you ever give up? I don't have any diamonds on me or in me."

Connors ignored him. His broad grin betrayed the pleasure he derived from subjecting Walter to the humiliating procedure once more. Two minutes later, the man shook his head and left without saying a word. Walter dressed and sat down again.

"Where did you hide it Boyce? It's not up your date, it's not in your clothes, it's not in your bag, so where the hell is it?" Connors was clearly getting worked up.

"Even with your super-cop brain, you must have worked out by now I don't have it."

Penisi suddenly spoke. "Was he travelling with anyone?"

Connors glanced at his offsider. Penisi read his mind. *We should have thought of the bleeding obvious. He's made a switch!*

Peters reached over and picked up the phone. "This is urgent. Find out who was sitting next to Walter Boyce on the Qantas flight just in from Singapore. If they're in the building, detain them." He replaced the receiver. "I can't do much more than that. If they're out of the terminal, they're beyond my jurisdiction."

"The London Met had a complaint about the theft of a large red diamond described as being priceless. They're sending someone out to talk to you and I dare say they'll ask for your extradition. You're in deep shit Boyce."

"And who am I supposed to have stolen the diamond from?"

"A Marcel Faroud laid a complaint that you stole a red diamond he'd given to his wife, the international model Chloe Faroud."

Walter grunted in indignation. "Well, you've satisfied yourselves I'm not carrying a diamond or diamonds, either on my person, up my person or in my luggage, I think you should ask the Metro boys for more information on Faroud's complaint. Where did he buy the diamond, where is the receipt, where is the certificate of authenticity that would have accompanied it? More to the point, when did he give it to his wife and on what occasion? I think Faroud would stumble at the first hurdle. Have they checked with Faroud's wife if she was actually given the rock by her husband? Does she or Faroud have any evidence I actually took the gem? I can assure you, Faroud has made a false complaint."

"Which implies you know something. Have you met Faroud?"

"Yes, I have. A very unpleasant experience."

"Is that all? What was your relationship with him? Why did you meet him?"

"I met him through a personal friend. Other than that, I'm not prepared to discuss this any further."

Watters had said nothing up to that point. He was sitting on a chair to one side, just observing. "You say you've met Faroud, so you must have also met a gent by the name of Massoud Farhangi? He was Faroud's security guard, or bodyguard, or whatever you want to call it."

"I recall he had some oversized gorilla with him, but he never introduced me to him, so I don't know if it was the man you're referring to. What about him?"

"His corpse was found in a London garbage transfer station along with items of expensive jewellery. Do you know anything about that?"

"Sounds like the best place for him if he was Faroud's bodyguard. That guy was one big, ugly mother."

"His throat was smashed in and his neck broken."

"Not my doing. Besides, the guy was way out of my weight division."

Watters nodded, but said nothing.

The door opened and an arm appeared beckoning to Peters. He looked to see who was standing behind the Customs officer.

"Show her in."

Walter held his breath, waiting for Annie to be shown in. Instead, a short, stout woman appeared. He recognised her as the school teacher who had sat next to him by the window on the last leg from Singapore. She chatted incessantly and was constantly climbing over him or excusing herself because of her prolapsed bladder. He had been subjected to hearing her full medical history, including her hysterectomy. He had even offered to swap seats with her, but she was immovable from her assigned position. She liked to be able to see out she said, although it was pitch black outside and at forty thousand feet, there was little to see.

"Do you know this man?" Connors smiled at her as he indicated Walter.

"Why of course," she beamed. "He's the lovely young man I sat next to all the way from Singapore—"

Connors cut her off; he could see she was about to relive the whole flight. "You got on in Singapore?"

"Yes, I was there for seven days. Lovely place, lovely people, but a little too humid for me. Have you been there? It's—"

"You live in Perth?"

"Yes. I teach at the Midlands High School. Do you know it? This is all very interesting and exciting. Why are you asking me these questions? Have I done something wrong?"

Connors realised he had drawn a blank and nodded to Peters.

"Thank you, madam." Peters escorted her to the door. "We don't need to delay you any longer."

"What has he done? Is he a drug smuggler—?" She was peering back over her shoulder trying to get a last look at the felon as Peters gently ushered her out. He poked his head in again.

"If you gents want me for anything further, I'll be out in the reception area. It doesn't look as though I can help you anymore."

"Just a moment!" Connors called as he followed him out and closed the door. "Could you get me a full passenger manifest for that flight and their seating details? There has to be a connection between Boyce and a passenger on that flight."

"I'll attend to it now."

Connors turned and went back into the room. "I've asked for a full passenger list. It may take a few minutes so he's all yours detective."

Watters opened his notebook with a practised flick and pulled a pen from his jacket pocket. "Okay Mr Boyce, let's go through your meetings with Faroud and the character who had his neck broken, Massoud Farhangi."

"I believe you're out of your jurisdiction with that one, detective. I don't intend to sit here and be interviewed by you regarding a case the London plods are enquiring about. Their case seems a bit thin to implicate me in the death of some thug picked out of a rubbish heap. If they want to talk to me, I'll let you know where I am at all times. If you have something to charge me with, then get on with it. If you don't, I'm out of here."

To Walter's surprise, Watters flicked his notebook closed and shoved it back in his shirt pocket. "You seem to know your rights."

"I'm learning fast." Walter began to rise from the chair.

"Just keep your seat there fella," Connors interjected. "I've got a few things to run over again. I want to see the diamond you showed Steiner."

"Well, you can't because I don't have it. Even if I did, I certainly wouldn't be handing it over to you. I've no doubt it would be the last I'd ever see of it judging by the rumours I've heard about diamonds disappearing from Argyle."

"You'd be well advised to button your lip if you know what's good for you," Connors replied, his florid face turning a deeper shade of red.

"Look Connors, you're really starting to get up my nose. As I've just said to your colleague, if you want to charge me with something then get on with it. You make your case; I'm not going to make it for you."

"Cocky bastard, aren't you? What about London?"

"London is for the London cops. If they want to lay charges or have me extradited, I've no doubt you or Watters here, would have already made the arrest on their behalf. It's obvious you're on a fishing expedition. I would guess Scotland Yard isn't too keen on Faroud's complaint, otherwise they'd be following it up properly rather than just having you and Watters trying to shake me down."

Connors reached behind him and pulled out his cuffs. He pushed his face into Walter's. "Well, consider yourself under arrest. We'll see if you're as smart as you think."

Walter felt the cuffs snap on his wrists. He was jerked to his feet and propelled out of the room. Half an hour later, he was being fingerprinted, photographed and his wallet, watch, passport and belt removed, before being shown to a holding cell. The solid metal door slammed behind him. The cell smelt of vomit and urine, although it looked relatively clean. He lay down on the single bunk. He was exhausted. At least he had a cell to himself. He stared at the hinged flap in the door, which he knew would be lifted every hour to ensure he wasn't hanging from a noose made out of his shirt or trousers.

It was early afternoon when the flap quickly opened and closed before the door swung open to reveal Elliott DiBrito.

"We meet again Mr Boyce," he beamed as he entered the cell. "I hear they're finally about to charge you with something, but Connors is still working on it."

"That's news to me. I wonder what he's going to charge me with. Apparently, I've stolen a couple of diamonds, one here and the other in London."

"They're not mere diamonds Mr Boyce. Connors is saying the rocks are worth millions. It's theft on a grand scale. That's impressive, even in this town notable for its corrupt white-collar executives and politicians putting their snouts in the trough."

"I'm not a thief. The diamond doesn't come from the Argyle mine. It was picked up on a remote property in the Kimberley many years ago, but the exact location is unknown."

"Connors is saying you showed the stone to a local diamond merchant. Why did you do that?"

"Because I wasn't sure if it was a diamond and if it was, I wanted an idea of its value, that's all."

DeBrito tapped his pen on his pad as he pondered something. "I believe I can get you bail, but you'll have to reveal what you've done with the stone. You may have to hand it into the police or to the court."

"I don't have it and if I did, I'm not handing it to the police because it would simply disappear. Connors would make sure of that."

"The court won't buy that line. Some magistrate will assume you know where it is and order you to hand it over. If you don't, you'll be held in contempt of court and thrown back in the jug until you do. No magistrate is going to let you out if he thinks you're going to run off with a diamond worth megabucks. You can bet Connors is going to be laying it on thick as to what a criminal you are."

"How long until I go before the court?"

DeBrito looked at his watch. "Anytime within the next hour. Connors will be preparing his brief of evidence right now. I'll have a word with him and see what he's got."

It was half an hour later when DeBrito reappeared. He was beaming. "I just can't fathom it. You're off the hook for now and free to go. Connors offered no evidence and withdrew the charges. He's received nothing from London so they're not looking for your extradition at this stage. From what I gather, the Faroud character who laid the complaint is on his way out here."

Walter realised he now had two threats to deal with; Connors, who he felt sure was after the diamond for himself and now Faroud, whose motives were equally obvious. Why had Connors withdrawn the charges when he had clear evidence Walter had shown it to Steiner and therefore the diamond did exist? He could think of no other plausible reason than Connors wanted it for himself. He was going to have to be very careful, but as long as Faroud was not bringing his two assassins with him, he felt he could handle him.

"You mean that bastard arrested me with no evidence? I should nail him for false arrest."

"As your lawyer Mr Boyce, I would advise you to leave well alone. Threatening Connors would be akin to prodding a brown snake with a toothpick, ineffectual and quite lethal—you didn't hear that from me. He's one tough cop, so don't mess with him. And before you go, can we talk about my account?"

"Sure, as soon as I get my wallet back. Then I'm off for a shower, a feed and a long sleep—in that order."

Walter retrieved his belt, watch and wallet from the desk clerk and paid the lawyer. Connors was nowhere in sight. He shook DeBrito's outstretched hand.

"I'll open an account for you Mr Boyce. I have a feeling you'll be requiring my services in the future."

"Thanks, but I hope I won't be needing you again."

Walter crossed the street and hurried up a side street without looking back. He weaved in and out of several laneways before hailing a cruising cab. Five minutes later, while stopped at traffic lights he observed the meter tab, dropped a note to cover it into the driver's lap and stepped out. He quickly walked through the foyer of a large office block and towards the banks of lifts. He got in and pushed the button for the first floor before finding the fire stairs down to the basement car park. He waited for several minutes before walking up the ramp and out into the laneway at the rear of the building. The electronics store had exactly what he was looking for. He then walked back to the Parmelia.

Annie was asleep when he let himself into the room. He did not wake her but quietly went into the bathroom, undressed and stood under the shower. The hot water washed away two days' worth of grime and sweat. His clogged, matted hair fell apart as he applied a handful of shampoo. He finally stepped out and reached for one of the large bath towels, wrapping it around himself as he made use of the complimentary shaver and toothbrush. He was beginning to feel human again.

"Well hello, Mr Brittan, where have you been?" Annie startled him as she wrapped her arms around his middle and pressed her naked body to his. "I've been so worried about you."

"You were only worried I may have bolted and left you to pay the bill. Isn't that true?" Walter smiled, enjoying the feel of her warmth on him.

"Don't be so sarcastic. I really did miss you."

Walter could see she meant it. "I'm sorry, but I had a rough time with the cops. They want that package I slipped into your pocket. You still have it, I hope?"

"Is that a red diamond? Is it really priceless?"

Walter nodded, combing his hair. "It certainly is. Carat for carat there is no diamond known that can match that particular rock and I believe there are more from where it came from."

Annie slipped her hands inside his towel and it dropped to the floor. "What do we have here, big boy?"

"It's a gun and it's liable to go off if you play with it."

"Well, I'm trigger happy and I think it's about time we got to know each other better, don't you?" She led him towards the bed. "How about you start by kissing me all over. I've had to put up with lily-white, chinless poms for so long, I haven't had a decent Aussie man in ages."

23

he phone rang, waking them from their light sleep. Annie looked at him in surprise. "Expecting someone?"

"Yes, but not so soon." Walter rolled over and picked up the phone.

"Boyce speaking." He listened to the voice on the other end. "Okay, I'll meet you in the foyer in an hour. I'm going to eat first, and I don't want to lay eyes on you until I've finished a steak and a bottle of wine."

"Who was that?"

"Unless I miss my guess, it's a bent copper wanting to make some sort of deal. I've been expecting his call."

He showered and pulled out a clean, but crinkled shirt and slacks from his bag. He looked in the mirror. "Rough, but I'm not concerned with appearances at the moment. Come on, I'm starving."

Annie handed him the diamond. "Take it. I don't want to be apprehended with this on me. It would be the end of my job." She disappeared into the bathroom. "I'll see you downstairs."

Walter looked around the foyer when the lift opened. It appeared to be almost deserted except for an elderly couple staring into the street from their lounge chairs. He had to risk it. He simply could not carry the diamond on him. He went up to the reception desk and asked for a padded envelope. He addressed it and slipped the wrapped diamond inside. "How often do they clear the mail?"

The clerk looked at his watch. "It will be gone in about half an hour, sir."

He slipped the envelope into the post box and then headed for the restaurant. He felt very uneasy as he picked a table with a clear view of the box.

Annie finally swung into a seat opposite.

"I was about to send a search party out for you."

"A girl has got to look her best. It takes time. All you guys have to do is shower, shave and shampoo."

"You look great."

"Thank you. Now cut the small talk and hand over the menu."

The steak was exactly as ordered, thick and rare. The Margaret River cab sav was exactly as expected, smooth and red. He sat back to savour the wine and he glanced across the restaurant towards the street. He saw the unmarked cruiser pull up in the no-parking zone and Connors emerge.

"Right on time," he muttered to himself. If he had been tipped off about the mailbox, Connors would walk up to the desk and demand it be opened. Walter breathed a sigh of relief as Connors swung straight past reception and into the restaurant.

Annie looked around, but Walter hissed at her. "Don't turn around. When he comes over, just get up and leave. Don't talk to him and don't let him engage you in conversation. Just walk away."

He reached into his shirt pocket and switched on the recorder. Annie nodded slowly and waited. Instinct told her when the person had nearly reached the table. She rose, tossed her napkin down and peeled off towards the restrooms.

Connors did not bother to intercept Annie, he just pulled up a chair and sat down. Walter could see his mood had not changed. He was his normal belligerent self.

"You didn't think you could shake me off did you? That's Anne Brittan, isn't it?" Connors cast a look at the departing figure. "She wasn't sitting with you, but across the aisle; that's how you got the diamond through. No doubt you've hidden it again. Very attractive indeed. I wonder how she'd stand up to a full strip and cavity search? I'd think she'd break down very quickly and confess to handling stolen goods. You'd be up the creek then Boyce. With her evidence to back up Steiner's, you'd have some explaining to do about the whereabouts of the gem."

"What do you want Connors?"

"I want to be a partner in the diamond you have and in the place where it came from. There must be more out there and you obviously know the location."

"I don't know what you're talking about, but if I did you'd be the last person I would be talking to, or making any deal with. You stink, Connors. You stink to high heaven and there's absolutely no chance of you and I ever being associated in any business dealings."

Connors lit a cigarette and puffed a cloud of smoke in Walter's direction. He grinned at the outburst.

A waiter walked hurriedly over to inform Connors he was in a no-smoking zone. Connors ignored him but stubbed the cigarette out on a saucer. "Don't test my patience Boyce or you'll find yourself back in a cell very quickly. You obviously think because I withdrew the charge, you're in the clear. Let me tell you the only reason you're sitting here free and not out on bail is because I want it that way—for now. I could have easily offered information and asked for an adjournment until I'd managed to put together a solid case. Because of the gravity of the crime, I could have you remanded in custody. Remand is not something involving a day or so being locked away before your case is heard, I could easily stretch it out for a couple of months. You're in some pretty deep shit stealing one of the most valuable diamonds on earth. Argyle pink diamonds have been turning up on world markets and they've not been legitimately acquired. The Argyle mine has lost tens of millions in revenue."

"You know a lot about it. I suppose you're involved?"

"Yeah, I've been involved in the investigation for the past three years."

"I didn't mean your involvement in the investigation, I meant involvement in the thefts."

Connors' face turned ugly. "You're giving me the shits Boyce."

"Am I really? I reckon you know all about the Argyle thefts, and you are involved."

"How do you work that out, smart arse?"

"In his excitement, Steiner showed me a couple of Argyle pinks, and lo and behold you're banging on my door the next morning. That's not co-incidence, that's collusion between you and Steiner. You know very well Steiner has pink diamonds of dubious provenance, so obviously you're in on it."

"What's your answer?"

"As I've already stated, I don't want to have anything to do with you."

"Listen Boyce, unless you want to wind up in the slammer this time tomorrow you'd better think about sharing your secrets with me. I want a share of that diamond and any further diamonds that turn up."

Walter eyed the officer. He could see he meant it. Either he dealt him in or he was in for a very rough time.

"You know very well the stone I showed Steiner has no relationship to anything mined at Argyle. Any expert would attest to that."

"I know that Boyce, Steiner told me so, but you're getting a little ahead of yourself. You see, Steiner would attest he believed the gem was stolen from Argyle. That will be enough to have you remanded without bail if you don't produce the rock. A couple of months down the track you'll come up for trial."

Walter thought for a moment as he finished his wine. "The way I see it Connors, even if I produce the diamond you could still have me locked up and then welch on your part of the deal."

"Not if you play ball with me."

"What sort of deal are you looking for?"

"I think half of everything would be a reasonable proposition."

Walter laughed. "You're out of your tree. You think I'm going to cut you in for half of everything? You're not thinking straight."

"Well, perhaps not half, but a fair percentage for keeping you out of jail."

"And if I tell you to get fucked?"

"Don't screw me around Boyce. You know the answer to that." Connors pushed his chair back as he made to get up from the table. "I'll give you until this time tomorrow to make up your mind. Either I'm in on the deal, or you're in for the most unpleasant experience of your life."

"And if I agree to your terms, are you going to do likewise with what you've got going now?"

"What do mean by that?"

"Deal me in on what you're creaming off from Argyle." It was a try on and he expected Connors to deny any involvement or knowledge.

"I'll think about that, but my first reaction is you've got yourself a deal. Now Boyce, we meet here tomorrow for lunch and it's on you. The answer had better be yes, otherwise don't pack a bag because they'll issue you with a pair of faded jeans and a nice orange shirt where you'll be going. And don't attempt to leave town again, otherwise I'll make it really hard for your travelling companion. I'll bet she won't like some dyke looking up her pussy when she's strip searched. And if she attempts to catch the next flight out, she won't be able to board until I've spoken to her. I've put a restraining order out on her. Do I make myself clear as to what will happen if you don't play ball?"

"Very clear. Say, what's your rank? Is it constable or sergeant, or what?"

"Detective Connors to you." Connors rose and slowly strolled out through the foyer.

Walter poured the last of the wine as Annie returned.

"You look pleased with yourself. What did he want?"

Walter waved his hand and shrugged. "Just someone wanting to do a little business."

"Don't shoot me a line of crap. That's Connors the bent copper you referred to?"

"Yes, he is and he's not making it very easy for me at the moment."

"In what way?"

"He's says if I don't give him a share of the diamond, he'll have me locked up for theft."

Walter explained the background of the theft of pink diamonds from Argyle.

Annie looked scared. "This is getting too hot for me. By taking that diamond from you in Customs, I'm already implicated so I think I'll haul out of here on the next available flight back to London. I'm not interested in getting a story on Chloe or that diamond if it means being dragged before a court as an accessory."

"You can't Annie."

"What do you mean I can't? This has nothing to do with me. I can leave anytime I like." Her voice trailed off as she saw him shake his head.

"You can't Annie. Connors has alerted Customs and he means business. You can't leave the country."

"What's so bloody funny? Why have you got that stupid grin on your face?" Annie was shaking with rage as she tried to keep her voice down. "Why did you drag me into this? Are you going to let him blackmail you?"

Walter watched absentmindedly as Connors took the parking ticket from under his windscreen wiper, scrunched it up and threw it into the gutter before getting in and driving away.

"I didn't get you into this, Annie. You were a willing accomplice. The only thing you did was carry the diamond through Customs. You didn't know what it was. Where's the crime in that? Now calm down. And to answer your question, I'm certainly not going to let him blackmail me."

"What are you going to do then?"

"I can't tell you right now. I have to listen to something up in the room."

As soon as they returned to their room, Walter took the small voice recorder out of his pocket and replayed the conversation as he held it up to his ear. "Got you, you bastard." He pumped the air and switched the recorder off.

He picked up the phone, identified himself and was put through. "Hi Mr DiBrito, Walter Boyce here. Can I post you something for your safekeeping? It's a recording, but I don't want you to listen to it unless something happens to me."

"You have my complete discretion on that Mr Boyce. Are you going somewhere?"

"I'm off to the Kimberley and home in the next day or so."

"Well, have a safe journey. Call me if you need any help."

He noticed the message light on the phone starting to blink as he hung up. "Not bloody Connors again I hope."

Annie glanced at her watch. "I think that will be for me." She picked up the receiver and pressed the message bank key. She listened and scribbled notes down on the hotel pad.

"That was Chloe phoning from Singapore. She's at Changi and just about to board a flight for Perth."

"Singapore. How does she know we're here?"

"I told her, that's how. I phoned her this morning when you were busy with the police. Luckily, Marcel was out. She told me she's leaving him, giving up modelling and coming back to Australia. She'll be here early in the morning and wants me to meet her at the airport."

"Faroud's not coming with her then?"

"She didn't mention him but if she's leaving him, I hardly think he'll be on the same flight. I don't know why she married him, although I've heard stories."

"And what are they?" Walter took a beer from the bar fridge, offered it to Annie but she shook her head. He popped the cap and settled down on the bed to listen.

"Pure gossip with a modicum of credence. Like any working girl she really had to network with the beautiful people. And once they accepted her, they wanted to be seen with her, but most of them are leeches wanting to score any fresh meat that catches their eye."

"Tell me more. I didn't realise such things went on."

Annie laughed. "You really are a country boy, aren't you? The world of fashion is rough and tough and you have to pay your dues to reach the pinnacle. It's like any part of the entertainment industry—and that's what modelling is really all about, entertainment of women with too much money, young women with money to spend they can't afford, and bored housewives fighting back the years with face creams, weight-loss diets, cellulose gels, nip and tuck operations to boobs and bums and even vulvas these days. Nothing is sacred or private. It's like the film industry. Even the big names have lain on their backs at some point in time to scale the heights of success and stardom. And never assume the guys are all straight. They may appear so, but any cavity will do, whether it be male or female."

"I never suspected Chloe would be into that scene." Walter was in disbelief.

"I'm not suggesting for a moment she was, but she sure rocketed to stardom fast. She's earned millions from modelling and endorsements and is one very wealthy lady. Chloe originally arrived in London to model for the LeClair

Agency, not a big agency, but certainly well respected. Paul LeClair, the effete vulture that he was, realised her potential and Chloe was soon in high demand. However, she was the proverbial lamb to the slaughter as LeClair engaged her on a fixed contract for three years. But as you can imagine, as her profile rose, LeClair was accordingly charging more and more for her modelling services. He was pocketing the lion's share of her ballooning income. At first she was happy and oblivious, but Constance Faroud, Marcel's then wife who also ran a small agency put her wise and Chloe engaged lawyers to look at her contract and accountants to try to extract the books from LeClair. The lawyers advised her she was locked in and there was nothing she could do."

"I note you referred to LeClair in the past tense."

"Yes, Paul died. Poor dear was found floating in a quarry. His boyfriend Cyrus Blomfeld shot himself, leaving a suicide note saying he had killed LeClair in a fit of rage in his apartment and then dumped the body."

"How do you know all this?"

"I covered the coronial inquest when I was with *News of the World*. A police confidante I had at the time gave me the full background of the contract Chloe had with LeClair. But there was something else he hinted at."

"Like what?"

"The police interviewed Chloe, as she was living in one of LeClair's apartments at the time. She was distraught, not about LeClair's death but about something that happened between her and LeClair that she wouldn't reveal. She wasn't a suspect in his death, so the police didn't pursue it."

"Probably an argument over money. The guy was obviously a faggot so she wouldn't have been worried about him cracking onto her."

Annie laughed. "The guys might all be straight where you come from, but that doesn't apply in London, or any other metropolis for that matter. In my short time as a journalist, I've come to the conclusion the whole world is bent to some degree."

"So what happened after LeClair died?"

"The agency folded so Chloe was a free agent."

"And that's how she wound up with Faroud?"

"No. Constance certainly tried to get her under contract, but apparently she was going to throw it all in and marry a Milanese squillionaire by the name of Pietro Malasardi. Unfortunately, Malasardi was murdered in Naples and she was dragged into the police investigation where she revealed the marriage proposal which was confirmed by his mother. Malasardi was walking out of the Grand Hotel Vesuvio when a motorbike pulled up, the pillion rider got off and pumped two shots into his head. No one was ever charged, but the Comorra mafia are a shadow behind all Neapolitan crimes. It was accepted that Malasardi had run foul of them, but the Comorra denied it."

"So Chloe was once again a free agent?"

"Yes, but she simply disappeared off the scene for about three months. Malasardi's death really shook her up. When she did surface again, she needed an agent and she could have signed with any of the majors, but she joined Picard's— Constance Faroud's agency. From that moment on, Chloe and Marcel were inseparable. It was obvious to everyone it had to be more than platonic, but Constance didn't bat an eye. If she was aware, she never let on."

"Do you think there was a link between LeClair's death and Malasardi's violent end?"

"A matter of months later, Constance was found dead in the park opposite their house. She often went into the park to unwind and relax. The autopsy revealed she was overloaded with drugs; not sleeping pills, but heroin. There was a single needle wound in her arm. The verdict was she had been given a 'hot shot', a massive dose that killed her within minutes. Faroud was a suspect, but nothing came of it as he wasn't in London at the time. Distance from the scene of the crime is always a strong alibi. The thing about London society and the whole modelling scene is that everyone's on drugs. You name it, they're smoking it, shooting it, snorting it or swallowing it. However, I would never have picked Constance Faroud. She was a darling, treated everyone with the utmost respect."

"If she was such a darling, how come she turned a blind eye to what her husband was up to with Chloe? What woman puts up with that?"

"Good question, but often the most intelligent people make mistakes only to realise after the event what they've committed themselves too. I don't know anything about Constance's background, but she did have Marcel's olive complexion so I assume she was also Lebanese. Perhaps it was an arranged marriage; it's very common in middle eastern countries. Who knows, it's irrelevant. But one thing I do know, I never saw her ever take a drink or appear to take drugs and I attended a lot of parties at which she was present. Never once did she ever let her hair down."

"What makes you think Faroud had something to do with her death?"

"Women's intuition. Within a couple of months, Marcel had moved in with Chloe. She had recently purchased the

Eton Square property and they were married very soon after. Chloe had shot into the big time, commanding huge fees but she was contracted to the Picard agency, so Marcel had a new wife, a steady income stream and her assets locked in as his. I made some extensive enquiries funded by *News of the World* because I was keen to dig something up of his background in Lebanon. I could find nothing, and neither could the private agency we hired. Their conclusion was he was a super-smooth conman with a false identity, but weren't prepared to put it in writing. I found out later that the real reason the agency dropped the enquiry was their agent had been beaten up when he started asking too many questions in a certain quarter of Beirut. I lost interest at that stage because I also received a couple of nasty threats suggesting if I persisted I would have my face altered, or worse."

Walter helped himself to another beer and sat down again, deep in thought. "If she's on the way here, is he following her, or is he already here? I wonder if he's travelling with one or both of his assassins?"

"Those guys undoubtedly have criminal records so I doubt they'll get through Customs. But it doesn't matter. Faroud will quickly find some thug to do his dirty work. People like Marcel Faroud don't have the balls to negotiate directly with anyone. He always has an enforcer at his side to get his message across. It's his way or you wind up dead in an alleyway. What are you going to do about Connors? Are you going to meet him in the morning?"

"I'm not looking forward to it." Walter drained his glass. "But unless I give it to him straight, I'm only going to be in for further blackmail."

"You must have a very strong argument. I'd love to hear what's on that recorder."

"No, I don't want to involve you further. Letting you listen to the recording could drag you into this. You can stand up in the witness box and truthfully say you have no idea what transpired between Connors and me. Let's keep it that way."

"Okay, take me down to the bar for a drink, then back here for a quiet evening watching television, or we could play hide the sausage again."

"Let's skip television."

24

The flight from Singapore arrived on time. They waited for Chloe to clear Customs. It was half an hour before she appeared, sporting large, dark glasses to avoid being noticed by any paparazzi. She pushed her trolley and searched the hall expectantly. Annie sprang to her feet and waved.

"Hi Chloe. How was the flight?"

"Don't ask me that inane question Annie. All I want is a shower and a nice bed," she replied as they embraced one another.

"Marcel not with you?"

"I certainly hope not. I don't want to ever lay eyes on that man again. I'm finished with the London scene and modelling too. I'll tell you about it later. Now let's go."

Chloe glanced over and saw Walter moving towards them. "Hello Walter. You still have my diamond, I trust?"

"I certainly do, Chloe and I'm hoping you'll show me where you got it from."

She nodded slowly. "I will have to think about that, but I know Gramps wouldn't agree."

"He's long dead," Walter protested gently. "Surely you don't believe in dreamtime myths, do you?"

Chloe fixed him with a cold stare. "It's not up to you whether I believe in it or not. I was burdened with a trust and I can adhere to it, or abandon it. You'll have to give me time to consider."

At first, Walter thought she might not be serious, but then he realised her grandfather's image and beliefs had probably risen to the surface stronger than ever now she was back in the land of her birth.

"Now, let's get out of here before someone from the media recognises me. I don't want any publicity."

Chloe and Annie made small talk in the back of the cab on the way to the hotel. The cabbie kept looking in the mirror, suddenly realising the identity of his passenger. "Hey you're Chloe the model. Wait 'til I tell my missus about this. You're more beautiful than the photos give you credit for."

Chloe graciously acknowledged his compliment. "Would you do me a favour?"

"If I can," the cabbie beamed.

"It's been a long flight from London and I'm very tired. I just want to sit here quietly and talk to my friend."

"Sure lady, but can I have your autograph please? I want to convince the missus it was actually you in my cab." He handed over a five-dollar note with a pen for her to sign it. "I promise I won't say another word."

Chloe signed and handed it back to the cabbie. He was silent for the rest of the journey.

Once she had checked in and the porter had disappeared with her bags, Chloe turned to Walter. "Could I speak to you alone?"

Annie took the cue and made an excuse to go up to the room.

"I'm sure Marcel will follow me if he's not already here. Do you know anything?"

"I heard he was on his way."

"He laid a complaint with the police you had stolen the diamond. When the police came to interview me, I denied it. After that, they were rather anxious to talk to Marcel, but he'd disappeared with the entire contents of my safe. Money, jewellery, the lot. We were at the end of the road in any case. I was sick of his gambling and womanising, so it was a small price to pay for my sanity and freedom. Have the local police spoken to you at all?"

"They most certainly have." Walter decided to take her into his confidence and told her everything.

Chloe interrupted him. "Did you say the policeman's name was Connors? I'm sure Marcel took a call from someone by that name. You say you're going to be arrested by Connors this morning. What are you going to do? I'm quite happy to testify the diamond is mine."

"I don't think that'll be necessary Chloe. What do you intend to do now?"

"First, I'm going home to see Henry. Did you know he's had a stroke?"

Walter looked shocked. "I had no idea. How did you find out?"

"Aunt Liz phoned me in London, but she didn't know how bad it was. I phoned her from Singapore to check on him, but there was no answer."

"There's a flight every morning to Wyndham. Too late today, but we could all go tomorrow. I promised Annie for all her help she could visit Venus Downs and do a background story on you."

"That's going to fall flat for her. I'm not going back to the world of modelling; I'm finished with it. I want to see Henry and spend a few days with him and then decide what I'll do from there."

"You're giving modelling away altogether?"

"Yes, I've enough in stocks and bonds and a bank account that Marcel didn't get his hands on, and the house in London is mine, so I won't starve."

"Do you intend to make Venus Downs your home?"

"I love Venus Downs, it's my home, but it's not my property. If I owned it, I would stay, but that's out of the question."

"I hope to inherit Venus Downs. Why don't you share it with me as my wife?"

Chloe looked startled. She reached over and touched Walter's hand. "That's very sweet of you, but I don't really think you and I were made for each other."

"Is that because of what happened between us? I've never forgiven myself for what I did. Johnny sure taught me a lesson."

"No, it's not because of that. I'm still married to Marcel and although I will file for divorce, I don't want to become involved with anyone anytime soon."

"I've always loved you Chloe. It's just I've never known how to show it."

"Do you love Venus Downs?"

"I do, but—"

Chloe cut him off. "Then why do you want me to show you where the diamond comes from? It's a site sacred to my grandfather. If you inherit Venus Downs, you'll also inherit all Henry's other properties. You'll be wealthy. Isn't that enough? Carl is dead, so you won't have to share it with anyone."

"Johnny wasn't your grandfather. He was no relation of yours."

"I've known that for a long time Walter, but apart from Henry, he's the only one who really showed me any real love. I don't know who my natural father was. You haven't answered my question. Why do you want to know where the diamond comes from?"

"The diamond came from somewhere on Venus Downs and if I inherit the property, then the source of the diamonds rightly belongs to me."

"I can follow your logic Walter, but Venus Downs is not yours yet, so there's no hurry. Are you going to give me my diamond back?"

"I don't have it on me."

"But you know where it is?"

"I do and it's safe. I'll give it back to you when you show me where you got it from."

"Walter, you profess your love and want to marry me, but you don't want to give back to me what is mine. I find that rather strange. It's no different to the blackmail Connors is apparently trying on you."

"I just want money Chloe. Real money. I've never had it and although Henry is a good man, I don't want to wait around for him to die. We could share what you know and get married. We'd be worth a fortune."

"You want me to share it with you first and then we'll get married. Is that what you're proposing? What if there's nothing but the single diamond you now have?"

"There's got to be more. I'm positive of it."

Chloe had observed his look of avarice. She had seen it countless times before in the expressions of the power and money-hungry people she had encountered. Walter was no different to Marcel.

"Walter, I'm tired. I'm going to bed. Why don't we meet for dinner tonight? Shall we say seven here?"

"Seven it is."

Walter posted the mini voice recorder with a covering letter to DiBrito and was sitting at the same table in the hotel's restaurant watching the street when Connors walked in and sat down opposite. His sagging gut matched his heavy jowls.

"Well, what's it to be? Do we have a deal, or do I arrest you now?"

"You really should give up smoking, start a diet and exercise, Connors. Otherwise you're going to drop dead soon."

The taunt immediately hit home. Connors began to rise, his hand reaching behind him for the handcuffs hanging off his belt. "You smart prick. It's yes, or you're under arrest."

"It's yes."

The big man sank back into his seat with a smile of satisfaction.

Walter paused for a moment, then continued. "What you don't realise, Connors, is that I recorded yesterday's meeting. It will be in the hands of my solicitor this morning, with instructions to hand it to the Internal Affairs boys if you arrest me. If you put those cuffs on me your career will be over some time later today. Bang goes the diamond, along with your job and pension. You've implicated yourself in the theft of Argyle diamonds, along with Steiner. You're in deep, deep do-do's, mate. Another bent copper put out of action. I wasn't trying to hide which hotel I was booked into; I was trying to shake anyone following me long enough for me to find an electronics store to buy the voice recorder. Here's the receipt. You'll note the date and time of purchase." Walter tossed the receipt onto the table in front of Connors.

Connors picked it up and studied it. "You're bluffing." He tried to mask it, but the shock on his face was clear. "It's illegal to tape anyone without their knowledge. You've just committed a criminal offence."

"I probably have, Detective Connors, but I'll only get fined or a slap on the wrist, whereas you face time in the slammer. You clearly identified yourself and the deal you were proposing to me. Of course, the most damning admission was your involvement in the Argyle thefts, along with Steiner. So I lied. We don't have a deal." Walter got up and walked away, all the while anticipating his arrest. He reached the lift and turned as he entered. Connors was still sitting at the table staring blankly ahead.

"She said she'd be here at seven," Walter remarked, looking at his watch. "It's nearly half past. I'll phone her room."

Annie watched as Walter walked up to the reception desk.

"Can you phone Mrs Faroud for me, please. She was supposed to meet me here at seven."

The clerk punched the computer and looked up with a deadpan expression on his face. "Mrs Faroud has checked out sir."

"Checked out? When?"

"She checked out at nine this morning, sir. She was only with us for an hour."

Walter stood in stunned silence, his mind racing. "Can I use a phone please?"

"Over there sir." The clerk indicated a row of phones.

Walter was shaking as he dialled the number. "Hello Liz, it's Walter. I was wondering if Chloe is with you?"

"No she's not here."

Walter caught the resentment in her voice. "Has she been there?"

"I don't like your tone Walter."

"I'm sorry Liz, but would you just tell me whether you've seen her today."

"Yes, I have. I drove her out to Jandakot airport. She said she couldn't wait until tomorrow to fly north with you so she chartered a plane. Henry's condition is deteriorating so she wanted to see him immediately."

Walter stood in stunned silence as he contemplated Chloe's actions.

"Are you there, Walter?"

"Yes. By any chance did you give her the package I posted to you?"

"Yes, I did."

"Why the hell did you do that?" Walter demanded angrily. "You were supposed to hold it for me."

"Because you always said it belonged to her, so I gave it to her. And Walter, don't ever contact me again."

The Cessna Citation put down and taxied towards a hangar with a helicopter parked outside.

"You're here Chloe," the pilot remarked as he stripped off his headphones. "And as you can see, Mark Snell has his chopper ready."

"Thanks very much. It was a pleasure riding up front and watching the landscape."

The pilot laughed. "I don't know that you saw much. You were asleep for most of the time."

Chloe nodded in agreement as she climbed out of the right hand seat. Five minutes later, she was seated in the helicopter with its rotors already turning.

"Chloe, you're one stunning looking lady. Has anyone ever told you that?"

Chloe ignored the tired remark and leaned back in her seat. She was in no mood for the suggestive but harmless banter that no doubt would follow if she replied. Half an hour later, the chopper put down at Venus Downs. Snell kept the motor running while he unloaded her bags.

"Look after yourself Chloe." He patted her on the arm, climbed back aboard and with a wave, the chopper lifted off.

She shielded her face from the dust as she walked towards the homestead. She could see Henry sitting in a wheelchair on the veranda attended by a woman who she assumed to be a nurse, and Dotti.

Chloe was horrified, but tried to hide her shock. The man with the strength and stature of an ironbark tree was no more. Here before her was a wreck, one side of Henry's face had completely collapsed, his eye socket and cheek sunken to the bone. His mouth was twisted and a constant stream of spittle ran down his chin. One side of his body was curled inwards with a useless claw of a hand resting on his chest. One eye was unseeing while the other gave a brief flare of recognition as she bent down to kiss him on his cheek. She burst into tears, then clutching her hand to her mouth, she turned away.

Dotti put her arm around her shoulders as she walked her down the veranda. "Nothin' you can do Chloe. You can talk to him, but he can't speak, but he sure glad to see you."

"How long has he been like this?"

"He had the stroke not long after Walter left. They had a heap big bust up."

"What about?"

"Dunno, but must have bin something to do with Henry finding him in his office goin' through his papers. I dunno if there was a fight, but sure as eggs there was a lot of yellin' going on. Soon after, Walter packed up and left."

Chloe composed herself and went back along the veranda. She sat down beside Henry and cupped a once huge fist in both her hands.

"I'm sorry about that Henry. I got a shock that's all." All she felt was a slight movement and barely perceptible nod of his head. The nurse wiped the drool from his mouth. Chloe did not know how long she had been sitting there lost in her thoughts when Dotti patted her shoulder.

"C'mon girl. I've made up your room."

The nurse followed them inside. Chloe turned to her. "I'm sorry for my rudeness, I'm Chloe. How bad is it? Will he recover?"

"There's no need to apologise. I can understand your grief. I'm Sarah Sullivan," she replied smiling. "No, he won't recover. He's had a series of mini-strokes followed by the major one that completely paralysed one side. He will never walk or talk again. He needs round the clock care."

"How long will he be like this?"

"I can't break this to you gently, or give you any hope. He could go on for a year, a month, or be gone in the next minute. However, according to the doctor, the next stroke will most likely prove fatal."

"The indignity of it must be killing him. It would be merciful if he just didn't wake up one morning, wouldn't it?"

"I can't answer that. All I can say is, it's only a matter of time. I can say though, he's thrilled to see you." Sarah turned and went back outside to her patient.

"You gunna stay for a while?"

"Yes Dotti. It's the least I can do, but I want to leave early in the morning for a few days, and then I'll be back to help. I'll stay for as long as it takes."

"Where you goin'?"

"You know very well where I'm going. I want to go and talk to Gramps."

"Can't it wait?"

"No, I must go tomorrow."

Dotti smiled knowingly and walked away, mumbling to herself.

25

She slipped off her footwear and shed her clothes before stepping into the clear waters of the billabong. The waters enveloped her and the surface spun off ripples from her splayed fingers as she gently stroked forwards. The water glistened and slid off her body and buttocks leaving her skin with a glistening, oiled appearance. Tiny goose bumps rose to give texture and accentuated her slender, muscular form. The years came back in a flash of memories. The lagoon she had swum in countless times as a child. It was her secret world where she knew she was completely safe with her memories. Her mind wandered in and out of the textures and corridors of the past, the telepathy of her ancestors, the events of her existence played over and over again, from the first time she had wandered alone on this land, and over the successive years. The dreaming was not of gods, but ethereal and inanimate beings that drifted around in the mists controlling every aspect of an ancient civilisation and life; the experience of the two worlds she lived in. Two worlds with which she was totally familiar and yet totally alien to. Two people with two identities, but one being.

After a while, she left the lagoon and lay down on a warm rock shaded by the overhanging cliffs. The tensions and stress fluidised and she felt them disappearing as she turned herself inwards into another world, her mind drifting into the twilight of unconsciousness.

She awoke with a start. It was cold, as the sun had disappeared from even the steepest face of the tallest rock formation. She was frightened at first, until her mind returned to the present as she lay, allowing the cooling strata beneath her reach up and gradually permeate until it was too cold for her to endure any longer. Shivering, she got up and dressed. She picked up her small backpack containing matches, a filleting knife, and a length of fishing line and hooks. She had neither bait nor food of any kind, which was intentional. She slipped on her sneakers and jumped from boulder to boulder until she was under the ledge of the tallest bluff. She gathered twigs and dead branches scattered around and made a fire. The dry material caught quickly and within minutes, heat radiated off the wall of the striated jasper cliff behind her. The jasper was mottled brown and white and the colours bounced and danced in the light as she watched, transfixed by the display. She could feel the sand around the fire becoming hot as she shoved at it with her bare feet. She laughed as she thought of her childhood when her feet were so hardened it was as if they were shod with an impermeable layer of hard rubber. Years of soft existence had seen them morph back to their original texture of an infant, feeling every unconformity and irritation. She scooped the sand away between the fire and the rock wall so she had an indentation the length and width of her body. Next, she wandered around the floor of the overhang picking up large stones, which she arranged around the perimeter of the fire.

After an hour, the quartz inclusions within the stones were cracking with the heat. Her pangs of hunger were growing more intense. Water alone was not going to sustain her. She had grown soft living in another world. Memories resurfaced of the days living off the land when she went walkabout in the wilderness with Gramps. She tore off a piece of cloth from the hem of her shirt and shred it into a succession of streaming fibres a few centimetres in length. This she tied around the shank of the hook. She studied her handiwork. Satisfied, she walked down to the billabong and cast the line out as far as it would go, before slowly dragging it back. The white fibres of the lure flashed in the moonlight as it trailed through the water. A dozen times, she repeated the exercise without result. And then, the process came back to her. She pulled in the line and stepped from rock to rock until she was just in front of a large boulder where the water below was blackest and deepest. Gently she tossed the lure in again and again, varying the speed with which she withdrew it. She chanted to the animal she knew was lurking, its eyes seeking out the intruder to its domain. The large mouth slowly opened and closed as it cautiously inched out to assess the risk and then unsure, gently settled back as the enticing life form disappeared again in a flash of white streaks. With each cast, it became more inquisitive about this strange morsel. It was not driven by hunger, but out of desire to strike and re-affirm its dominance over its territory. It had already glutted itself on lower life forms within the lagoon, on insects that darted across the surface or landed momentarily, and on larvae and worms which thrived in myriad abundance on the bottom and edges. It did not need to eat, nor was it forced to actively search for food. It was full-bellied and lazy, but the lure of the flashing strands so near to its lair was too much to ignore. The intrusion had to be dealt with. Slowly it inched back and forth from under the lee of the boulder, hesitant to be suddenly exposed to some unforeseen predator.

Chloe could now see the form as a silvery outline as she enticed it to rise. It heard the soft chant and moved as if drawn by some primal calling, but hesitated and drew back, as if unsure the call was not the sound of danger. Gently she enticed it from under the boulder again, all the time recalling the language, dialect and intonations of her grandfather. She was searching for her memories, unexposed secrets of the land unknown to anyone except those chosen to learn and accept. She was comforted, as shred by shred the ancient dreamings Gramps had taught her emerged. She had much to remember as she untangled it from the life she had just abandoned. She snapped back to the present as she noticed the shape of the fish had disappeared from her wandering mind. She returned to her concentration and gradually coaxed it out of its lair again, her voice gently soothing the animal and calling it to the surface. The bait was a secondary motivation for the fish as the chant mesmerised its attention. It slowly inched its way out from under the safety and its form became once more visible in the bright moonlight. It finally ingested the lure and Chloe made one savage tug to ensure it was embedded on the hook. The large fish slowly rose to the surface as she talked to it and pulled it out. With deft strokes, she gutted and filleted it, all the while chanting in a soft voice to the spirits of the dreaming.

She laid the fillets in the hot embers, occasionally turning them over with a stick until they were cooked. No fish fillets from the best restaurants in London, Paris, or New York had ever tasted better. None were as fresh and succulent. She sat back against the rock face and studied the heavens. Countless millions of pinpoints of light interspersed with more distant coalescing bodies of merging galaxies, generating the cold blue haze at the fringes of the surrounding horizons.

She recognised the giant lizard, the serpent, the fish, the wedge-tail eagle and a myriad of other dreaming animals within the celestial constellations. Her mind was completely divorced from her life of only a few days ago and she chuckled at the thought of her London and Paris friends and acquaintances contemplating her in her current surroundings.

She took two sticks and flicked the hot rocks surrounding the fire into the indentation she had scooped out. Next, she covered the rocks with a thick layer of sand and pushed the remains of the fire on top. She then stoked the hot embers again, adding more wood to heat the sand above the stones and locking in the heat from that source. She watched as she let the fire die down completely and then scooped away the ashes, leaving a small indentation in the sand covering the hot rocks. She tested it until she believed it was cool enough to lie down in. The heat radiated from below and it was only minutes before her contemplation of the planets faded, and her eyelids closed into a deep, exhausted sleep. She didn't notice the chill breezes that enveloped her as she lay below the rim of the surrounding sand, the heat of the stones and sand warming her from below. She awoke a few times to change her position and contemplate her surroundings. At first she felt alarmed, until she realised she was far removed from the cosseted surrounds to which she was accustomed. She drifted off again, safe in the knowledge Gramps was looking down on her.

The overpowering chatter and screeching of swarms of budgies, finches, sulphur crested cockatoos and corellas woke her as they crowded the edges of the billabong, bathing and splashing in the shallows. The beaks of the finches barely broke the surface, as they dipped quickly and threw their heads back to swallow, all the while nervously aware and looking for any possible danger. The cockatoos were slower in their actions, comforted by the lookouts posted in the surrounding trees to watch and screech the intrusion of any predator. The budgies and smaller parrots took no notice of the frenetic finches, content in the knowledge the lookout would give ample warning.

Chloe watched from the rim of her sleeping pit, which was still warm and comfortable. She marvelled at the colours and sounds of nature before her. Suddenly, with an almost unanimous screech and whirl of sound, the lagoon was empty as the birds took to wing. She looked around to see what had frightened them and saw a goanna several metres in length lumbering towards the water, its long pink and blue tongue sensing the air for prey or danger. It was followed by another smaller goanna, which kept its distance from its larger relative. Both sank their heads into the cool, clear water. At that moment, she grabbed a heavy stick and sprinted towards the smaller of the two. In an instant, it saw her coming and tried to dodge around her in its haste to regain safety amongst the rock ledges that were its sanctuary and home. She swung the club with a savage blow that caught the animal behind the head, stunning it. With a quick movement, she picked it up by the tail and swung the metre long reptile in an arc before crashing it down on a rock. All movement from the unfortunate creature ceased. She noted the larger and more dangerous animal, scurrying for safety.

Chloe stoked the still smoking embers of the fire with handfuls of dried spinifex and twigs and fanned it back into life with her hat. On this, she tossed larger pieces of wood so within minutes the fire was generating the necessary hot embers she needed for preparation of her morning meal. She felt hungry and her hunger increased as she finally laid the dead monitor on the hot coals and watched it roast. She had not gutted it; the juices of the internal organs would add moisture to the soft white flesh. She turned it with a stick from time to time to make sure it was not burning. Finally, she pulled the cooked carcass out of the embers, peeled away the blackened skin with her knife and cut into the white flesh. It was just as she remembered: delicious.

In recent times, she would have been revolted by the sight of the skeletal remains, the blackened eye sockets now two empty pits, the jaw drawn back in the strained rictus of death and heat with tiny teeth visible, straightened legs and clawed feet burnt to reveal bone and the burst gut spewing forth a gelatinous mess. However, these were not recent times. These were the times of her childhood and youth, times of living close to nature and the earth of her ancestors, the times of living off what the land provided, rather than supermarket shelves. She pulled the remains of the animal back onto the embers and stoked it again with dried branches. She watched, fascinated, absorbing the cremation of what was an hour before, a living creature. The cycle of life and death.

The birds deserted the billabong as the early morning heat began to surmount and penetrate the depths of the ravines.

The avian world belonged to the crows and soaring wedge-tail eagles from this part of the day. The crows lived on the carrion, dead kangaroos, wallabies, bandicoots, snakes and goannas, and anything else that had recently died and was now putrefied enough to attract the attention of the packs of black, raucous scavengers. The wedge-tail's soared on a relentless wave of thermals, looking for living prey, small wallabies, mice, snakes and lizards. Their unsuspecting prey only became aware of their fate the precise moment the talons dug in and lifted them to an erie, to be torn to pieces by the powerful, curved beak of the magnificent bird, and fed to its young.

Chloe shed her clothes and once more stepped into the cool waters. She swam the hundred metres of the billabong's length with practised strokes, stopping occasionally and rolling on her back to look up at the steep cliffs and wonder at the gnarled trees fighting for existence, clinging to the sheer rock walls. She watched as an eagle landed on a ledge high above with a snake writhing in its talons. She swam slowly back to her camp and lay on the warm sand. It clung to her body as she rolled over to cover it entirely. She laughed at the memory of the games she played as a child when she would roll in the sand and then jump into the water, repeating it over and over, all the time imagining she was changing the colour of her skin. Johnny would sit on the bank and laugh at her antics, such was the simplicity of their existence. Gramps remained a vivid memory, his love and understanding, his teaching and guidance, an all-permeating experience never to be forgotten.

It was her final memory that haunted her and flashed periodically like an explosion in her brain. It was as clear as though it only happened yesterday. The momentary effect of that occasion was the most traumatic experience she had ever endured. It had been a gunshot. She was used to the sound of rifle fire. She knew Gramps was gone; she would never see him again. The shattering of her life and the total loss of one facet of her innocence and gaining of an understanding of man's brutality emerged. The memory of that day exploded out of the darkness of her subconscious as she quickly picked herself up and dived once again into the billabong. It washed away the sand in an instant, but the memory remained intact. It would never leave her no matter how hard she tried to erase it.

She fished again late in the afternoon when the insects swarmed over the surface of the lagoon and the black bream rose to feed. Her lure hardly touched the water before it was almost jerked from her hand, such was the force with which it was taken. She wrapped the line around the stick and quickly reeled it in. Once again, she filleted the fish and threw it onto a large, flat stone that had been heating in the fire for several hours. She had spent the morning collecting water lily bulbs and picking wild fruit and berries. She located a sugar-bag beehive halfway up a blood-wood tree and fashioned herself a honey dipper by using a long stick with a knobbly end, which she pushed down into the tiny hive and withdrew, covered in the golden nectar and pieces of wax. She drew the stick sideways through her mouth and repeated the process until she had her fill. The tiny, stingless bees flew around angrily, unable to retaliate at her intrusion and theft. They were part of the dreaming, not to be harmed as she brushed them off. The simple foods of her childhood were all that was needed to sustain life.

The night repeated itself as it had done since time began, but she still lay in wonderment and gazed up contemplating which one of tiny lights was Gramps. Each of them was one of her forebears. The stories and legends of the dreaming were never ending, and she was sure Gramps' fertile imagination was the source of many original stories, for experience now told her no one could recall in such detail the multitude of legends he professed to protect.

She was awake as the first rays of dawn touched the tips of the cliffs and slowly worked their way down to embrace and then flood the landscape with bursting light and life. Within minutes, the birdlife was once more chattering around the water. She lay still, not wanting to disturb them as she marvelled at the variety of colours and hues.

Yesterday, she had only noticed the budgies and parrots for their colour, but today her eyes became aware of the varieties of finches: zebras, spinifex, strawberry and the spectacular Gouldian with its mauves, greens and yellows clearly outlined as though painted, noisily establishing their territorial rights to a particular portion of drinking space. Their flight and actions so quick, it was possible only to catch a glimpse of colour as the tiny birds flashed through the sunlight to drink and then take flight again a second later. She watched and sure enough, the same old goanna strode into view with its tongue searching the air like a blind man with a stick, its fat legs splayed akimbo and its spine twisting back and forth as it approached to drink. It had the billabong to itself, as all the birdlife departed in a melding cacophony of sound. The goanna looked in Chloe's direction before turning and ignoring her as it slowly stumped off up the bank towards the cool of an overhanging ridge. She took some of the fruit and berries out of her pack and sucked on them as the sunlight began to seep through the crevices, dispersing its rays in flickering patterns on the surface of the water. She felt comfortable she had adjusted so quickly to the environment again, but she would not feel at ease until she fulfilled the purpose for which she had set out.

She picked up her bag, put her few possessions inside and started to walk to the east into the still rising sun. She kept to the shelter of the cliffs as much as possible, but she knew she was about to start crossing a broad flat plain before she reached another range of hills a full day's walk in the distance. She kept a steady pace as she cleared the last of the range she had been walking through and out onto flat featureless ground ahead. The spinifex pricked at her legs through her soft cotton trousers as she brushed past, blood appearing in hundreds of little well-heads that oozed briefly and then congealed. The small bush flies were thick, seeking out any moisture on her face, neck and back where the sweat soaked her shirt. She plucked a branch from a lone sandalwood tree and began to swat the annoying insects in a futile effort to keep them at bay. She sucked in the scent of the sandalwood, a reminder of the perfumed life she had left behind.

Chloe could feel the thirst coming on, something she had never experienced as a child as there was always abundant water to be found when she was with Gramps. She had not packed a water bottle because in the back of her mind she knew she would be able to look for the indicators her grandfather had taught her. Countless white men had died in this country within sight of water, but unless they had been taught to recognise the signs clearly visible to the native eye, there was little chance of survival. She got up and walked on, searching for what she knew was there. The barely discernible rise finally came into view, a pile of nondescript rocks and a soak that always contained water. It was as though she had been here only yesterday. Nothing had changed. She picked her way through the flint hard strata and halfway around the outcrop until she found a barren circle of red earth with concentric circles where moisture rose and then evaporated in the heat of the day.

She sank to her knees and began to scoop away the loose earth and sand. It was easy digging, but exhausting in the midday sun. She realised she should have set out at dawn and not waited to take in the beauty of the wildlife. It was not long before the hole began to fill with dirty brown water. She dug a little deeper and then sat back on her haunches to watch the liquid fill the hole before slowly starting to clear as though being circulated through an unseen filter. She cupped some in her hand and sampled it. Satisfied, she leaned down and drank deeply. Once again, she laughed as she thought of her international friends seeing her leaning into a water hole in the middle of an Australian desert with her backside in the air. Not very dignified, but she felt smug in the knowledge she could survive in both worlds, something none of her 'friends' could envisage or understand. She continued to take small drinks to completely re-hydrate herself. Satisfied at last and with the sun gradually dropping to mid afternoon, she filled in the hole and smoothed over the surface until once again it was just an innocuous patch. She picked up her pack and set off at a paced walk. She was finding herself again. The anxiety of not being able to find further water soaks disappeared the moment she had recognised the marker for the first one. It all fell into place, the vital signs were like traffic lights to the natives, but completely invisible to those unfamiliar with a nomadic existence.

It was several hours before she reached the next outcrop and water source. She dug down and watched the water slowly rise through the cleansing sands, before gathering dead branches to make a lean-to shelter and debris with which to make a fire. Inside the lean-to, she dug her familiar sleeping depression. She wandered in every direction searching for rocks that would retain heat, eventually gathering the quantity she needed. Next, she walked around hitting the large spinifex clumps with a stick looking for a source of live food these clumps often concealed. Half an hour of looking only produced a blue tongue lizard the length of her hand, which was barely a mouthful. She watched as the beautiful animal with its vivid blue tongue puffed up its brilliantly mottled and smooth scaly body and hissed harmlessly in anger as it sought refuge in another growth of spinifex. The animal was easy prey, with no defence against any predator except for its menacing mouth wide-open hiss as it challenged its tormentor. She was about to give up and settle on the unfortunate animal when her sharp eye caught sight of the very end of a slender tail poking out from under another clump of dry spinifex. She shuddered, but hunger overcame the thought of danger. She knew exactly what the tail belonged to and she trod gently as she walked to within and arm's length and then stooped down with extreme care, as she did not know where the head of the reptile lay. She quickly grabbed the tail and with a firm and violent pull tore the large mulga snake from its concealment. It swung its vicious head towards her and jerked its length in an upwards movement in an attempt to find a soft target for its deadly fangs. She anticipated the movement and shook the snake with a sudden upwards arm flick and then with a practiced movement, swung it over her head and commenced the downwards snap to break its spine. However, she didn't have as much of the tail, nor as firm a grip as she thought. The snake twisted in mid-air and dropped almost at her feet. She sprang back in anticipation of the strike that would occur the moment the reptile gained leverage. It recovered in an instant and came for her, its head rising and readying to strike as it advanced. She spread her arms and legs wide in anticipation of when it would make its move. She saw its body stiffen and a millisecond later, it struck, but she had already sensed the move and sprang backwards. She slowly circled, looking for another opportunity to grab the tail of the enraged viper. One false move and she knew she would be dead within the hour. Those fangs packed enough venom to kill a dozen men, let alone a lithely built female. Death would be very quick. The snake suddenly saw its opportunity and threw its full length forwards. It missed and fell flat. In the instant it took to recover and recoil for another strike, she had grabbed its tail, swinging it high over her head before jerking it back and down in a long looping motion. She heard it crack like the snap of a bullwhip and she knew it was dead. She coiled it into the hot embers of the fire.

The wind began to flow in across the plains and with it came the cold. She pushed the rocks she had gathered into her sleeping depression and curled up in her shelter. The chill factor of the wind intensified the cold. Even the heat of the rocks was not enough as she shivered through the night. As the first rays of light appeared on the horizon, she took a long drink and started out at a brisk walk into the rising sun. Within a short time, she started to feel the warmth from her body's exertion and the effect of the sun hitting her full in the face. It had been a bone-chilling night, but she revelled in her freedom. There was no happy medium in the desert; the sun was relentless and debilitating during the day, and the cold equally as enervating when darkness fell.

By late morning, she had reached the next range of hills and once again she was enthralled by their timeless majesty. They were not impressive because of their height, rather it was the vivid colours that ranged in hue from the lightest of yellows through to reds, ochres, soft mauves, dark purples and greys, depending on how the light caught them. The deepest chasms concealed beautiful waterholes teaming with fish and birdlife. She spent the afternoon fishing for red-claw crustaceans using her shredded material hook. The inquisitive creatures would grab onto the white cotton threads in the belief they concealed some form of food. She would gradually pull the unsuspecting creature with its dominant red-claw, closer and closer and then with a quick jerk, fling it up onto the bank. When she had gathered about a dozen, she built a fire and roasted them.

She was warm that night, as there were plenty of dry branches for the fire and large jasper rocks to heat and place in her bed. The cold winds did not penetrate through these secret gorges. If she had come by horse, she would have skirted this range of hills, but that was why she walked—to absorb their magnificent timelessness. She began to feel a strange power overtaking her. All Gramps' stories of the dreaming began to well up as she drifted back into her culture. She was confused. Why did this feeling seek to overtake her? She knew her heritage was in fact not native, but mixed blood from several cultures. Why did the minority of her lineage subjugate the majority of Western culture in this timeless setting? She realised there was a vast chasm separating the two and she was retreating back to where she came from, in a seamless flow. She would not be going back to her previous life.

She awoke early and moved on, picking her way along animal tracks through the ravines and gorges where kangaroos, rock wallabies and the predatorial footprints of dingoes left a defined road to the waterholes. She began to notice the gradual changes as certain of the rock overhangs and cave entrances displayed primitive drawings of animals, hand stencils and mystical figures. They were nothing unique, but few white men except dedicated anthropologists had laid eyes upon them. Gramps had brought her this way several times in the past, but it was the more spectacular paintings she remembered, the mystical robed figures and the rainbow serpent that she sought.

She stopped in confusion some time later when she realised she was heading in the wrong direction. She retraced her steps, looking for a branch in the dry water course she had been following. She sat down and searched her memory. Her head in her hands, she took herself back, dredging through recollections of each time she had walked and ridden through with Gramps. Then in her subconscious she heard a voice, the voice of her grandfather calling softly to her. The voice was directly in front of her. She slowly took her hands away from her eyes, half expecting him to be standing there. She shaded her eyes again to shake off the illusion. He called again and she glanced up and back over her shoulder.

It was then she saw the entrance. It was above the level she had been walking along; a vast monsoonal flood having inundated the gorge in past years and swept away metres of alluvium. She was standing many metres below the previous floor of the gorge.

"Thank you Gramps." She smiled as she picked up her pack and began to walk up the slope, the smooth, water worn rocks affording easy hand and footholds. She finally crested the rise and sat down, panting as she studied the surrounds. They were unfamiliar as she got up and followed the narrow gorge until it finally opened into a large amphitheatre about fifty metres wide. She remembered it, and walked slowly and quietly so as not to disturb the ambience. The spirits of the dreamtime and her ancestors were everywhere, calling to her from every rock, every tree and all living but hidden creatures. She watched as a pair of spinifex pigeons, flushed out from where they were hiding under a clump of dry grass, ambled in front of her as though loathe to take to the air. She slowed down to let them gain distance and then slowly walked on. She took off her sneakers to feel the warm sand between her toes, her bare feet leaving distinct impressions in the red earth. She talked softly to the pigeons where they had stopped and settled under another growth of spinifex. A frill-necked lizard, a miniaturised progenitor of the dinosaurs that once roamed the land, hissed ferociously as it adopted its aggressive stance with flared collar and gaping mouth, before scuttling for cover within a cluster of rocks. The trail of a mulga snake was visible where it had slithered along the cool sand of the evening and early morning looking for small prey. It would have only taken minutes to find its hiding place, but it was safe because it was within the realm of her grandfather; she would not harm it. She stopped frequently to listen to the birds and watch the rock wallabies as they leapt from outcrop to outcrop high above her and far out of reach of predatory dingoes.

26

It was late afternoon when she walked out of the gorge, heading for the outstation with its nearby permanent spring providing water and shelter under the ancient eucalypts. On reaching it, she tossed her bag down under the tree where she had last camped with Gramps. She gathered stones and wood for a fire, made her camp and then out of curiosity walked up the rise towards the old outstation.

She suddenly checked herself, and stood stock-still as she noticed the wheel of a motorbike protruding from the far side of the building. She looked around, but could see no one as she cautiously approached the open door and looked inside. A sleeping bag lay on the floor and clothes were tossed over a chair. There were cans of food and utensils on the table. She began to back away when she heard the voice behind her.

"Hello Chloe."

She spun around in shock as she recalled the soft brogue from all those years ago.

"What are you doing here?" Chloe stammered. "You're Father Murphy, aren't you?"

"Dion Murphy is the name. I was a priest, now I'm a geologist. I'm looking for diamonds. A special diamond, to be exact. You know what I'm looking for, don't you?"

Chloe shook her head. "I don't know anything about diamonds, or where to find them."

"I think you do, but you might not be aware of what you'd found at the time. I'm looking for red diamonds like the one I saw in your room."

"You saw one in my room? What were you doing in there? Did Henry say you could search my room?"

"No, Walter showed it to me. I'd seen it before that, but not closely. He asked me what it was and I told him it was a diamond."

"And you think it came from here?"

Murphy nodded. "It came from somewhere around here, of that I'm sure. You haven't answered my question as to why you're here. You're a famous model and yet here you are, thousands of kilometres from where you should be."

"Look Father, I mean Dion, I want to get the fire going and prepare something to eat before it gets too late."

"You can sleep in the shack if you like. You'll be perfectly safe." His voice was reassuring, but Chloe wanted to keep her distance.

"Thank you, but I prefer to sleep out under the stars."

"Suit yourself, but it looks as though you're travelling very light. I've got plenty of food. Why don't you prepare your site and then come back and have dinner with me?"

Chloe thought about it for a few moments. "Thank you, I will. I'll just go and get my fire going and prepare my bed for the night."

Dion ladled out a bowl of soup from a pannikin into a single bowl when she returned. "I stocked up on dried food, so I just boil water and add the ingredients. I've also learnt how to make damper. Help yourself."

"But I've taken your bowl."

"I'll just have mine straight out of the pannikin."

Chloe needed no second bidding as she tore off a bit of damper and dunked it into the thick, soupy mass.

"Is this where you often came with your grandfather?"

"I went all over Venus Downs and beyond with Gramps. Why do you ask?" Chloe was wary of where his questions were leading.

"No particular reason. I just wondered whether you'd been here when I first saw you at the homestead. You'd just arrived back with your grandfather from a week or more away, according to Henry."

Chloe finished the last of her soup and mopped the bowl with another piece of damper. "Yes, we had been away for a week. Gramps wanted to show me some more of his sacred sites."

"And one of them was around here someplace. Am I right?"

Chloe shook her head. "I can't tell you that. I can't tell you anything about what he showed me, or where."

"You mean you cannot, or will not?"

"Both, and there's no point in pressing me on that. The sites are sacred and I would never divulge their location."

Dion fixed her with an amused look. "But I know you did come here on that occasion."

"And how do you know that?"

"Because someone mentioned it while we were having dinner that night."

"Well, it certainly wasn't me and it wouldn't have been Gramps because he never ate in the homestead."

"It must have been Carl or Walter then?"

Dion didn't miss the startled look that flashed across her face for an instant. She recalled Gramps pointing out the crushed ants. Gramps said they were being followed, but who was it?

Dion was studying her intently. His voice had taken on an even softer tone as his eyes bored into her. "You're very beautiful. Your face is as lovely as your body."

"But you've never seen my body." Chloe gave a dismissive flick of her head.

"You're wrong. I saw you completely naked once, holding a red diamond up to the light."

It came back to her in a flash. She hadn't imagined it when she thought someone had been at the window of her room that day.

"You're sick Dion. How do you justify a priest looking at a seventeen year-old girl in the nude?"

"I'm not sick for wanting to look at someone as beautiful as you. I admit it's not what priests should do, but a life of celibacy doesn't prevent a priest from lusting after the flesh."

"So you saw me in the nude and you saw me holding up the diamond, which I didn't even know was a diamond at the time."

"And neither did I, but I suspected it immediately from the lustre of the stone. If it were just a red stone you'd picked up, it would have been pitted and opaque from the ravages of time, but a diamond never loses its lustre. Nothing is harder than a diamond."

"But you haven't seen the stone since, have you?"

"Walter showed it to me. I've handled it. It's a priceless gem and I want to know exactly where it came from. There must be more."

"Walter has the diamond now," she lied.

"He may have the diamond, but he's not here so it will be first in best dressed. If I can locate the source, I will immediately apply for an exploration licence over the area. It will be worth millions. Are you going to help me?"

Chloe could see she was in a dangerous situation. "What's in it for me?"

Dion laughed. "Of course I'll share it with you, that goes without saying. We'll take out the licence in both names."

"I'll think about it. Thanks for dinner." She got up to leave and was about to walk out when she saw something familiar lying on the floor. She stooped in shock and picked it up. She was not mistaken. She knew exactly who it belonged to. "Where did you get this?"

Dion let out a heavy sigh. "I picked it up from a pile of human bones on a ridge about ten kilometres from here. Do you know something about it? I first saw the bones when I was there several years ago, but I didn't tell anyone about it at the time. I was up there again a couple of weeks ago looking over the terrain when I noticed the buckle."

"It's my grandfather's belt buckle. I saw him making it when I was a child." The prancing horse stood as a proud centrepiece. She turned it over and rubbed the initials JQ engraved on the back. "Was there anything else there?"

"Nothing at all, except the buckle and the bones, which looked as though they'd been there for years."

"Did you bury them?"

"No, I didn't. I thought it best not to disturb them. I was going to mention it to Henry the next time I saw him."

"Would you show me where they are?"

"Of course. It's only a short ride there on the bike. We'll go first thing in the morning."

Chloe nodded as she thrust the buckle in her pocket and walked out. She lit her fire and piled around the rocks to heat up before placing them in her sleeping hollow and covering them with sand. Her actions were automatic. All she could think about was finding her grandfather's bones and burying them. She lay back and looked up at the stars for hours. Her mind was churning relentlessly. Sleep would not come.

"Hey Chloe, breakfast is ready!" The shout woke her. Dion was standing at the door of the shack with a bowl in his hand. "I hope you like porridge, damper and jam?"

Chloe slowly stood up, shook herself and stretched. She felt filthy, but was not concerned about her looks as she walked towards the shack.

She took the offered bowl and sat down. "Thank you."

"That's okay, I've got plenty of food. Here, pour some treacle over it. How long do you plan to stay out here?"

Chloe took the bottle and poured the golden liquid over the porridge. "I don't know now. I was planning on a couple of days, but I will have to attend to Gramps first."

"Have you thought about my proposition?"

"I have, but give me until tomorrow to decide."

"Very well. When you've finished, I'll take you out to where I found the buckle."

An hour later, she climbed off the back of the motorbike and looked up at the ridge.

"I'll come up with you, or wait if you like."

"No, I don't want you to show me, and don't wait for me as I will be some time. It will only take me a couple of hours to walk back this afternoon. I just want to be by myself."

Dion nodded, gunned the motor and took off, leaving a cloud of dust behind him.

Chloe slowly picked her way through the rough ground, strewn with scree and broken rocks shattered by the relentless heat and passage of time. Finally she crested the ridge, which levelled out onto the small plateau. She looked around for the outcrop Dion had described and slowly approached it.

The skull was lying on its side, the empty sockets of the eyes staring directly at her. She let out an anguished cry of despair and burst into tears as she slumped to the hard ground. Why had Gramps come up here to die? Was he hiding an illness and just went walkabout to conceal it, and be with his ancestors? Her thoughts reached back to the day he told her not to come looking for him should he not return to their camp. He was hiding something, but what?

She stopped crying to study the skull and scattered bones. Surely, he would have picked a place where his ancestors had come to die, but there was no sign of other remains. Something caught her eye. She leant forwards to prize it out of the clinging earth. It was the empty casing of a rifle cartridge. She was idly polishing it against her clothes when a sudden thought seared a shiver of realisation into her brain. She was shaking as she slowly got up and studied the skull before reaching down and turning it fully upright. The entire back of the skull was missing and as she brushed the earth off the temple lying closest to the ground, she saw the neat, round hole where the bullet had entered. She put her hands to her face and sank to her knees, distraught with grief. Chloe realised she had not imagined the sound she had heard that day so long ago. It was the shot that killed her grandfather. He must have known someone was following them and wanted her out of harm's way until he discovered who it was. There could only be one answer: Carl. It couldn't have been anyone else. It was just too contrived that he happened upon her bathing in the billabong. He had followed them. The memory of their lovemaking came flooding back, the softness, the tenderness, the passion. How could he murder someone in cold blood? What was his motive? She had experienced a side of him he never openly revealed. She believed he had really been a loving individual whose emotions had been suppressed by the neglect and abuse of his early upbringing. He had told her everything as they lay in the grass afterwards. But now, she realised he must have been a twisted psychopath who claimed he loved her and wanted to marry her, yet he had murdered her grandfather. Carl was dead. He would never answer for his crime. She searched her memory for what he was carrying on his horse, but could not recall if he had a rifle scabbard attached. It was rare for anyone from the station to go about armed. If they wanted a pig, they would pick a young one and simply ride it down. She had seen the native jackaroos and Carl and Walter do it often. They would gallop after the animal, swing from the saddle when they drew level and wrestle it down. They would quickly tie its legs before throwing it across the saddle. They only carried guns if they wanted to get rid of the wild bull camels responsible for the propagation of the feral herd, or for destroying badly injured cattle. She was sure she would have noticed if Carl had been carrying a gun, but it had to be him.

Chloe carefully gathered the bones and piled them in a heap before scooping out all the earth she could and placing them in the small depression. She spent the rest of the morning gathering rocks and piling them on top to make a cairn to the mark the final resting place of her grandfather.

Dion had dragged the table outside dand was bending over a topographical map studying the contours and ancient drainage patterns of the landscape. He did not hear the footsteps approaching from behind.

"Hi there priest, how's it going?"

Dion spun around to see Walter standing behind him with his hands thrust into his jeans pockets.

"Do you always creep up on people like that? You gave me a hell of a shock." He began to cover the maps and papers he was studying.

"Nobody at the homestead mentioned you were out here."

"That's because I didn't call in to tell them. I didn't want anyone asking questions."

Walter grunted. "What are you doing here?"

"That's obvious, isn't it? I'm trying to find the source of that diamond."

"Having any luck?"

"Yes, I'm very close and I should know more this afternoon."

"You'll know more? What are you talking about?"

"Chloe is here."

Walter looked around. "She's not here at the moment then?"

Dion shook his head. "No, she's gone to bury the bones of her grandfather. I showed her where they are."

"How does she know the bones are of old Johnny Quartpot?"

"Because I picked up a belt buckle near the bones and Chloe recognised who it belonged to."

"So who are you working for?"

"I'm working with a group in Perth. They're funding everything and we split what we find."

"You mean, you're working with Connors and Steiner? Am I in on the deal?"

If Dion was shocked at what Walter knew, he didn't show it. "No, I got a better offer Walter. Our deal was you would get

Chloe to lead us to the source of the diamond. To this point, you haven't. Anyhow, I got into a spot of bother in Perth. You probably read about my trial, no doubt. I was cleared, but they wanted to throw me out of the country as an illegal with a false passport. Connors had some documents I'd acquired that would have not gone well for me if they'd come to light." He swept his hand over the papers he had covered. "Combined with that and the fact I don't particularly want to go back to Ireland, we came to a compromise. You can guess the rest."

"So we both now know where the diamond came from?"

"Yes, it's somewhere very close to here. I believe she may show me. But tell me, why are you here?"

Walter sat down and rolled a cigarette. "I've been tracking her for a couple of days. She's got the diamond and I followed her here."

"But why would she bring it back here?"

"That's simple. The gem is sacred and she's going to put it back where it came from."

"How did she get hold of it? She told me you had it."

"That's a long story, but she gave me the slip. I wasn't counting on her being one jump ahead of me."

Dion laughed. "I thought you were smart. You had the diamond and then she took it back off you?"

"Yeah, she thinks she's smart, but I'll get it back—along with the source."

"You're in an aggressive mood, I can see that. You should calm down and see if we can't talk some sense into her when she gets back."

Walter stood up, shaking his head with a look of disdain. "You dumb bloody Irish spud-muncher. Don't you realise she's not coming back. She's got a diamond worth millions on her and you let it slip through your fingers."

Dion rose, his fists clenched. "If you're that smart, why didn't you catch up with her?"

"I lost track of her when she diverted through a gorge for some reason. It took me a day to pick up her tracks again and then I realised she was heading for this outstation. I wasn't more than ten minutes away when I heard you go off on the bike. If you hadn't been here, I would have followed her today. She would have led me right to where the diamond came from."

"So what are you going to do now?"

"I'm going to try and pick up her track. It should be quite easy now I know where you took her. I can tell you she won't be returning here."

"What about our deal?"

"It's off Murphy. The deal was between you and me, not your syndicate. Too many people wanting a share and knowing what I know now, I think I'll just keep it all for myself."

"You'll have to get past me first."

"Then I'll have to deal with that eventuality, won't I?"

Murphy tensed for a fight, but Walter grinned and slowly walked past him and into the shack. He pulled over the chair and reached up into rafters where they joined the wall bearers. It was still where he had left it all those years before in a place that could not be seen from the floor of the shack. And it was still loaded. He retrieved a handful of extra cartridges and walked back outside.

"Oh, Mother of God," were Murphy's last words as the gun was levelled and a shot rang out.

27

Chloe's head jerked towards the distant sound resonating in her brain. It matched that of what she had heard the day Gramps disappeared. Frightened, she looked out across the plains towards her destination. She would reach it by late afternoon. She picked up her kitbag and began to descend through the strewn rocks, heading directly south and away from Dion and the outstation. She had almost reached the bottom when a patch of loose scree gave away. She felt her ankle collapse sideways as she tumbled forwards, trying to stifle the cry of pain. She lay there for some time as the agony intensified. Her arms were grazed and bleeding from where they had taken the brunt of the fall. She inched herself down to retrieve her hat to protect her head from the relentless sun. She took off her sneaker, exposing a foot already badly blistered from the grinding action of sand in her inadequate footwear. She ripped a piece off her shirt and bound her ankle as tightly as possible before easing the tattered footwear back on. She had to get moving if she hoped to get to her destination before nightfall. She shuffled down feet-first with her backside kept off the ground by the weight of her hands and arms holding her up for support. Finally, she saw a stout stick and used it to pull herself up for support. The pain was excruciating as she hobbled forwards, trying to keep the weight off her damaged ankle. She cursed herself for being so careless and not watching where she was walking.

Exposed and in danger in the open, she hobbled on towards the safety of the red bluffs. Normally, she would have covered the distance in half an hour but the sun was already setting when she stumbled into the sheltering comfort of the overhanging bluff. She sat down and looked back in the direction of the outstation. She watched, but there was no sign of movement, except for a barely perceptible breeze through the spinifex. There was no sound of a motorbike signalling danger as she staggered to her feet again and stumbled on.

Finally, she located the entrance to the small chasm. It was if she had only walked it yesterday with Gramps. His spirit was all around her and she began to feel safer as she rounded a bend and saw the small waterhole filled from an underground spring gently bubbling up from some artesian source deep below. She took off her sneakers and thrust her feet into the cool water, watching as tiny fish began to nibble at the dead skin of her blistered heels and toes. She raised each foot and tore away the dead skin with thumb and forefinger, wincing in pain as the blisters began to bleed before shoving her feet back into the water for little relief. She stood, pulling down a veil of denial over the pain and began to gather wood for a fire. The fire radiated off the chasm walls as she chewed on a few pieces of Dion's damper she had thrust into her bag that morning. Exhausted, she finally slumped down onto the bare earth, drifting off in the knowledge the spirits were all around her, and feeling safe in their presence.

She woke with a start. It was too quiet. There were no signs of wildlife, no crows noisily marking their territory, no finches, chattering parrots, or budgies, contributing to the melee of sound that should have been present. She carefully raised her head and looked around. She remained still for some time, detecting no sounds or movement, but there had to be a reason why the birds were not present. Instinct and fear told her she was in danger. She was being followed, or someone had already detected her presence and was laying low, watching what she would do. It could not be Dion, she was sure of that. There was only one person it could be; she knew he had the tracking skills of a native, but where was he? She tied the laces of her sneakers together and slung them around her neck; she could not stand the pain of putting them on, so with the aid of the stick she got up and walked further into the chasm, stopping often to listen. As she penetrated further, she began to recite the incantations that Gramps had taught her from childhood. Above all, she called out to her grandfather to look out for her.

She walked on, oblivious to the pain in her feet and ankle, noting every familiar rock outcrop or bluff, all the time aware of danger. She knew it was Walter tracking her, but how far behind was he? It was slow going keeping to the shadow of the cliffs as she climbed steadily upwards. By mid-morning, she saw what she was looking for, a gently dipping rock face that curved down and around like a spiral until it flattened out onto a small plain. From there, it dipped and then spiralled down again until it finally opened out onto a small patch of desert. She descended the time worn path of an ancient watercourse carved out and smoothed by millenniums of monsoonal rain, which disappeared as quickly as the parched earth absorbed it. She was careful to only step on rock and not loose scree or earth until she reached the bottom of the curved structure, the trail left by the dreamtime giant frill-necked lizard as it dragged its tail over the earth.

Anyone following and watching her from above would think she had simply vanished as she stepped inside a fissure in the sheer rock face behind the familiar, dry watercourse. She was in total darkness as she squeezed her way through, holding her hands in front to feel for an impenetrable wall as her feet searched for the rim of a cylindrical pipe carved out by water. She found it, and putting her hands on the ceiling to steady herself, walked down its length. She picked her way along another channel, faintly lit by a fissure in the rock high above, and into the bowels of the frill-necked lizard, then finally into the opening of a large, circular vent—the mouth of the giant lizard. She came out into daylight and looking back and up, she could see the giant frills of the lizard's defensive hood standing proud above her in the form of sharply jutting pinnacles of distinct grey strata. In front of her and opening into a flat area were rocks jutting upwards, the teeth of the reptile, while the flat stone area was the tongue of the giant mythical creature, which had been cast in stone, lying in wait for any threat to the rainbow serpent. The legend was as vivid and real as the first time Gramps had revealed the existence of this sacred place to her. At first, they had seemed like non-descript rocks that meant nothing to a child, but when the revelation was gently unfolded like the pages of a book being turned, she was struck by the awe and mysticism of her surroundings. It was timeless, for indeed it was truth and not myth and was to be treated and revered as such.

Chloe had often reflected on the stories and queried the creativity of the primitive human mind to construct such legends, but here in the presence of the dreamtime lizard, her ethnic roots returned and she felt the powerful pull of her ancestors. Just beyond the gaping mouth of the lizard resided the most powerful totem of them all, the rainbow serpent with its piercing look of evil and doom. She sat and slowly looked around the walls of the totally enclosed circular forum. As her eyes adjusted to the light, she saw the distinct beginning of the tip of the tail of the multi-coloured serpent, contrasting with its dull surroundings. She walked down its length as it grew larger, until the reptile ended with the familiar fanged head about to strike, its two malevolent, bright red eyes fixed on the intruder. At the head of the snake was the familiar cluster of stunted trees gathered around a waterhole. She remembered the ancient boab tree. The figure in the flowing gown with the red pendant around its neck was just as mysterious as when she had first seen it.

Whereas the area had been barren on her last visit, it now contained a large billabong at its southern end. Chloe gathered wood to make camp and prepared her sleeping hollow. She went down to the lagoon, stripped off and swam for an hour as the warm waters soothed her tired body. Ducks and other waterfowl moved away as she approached, but were not alarmed by her presence. She got out and sat on the soft earth, enjoying the solitude of her surroundings. She was hungry as she slowly walked back to retrieve her last piece of damper. She was about to eat it when she stopped, picked up a large piece of wood and walked back to the water's edge. The birds approached and she threw small pieces of damper into the water. She waited until a fat duck had dipped its head for a morsel when she struck with speed and force. She prayed the spirits would forgive her as the birds scattered in fright and she took hold of the unfortunate waterfowl. She hummed to herself as she plucked and gutted it before putting it on a large rock facing the flame of the fire she had earlier prepared. She gazed into the fire, mesmerised as the flames flickered and danced. The presence of her grandfather drifted in and out of the shadows beyond the light. She felt herself trying to catch a glimpse of him by quickly lifting her gaze from the fire but he was always too quick and would disappear in an ephemeral mist. The flesh of the bird was stringy and tough, but she didn't mind; it was enough to relieve her hunger.

The sun was already bathing the secret space in soft morning light when she awoke. She immediately relaxed, as she was under the protection of the rainbow serpent. She was the sole arbiter of this sacred place and would never reveal its existence to anyone. The secret would remain with her.

A pair of spinifex pigeons were already foraging in the long grass, softly cooing to each other, confirming their life-long bond. Finches, budgies and parrots crowded the edge of the billabong. It was another three months until the wet season, but the grasses now were long and dry, the seeds providing the life-giving source for birds and small rodents. Fires would soon sweep through the plains as lightning strikes spontaneously ignited the grasses and spinifex. The conflagration would flare within minutes as the updraft of the superheated air sucked in oxygen and fire leapt forwards faster than man or any animal could run. Kangaroos and flightless emus would invariably be overrun as the fire didn't burn on a continuous front but leapt around the landscape seeking dry material to add to its explosive force. Animals would panic as their retreat was cut off and they frantically searched for an escape, only to be met with an encircling wall of flame. The fire meant food for hordes of crows that feasted on the roasted remains and for the kites and wedge-tail eagles, it meant live food as the rodents and snakes forsook the safety of their seclusion within the rocks and crevices, oblivious to the threat hovering above as they frantically searched for safety. The devastation of the blackened earth and charred stubble would remain a cruel testament until the rains came, grasses and desert flowers would spring to life overnight and the animals would miraculously appear again.

Chloe rose and walked down to the edge of the billabong, watching in awe of nature as the birdlife took flight. She took off her clothes and walked into the water. It was cold and refreshing. The pain in her ankle was easing, but was still too swollen to travel far. She would wait a few days before heading home again. In that time, she would accomplish the task she had set out to do. She struck out in a gentle breaststroke, casting her eyes upwards at the majesty of the lizard's frills. She noticed a couple of large goannas approach the water and begin to drink. Each was an ancestor and she softly called to them from the centre of the billabong. Afterwards, she sat on a rock and trolled for red-claw crustaceans. They were large and plentiful and within a short time, she had enough for a meal. She walked about the edge of the water to a patch of damp ground where she could see the dying stems of a yam tuber, which she dug up. She broke off dead branches of the stunted mallee bush and pulled out four fat witchetty grubs.

Finally, contented and at peace in her surroundings, she slowly walked back to her campsite, throwing her catch into the embers of the fire. She pulled the grubs out of the embers with a stick and biting into the blackened casing, chewed on the custard like contents. They were delicious and brought back memories of years gone by. Next, the red-claws were dismembered and sucked for every morsel of soft white flesh. The small, sweet yams finished her meal and she sat back in the overhanging shade and looked out at her surrounds. An involuntary shudder passed through her. She was putting it off, but she knew she had to do it. The more she tried to put it to the back of her mind, the more it surfaced in her subconscious. Slowly, her gaze was pulled back to the eyes of the giant serpent. It was commanding her to return what rightfully belonged to it.

Chloe got up, took the daimond out of her pack and slowly walked towards the hideous head of the painting above the familiar boab tree. Directly below the head was the cleft in the rock at ground level with a circular opening not much bigger than a clenched human hand. The soft sand in front of the opening had numerous lines running out in multiple directions where they disappeared into the high grasses. They were the tracks of the rainbow serpent's guardian, the lethal king-brown, as it ventured out in the early morning and evening in search of rodents and frogs near the billabong. She squatted down in front of the opening and began to slowly chant to the spirit within. She knew it would respond and several minutes later, she saw the first slight movement in the darkened entrance as the snake's flicking tongue tested for movement. She could feel the sweat running down her brow for she now no longer had a protector. She was on her own and afraid, but she suppressed her fear as the head of the snake emerged. It checked, its tongue flicking the air for unforeseen movement and danger, its scaly pattern reflecting the light and burnished sheen of nature's most dangerous. It reared up as its beady eyes became aware of the crouching form and its tongue flashed faster. She grimaced as she anticipated the lightning strike that would be impossible to avoid and the agonising death that would follow. At least death would come within minutes as the venom shut down her central nervous system. Paralysis would follow and her life would be extinguished as quickly as the throwing of a light switch. But until the moment of death, the torment would appear long and excruciating. This was not a common brown or death-adder. Gramps had taught her to handle those. This was the most lethal of all snakes and here she was completely unprepared, exposed and defenceless, inviting it to strike. The snake slithered towards her as she kept up the almost inaudible chant. It flattened and slithered through the dry grass clumps around her, its two-metre length lightly touching her legs as it encircled her and disappeared back into the crevice. She reached in and pulled out the clay bowl. The eyes of the rainbow serpent were exactly as she remembered them, a large gem dominating the grouping. She held her diamond up to the light one last time before placing it into the bowl. She placed the bowl back in the crevice. The eye of the rainbow serpent was back where it belonged, never to be disturbed again.

An explosion of dirt and dust blinded her as the crater of the bullet opened near her hand. She spun around, shaking in fear and shock as she jumped to her feet. Walter was standing metres away, casually reloading. The ejected shell casing spun into the air.

"Hello Chloe. I see you have my diamond."

"It's not yours, Walter. It belongs to the rainbow serpent and this sacred site."

Walter laughed derisively. "It belongs to me now." He looked around the grey walls of the enclosure. "Dion said the diamonds would come from a pipe in a grey material and this looks like what he described. Looks as though I've hit the jackpot."

"How did you find this place?"

"Chloe, with a bum leg and a walking stick you might as well have left flags for me to follow. Mind you, the entrance behind that old waterfall slowed me down until this morning, but I eventually found it."

"Is Dion with you?"

"No, we had a little disagreement as to his eventual interest in this venture so he's no longer involved."

"You murdered him too, didn't you?"

"Well, let's just say he's no longer with us. It was self-defence but tell me, who else am I supposed to have murdered?"

"You murdered Gramps," Chloe's voice was low and full of hatred.

"And how could you prove it was me?"

Chloe walked forward and picked up the spent shell casing Walter had just ejected. Then she pulled out the casing from her pocket, compared them and tossed them at Walter's feet.

"Identical, both from the Martini Henry you're carrying. I found this one near Gramps' remains. He'd been shot in the head. Until this moment, I thought Carl had done it, but now I know it was you."

"Very astute, Chloe."

"I also realised you murdered Carl. I was watching you both as you were loading those bulls. You purposely opened that gate when he was trying to retrieve his shirt. And now you're going to kill me too, aren't you?"

"That is the sad reality of it, Chloe." He began to level the gun. "Venus Downs is mine now, along with the diamonds I just saw you shove into that hole."

"Not while Henry's still alive. Are you going to murder him too?"

"Henry's dead. He had a terminal stroke the morning you left the homestead. Once I've dealt with you, I am the sole heir to Venus Downs and all that's on it. You didn't know Henry was your natural father, did you?"

Chloe shook her head in bewilderment. "No, no I didn't. How do you know that?"

"He caught me in his office one day going through his papers. I found a copy of his Will. It named Carl, you and I as the beneficiaries of his estate. He revealed you were his daughter, the result of some gin he'd been shagging. We had an argument and that's when I decided to head for London to talk to you. He'd threatened to kick me off the property and out of his Will. Fortunately for me, he's now dead, so I don't see why I should share anything with you."

"Gramps always said you were just as dangerous as Carl."

"There's one final thing I've always dreamed of doing with you, and I'm going to do it now. You and Carl really put on a show that day down by the billabong. It's a pity I couldn't stay and watch the whole performance, but I had to get back to the homestead ahead of you. I had to jerk off just to get over the frustration of missing out. Now I think I'll try the real thing." He put down the gun and moved towards her, unbuckling his belt.

Chloe forgot the pain of her ankle and sprinted away, followed by Walter's peal of laughter.

"You can't get away, Chloe."

She stopped, realising her position was hopeless and sank to the ground in despair.

"Come back here. I'll undress you and put a diamond in your navel. I want to admire two beautiful objects as nature intended."

Chloe stifled the warning in her throat as she saw him lean down and thrust his hand into the crevice.

He let out a piercing scream and she saw his look of abject terror as he flung himself backwards, looking at where the fangs of the snake had penetrated the veins on his wrist. His screams and expression of disbelief continued as the snake followed, striking him again and again as he tried to regain his feet. Satisfied, it slithered back into the crevice, its job as protector complete.

In desperation, Walter looked around for his rifle. Chloe realised he did not intend to shoot the snake; it was already too late for that. He was going to take her with him. She ran over, picked up the weapon and moved away.

As Walter lay dying, Chloe sensing another presence, looked up as a willy-willy, a swirling cloud of dust and debris erupted from the centre of the amphitheatre, drawn up by the vacuum of heat and the spirits. It died as Walter took his last breath, and she knew, at long last, she was safe. Gramps was looking over her.

———————